Julie Shackman is a forme Scotland with her husband

 twitt

Julie Shackman is a former journalist and writer. She lives in Scotland with her husband and sons.

🐦 twitter.com/G13Julie

A SECRET SCOTTISH ESCAPE

JULIE SHACKMAN

One More Chapter
a division of HarperCollins*Publishers* Ltd
1 London Bridge Street
London SE1 9GF
www.harpercollins.co.uk
HarperCollins*Publishers*
1st Floor, Watermarque Building, Ringsend Road
Dublin 4, Ireland

This paperback edition 2021
First published in Great Britain in ebook format
by HarperCollins*Publishers* 2021
Copyright © Julie Shackman 2021
Julie Shackman asserts the moral right to be identified
as the author of this work

A catalogue record of this book is available from the British Library

ISBN: 978-0-00-845577-4

This novel is entirely a work of fiction. The names, characters and
incidents portrayed in it are the work of the author's imagination. Any
resemblance to actual persons, living or dead, events or localities is
entirely coincidental.

Printed and bound in the UK using 100% Renewable Electricity at CPI Group (UK) Ltd

Chapter One

"Mac, you've done it again!" I grinned into my mobile. "You've forgotten your notebook."

I glanced round to where his leather-bound journal was lying on the glass coffee table. Beside it was a framed photograph of the two of us by the shores of our local loch.

Mac's chestnut hair was streaked with the faintest slivers of grey and we had been laughing as we took the impromptu selfie. His hooded, pale blue eyes were crinkling against the sunshine and I was nestling against him, my freckles popping across my nose and over my cheeks.

My dad, Harry, would often cast wary looks at Mac whenever he visited us. "Doesn't the age gap bother you, Layla?" he would hiss out of the corner of his mouth. "I mean, the old goat's only a year younger than me."

I paused before I spoke again into my mobile, my rose-gold morganite engagement ring flashing as I moved my hands. "So, anyway," I continued, pulling my attention back to Mac's voicemail. "I hope your meeting with your agent goes well, even though you have left your notebook behind. Ring me when you're done. Love you."

I rang off and headed back to my desk, an old oak affair that sat at the furthest end of my cottage sitting room. Through the cream-painted sash windows, I could see the spooling waters of Loch Harris in the distance.

On a clear April morning like this, the odd smudge of an angler's boat could be glimpsed between the tangles of woodland that surrounded it. Clumps of daffodils were springing out of the ground, like lemon trumpets.

Loch Harris was the epitome of craggy and mysterious Scottish beauty, with its sprinkling of old stone cottages, churches with stained-glass windows, and an eclectic handful of shops. It was a popular destination for tourists, thanks to its myriad dramatic walks, as well as the expanse of mirrored loch and the magical spectacle of Galen Waterfall, located only fifteen minutes' drive away.

Mac and I lived together in what had originally been my family home, before my family had been blown apart. When I was seven my mother, Tina, decided that life owed her far more than Loch Harris could ever give her, and she swept out of our lives.

For the past twenty-two years, she had been this unfamiliar, strange entity who sent me the odd birthday and Christmas card from her life in London – and, to be frank, I was more than happy to keep the arrangement that way.

Dad had raised me alone, albeit it with the support of my late paternal grandparents.

I still remember, despite the absence of my mother, this little whitewashed cottage reverberating with the sound of music. From an early age, I recall my dad's assorted albums littering the carpet in the sitting room and him proudly cleaning the record sleeves. "Forget any jewels," he would say to me. "These are all the treasures you will ever need."

Eric Clapton was my dad's hero – hence him naming me after Clapton's most famous song.

When I had mentioned to Dad that I wanted my own place, he'd been content to leave the painful memories of my mum behind and had insisted I stay in the cottage. He took up residence in my late grandparents' home, which was just a little further down the lane.

I scooped a hunk of my wavy, light brown hair behind my ear and used the mouse to scroll down the new messages that had materialised in my email inbox.

I had a couple of deadlines looming: one was a book review for a Glasgow evening newspaper, and the other was writing up an interview I'd conducted with a debut crime writer from the Netherlands for an online magazine.

Procrastination was the enemy when you were a freelance writer.

I reached over to snatch a pen from my tub and saw Mac's spidery, dark handwriting. He'd jotted down a random note on a scrap of paper.

Hendry raised the gun, his knuckles white. Fragments of sunrise highlighted the flickering silhouette of the murderer...

Mac was working on his next political thriller, currently titled *Injustice*.

The success he had been having for a number of years now was impressive, but even the great Mac Christie, with his debonair smile and easy charm, doubted himself at times.

He would sit and write in the spare bedroom and I often heard his fist thump on his writing desk, followed by a cacophony of swear words raining out through the door.

I fiddled with my engagement ring before opening YouTube and clicking on some of my favourite songs to listen to as I worked.

Whereas Mac could only write in silence, I found I worked most productively when I had heart-tugging lyrics soaring around me.

"Do you have to have that cranking out at that volume, Layla?" Mac would yell from across the hall. "This isn't the O2 arena."

I often indulged in daydreams in which I owned my own music venue. When I'd confided in Mac about it, he'd said, "Urgh! Not all that manic rock, surely? I could understand a sedate jazz club, but not the sound of someone being unceremoniously tortured for four minutes."

"If it's too loud, you're too old," I had teased back.

Mac had abandoned his desk and pulled me towards our bedroom, where he'd proceeded to show me how youthful he actually was.

After having rattled off a very complimentary review of the historical romance I'd been asked to read, I padded out of the sitting room and into the kitchen to rustle up some lunch.

My dad, though a landscape gardener by trade, was very handy, and had transformed the dark wooden fitted cupboards we'd suffered with for years into the wash of palest lemon we had now, ably assisted by a few of his local tradesmen friends.

I had dotted several potted plants on the deep brown worktops, ranging from sprouts of heather to trailing ivy, stationed an old-fashioned yellow silk lamp in the corner, and chosen a stainless steel oven and fridge to replace our original white goods that had seen better days.

My bare feet slapped on the burnished wooden floor as I drifted from the cupboards to the fridge. Mac hadn't returned my call. Maybe he hadn't received my message?

I cranked open the fridge door, reaching for a loaf of seeded bread, smoked salmon, and some leafy salad.

A sharp knock at the front door managed to fight its way over the sound of Stevie Nicks singing about paper flowers.

Through the frosted glass, I could make out the shimmery silhouette of a tall man.

A grin broke out across my face.

"Mac," I started, tugging at the handle. "Have you forgotten your key as well?"

I blinked several times at the sombre eyes of Tom, our local policeman.

A kind-faced policewoman, whom I didn't recognise, lingered at his back.

Chapter Two

My fingers clawed at my engagement ring. "There must be some mistake."

Tom laced his fingers together. "I'm so sorry, Layla."

I lurched from the chair and paced up and down in front of the two concerned police officers. "No. I don't believe this."

They stared up at me from the sofa, empathy etched into their expressions.

"But none of this makes any sense," I stammered, my mind careering in all directions. "Mac was meeting his agent in town. Why would he be in some hotel in Stirling?"

My heart felt like a cold lump sitting in my chest and the colours of my sitting room were beginning to swirl into a smudgy claret and grey haze.

Tom stood and patted me on the arm. His companion, who had introduced herself as Constable Emma Nicholson, gave me the briefest of sympathetic smiles. "I think you should take a seat, Layla."

I stared at her for a moment before nodding slowly and lowering myself back into my armchair.

Emma glanced at Tom out of the corner of her eye. There was an embarrassed silence. "Mac wasn't with his agent when he suffered the heart attack."

My brows knitted together. "Sorry, I don't understand."

Tom and Emma exchanged another brief look, which made my breath judder. What was going on?

"Mac collapsed in a room at the Brookman Hotel – and there was someone with him at the time."

Tom's words pierced me and the breath caught in my throat. "Are you trying to tell me he was with another woman?"

Emma's pale blue eyes blinked. "Yes. Yes, he was."

Tom dropped his light gaze to my wine-red carpet and then looked back up at me. "Mac was with Hannah Darley-Patrick."

This was ridiculous. None of it was making sense. "No," I struggled. "That can't be right. She's his ex-wife."

Tom and his companion said nothing.

"What were they doing?" I rasped, silently chiding myself over the stupidity of my question.

There was yet more silence.

I surprised myself by letting out a gravelly laugh. It sounded alien, as though it didn't belong to me. "Oh no. They were in bed together, weren't they?"

Emma inclined her head. "I'm very sorry, but yes, it would seem so."

I dragged my palms down the front of my jeans and shot out of my chair again. "This can't be happening," I murmured, my engagement ring flickering on my finger. "So, you're telling me my fiancé had a fatal heart attack while he was shagging his ex-wife?"

Tom and Emma sprang up from their seats to stand in front of me. "We're so sorry, Layla," emphasised Tom again.

Shock and anger were battling it out inside of me. "Not as sorry as I am."

Emma hovered in front of me. "Is there someone we can call for you? You shouldn't be on your own right now."

I traced my disbelieving fingers up and down my arms. I tugged needlessly at the hem of my jumper. "Harry," I muttered. "You could ring Harry."

"Harry Devlin is Layla's Dad," explained Tom to Emma.

"And Faith," I added in desperation. "I want Faith."

As I muttered those words, the irony wasn't lost on me.

Mac and I had first met when I was assigned to interview him for a lifestyle magazine almost two years ago.

He was this louche, charismatic, older man with a ready smile and a prominent nose that only seemed to enhance his character.

Mac had flirted outrageously with me from the beginning of the interview, and as I was departing the Edinburgh restaurant where we'd met for lunch, he'd snatched my mobile from my hand and entered his number.

I remember feeling warm and fuzzy with flattery and admiration for this political thriller writer, and after allowing a couple of days to pass, I had rung him.

After a few dates, Mac insisted on visiting me in Loch Harris and was swept away by its silvery waters and swathes of forestry.

He said he had been energised by its beauty and I was delighted when he announced he was renting one of the plush new holiday apartments that had sprung up close to the town.

My dad had been sceptical of Mac from the beginning, especially when he learned that he had been married before. "But there's a twenty-five-year age gap between the pair of you," he would protest. "He could be your father."

"But he's not, is he? You are."

I recalled Dad sucking in the air through his teeth. "And now you're moving in with him?"

"Correction, Dad. Mac is moving in with me."

My father had pushed his tanned hands into his combat trouser pockets. "Stop being so pedantic."

Then he had reached out and given me a protective hug. "This must be boosting the old codger's ego no end, being seen with a gorgeous twenty-nine-year-old."

"Old codger?" I laughed. "Really?" Dad's sombre expression made me laugh louder. "Mac's only fifty-four, Dad, not ninety-four. And you're only a year older than him."

A flush appeared across my dad's weather-lashed cheeks. "He's been married before, love."

"Well, so have you," I pointed out, trying not to pull up images of my mother.

Tina was like this faceless silhouette at times, who had lingered on the outskirts of my life, before she'd taken off to

London, leaving my shattered Dad and her confused young daughter behind.

The less I thought about my mother, the better I always felt.

"That's an entirely different situation," argued my dad.

"No, it isn't. He's over fifty, Dad, just like you. At that age, baggage is only to be expected."

Now, that baggage – in the shape of Hannah, his ex-wife of twenty-four years – had reared her head in all its severe, black-bobbed glory.

Once Tom and Emma had departed my cottage, I slumped against the front door.

My attention fell on my engagement ring. The rose-gold band seemed to grin up at me. It might as well have sprung from a Christmas cracker.

What had meant so much to me was now taking on a meaningless, cheap hue.

As Mac's life had drained from him, he hadn't been here in Loch Harris with me. He'd been thrashing about in a hotel bed with her.

Chapter Three

"I could kill him!" thundered Dad into his mug of tea.

Faith, my best friend, folded her arms. Her three gold bangles jangled together. "Well, something tells me that's going to be rather tricky, Harry."

"You know full well what I mean."

When I emerged again from the bathroom, snuffling into a hankie and still sporting a face that resembled a melted waxwork, Dad and Faith dumped down their respective mugs of tea and rushed towards me.

I gazed past Faith's shoulder, the grey and blue twists of the loch visible out of my kitchen window. "Why was he with her? What was he doing with Hannah when he was supposed to be meeting his agent?"

Faith shoved a lock of her strawberry-blonde hair back behind her ear. "There'll be time to mull over all that later. Right now, you just need to focus on yourself."

"But how can I? I've just found out that my fiancé died

while he was shagging another woman! And not just any woman at that..."

My dad's lips morphed into a hard line. I noticed he was wearing his favourite Pink Floyd T-shirt.

"Have you heard from her? The ex?" he asked.

I dabbed ineffectually at my eyes with a corner of my hankie. "Not yet, but I'm sure I will at some point."

My dad and Faith exchanged wide-eyed glances. "You don't have to speak to this Anna, if you don't want to, love," he said.

"At least not yet," added Faith.

"Her name's Hannah, Dad. And how can I not speak to her? She was the last person to see Mac." A dry croak shot out of my mouth. "Well, I say see, but we all know what they were doing and it wasn't a sodding crossword!"

Dad gathered me into his arms. He smelled of damp earth and there were faint traces of dirt under his fingernails.

I let out a series of heaving sobs, until I was able to take a few breaths. "You need a haircut," I mumbled into his shoulder.

Dad's chest lifted. "I was going for the rugged landscape gardener look."

I jerked my head up and eyed his collar-length salt and pepper waves. "Actually," I conceded, rubbing my red nose, "it does quite suit you."

Dad's arms tightened again around me. "You do know we're both here for you, don't you? Anything you need, you just have to ask."

Visions of Mac's hooded blue eyes drifted in and out of

my mind. I reached up and kissed Dad on the cheek. "I know."

Then I flinched as Hannah's powdered and pointed expression interrupted me again. She refused to leave me alone. Everywhere I turned in the cottage, I could see her and Mac in bed, going at it like two battery-operated bunnies.

I made an attempt to gather myself together. I knew what Faith and Dad would say to my suggestion, but decided to air it anyway. As far as I was concerned, it was just putting off the inevitable. "Actually, there is something I need."

"What is it?" asked Faith.

I swivelled my wet grey eyes on her. "I really do need to speak to Hannah. *Now*."

Dad and Faith's appalled expressions followed me out of my sitting room.

"What are you doing?" asked Faith gently. "What are you looking for?"

I ventured into our bedroom further down the hall, deliberately averting my gaze from our bed, with its coffee and cream covers and two vanilla-coloured scatter cushions. There was the faintest ticking noise from the alarm clock.

Lying on top of the white bedside cupboard on Mac's side was his contacts book. "I knew it was in here," I mumbled.

"What is?" pushed Dad, lingering in the doorway. "Look, darling, you've had a terrible shock. Why don't you go for a lie-down and I'll bring you a fresh cup of tea?"

I shook my head. "That's the worst thing I could do. When I close my eyes, I just see them together."

I rifled through the alphabetical pages until I came across Hannah's mobile number under her new married name. A thought struck me. Not only was I wounded by all this, but her new husband Mark would be too.

But the selfish, furious part of me didn't care.

Dad heaved a concerned sigh. "Layla. Think about this. It's not really the right time—"

"So when will be the right time, Dad? You tell me when will be the right time to ask my fiancé's ex-wife why he was in bed with her when he died?"

There was a weighty silence.

"My mobile is up on the mantelpiece," I said to Faith, heading out into the hall. "Just by that photo."

Faith hesitated for a moment before walking past me into the sitting room and reaching past the grinning picture of Mac. She handed the phone to me.

Mac's gaze sprung out of the picture frame. He had such a ready smile. The lights of New York were popping behind him.

Ignoring the silent pleading of Dad and Faith, I set my phone down on the coffee table and rifled through the pages again until I located Hannah's number. A ball twisted in my stomach at the sight of Mac's spidery, dark handwriting.

My cheeks were hot and tear-stained. "Faith, you couldn't make a fresh pot of tea please?"

She inclined her head, as if accepting defeat. "Of course I

14

can, and I'm making you some buttered toast too. No arguments. You need to try and eat something."

While the dial tone began ringing in my ear, Faith encouraged Dad to join her back in the kitchen. "Come on, Harry. Layla has made up her mind."

Dad shot me a concerned look. "Oh, I can see that."

I watched the pair of them meander back into the kitchen and begin pottering about with mugs. I knew they were worried, but ignoring what had happened wasn't going to help anyone, least of all me.

My thoughts were rudely interrupted by the sudden husky tones of Hannah bleating, "Hello?"

Chapter Four

"Hello?" she repeated again. "Who is this?"

"It's me. Layla," I said, as I began to pace.

"Layla," she repeated in a flat tone.

I clung to the silence for a moment before a surge of resentment swept over me. I caught a glimpse of myself in the oval mirror above the fireplace and wished I hadn't. I looked like a negative of the real me – pale with soulless eyes. I managed to force out the first few words that popped into my head. "You owe me an explanation."

I needed to hear what had happened. I needed to hear it from Hannah.

"I don't think now is the best time to discuss this," she replied evenly.

Anger flared in my chest. "So, when would be the best time? How about over afternoon tea? Or would 3 p.m. next Wednesday suit you better?"

"There's no need for sarcasm."

My fingers clutched my mobile tighter to my ear. "Don't you dare stand there and tell me how I should be feeling right now." I dragged a hand through my wayward hair. "I've just been told that my fiancé died while shagging his ex-wife. I think I win in the emotional stakes, don't you?"

A cracking sob seeped down the line. I scrunched my eyes up tight and opened them again. Early afternoon sun was washing over my bare toes.

"I'm so sorry," she swallowed. "The last thing Mac wanted to do was hurt you. But we had so much history and you can't extinguish twenty-four years just like that."

Realisation punched me in the stomach. "Is this your way of telling me this wasn't a one-off?"

From the kitchen, Faith clattered down her mug and Dad's eyes widened.

"Let's not ... let's not talk about this now, Layla," faltered Hannah. "It's all too raw."

Her audacity was breath-taking. Didn't she realise what she'd done? "You are in no position to stand there and dictate to me."

Tears jostled at the back of my eyes. "How long?"

There was a sniff and then the sound of rustling.

"I asked you a question."

Hannah's sigh was like a gust of wind. "Eighteen months."

My shoulders stiffened under my pink jumper. Faith searched my expression from the kitchen, but I just stared back at her. "But that means all the time that Mac and I were together..."

"He loved you, Layla. He really did. But Mac and I shared so much while we were married…"

I lowered my mobile, not able to drag my eyes away from the engagement ring glistening on my left hand.

Hannah's disembodied rasp intruded again. "Layla? Layla? Are you still there?"

Chapter Five

F aith's fingers, slicked with pink polish, tapered up and down the sleeve of my black jacket. "Are you ready?"

My shoulders slumped. "Not really."

"I expect you're not. That was a stupid question."

Dad, his crisp, white shirt emphasising the rich chestnut of his tan, came towards me and hovered.

I gave a brief nod and then we rustled down the hallway in our funeral garb. As I passed my hall mirror, I stole a quick glance. There were smudges of hurt clouding my eyes. Perhaps it was because I'd pulled my hair back in a bun, but my jaw appeared more pronounced. Still, that was no surprise. I hadn't been eating properly since Mac had died just over a week ago.

I applied a shaky extra dash of lipstick before pressing my lips together and exhaling.

The funeral car negotiated the country lanes like a shiny black snake. The familiar bursts of hedgerows and curve of Loch Harris blended into each other like a Monet watercolour.

How was I supposed to feel? Was I supposed to be angry? Heartbroken?

Dad clutched my hand as he sat beside me on the back seat, his coarse skin acting like a comfort blanket. I appraised his navy suit through a watery smile. "You look very dashing, Dad."

He rolled his eyes up to the roof of the car. "Well, I couldn't turn up at a funeral in my Motorhead T-shirt, could I?" He raised a finger and traced it around the inside of his collar.

Beside my dad, Faith leaned forward to look at me. She'd tamed her blonde locks into a chignon and was tugging at the hem of her dark skirt.

"Mac fell in love with Loch Harris from the first moment he saw her," I blurted. "Ironic really that he turned out to love the place more than me."

Dad and Faith squirmed in their seats.

"He thought it was such a gorgeous place that he said he wouldn't mind being buried here. I didn't think it would happen for a long, long time. I thought we would have years and years to explore together."

Faith slid her arm across and folded her fingers around mine. "You'll get through this. We're here for you."

I nodded, not convinced in the slightest. "Did you manage to reach Mum?" I stuttered after a pause. "Did you tell her?"

Dad's freshly shaved jaw tightened. "I rang her and left several messages, but she hasn't got back to me yet."

"OK. Thanks."

I turned back to the window, blinking.

I don't know why I had even bothered to ask Dad such a stupid question. Of course she wouldn't be at the funeral. No doubt she had many more pressing issues to deal with – like organising yet another of her charity lunches in some swanky London hotel.

What would it be this time? Raising money for traumatised hamsters? Highlighting the plight of the middle classes, who hadn't had a holiday for three months?

I could feel resentment tightening in my chest as we approached the church. Pity Tina didn't consider her own daughter a priority, or the funeral of her almost son-in-law.

She had only met him once, when I'd accompanied him on a book signing to London three months after we'd started dating, and Mum had insisted on meeting up for a bite of lunch afterwards.

I recalled the way she had openly flirted with him, dangling her strappy heel off the end of her foot and remarking in that raspy way of hers, "He's far more my age than yours, darling!"

More painful reminders of Mac gripped me again, silly things that I took for granted – his languid, confident walk, the way he would bark with laughter at Monty Python…

What a bloody mess it all was.

We eased to a halt in front of the red scalloped porch and granite steps of Loch Harris church. They led up to a gothic oak door studded with two imposing Celtic crosses.

I flinched at the sight of the mourners dotted around the church entrance. They were hunched in conversation or milling around the cemetery in quiet contemplation, black coats flapping gently and the odd hat surfacing amongst the sea of heads.

I recognised the long and lean angles of Mac's literary agent, Garth Keller, who was offering polite smiles to Mac's fellow author friends and various members of his publicity team.

Mac's parents had both passed away some years ago, so family members were in short supply, however, I was sure I'd glimpsed Mac's younger sister, Lois. She was sporting a Spanish-style, black lacy affair on her head.

A glimmer of a flash made me shuffle forward in my seat. Dread pooled in my stomach. "Photographers."

Dad jerked his head round and peered out of the rear windscreen. "There's only a couple of them, love."

"A couple is enough."

Faith flapped her hand dismissively. "Don't you worry about them. Garth said he'll take care of it."

"Garth? So, you've spoken to him then?"

Faith offered me a smile. "I rang him a few days ago. I hope you don't mind. Mac's publicity team said a couple of reporters owe them a favour or two that they would call in."

I blinked. "Is that why the details of Mac's death seem to have been buried – if you'll pardon the pun?"

Faith nodded, shooting my dad a glance. "I know Garth Keller can be an arrogant swine, but he has his uses."

I jumped back as the driver materialised at my window and eased open the car door. I felt like a new-born fawn, all shaky legs and startled eyes. I gulped in the earthy scent of lavender heather and damp grass.

Dad and Faith emerged and stood either side of me, and I paused for a moment on the gravel. A shimmer of late morning sun was striking a helmet of sharply cut raven hair over by the church door.

Hannah.

I dropped my head and eyed the engagement ring on my left hand. "Why am I still wearing this bloody thing? It doesn't mean anything. Not anymore."

Dad slid his arm around my waist and gave me an affectionate squeeze. "There will be plenty of time for starting over. Just let's get through today." His grey eyes flickered over me. "Ready?"

I eased the ring from my finger. Its absence left behind the faintest trace of pale empty skin. Dad and Faith exchanged charged stares as they watched me fire open my quilted clutch bag and push the ring inside it.

"Now I am."

Chapter Six

I tried not to focus on Mac's pale oak casket through the polished glass of the hearse.

He had never been a hearts and flowers type of person, and considering he had been having sex with Hannah when his heart gave out, I hadn't had the urge to spend lots of money on a lavish wreath for him.

Dad had joked darkly that he could lay his hands on a "bloody great clump of giant hogweed", and although rather tempting, I decided in the end to go for a simple, circular wreath decorated with purple and lilac flowers that included liatris, freesias and tulips.

The florist had interwoven it with lime green eucalyptus and aspidistra.

My floral tribute was seated at the front of Mac's casket, with a riot of white and yellow lilies, tied with navy and green tartan ribbon, positioned on the other side. Its trumpet-shaped blooms were pressing against the window and almost obliterated the view of Mac's casket from that side.

I could guess who that ostentatious display was from.

Sat beside my floral tribute was one from Lois, Mac's sister. She had opted for an open book, crafted from yellow and white carnations, altogether a more modest and tasteful affair.

I could see myself reflected in the hearse glass, all pressed-together lips and wide eyes.

"Layla!"

Lois rushed towards me, her pale face etched with relief at seeing someone she recognised. She gathered me into her arms. Then she took a step backwards in her black kitten heels. She clutched both my hands in hers. "How are you bearing up?"

My brow furrowed. "I honestly don't know what I'm feeling right now."

"I'm not surprised."

She offered greetings to Faith and Dad who were standing behind me. "I think nearly all these people are Mac's literary associates."

"Well, not quite all," I observed, indicating Hannah who was holding court amongst a small group.

Lois narrowed her dark eyes. "Oh, her! I'm so sorry she's here. I didn't want her to come but—"

"It's fine," I interrupted. "Well, that's a lie. It's not fine, but she was his wife for twenty-four years." I swallowed a ball of resentment. "And she was with Mac at the end. Well, under him at least. Or maybe she was on top? Who knows…"

My voice splintered and Dad pulled me into a fierce hug. "Don't go there, darling. It's not worth it."

Faith nodded beside me. "Harry's right ... Oh shit. Cruella is coming over."

Hannah was stalking across the gravel, parting the fellow mourners like a praying mantis in a black velvet trouser suit, needle-thin heels, and a Missoni hat. It was decorated with a silk crochet scarf of gold and turquoise that fluttered out behind her as she moved.

I could feel my jaw tightening.

"Hello Layla," she murmured, through a slash of red lipstick.

I inclined my head. "Hannah."

"I think we should go in for the service now," ground out Faith as she delivered a swift glare at Mac's ex-wife.

Dad took me by the arm but I gently unfurled his fingers from my sleeve. "Why?" I asked her. "Why get engaged to me if he was still hankering after you?"

Lois, Faith, and Dad swivelled their icy attention to Hannah.

Hannah's ruby nails clutched at her tasselled purse. "He loved you in his own way," she rasped in theatrical tones. "He really did. But I was an itch that Mac still needed to scratch."

"Oh please," burst out Faith, taking a protective step in front of me. "Spare us all the old clichés."

"It's the truth," insisted Hannah. "Mac loved being seen with a much younger woman. It boosted his ego. But when it came to a meeting of minds—"

"So that's what happened last week," snorted my dad,

folding his arms. "You and Mac were having an intellectual debate when he keeled over."

Hannah fidgeted. "You know that isn't what happened."

"I don't know why you insisted on coming along today," hissed Lois, aware of the curious looks from the other mourners drifting past. "Couldn't you have put other people first for once in your life?"

I snatched a steadying breath, and from the corner of my eye, I noticed a man about Mac's age observing our exchanges with more than a passing interest.

He appraised me from under silvery brows. Was he a journalist?

I turned my head away. That was the last thing I needed. "I've had enough of providing the pre-funeral entertainment." I turned to Lois, Faith, and Dad. "Let's go into the church."

Hannah took a step forward, her heels grinding into the pink gravel. "We just couldn't help ourselves. I'm sorry."

I stared at her, incredulous. Dad and Faith were ushering me further into the cool air of the church, when the man with the impressive eyebrows stepped into my line of sight. "I'm so sorry to interrupt you Ms Devlin, especially today of all days, but I'm David Murray, a friend of Mac's."

He smiled kindly and slid his fingers down his slate-grey tie.

"Can't this wait?" insisted my dad. "Layla has a lot to deal with right now."

"I appreciate that, sir, but not only was I Mac's friend, I'm also his legal representative."

David Murray glanced over at Hannah. "Once Mac

became a successful author, he insisted I ensure all his financial affairs were in order."

He fixed me with an earnest look. "Your late fiancé was most insistent that his final wishes be carried out immediately, should there be any..." His cut-glass timbre tailed off and he jerked his thatch of steel hair in Hannah's direction. "To limit the chances of there being any dubiety, shall we say."

I blinked at him, not processing what he was saying. "Mr Murray, I don't understand."

"Please. Call me David." He gave Faith and Dad a smile. "I'd really appreciate a word with you after the service."

I flapped my hands in defeat. "Yes. Why not? I mean, there's bound to be lots of loose ends to tie up."

"Are you sure?" asked Dad. "You don't have to do anything you don't want to, Layla, especially not today."

I grasped my clutch bag tighter to me. "I know, Dad. But the sooner I can try to put all this mess behind me, the better."

Chapter Seven

I was relieved to escape the confines of the church once the service had trickled to its end with a rousing rendition of 'Amazing Grace'.

The smell of beeswax and candles was making me feel nauseous.

As I emerged, blinking, into the sunlight, golden shots of colour lit up the stained-glass windows. The shards of ruby and buttercup seemed to bleed into one another.

Mac was interred within sight of the Loch Harris Fells, and as soon as Reverend Callan concluded proceedings at the graveside, Faith and Dad melted away, together with the other mourners, to give me some privacy.

I stared down into the grave, at the gold plaque winking up at me from the coffin lid.

MacKenzie Terence Christie
Born 18 January 1965
Died 2 April 2020

My emotions were running riot. What was I supposed to feel right now? Was I supposed to throw myself down on the grass and let out wretched sobs? I felt cheated, angry...

My thoughts travelled to the surprise party I had been planning for Mac's next birthday – a New Year's bash out on Loch Harris, with a hired boat, a ceilidh band, and fireworks.

A dry laugh threatened to erupt out of my throat.

"Layla, we are so sorry."

"Layla, if there is anything we can do..."

I jerked my face up from the graveside to see a cluster of Mac's writing buddies surrounding me with hesitant yet concerned expressions. Did any of them know about Mac and Hannah? Were they pitying stares?

"Let's get you in the car," interrupted Dad, guiding me through the throng. He addressed the group of solemn faces. "Thank you very much for coming and please feel free to join us at the wake."

Murmurs followed us as he led me away. "I've asked Lois to join us in our car so we can all go to the wake together."

Catching sight of my slumping shoulders, Faith excused herself from speaking to Reverend Callan and hurried towards me. She pinned me to the spot with caring hands. "Just put in an appearance and we will leave whenever you want to, OK?"

I answered her with a watery smile. "Thank you. I don't think I could have got through all this without you and my dad."

My father sighed. "We're a team Layla, you and I. We always have been."

We approached the black Daimler, where Lois was hovering. "Thanks ever so much for insisting I travel with you."

Dad flapped away her gratitude. "Don't be silly. I suppose we're all family – in a way."

I cocked an eyebrow. "Or at least, we were meant to be."

Ignoring the tilt of Hannah's grey hat amongst the throng, we all clambered into the car and focused on the avenue of trees and the assorted mourners drifting back to their parked vehicles.

Images slipped past the window, and with that came the realisation that Mac was gone and all I was left with was the empty promise of an engagement ring rattling around inside my clutch bag and a lasting image of him collapsed on top of his naked ex-wife.

As if reading my thoughts, Lois shifted round in the front passenger seat to look at me. She didn't say anything. Neither did I. We swapped meaningful stares.

Dad and Faith were bunched up beside me on the back seat. Faith's silk shirt was a little rumpled and I noticed that my dad had loosened his tie.

I was so conflicted, so charged, that I couldn't even muster up the energy to think about Mac's solicitor friend. Whatever it was, I would do it. All I wanted was to see the back of this dappled morning in April.

During the funeral arrangements, Lois had mentioned The Aldebaran, an old hotel on the outskirts of Loch Harris, as a possible venue for Mac's wake.

"Mac always said the place had so much character," explained Lois. "He even said it had influenced him for the setting of his next novel."

And so it was that I found myself, my dad, my best friend, and the woman who had almost become my sister-in-law being driven into the semi-circular car park of The Aldebaran.

I was relieved to see we had arrived first.

"I think we all deserve a bloody big drink," exclaimed Dad, thanking the driver. He linked arms with me and Faith, and Lois followed up the rear.

The architecture of the hotel was dove-grey brick that twinkled prettily under the west coast light. Sash windows blinked out like inquisitive eyes, and underneath the canopied green and blue tartan entrance sat two fat shrubs in cream pots.

We all filed in and were directed by a member of staff to the right-hand side of the chrome reception area.

A function room boasting the name 'Selkie' was laid out with tables adorned in starched white tablecloths, and members of the hotel staff were placing platters of miniature seafood canapés, assorted sandwiches with tuna, brie, and egg, mini tartlets, and focaccia onto the tables.

On a smaller side table was an array of freshly baked fruit, plain, and cheese scones, lemon shortbread, and slices of cheesecake.

I gratefully accepted a glass of white wine offered by a passing waiter and took a generous mouthful. The crispness hit the back of my throat. Faith came up to join me, also clutching a glass of wine.

"I like the name of this room," I commented. "Did you know selkies were mythical Scottish creatures who could transform themselves from seal to human form and back again?"

Faith picked up a plate and napkin. "So they say."

"Kind of ironic really. That's what Mac was doing. He was leading a double a life with Hannah and I knew sod all about it."

Faith's pink mouth popped open to reassure me, but I waggled my wine glass. "I just want to get this bloody charade over with."

Murmurings made us both swing round. The remainder of the mourners were wandering in, exclaiming politely at the midnight-blue carpeting, ivory walls, and chandelier dripping from the ceiling.

"You need to eat something," ordered Faith, thrusting the napkin and plate into my free hand. "Go on."

I pulled a face and tried to summon up some enthusiasm for two goat's cheese and red pepper tartlets. Faith frowned at my plate. "Is that all you're having?"

"Who are you now, my mother?"

Faith pushed an escaping hair back into her chignon. "You can ill afford to lose any more weight."

"I'm hardly fading away before your very eyes," I answered, pointing to my bottom.

"No, but your face is definitely thinner than it was."

I rolled my eyes up to the cornice ceiling and plopped a tomato and mozzarella sandwich onto my plate. "Happy now?"

"Not really, but I will be when I see you actually eat it."

I nibbled at one of the tartlets, realising I was hungrier than I thought. I moved on to the other tartlet, and was about to take a bite of the sandwich when David Murray appeared at my shoulder. He was carrying an apologetic expression. "I'm so sorry to trouble you again Ms Devlin..."

Dad, who had returned with Lois – both carrying cups of freshly brewed coffee – stopped short. "Do you have to do this now?"

I put down my plate and ran a weary hand over the top of my head. "It's fine. Whatever it is, let's get it over with."

David Murray nodded and smiled. "Thank you."

He shot out a hand and indicated towards the function room doors. "There's a quiet spot just past reception. We can talk there."

He strode ahead of me and held the doors open. Dad, Lois, and Faith watched me leave.

There was the faintest tinkle of pan pipes seeping through the public address system as I straightened my skirt and sat on the quilted sofa opposite. A hunk of chestnut coffee table separated us and out of the floor-to-ceiling window, I could see assorted flowerbeds and soaring lawns.

"I've been taking care of Mac's legal affairs for years," began David Murray, steepling his fingers. "He was always very clear on what he wanted."

My skin prickled. "Yes, that's very apparent."

David eyed me for a moment. "He did love you, Layla."

"But evidently, not enough."

David Murray dragged a hand down his face. He had

kind, hooded eyes and a soft expression. "He and Hannah had such a unique relationship…"

I let out a growl. "If you're here to defend him, I don't want to know." I shot up from the sofa. "In time, I might be able to forgive Mac, but right now, I can hardly bring myself to say his name."

David rose to his feet. "I understand."

"Do you? Do you really?"

He beckoned for me to sit down again. "Please, Ms Devlin."

I blew out a cloud of frustrated air and sank back onto the sofa. "If you have papers for me to sign, I will need to discuss anything with Lois. She is his sister, after all, and the only family Mac has left."

David Murray swished open his suit jacket, revealing a flash of caramel silk lining. He plucked out a slim white envelope and offered it across the table.

My breath fluttered in my chest at the sight of Mac's terrible handwriting. He had written my name in black ink on the front of it. It was all leaning letters and exaggerated loops.

"Mac told me that were anything to happen to him, you were to be given this straight after the funeral."

I took the envelope and stared down at it.

"He said he hoped it would explain everything."

I was aware of my heartbeat pounding in my ears and of the faint clatter of coffee cups in the background.

I turned over the envelope a few times in my hands, feeling its smooth straight edges. I knew Mac had always loved a touch of the dramatic, but this…

I looked across the table at David Murray, trying to read his expression and failing. He gave the briefest nod of encouragement and I switched my attention back to the mysterious envelope in my hands. Then I surprised myself by feverishly ripping it open.

Chapter Eight

M ac's handwriting swam along the paper in front of me.

I searched David's face.

"I'm aware of its contents," he admitted.

I cleared my throat and began to read.

Dearest Layla,

If you are reading this then that means the secret I have been keeping from you will have to be revealed – and for that, I am truly sorry.

It also means we won't be spending the rest of our lives together.

I tried to bury a painful ball clustering at the base of my throat. Was this some sort of twisted joke on Mac's part?

I lowered the letter and stared across the table at David. From behind him, a couple of mourners appeared.

"Would you like a tea or coffee, Layla? Or perhaps something stronger?"

"No," I faltered, the letter feeling alien in my fingers. "No, thank you."

I lowered my eyes and started reading again.

You need to understand that meeting you made me feel twenty-eight again and I will always be grateful.

A few more hotel guests wandered past us, their shoes resonating on the black and white tiled floor.

Despite what stories you might hear, please know that I love you.

It's true that Hannah and I always felt that we had unfinished business…

His words pricked me and I blinked several times. "Why is he doing this? Why is he saying all this now?"

David nodded his understanding. "I know it isn't easy, Ms Devlin, but please read to the end."

I let out a weary sigh and turned my attention back to Mac's last words.

… but know that despite any feelings I still had for Hannah, you mean the world to me.

I frowned, tears gathering on my lashes as I waved the piece of paper dismissively. "Oh, please Mac. Spare me the Elizabeth Taylor and Richard Burton routine."

David Murray fiddled with the buttons on his suit jacket. "Please don't think I'm interfering, but he really did love you."

I eyed him. "Are you telling me you knew about him and Hannah?"

"No, not at the beginning. Not until he asked me to revise his will."

I shifted on the hotel couch. "And when was that?"

David dragged a hand down his face. "Two months ago."

"Two months?" I echoed. "Why on earth would Mac have altered his will as recently as two months ago?"

Now it was David's turn to shift on the opposite quilted couch.

I flapped the letter in mid-air in disbelief. "He wanted both of us. Was I the only idiot not to know what was going on?"

"You're not an idiot," assured David in hushed tones. "Mac was an expert at managing to keep his private life private, even when his novels became a big success."

I waved the letter savagely. "You're telling me!"

David lifted a manicured finger and pointed to the letter. "Please. Layla."

My shoulders slumped in defeat and I turned back to Mac's slanting, black scrawl.

I know there is nothing I can say to apologise for my behaviour, so that is why I have named you as the sole beneficiary of my book royalties.

39

Lois will receive the advance for my last novel, Improper Justice.

My hand flew to my throat. "What is this? Mac has left me his royalties?"

"Yes," confirmed David. "The whole lot. It's one hell of a back catalogue, but I'm sure I don't have to tell you that."

Waves of shock swamped me. What was this? Some sort of bribery from beyond the grave?

"That amount of money" carried on David, "excluding the sales from *Improper Justice,* which will be included later after its release, will be in the region of—"

"I don't want it," I choked. "It's guilt money and I don't want anything to do with it."

"Layla, I know Mac behaved like an utter idiot, but he was adamant he wanted you to have it." He leaned forward, his side sweep of grey hair catching watery sunlight through the window. "It will ensure you have a very comfortable future."

I felt like laughing. "What future? I thought I had a future with him." I slapped the letter back on the table in front of me. "If I accepted that money, I'd be condoning what he did."

"No, you wouldn't. You know that after Mac was diagnosed with his heart condition—"

I slumped back on the hotel sofa, winded. "What heart condition, David? What are you talking about?"

His jaw sagged. Alarm shot through his eyes. "Oh shit. Don't tell me you knew nothing about this either? Mac said he was going to tell you…"

I folded my arms, anger and pain ready to erupt. "Well, he didn't."

"You have got to be joking." David rubbed his face. "I'm sorry. I assumed you knew."

"Well, evidently not."

"Mac was diagnosed with a heart condition a few months back."

"This just gets better and better," I gasped, momentum gathering. I felt as though my insides were being squeezed.

My attention fell to Mac's letter on the table. "First, I find out he's been sleeping with his ex-wife the whole time we were together and he left me a pile of cash out of guilt. Now I discover he was ill and never told me!"

"He wasn't ill," clarified David. "But he was supposed to take things easier and be mindful of his condition."

My hands balled into fists on my lap. "And he did that by energetically shagging Hannah and killing himself in the process?"

An awkward blush swept up David's cheeks.

"Does Hannah know? About his heart?"

"No," assured David emphatically. "Mac was adamant he wasn't going to be treated differently, so he kept it quiet."

"Even from Lois?"

David nodded again and pressed his lips together. "I did tell him I thought he was being ridiculous on more than one occasion, and then he said he would tell you – but obviously, he never got around to it."

I felt as though I were being swallowed by a huge, dark shadow. I didn't know Mac at all.

I jumped out of my seat, my legs swaying in my heels. I wanted to get away from here; I didn't want to be anywhere near that letter. "I told you. I don't want that money. I don't even want the memories I have of him."

David rose to his feet and straightened his tie. "Layla, I know this must all have come as a terrible shock to you."

"That's an understatement. You cannot begin to imagine what is going on in my head right now."

David sighed and thrust his hands into his suit pockets. "I know this must be a hell of a lot to digest, especially today, but Mac insisted that you be told at his funeral. He didn't want Hannah getting wind of any of this."

"He didn't want Hannah getting wind of what, exactly?"

I spun round on my heel. Oh no. She must have been listening around the corner.

She barrelled towards David and me in her ostentatious hat.

I reached for Mac's letter and stuffed it into my jacket pocket. I didn't want her seeing it.

"This is a private conversation, Hannah," said David. "I was planning to speak to you next week."

"Next week? What is this? It's not a bloody bus queue!"

David frowned and lowered his voice. "Can't you exhibit a modicum of decency? It is Mac's funeral, after all."

Hannah folded her bony arms and eyed me. "Well, I want to know what's going on. I bet certain people will do very well out of Mac's demise."

I turned back to David. "I don't want it. I don't want anything from Mac. Not anymore."

Hannah's nostrils flared out of her heavily made-up face. "I was his wife for twenty odd years. I have a right to know what the hell is going on here."

David shot me a questioning gaze, and I nodded. It made no difference to me now, anyway. And after the emotional demands of the funeral, the last thing I needed was one of Hannah's melodramatic meltdowns in full public view.

David indicated for Hannah to sit down and she tilted her powdered chin up in triumph.

I could feel my body stiffen as I sat again. I kept my watery gaze focused on David across the table. I had seen enough of Hannah's long nose and pinched mouth to last me the next forty years.

When he told her about Mac leaving me all current and future royalties from his novels, her nails reached for the dangly bracelet dripping from her wrist. Her appalled expression twisted from me to David. "But that's ridiculous," she spluttered. "There must be some mistake."

She opened and closed her mouth for a few moments, inwardly processing what David had just told her. "That's an extortionate amount of money. Why the hell would he leave it all to you?" I could see her chest rising and falling. Her voice was growing bitter. "No, that can't be right. What did Mac leave to me?"

David settled back on the other quilted couch. "You'll recall that Mac owned an estate in northern France. He has bequeathed that to you."

Hannah was blinking so furiously, I thought she'd

developed a nervous twitch. "You call that apartment an estate? It's *in* a state, more like! It's as big as a minute!"

"It's well maintained and in a good location," replied David evenly. "If you don't wish to keep it, I'm sure you'll be able to sell it quickly."

Hannah swung her curtain of bobbed hair towards me. She couldn't contain her fury. "So I get a pokey flat with a rusty balcony and she gets her hands on all his royalties. This is ludicrous!"

She threw her head back, almost losing her hat. "That estate, as you call it, was Mac's first writing retreat. It's a sodding bug hole!"

"I think that's an exaggeration, don't you?" asked David.

Hannah glowered under the brim of her designer hat.

I had never been to the northern France flat, but Mac had shown me photos of it. It was a modest, cream and beige balconied affair close to a main street and a public park.

Mac had been able to afford it at the time thanks to his redundancy package as a political columnist for one of the London broadsheets, and it was there that he had written his first two novels.

Once his writing career had begun ascending, he'd rented it out as holiday accommodation.

Hannah shot forward, making the silk lining of her jacket rustle. "I want to contest Mac's will."

"Oh, for pity's sake," I blurted. "Have you no shame? First, you shag him to death and then you sit there like Vampira, making demands?"

Hannah's hard gaze ran over me. "You've always been jealous of what Mac and I had."

"What?!" I shifted round to confront her, my hot cheeks burning.

"Ladies," warned David, indicating to our surroundings.

I noticed a couple of hotel guests frowning over at us while they browsed a rack of newspapers.

I fell silent, but Hannah rallied over the sound of the tinkling piano music that was now playing over the public system. "So, how do I get the ball rolling with contesting this ridiculous situation?"

David's lips carried an element of amusement. "It would be a costly and lengthy process to contest this in court." He dashed an imaginary piece of fluff from his suit trousers. "I understand that your current husband's property business has been the recent subject of an alleged financial scam. Is that correct?"

Hannah's arrogant air began to slide. She paled under her make-up. "What are you implying, David?"

"What I'm trying to say is that if the rumours are true, Mark's property portfolio is in jeopardy, because of the losses you have sustained."

He leaned forward and smoothed down his sliver of a tie. "Mac was of sound mind when he dictated his will and was not experiencing any sort of incapacity or circumvention."

"And your point is?"

David slid a loaded glance my way before continuing. "If you insist on proceeding with a contest of the will, it could cost you and Mark a considerable amount of money, not to mention the negative publicity these sorts of cases attract. As for the fact you were—"

Hannah's mascara-lashed eyes rolled. "All right! All right!"

I could see her digesting this, like a giant cobra swallowing a rabbit.

"Does Mark know about you and Mac?" I asked.

"No," she ground out. "No, he doesn't. At least not yet. He's been in Dubai for the past few weeks on business."

She squirmed beside me as the function room doors creaked open further down the hallway and more urns of coffee and tea were ferried in by waiting staff.

I could see her mentally processing all the possible implications. "He's not due back for another fortnight."

David silently raised his hands and lowered them again.

"Oh, for pity's sake," spat Hannah, leaping to her feet. "Talk about being shafted in more ways than one!"

I snapped my head up to look at her. How could she be so insensitive?

A white rage took hold of me and I jumped up to confront her. Hannah's feelings were of no consequence to me.

"Layla," said David in a warning tone.

I shook my head at him, vengeful tears brimming in my eyes. "No. She needs to know."

Hannah's expression took on an apprehensive edge. "Know what? What are you talking about?"

I wanted to see her reaction. I wanted her to know what it felt like to be subject to Mac's deceptions. I looked her square in the face. "Mac had a heart condition and it is *your fault* that he is dead. You literally shagged Mac to death."

Hannah froze. "What? No. You're lying. He would have told me." She whirled round to David. "It's not true, is it?"

David dropped his eyes to the glossy floor for a moment. "I'm afraid it is true. He didn't want anyone to know. Not even Lois."

My shoulders sagged with emotional exhaustion after revealing the truth to her. Part of me felt satisfied by her stunned reaction, whereas the other half experienced a surge of guilt.

Hannah hovered, myriad emotions flitting through her eyes before she settled on strained defiance. "Thank you for the legal advice, David."

Then, ignoring me, she whirled away.

My eyes followed her until she had barged back through the function room doors and into Mac's gathering again.

"I'm sorry," I gushed to David. "I shouldn't have told her – especially not like that – but she was so insensitive..."

The solicitor nodded. "It would have come out sooner or later, I'm sure, and she was being her usual brittle self."

"Thank you," I managed after a pause.

David pushed his hands into his trouser pockets. "You're welcome, Layla. A contest of Mac's will is the last thing either you or Lois need right now."

He tipped his head to one side. "So, about the royalty money Mac has left you..."

I wrapped my arms around myself. "This doesn't change anything. I still don't want it."

David's expression collapsed. "But Layla, don't you think you're being rather stubborn about all this?"

I shook my head fiercely. "Our relationship was a sham. It's guilt money and I don't want it."

His reply was gentle. "Give yourself some time. Once you've had time to think it through—"

"I don't need to think anything through," I swallowed, dashing away a tear with the back of my hand. "I'm thinking very clearly now."

I pulled Mac's letter out of my jacket pocket and threw it onto the wooden coffee table. "I don't want a penny from him. I wish I could forget I ever met him."

And with that, I hurried back down the corridor and towards the function room in a haze of tears.

Chapter Nine

I burst through the wooden panelled swing doors so hard that I was in danger of dislodging the blue and gold 'Selkie' name plate that was attached to them.

As my eyes scanned the crowd of mourners, I noticed abandoned plates, screwed-up napkins, and loosened ties.

Faith was lingering by the stack of white ceramic coffee cups, chatting to Lois and Dad.

"I'm going to head off now," I managed through a watery smile.

Dad took one look at me and set down his crumb-filled plate on the nearby pastry table. "What happened, lovey?"

I studied each of their worried faces.

What the hell had Mac been thinking? Why hadn't he told me about his heart diagnosis? He had been leading this other life when he wasn't with me, and it had been a reckless, selfish one that had left me without my fiancé and Lois without her brother.

Oh shit! Lois. Guilt crawled all over me. I had to tell her

about Mac's heart condition. This wasn't just about me. She had every right to know.

"Layla?" asked Lois, studying me. "Are you all right?"

I felt suspicion nudge me. Could Lois have known about Mac's illness after all? She hadn't known about his affair with Hannah – or, at least, she said she hadn't.

Who could I trust? Who could I confide in? Despondency thudded in my head. I opened and closed my mouth.

"Come outside, all of you," I said after a moment. "There's something I need to tell you."

Leaving behind the thrum of conversation, I slid out of the function room, with Dad, Lois, and Faith following me.

I headed for a secluded set of couches just around the corner from reception.

They each took up a seat on the biscuit-coloured sofa opposite, and the sight of them, all decked out in their funeral best and sitting side by side, almost made me smile. They reminded me of three grim-faced solicitors.

"As you know, I've spoken to David Murray." I clasped my fingers together in my lap.

"And?" asked Dad.

I secured my bun tighter and then, in a gush, explained Mac's heart condition.

My words were met with silence, only punctuated by the thrum of pan pipes from the reception area speakers.

Lois, Dad, and Faith blinked at each other, like three bewildered owls.

"Did you know about his heart, Lois?" I asked. "Mr Murray seemed to think you didn't, but did he tell you?"

Lois shook her swish of hair, her disbelief evident. "No! This is the first I've heard of it. The stupid man! Why didn't he tell us?" A hot flush popped on her cheeks. "The stubborn idiot." Tears clustered in her eyes.

Dad patted her hand.

"He must have had his reasons for not saying anything," pondered Faith, "although I have to admit I'm struggling right now to see what they might be."

Dad fired an agitated hand through his hair. "Layla was his fiancée. They were supposed to be getting married next year. She had a right to know."

I turned my watery gaze to the far side window. There was a small fountain sprouting water in a silvery gush, in the shape of a leaping fish. "He didn't even tell Hannah. She was every bit as shocked as me."

Lois blinked back more tears and arranged her pink-slicked lips into a firm line. "That would be a first. Very little seems to shock that woman."

I toyed with the lapel of my jacket. "There's something else too."

Faith's plucked brows hitched upwards. "As if that wasn't enough for you and Lois to contend with – and to be told that on the day of his funeral too."

Lois leaned across the polished table and cupped one of my hands in hers. "What is it, Layla? You said there's something else?"

I sucked in a cloud of air through my teeth. It just seemed like a torrent of revelations were being dropped from the heavens today – literally. I squeezed Lois's hand. "It seems that after Mac found out about his heart, he was determined to get his affairs in order. Mac has left you his advance for his last book – and he has bequeathed all his royalties from his novels to me."

Lois blinked several times. I turned to Faith and my dad, who were gawping at me.

"Well, that's great," said a shocked Lois after consideration. "It's the least he could do for you, under the circumstances." She jerked her head towards the 'Kelpie' function room. "Thank goodness that mercenary bitch won't be getting her hands on it." Then she paused. "I just hope Mac had the common sense not to leave her anything."

Dad and Faith joined in, chorusing their agreement. Their mouths popped open with surprise when I told them Mac had bequeathed his northern France apartment to her.

"Oh, I bet she didn't like that," smirked Lois. "There are no gold taps or chandeliers."

"I don't want it," I cut across their conversation, making the three of them start. "I don't want any of his guilt money."

Dad, Faith, and Lois looked perplexed. "But, love—" began Dad.

"I've already told David I'm not accepting it," I interrupted, lacing and unlacing my fingers in my lap. "The relationship – the engagement – it has all been one huge lie."

A crackle of my dry laughter made them frown with concern. "Unfortunately, I can't tell Mac what he can do with his royalties, so I'm telling you three instead."

Faith rubbed at her forehead, perplexed. "But sweetie,

do you realise how much money that is? I don't mean to sound mercenary, but it's probably a life-changing amount."

I levelled my gaze at her and told her exactly how much.

Faith's hands flew to her mouth. "Bloody hell, Layla!"

I shrugged. "It means nothing to me, because evidently our relationship, such as it was, meant nothing to Mac."

Dad threw his hands into the air. "You need time to digest all this, darling. It's been a horrible time for you. Going through the funeral today was bad enough, but to have Hannah and then this heart thing dropped on you as well…"

"I don't need time, Dad." I smoothed down my shirt. "I can't stay in Loch Harris after all this. There are too many bad memories."

Faith exchanged wary glances with my dad. "What are you saying? You're thinking of leaving?"

"You've lived here all your life," reasoned Dad. "You always said you loved it here and would never leave."

I tilted my chin up, tears catching in my throat at Dad's fallen expression. "Yes, well, things have changed. Mac saw to that."

I rose to my feet, my heart in the pit of my stomach. "Leaving Loch Harris is the only way I can move on."

Chapter Ten

The following couple of weeks passed in a haze.

I tried to keep occupied by getting the cottage valued, reviewing two new albums, interviewing a controversial street artist for one of the broadsheets, and writing a feature about the financial hit Loch Harris had taken due to the shaky economy.

"Maybe it's a blessing I'm moving on," I'd remarked to Dad one evening over a plate of lasagne and crusty garlic bread.

"A blessing for who?" he'd barked. "For me? You? Or Loch Harris?"

I knew I had to make a start on clearing away Mac's collection of blown-glass paperweights and, over a mug of builder's tea, I gathered my resolve to do just that.

I studied them as I wrapped them in brown paper, before carefully placing them in a cardboard box. When he was alive, Mac had guarded them jealously; he would set them on shelves around the spare bedroom, like an array of invaluable orbs from an alien planet. Lois had agreed to take them.

Just a couple of days after the funeral, Lois had volunteered to come over from her home in Fife to help me sort through his things. "You are not doing all that on your own," she had insisted.

And so, like the kind and organised whirlwind that she was, Lois arrived armed with warm scones to give us some sustenance, and we quickly packed away his golf clubs, notebooks, and book collection before turning our attention to his wardrobe.

"Is there anything you would like to keep?" I had asked her, dragging a weary hand through my ponytail.

Lois had surveyed Mac's clothes, lying in a heap on the bed in the spare room. There were his casual checked shirts, an array of richly coloured ties, his Pringle jumpers – the patterns and materials merging against each other, sleeves criss-crossing. "I'll take his Celtic cross cufflinks, if you don't mind."

Then her forlorn eyes had strayed to his paperweights jostling on the shelves. "I wouldn't mind taking that jade and blue one. Mac called it Neptune as he always said it reminded him of the sea."

I blinked at her. "I didn't know that."

I shouldn't have been surprised. There was so much about Mac I'd thought I known but didn't.

Lois had squirmed under her lavender shirt, detecting the hidden meaning in my words. "Let me know which clothes of his you want to keep and I'll bag up the rest for the charity shop."

I cast my attention across the ties, crisp shirts, and sharply cut jackets. Part of me didn't want to keep any of it.

Against my better judgement, I reached over and picked up one of Mac's silk ties in steel grey – the one he had been wearing the first time I met him.

I recalled how it had complimented the shade of his eyes and I had found it very difficult to concentrate on the interview. The material slithered through my fingers as I stood there, remembering. I placed it to one side. "I'll keep this one."

It was then that Lois had made another valiant attempt to try and talk to me about the money Mac had left for me.

"Please Lois," I'd begged, snatching up one of Mac's polo shirts. "I've told you already. I'm not accepting it."

She had grudgingly agreed to drop the topic, but I'd seen in her dark eyes that she wasn't surrendering just yet.

Lois had stayed the night and departed the next morning after breakfast. After a prolonged hug and a promise that she would ring me that evening, she vanished in her little mint-green Honda Civic.

I had watched her melt out of sight past the line of trees, the mid-April sky making promises it might not be able to keep.

Lois had insisted on ringing me frequently to make sure I was OK, or at least as OK as I could be, under the circumstances – I suppose it wasn't every day that your fiancé collapsed and died while on top of his ex-wife. I appreciated her concern, but resisted making any firm arrangements to see her again, at least for the time being.

She reminded me too much of Mac.

I gave myself a mental shake and turned my attention back to the matter in hand: Mac's paperweights. I sealed the lid of the box with a thick strip of Sellotape.

I sat back on the living room carpet, the silence seeping into my skin. The house was too quiet, so I got up and fetched my phone.

As some 1970s American rock music blasted out, I moved towards my writing desk at the back of the sitting room and stared out of the window.

The trees were pricking snatches of powder blue sky and the loch lapped gently against the shore in the distance.

The number of arguments Mac and I would have – not only about my choice of music, but the volume at which I would play it – came back into my thoughts.

Thanks to Dad, I had grown up surrounded by music – heart-tingling lyrics and mind-blowing riffs. Once I moved away from Loch Harris, maybe I could try and focus more on freelance music journalism?

Leaving the area would be painful, but surely not as painful as staying. I had to leave. I had to move on.

I pushed my hands into the pockets of my jeans.

Through the tree tops, I could see the church spire. I hadn't been up to the cemetery since Mac's funeral. I dropped down into my swivel chair and rocked backwards and forwards.

I switched on my PC and listened as one track drifted to an end and another one began.

It all came crashing back: Mac twirling me around the sitting room; his melting smile and deep, rumbling laugh while one of his pretentious jazz instrumentals wound its way around the cottage; the fine lines that deepened around his hooded blue eyes when something amused him.

Tears slithered down my cheeks. Why was I crying for a man who had kept secrets from me?

I silenced my music and then took myself through to the kitchen. Rummaging around in my cutlery drawer, I located a pair of scissors and then ventured out the back door.

My modest patch of back garden, with its few feet of wild cherry hedging studded with white flowers, housed a corner of herbs and a bed thrusting with amber and red germini, purple pansies and hybrid tea roses in lemon and sorbet-pink.

I couldn't take any credit for the riot of colours on display. My gardener dad had woven his magic.

I tried not to question what I was doing as I selected four of the germini and two of the prettiest roses, snipping the stems with the utmost care.

I paused for a moment, breathing in their heady scent before taking the cut flowers back into the kitchen and securing them together with a strand of white ribbon I found in my bits and bobs basket.

Then I filled an empty bottle with water and fetched my shoulder bag from the hall.

My dark purple Nissan Juke was parked by the side of the cottage and I opened the door, placing the bottle of flowers in the passenger seat and wedging them upright with my bag.

I drove towards Loch Harris Church, switching on the car radio to fill the silence and stop the circling questions in my head. The drone of the presenter's voice was oddly comforting.

I dislodged all the questions my mind was asking and steered right, towards the side lane that led into the church car park.

Relief flooded through me. There didn't seem to be anyone else around on this Saturday morning.

I fetched my bag and the flowers and picked at the ribbon I'd secured them with. Then I slid on my sunglasses and negotiated the paths that snaked between the headstones. Mac's grave was just up on the right.

My pink and white trainers crunched over the gravel as I found myself fiddling with some of the petals. The white ribbon that held the flowers together fluttered in the breeze.

Life continued as normal around me. There was the burr of a wood pigeon and the distant parp of a car horn. I blinked and found myself in front of Mac's grave.

Lois had deposited a bouquet of white lilies when she had visited me. They rested their heads against the cool stone, their thick green stems stretching out of one of the two narrow vases either side of the grave inscription.

I crouched down to decant the water into the vacant vase, before easing my assortment of bright blooms into position.

I got to my feet again and took a couple of steps backwards. Around me swelled the Scottish countryside.

Hitching the strap of my bag tighter over my shoulder, I tried to fight my images of Mac – flirty, twinkling, with that rumbling voice. "Why?" I asked aloud. "Why did you have to do what you did?"

Burying a sob, I turned on my heel and walked robotically back to my car.

Chapter Eleven

"You are not staying in on your own again this Saturday," insisted Faith later on that afternoon. "It's the law."

I rolled my eyes at the other end of the line. "In case you hadn't noticed, Ms Robertson, we live in Loch Harris, not LA."

"How dare you!" teased Faith in mock indignation. "This is a heaving, vibrant metropolis with a total of two watering holes."

"Exactly. There's not even a music venue in these parts."

Faith sighed in my ear. "OK. I'll admit we aren't overrun with entertainment round here, but don't try to use that as an excuse to be a boring, old fart."

"Gee, thanks."

"We'll go for a walk and then, if you're lucky, I'll treat you to one of Rab's bar suppers."

I made a grunting noise. "You'd better not be trying to get me out tonight as an excuse to nag me about that money

Mac left me. I've already told you, I don't want anything to do with it."

There was a theatrical gasp. "How could you even think such a thing?"

I played with the buckle of my belt. "I take it the Loch Harris tourist information office isn't busy right now, since you're on the phone to me at 3 p.m. in the afternoon."

"It's nowhere near as busy as it should be," admitted Faith. "If the town wants to survive as a tourist destination, it's going to have to move with the times."

"Yes, well, that won't be something I'll have to consider for much longer."

Faith's stony silence made my stomach lurch. "Please don't be angry with me," I pleaded. "I don't want to go."

"Then don't!"

I rubbed at my forehead. "I can't stay here. Not now. Not after all this."

"We'll talk about all that later," she soothed.

"Faith, there is nothing to talk about."

"I'll come by your place for 7.30 p.m.," she breezed, "and we'll get a taxi into the village. The first round is on you."

We stepped out from Duncan's taxi as the Saturday evening sky twisted into coils of vanilla and peach.

"Sorry about your Mac," called Duncan out of the cab window.

It turns out he wasn't my Mac, I thought darkly. "Thanks Duncan."

Faith slid her arm through mine. "Right, Miss Devlin. The heaving metropolis that is Loch Harris is your oyster. Which drinking establishment are you keen to visit first?"

I cocked one dark brown eyebrow at her. "Faith, I don't mean to put a dampener on tonight's proceedings, but in case you have forgotten, we've only got two pubs to choose from."

"I know. So which one of the two will we visit first?"

I paused just outside our post office, with its array of hanging baskets and bevelled windows. My shadow licked across the pavement and onto the quiet road. "Could we just go for a walk first, down by the loch?"

Faith nodded and smiled. "Sure. Whatever you want to do."

We crossed the road and headed past the sprinkling of shops. There was one selling homeware, inspired by our changing seasons, then there was our local supermarket, sandwiched in between the pharmacy and our celebrated little tea shop, The Busy Bean, where your cholesterol levels rose simply by looking through their window at the sumptuous baking.

Tourist information, where Faith worked, was located up the cobbled lane and just past the post office.

The tourist information office was a sweet little place. It had formerly been a shoemaker's, but had been transformed with potted plants, sash windows, and paintings by local artists displayed for sale on its buttercup-yellow walls.

Faith took pride in being the 'public face of Loch Harris', providing glossy maps and proudly carrying her knowledge of the area as a badge of honour. However, if Loch Harris wasn't doing as well from the tourist industry as it had done in the past, it didn't bode well for Faith and her colleagues.

We cut down a short embankment fringed with thick trees. It was just beyond there that Loch Harris spread out like a silver mirror. It was almost as if the water had scooped out its own heart-shaped enclave from the jutting rocks.

No wonder Mac fell in love with this place as soon as I brought him here, I concluded to myself. It was so different to the flashy eateries and sharp apartment lifestyle he was used to in Edinburgh.

A melancholy thud hit me and I blinked. It was going to take time to come to terms with everything. It was the betrayal of it all. Not just that Mac had been having an affair with his ex-wife, but also that he hadn't even disclosed his heart condition to me.

It was approaching a month now since Mac had passed away. "Still very early days," I was often reminded.

Faith spoke, bringing me back from where I was lost in thought. "You're not worried about facing people, are you, Layla?"

I drew to a halt by the railings. "Yes. No. I mean ... I don't know."

Faith squeezed my arm and stood beside me, overlooking the fantastic spectacle of the first tourist viewpoint. "You've got absolutely nothing to feel embarrassed about, do you hear me? All this mess was Mac's doing and now he's gone—"

"And I'm left to deal with the aftermath."

"But not on your own," she emphasised. "You've got your dad and you've got me. You've also got Lois." Faith studied the trees. "I know there are some right nosey buggers round here, but most of them mean well."

I gave a small smile. That's how Mac would often describe a few of the locals, despite my protests to the contrary.

I glanced over my shoulder and recognised two ladies from the local rambling association. They were sporting their usual walking boots and crinkly waterproof jackets, and were hovering by some trees.

They both looked over and began chattering in earnest, flicking me intrigued glances. It was obvious I was their topic of conversation.

They spun away from me to examine a branch when Faith realised they were gossiping and turned full-on Rottweiler. "Some people have got nothing better to do. Heard enough, have we?"

I buried a smile as the two ladies scurried up one of the embankments and vanished. Maybe Mac had a point about there being a very fine line between the Loch Harris community spirit and rampant nosiness.

Faith squinted a little as the evening light trickled up and over the fells, which were spread out behind the loch in a series of heather-dotted peaks. "Whenever one of us is in trouble, you know we are always there for one another."

I swivelled my eyes to her. "I got that impression by the

way you just verbally abused those two women." I admired a brazen little robin flitting about in the branches. "Is this your clumsy way of trying to persuade me to stay?"

Faith clapped her hand to her chest. "How could you think such a thing?"

We tapped down some steps, which led us onto the path that wound its way around the Loch.

"Hi Faith. How are you?"

An attractive, sandy-haired man was ambling towards us. He was hand in hand with a cute little boy, who looked around four.

Faith's face became smeared with pink. She let me have a shifty glance out of the corner of her eye. "Hi Greg. I'm fine, thanks. How's you?"

My attention travelled between the two of them.

Greg nodded at her. "Oh, I'm not bad, thanks."

He indicated to the little boy down by his side. "Sam wanted to come down and feed the ducks before bed, but we're not having much luck finding any at the moment."

Sam gazed up at both of us with inquisitive blue eyes. He had corn-blond hair and a wide smile. He waggled a little bag of breadcrumbs. "I think they've all gone to sleep."

I grinned down at him. "I bet they'll soon wake up again if they know you're here, isn't that right, Faith? Faith?"

She didn't answer. She was too busy peering at Sam with a look of mild horror.

Greg smiled briefly at me, but I sensed he wanted to speak to Faith alone, so I edged several feet away to admire the shimmering vista of the Loch.

I could hear Greg's hesitant voice. "I really enjoyed the other evening. Did you?"

Faith sounded exasperated. "Of course I did. Why?"

I glanced across. Oh, I knew the look Faith was offering him. It was her don't-push-me-as-I'm-frightened-of-commitment face.

"It's just you said you would call me but you haven't."

"I've been really busy."

My heart thudded in sympathy at the sight of Greg's resigned nod. "It's nothing to do with me being a single parent, is it?" Greg nodded towards his little son, who was hopping from foot to foot and singing something about a baby shark.

The colour of Faith's cheeks deepened and she reached up to fiddle with her hair. "No. Don't be silly. Not at all."

I sighed to myself. Why was she lying to him?

I watched as she brushed a non-existent hair out of her eyes. "I'll call you in a day or two, OK?"

Greg didn't appear at all convinced. "I'll ring you tomorrow, if you like?"

"I'm not around much," she flustered. "I'm working."

Now it was Greg's turn to appear embarrassed. "Oh, OK. Right."

"I'll call you," insisted Faith, offering a hasty goodbye and steering me away up the path.

Once we'd turned the corner of a hedge, I pulled up. "What was all that about? I didn't know you were seeing someone."

Faith flapped her hands. "I've been out with him a

couple of times. It's no biggie. I didn't mention it because you've had all this going on with Mac."

I stuck my head around the corner of the hedge for another look at Greg and his little boy. Greg's shoulders were slumped and he was feigning interest in something Sam was telling him about a stone he'd picked up.

"He's cute," I observed.

"Which one?"

"Both of them, as it happens." I frowned. "Greg seems vaguely familiar."

Faith started to move off. She was playing with the fastening of her clutch bag. Her reluctance to discuss Greg and his son was palpable. "He works as a ranger with the forestry services round here."

I eyed her. "He seems a nice guy."

"Yes, he is."

I blinked at her. "He's very good-looking and also seems really keen on you, so what's the problem? Do you like him?"

Faith squinted in the lavender light. "Yes, of course I like him."

"Then what's with all the off-hand behaviour? As soon as you spotted him, you looked like you had just stepped on a plug. Talk about mixed signals."

Faith appeared to be inwardly debating whether to confide in me. She moved across to a nearby wooden bench that overlooked a section of Loch Harris and plonked herself down on it. I joined her.

She continued to stare across the murmuring waters of the loch, before finally revealing that she had met Greg

McBride when he had dropped in to the tourist office a few weeks back to deliver some new forest walk maps.

"You know how it is," she blushed, "when you first meet someone and you're attracted to them, and it's all flashing eyes and teeth." She sighed. "Anyway, he popped into the office again a couple more times on some pretence or the other and then he asked me out."

"And?"

Faith explained that she and Greg had been out on a couple of dates. "We went for a drink to a little country pub in Finton a few days ago. We had a lovely evening. Greg's handsome and funny..."

"I sense a 'but' coming. Is it in the form of a cheeky-faced little boy?"

Faith tilted her head back and then turned to look at me. "Shit, Layla. Are you part witch or something?"

I rolled my eyes up to the setting sky. "No, I just know my best friend."

Faith's profile was troubled as she stared at the rugged vista of hills reflected in the loch. "I must sound a right cow, but you know what a commitment-phobe I am at the best of times."

"Oh, I do. Only too well." I chose my words carefully. "Is it so bad that he has a child?"

"Of course not," she answered, squinting ahead.

"Then I'm confused. What's the problem? Is he still married or something?"

"Divorced," clarified Faith quickly. "His ex decided she wasn't cut out to be a mum and took off to Canada with someone she met at work."

"Bloody hell. Poor guy and that lovely little boy."

Faith made me jump as she suddenly slapped her hands down on top of her thighs. "I'm the problem, not Greg and certainly not Sam."

I attempted to lighten the darkening mood. "If I can unravel this, what's the star prize?"

Despite herself, Faith flashed me a smile before her pensive expression took over again. "You said so yourself. I'm frightened of commitment. What if things start to get heavy and then I finish with Greg? I wouldn't just be hurting him, would I?"

I pulled my jacket tighter around myself against the crisp loch breeze. "Ah. Now we're beginning to get somewhere." I playfully nudged her arm. "So, the Ice Queen does have a heart after all."

Faith poked out her tongue and nudged me back. "That's why I didn't ring Greg back. I started thinking that if things got serious and I backed off, it's not just him I could hurt, but Sam too." She pulled her glossed lips into a line. "I would feel so guilty."

My eyes raked over her. "So, Greg was straight with you from the beginning and told you he had a child?"

"Yes, about halfway through the evening of our first date. I didn't think too much about it at first, but then on our second date, he forgot his wallet and had to go back into his house to collect it."

Faith shrugged her shoulders. "Greg's mum was babysitting and I caught a brief glimpse of Sam waving from the window. And now I've seen him for the first time up close…"

"Don't you think you're getting a bit ahead of yourself here?"

After a considered pause, Faith shifted round on the bench. "I really do like Greg. He's not like a lot of the other guys I've been out with. He talks about wild birds and trees and he has a wicked sense of humour." Her eyes clouded over. "And he loves Sam so much. I can see why. He's adorable."

Realisation dawned. Well, who knew?

Faith Robertson, the femme fatale who left broken men in her wake, had finally met a man who had got to her. But this time, he wore frog wellingtons and sang songs about baby sharks.

"You're overthinking things," I said, patting her hand. "Why not give this a chance? Phone Greg tonight and arrange to see him again. Maybe you could even suggest the two of you take Sam somewhere?"

I frowned as Faith got to her feet and switched the conversation back to me. That's what she always did when she felt she was at risk of being exposed.

I would speak to her about Greg again, I decided. She couldn't let this chance of happiness slip by, just because she had been cautious in the past.

I got up and followed her up the path.

"Layla. Layla! Are you listening to me?"

I blinked back. "Yes, sorry."

She straightened her shoulders. "I do think you would be making a big mistake leaving here," she announced in a rush, not able to help herself. "And for what it's worth, I also think you're being stubborn and stupid not taking that money."

I stopped on the path. My white quilted shoulder bag almost slid off my shoulder. "Ah. Here it is. I wondered when you would bring this up again."

"Well, can you blame me? I think it's the least you're entitled to."

"I was entitled to a proper relationship. I was entitled to the truth."

We stopped and turned sharply away from one another. I drank in the moody vista. "We were engaged," I said after a moment. "I was all set to marry him and yet I didn't even know he had a heart complaint, let alone that he was sleeping with Hannah. What does that say about the relationship we had?"

Faith's chest rose and fell under her denim jacket. "Look, I don't know why Mac didn't tell you about his condition. He must have had his reasons, stupid though they were."

I shook my head in despair.

"But this money he's left for you; if you don't take it, Hannah will try to get her hands on it."

"She's welcome to it."

"But in the future, you might not feel like that, and then it could be too late." Her voice softened. "Once you've come to terms with all of this, you might well regret not taking it and doing something positive with it."

"Like what?"

Faith flapped her baby-pink nails in the air. "I don't know. Maybe a lap-dancing club for the Loch Harris pensioners?"

I made a squeaking sound and she laughed.

We moved on again, the shale path opening out onto mounds of grassy hillocks.

"Don't let Mac rob you of your future," advised Faith. "You were not responsible for his behaviour."

"No," I faltered, "that's true. But I am responsible for my own life." I pushed my hands into my trouser pockets. "And that's why leaving Loch Harris and not taking that money is so important. It would be a fresh start for me on all fronts."

Faith's mouth flatlined.

"Now, let me buy you a drink."

She struggled to smile, her shoulders slumping. "Go on then."

———————

We were rounding the loch shore, its rhythmical waves caressing the shingly stones, when Faith shot out a hand and clutched at my arm. "Did you hear that?"

"Hear what?"

"A banging noise."

We paused and I cocked my head. There was a rhythmic hammering and it was growing louder, echoing through the trees.

"I hope it's not someone burying a body," muttered Faith. Then she coloured up. "Oh shit! Sorry, Layla. Me and my size sevens."

"Don't worry about it."

We trampled along the path that trickled by the loch.

Birds were still zinging about in the branches overhead and there was the odd rustle of disturbed leaves.

"I've got my nail file, so we could manicure him to death," joked Faith half-heartedly.

I rolled my eyes. "Come on, Lara Croft."

The swathe of woodland opened out to reveal the old boathouse, where Norrie Erskine, an elderly stalwart of the Loch Harris community, had his angling business.

It was a stunning location, with the Loch Harris waters rippling at the end of the jetty and billowing trees, looking like they were perched on top of lollipop sticks, peppered across the skyline.

We discovered that the enthusiastic hammering was coming from Victor Prentice, the local estate agent, who was hammering a For Sale sign into the grass beside the boathouse steps.

He heard us approaching and beamed. "Evening ladies. Good one for it."

"Evening Victor," said Faith, pointing at the blue and white sale sign. "What's all this?"

I turned and caught a glimpse inside the boat shed through the creaky door which was swinging open.

"Norrie has had enough and has decided to sell up," explained Victor, puffing a little. "End of an era," he observed sadly. "I've been coming up here for my angling equipment since Julius Caesar was a lad."

I took in the tired, ice-blue slated roof and dusty windows.

The boathouse was positioned on a long planked jetty and possessed spectacular views of the loch. There were moulded rocks and sprays of majestic woodland all around it.

"I didn't know Norrie was selling up," I said to Victor. "Dad hasn't mentioned anything."

Victor jerked his balding head at the boathouse. "It's all been rather sudden, lass. He only just decided."

He dropped his voice an octave, before glancing around. I don't know who he expected to be listening in. We were in a copse and there wasn't another soul in sight. "Norrie wants to take things easier now, but neither of those two lads of his are interested in carrying on the business." Victor looked pained. "We'll have to go into the city now to get all our angling bits and bobs."

Dark thoughts clouded in his small, button-like dark eyes. "Don't fancy having to run the gauntlet of bloody muggers and graffiti artists, just to buy my 3D Twitch Minnow."

Faith and I fought to hide smiles.

"I tell you, ladies," announced Victor, hooking his thumbs into his quilted waistcoat, "we need to inject some life into this place, otherwise Loch Harris will end up like a morgue."

"Not when we've got Loch Harris' answer to Tom Jones," said Faith with a straight face.

Victor was confused. "Who?"

"I think she means Big Bob and his Bobcats."

"Oh right."

While Faith and Victor proceeded to discuss Big Bob's temporary and unsuccessful diversion into performing Ed Sheeran covers at the local pubs, there came a sudden burst of bagpipes from somewhere near the buttery shoreline.

"That's young Hector Fleming," said Victor, anticipating my question. "He often comes down here to the loch to play. Poor bugger can't get a look in at either of the pubs for a gig."

He leaned on top of the For Sale sign. "I tell you, if things carry on like this, you won't recognise Loch Harris soon. There will be bloody tumbleweeds blowing along the High Street."

"Oh, don't say that, Victor," I answered, trying to smile.

Victor raised a sceptical eyebrow. "Mrs McNab is even talking about taking early retirement and closing up."

Mrs McNab's crockery shop was entrenched in Loch Harris history. Her great-grandparents had owned that business, and her grandparents and then her parents had continued the tradition.

My mouth dropped open and I turned to Faith, alarmed. "She can't do that. The Crockery Rockery is an institution around here."

Victor gave a shrug of his shoulders. "She said she used to shift a lot of Loch Harris and Galen Waterfall inspired tea sets to tourists, as well as those Scottish-themed mugs in her window, but since visitor numbers have dropped…"

A despondency settled in my stomach. Good grief. I knew Loch Harris could be busier, but I didn't realise things were that serious.

I had been born and raised here. If only there was something that could be done to bring a bit of life back into the area. Surely someone with a bit of cash behind them would be able to see the potential of Loch Harris...

I drew up, weird thoughts catching me unawares and tripping through my head.

Visions of a deserted Loch Harris, with its gift shop trinkets sitting unsold in the windows, shuttered tea rooms, and dinky bed and breakfast accommodation flashing desperate Vacancy signs, cartwheeled in front of me.

I examined the boathouse, splashed with sleepy sunlight. Then I found myself taking a few tentative steps up to the creaking door. *What the hell was I thinking? What was I doing?*

I was going to move away. I was going to sell the cottage and leave behind the ghosts that Loch Harris now carried for me. I was going to start over somewhere else. "Victor, would you object if I took a quick look inside?"

"Not at all, lass. Be my guest. I've got to ring Diane and tell her I'll be home a bit later, before I lock the place up."

Faith wandered over and squinted at me. "Why are you looking like that? What is it?"

I didn't answer her. I went inside, with only the echo of my tapping footsteps on the wooden floor for company.

The interior of the boathouse was deceptively long, running out a fair way towards the water because of the jetty. It was the colour of a washed-out pebble.

Spirals of dappled evening light trailed through the two windows in the wall, and through a larger window down at the far end. It was like a dusty, empty shell.

There was a large storage cupboard at the back, with a

smaller cupboard next to it. To the right of that was a generous-sized bathroom.

There were hooks running down the walls from when Norrie had displayed his array of fishing rods and equipment and there was a semi-circular Formica counter halfway in.

Outside, the landscape rolled out before me, weaving and dipping in a carpet of silvery water and craggy hillsides.

From over my shoulder, I could still hear the drifting throb of Hector's bagpipes. Victor's comments about Hector struggling to secure a gig echoed in my mind.

I drank in the soaring views of water and sky again. What the hell was I thinking? Where were these random thoughts coming from? I couldn't even blame a sojourn to the pub, as we hadn't made it that far yet.

Faith materialised at my shoulder and I jumped. "Crikey. You almost made my hair turn white then."

"What are you up to?" she asked, her eyes narrowing. "I can see there are cogs turning." She stared at her surroundings. "Don't tell me you're a secret angling obsessive?"

I forced a smile, flustered. "Oh, you know me. Just being nosey."

Faith made for the door, seemingly satisfied by my explanation. "Come on then. Are you ready for that drink?"

I didn't reply. I was too spellbound by the loch spread out at the end of the long wooden jetty and the way the old boathouse was surveying it. "I never realised this place had such a fantastic view."

"Yes, it's not bad, is it?"

She rested one hand on my shoulder. "I suppose you don't appreciate things like that as much, when you see it all the time."

I nodded silently.

We said good night to Victor and then Faith linked arms with me again and started to lead me away from the boathouse.

"Are you OK?" she asked, as we made our way back along the shale path.

But I didn't say anything.

I was too occupied by the stream of crazy ideas running through my head.

Chapter Twelve

I lay in the spare room bed that night, like an agitated starfish.

I still couldn't face returning to my bed – *our* bed.

It all felt so false and contrived now. I kept remembering myself lying there beside Mac, laughing about our wedding plans and seeing his blue eyes flash in the dark. Then there was his sweep of greying hair indented against the pillow.

He was confident and solid...

I stopped myself. The rose-sprigged curtains were too thin. I could already see wisps of the sunrise feeling their way onto the duvet cover.

Over in the far-right corner of the room sat Mac's writing desk and swivel chair, as though they were waiting for him to return.

I was used to seeing it littered with his pens and notebooks. A coffee percolator would be stationed by his laptop and there would be a flurry of Post-its with arrows drawn on them, indicating plot twists and turns for his latest novel.

Now it was empty, except for the drizzle of early light striking its surface.

I averted my eyes. I would speak to Lois about what she wanted to do with it. I preferred not to keep it. It was still too much of a painful reminder, and I was sure Lois would be more than happy to inherit it.

I wriggled under the duvet and let out a sigh. *What was going on inside my head?* I'd decided to move on. I was going to leave Loch Harris and begin again.

But if I was so certain about my next steps, why was that great hulk of old boathouse nudging at the corners of my mind? It just wouldn't go away.

I shoved a frustrated hand through my hair, sending it flying back off my face.

Faith's remarks about Loch Harris being in urgent need of an injection of something new flitted around inside my head.

Could I just walk away from the area, when there was a chance I might be able to do something? What if there was a possibility that I could help?

Fuming with Mac for putting me in this position, I threw back my bedcovers with an irritated, "Sod it!"

Even though 5 a.m. had only just clicked up in red neon on my alarm clock, I jumped in the shower and washed my hair.

I tried to focus on the hot needles of water pounding into my body, but it was useless. Images of Mac and the boathouse jostled for position.

I fired my damp hair back into a high ponytail and clattered about in the kitchen. I didn't feel hungry, but managed a modest bowl of cereal and a glass of fresh orange juice before I switched on my computer and raced through my emails, noting a couple of new freelance commissions that had arrived for me.

My dad's house was only ten minutes' walk down the lane, so I set off at a leisurely pace, with only the thrum of birdsong for company.

As it was Sunday morning, the church bells would soon echo around the loch and surrounding treetops.

When I was little, I used to love rolling down the hills and tumbling through the clusters of heather, and Dad had taken great delight in pulling together modest but mouth-watering little packed lunches for the two of us to take on our adventures.

We'd shove them in our rucksacks and then thump off down the lanes in our walking boots. He'd become very adept at doing my hair into pigtails and, as they swung about my shoulders, I'd gaze up at this bear of a man, with his rock music T-shirts and ready smile, and think how much I loved him.

Usually, on a day like this, I'd drink in the thick hedgerows and crafted dry-stone walls, but this morning all I wanted to do was speak to my dad.

My late grandparents' cottage peeked out as I rounded the corner. Visions of me scampering around their patch of front lawn scoffing local strawberries and darting in and out of their trellis porch swam in front of my eyes. I smiled to myself.

The cottage was set back a little from the road, an off-white affair with a black roof and double chimney breast. Dad had cultivated the side rockery, so that it added an extra splash of colour in the shape of stout, lush shrubs.

He'd painted the front door and surrounding woodwork in sky blue so that it was much more vibrant and welcoming than the plain charcoal my grandparents had opted for.

I was about to knock on the door, when I heard a clatter from the back garden.

I eased open the black iron side gate and saw a glimpse of Dad's legs fired out in front of him.

There was a mug of coffee stewing gently on the wrought-iron table and the remnants of toast on a plate. His head was bowed over one of the Sunday newspapers. I could make out his jutting chin from behind that curtain of hair.

When he sensed movement, he swung his head up. "Layla, love!" He stared down at his chunky wrist watch. "Bloody hell. It's not even half seven yet. You're up and about early."

He stalked over and enveloped me in his tanned arms.

"Morning, Dad," I smiled as he planted a kiss on my cheek. "I couldn't sleep."

I gave him a kiss back and studied him. "Sitting there, you still look like a Seventies rock star, rather than a landscape gardener."

He broke into a wide grin. "One does one's best." Dad pointed to his coffee. "Would you like one or would you prefer one of those herbal tea things you've started drinking?"

"Oh, a herbal tea thing would be great, thanks."

He rolled his eyes good naturedly and vanished through the open back door.

I felt as though I'd only just closed my eyes and raised my face to the blossoming sunshine when Dad reappeared with one of his ceramic mugs for me and a fresh coffee for himself. "Camomile OK for you?"

"That's perfect. Thanks."

Dad sat in the garden chair opposite. "Go on then. Spill."

I reached into the pocket of my top and plucked out my sunglasses. It was a relief to retreat behind them, and not just because of the early morning glare.

Dad's brows knitted together. "Come on. Out with it. You're making my garden look untidy."

I was losing my nerve. Maybe all these mad thoughts were a result of delayed shock or grief. "Out with what?"

Dad pushed his crumpled newspaper back across the table. "Why have you rocked up here so early on a Sunday morning?"

"I told you, Dad. I couldn't sleep."

I buried my face in the warm, flower-scented brew of my tea. Right now, I needed all the relaxing camomile I could get. "Oh, I'm just being stupid," I blurted. "I'm still a bit all over the place."

"About Mac, you mean?"

I shifted in my chair, the sleepy sun working its way up my arms. "Yes. No. Well, a little."

"Well, that's understandable," answered Dad. "What that bastard did to you…"

He must have noticed my mouth sag, because he stopped himself. "Sorry, darling. I know I shouldn't speak ill of the dead, but my loyalty is to you."

"I know."

"You were too good for him," he insisted.

"Not that you're biased or anything."

Dad's mouth hitched upwards at one corner. "Of course not." Then he reached over to the table to cradle his mug. "It does make you think, though. Mac was only a year younger than me."

I watched him take a sip of his coffee. "So, are you going to tell me what's up," he asked again, "or do I have to guess?"

I drank some of my tea and carefully placed the mug back down on the table. "Maybe I thought I knew what I wanted. Or perhaps I was just trying to convince myself that I did."

"Layla, you're not making any sense, love." Dad leaned forward. "You know you can tell me anything."

I admitted defeat and swiped off my sunglasses, stashing them on top of my head. "I'm probably making a big mistake again, but I don't think I'll be leaving Loch Harris after all."

Dad's face broke into a grin. "Oh, sweetheart. I'm delighted to hear that."

Then Dad reined himself in a little. "I know that might sound selfish, but I honestly think you were making a big decision far too soon – and that's understandable."

Dad pushed his hand across the table and squeezed mine. In the distance, there was the faint sound of cattle high up in the fields and the whirr of a car engine out on the road. "In the end, I think you'll be pleased you didn't leave."

Dad reclined back in his chair, his crinkly grey eyes dancing with delight. "This calls for a celebration."

He slapped his hands down on the edge of the table. "You'll see that your freelance writing will pick up and things will sort themselves out."

I steeled myself to tell him about my absurd idea. I still wasn't sure myself whether I was doing the right thing, but my heart had other ideas. "I'm not planning on spending as much time on my freelance work, Dad. At least, if things work out as I hope they will, I probably won't have the time."

"Oh?"

I pressed my lips together. Even as I began to utter the words, I couldn't quite believe it was me talking. "I've been doing a lot of thinking and I've decided to accept Mac's money after all."

My dad nodded ferociously. "Good for you, Layla. I think that's sensible. What made you change your mind?" He steepled his hands together. "It will be a good nest egg for you to invest for the future."

I cleared my throat and took a mouthful of camomile tea. "I'm not planning on investing the money, Dad."

His brown brows rose up. "Oh, what are your plans then, if you don't mind me asking?" He broke into a smile. "Are you thinking of going travelling? You know, I think

86

you should take yourself off somewhere exotic on holiday for a few weeks."

My stomach surged with adrenalin. "No. I'm not planning a holiday."

"Oh, you've got me intrigued now."

I tilted my chin upwards and pinned on a smile. Excitement and trepidation squirmed around inside of me. "I've decided I'm going to buy Norrie's old boathouse and turn it into a live music venue."

I don't think I have ever seen my dad look as shocked.

Chapter Thirteen

There was nothing but a charged silence.

"Dad? I thought you'd be pleased."

"I am," he insisted, not sounding convinced. "I'm delighted you aren't moving away. It's just that starting your own music venue is bloody hard graft."

I studied him from across the table, the stippled, Sunday morning sunshine catching the angles of his face. "And this coming from a rock drummer."

"Exactly. Look, darling, when I was in Battalion, we saw first-hand what long hours and commitment those places had to put in."

I snatched up my tea and cupped it in my hands. "So you think I'm not up to it?"

"Stop putting words in my mouth, Layla."

I took a sulky drink. "So, what are you trying to say then?"

Dad blew out a cloud of air. "I don't mean to rain on your parade, love, but Loch Harris is hardly Nashville."

"I realise that, but it needs something to give the area a boost and attract more visitors."

Warming to the idea, I leaned forward. "I wouldn't be competing with Sydney Opera House. What I had in mind was a cosy, intimate, live music lounge. It would be somewhere where bands and singers can really connect with their audience."

I smiled when I thought of the dazzling view of the loch with which Norrie's business was graced. "And that old boathouse is in such a stunning location."

Dad drained the last of his coffee. "I'm not doubting your enthusiasm for a moment, and I know you inherit your love of music from me. But a lot of those musician types..." His rumbly voice tailed off.

I fidgeted with my trainers under the garden table. "Dad, you're one of those musician types."

He tried not to smile. "That's my point."

I then realised he was in protective father mode. "Oh, don't tell me this is your way of warning me about getting my heart broken by some long-haired Lothario?"

Pictures of Mac and Hannah swept in front of me and I straightened my shoulders. "The last thing I need is another relationship."

I smiled at my dad. "I thought you'd be delighted. This means I'll be staying in Loch Harris."

"Don't be daft, lass. You know I don't want you to leave."

I swallowed the last of my tea and put down my mug with a decisive clatter. "I'm going to put that money to good use. And this music venture would be good for Loch Harris."

A flare of determination caught me off guard and I jumped to my feet.

"Where are you off to now? I thought we could pop down to The Fiddler's Rest for a cooked breakfast. My treat?"

I darted round to where Dad was sitting and threw my arms around his solid neck. "Could we do it another day? I'm going to see Norrie about the boathouse and I'll ring David Murray on the way."

Chapter Fourteen

Norrie Erskine resided in a grey-bricked, red-shuttered affair ten minutes further down the lane from Dad.

I paused on the grass verge and left a bit of a garbled message on David Murray's mobile, explaining that I'd had a change of heart and would now accept Mac's money to plough into a new business.

Even though it was Sunday, I knew solicitors very rarely took a day off, so I asked him to ring me back as soon as he could.

My trainers slapped along the deserted road. It was coming up for 8.30 a.m. and I hoped Norrie was up and about.

As I approached his house, I stuffed my sunglasses into the back pocket of my jeans. I entered by the stout, red gate and strode up towards the front door. There was a pane of Charles Rennie Mackintosh-style stained glass in the centre of the door and I could just make out two hazy fingers drifting backwards and forwards behind it.

My hand hovered in mid-air in front of the gold doorbell. *Did I really know what I was doing? What was I letting myself in for?* I was a freelance writer for pity's sake, not a stalwart of the music industry.

But what I lacked in knowledge about the practical side of things, I more than made up for with my love of music, my enthusiasm, and the valuable contacts I'd accumulated over the years, thanks to my freelance submissions. Dad still had music connections from his time with Battalion too.

My hand remained frozen in mid-air, my rose-gold bangle suspended from my wrist. Despite Dad's concerns, I knew he would help me. He still kept in touch with many of his old rocker mates.

Then there was Faith.

Goodness knows what her reaction would be to my wild idea, but she was such a practical and positive soul, I was certain she'd be happy to support me. Given the fact that my crazy, exciting venture would mean I would be staying in Loch Harris, surely it would delight her every bit as much as my dad.

Refusing to engage with any more doubts, I tilted my chin and knocked on the door.

"So, lass, you say you want to buy my business and turn it into a music shop?"

"Not a music shop," I clarified, eyeing Norrie's wife Clem, who was bustling in with a tray set with tea, despite me declining her kind offer. "I'd like to turn it into a venue for live music."

Clem's hand shot out and clutched at the handle of her tea pot. "Oh my goodness, Layla, it wouldn't be all that gangster rap, would it?"

Gangster rap?

I was mightily impressed that Norrie's seventy-year-old wife, a retired clerk of Loch Harris post office, knew of this particular musical genre.

I pressed my lips together so I wouldn't laugh. "Not at all, Clem. I can assure you there wouldn't be anything like that."

Her plump face mellowed with relief and she busied herself by pouring a stream of tea into three rose-sprigged cups.

Norrie sat opposite me in his bottle-green velvet chair, like an inquisitive gnome.

He smoothed a flat hand down and over his wisp of white, combed-over hair. "I don't know that we need another music place in Loch Harris." He shrugged. "We've got the twice-weekly appearances of Big Bob and The Bobcats at The Fiddler's Rest."

Oh, good grief.

I knew I was possibly getting a bit ahead of myself, but I had bigger plans in mind than Big Bob's fiddling quartet. They were a talented bunch, but had a tendency to play their tried and trusted favourites of 'Rock Around the Clock', 'Mona Lisa', and 'Sweet Caroline' on a continuous loop.

Although I was still waterlogged from the tea Dad had

given me, I accepted Clem's offer of a cup and saucer and took a few polite sips. "My idea would be to have a music venue that's totally different to what The Fiddler's Rest offers."

Clem and Norrie exchanged concerned glances and I felt obliged to explain. "I know it's going to take a lot of hard work and effort, but I think we could make the old boathouse a place where singers and bands will want to appear."

I cast my eyes around the older couple's sitting room, which was brimming with chintz furniture and photographs of Norrie proudly holding his various catches over the years. There were also photos of their two hardy-looking sons and their offspring.

"I want it to have a cosy, intimate atmosphere for real music fans. It boasts such a spectacular view of Loch Harris, who wouldn't want to come and see it for themselves?"

Norrie rocked back in his armchair and surveyed me from under his caterpillar brows. "Aren't you getting a bit ahead of yourself, lass? I might have had many other expressions of interest already."

I blushed at my gushing enthusiasm. Oops. I'd been so consumed by my ideas that I hadn't even thought that there might be other interested parties. *Oh bollocks! Maybe I'd blundered in here, instead of deploying more subtle tactics.*

"Have you?" I asked in a quiet voice.

"Have I what?"

"Have you had any other enquiries about the boathouse?"

Now, it was Norrie's turn to colour up. He cleared his throat. "No."

Clem frowned as she sank into the armchair next to Norrie and swiped his arm.

"Ow, woman! What was that for?"

"For teasing the poor lass."

Clem set her teacup and saucer down on the coffee table. It was decked out in a burnt-orange cotton tablecloth that reminded me of an amber traffic light. "We haven't had any other offers or folks asking about it. The old heap hasn't even gone on the market yet."

Norrie appraised her with indignant hazel eyes. "It is not an old heap. I don't understand for the life of me why neither Ross nor Scott wanted to carry on with it."

Clem rolled her clear blue eyes up to her puff of white hair. "They've got their own lives to lead and neither of them lives locally."

There was a few seconds' pause before Norrie burst out. "I don't mean to sound nosey, Layla—"

"But you will anyway," supplied an irritated Clem beside him.

"But how will you be able to pay for all this? I mean, we all know of Mac's passing – we're so sorry for your loss – and there were rumours he'd left you—"

Clem gave Norrie a sharp tap on the trouser leg with her pink slipper. "Will you mind your own business, man?"

Norrie shifted in his seat, suitably chastised. "I shouldn't have said anything, lassie. My apologies. It's just that starting up a business back in my day was hard enough. Nowadays, the financial pressures are even worse."

A wavering image of Mac threatened to upset me. I gave my brain a mental shake. "Let's just say that Mac's will did contain a financial surprise for me."

Clem didn't push it any further, but when Norrie opened his mouth to interrogate me again, she pushed a plate of clotted cream shortbread fingers under his nose. "Biscuit, Norrie?"

He didn't dare refuse.

We exchanged handshakes all round. Norrie said he would contact Victor first thing the next morning and I promised to get everything sorted with David Murray as a priority.

Then I raced back up the lane on excited legs, still reeling from what I had just done.

I stopped by Dad's house to tell him. I felt like I'd been awake for hours – in truth I had – and it was only just after 10.30 a.m. Tiredness and anticipation clouded me.

Dad had changed into his trusted gardening gear of a frayed, moss-green T-shirt and his combats, and he was delving his gloved hands into the rich, chocolate-coloured earth in the back garden.

I smiled at the look of concentration on his face as he tore at weeds and tossed them into a nearby wheelbarrow.

"Dad, you are now looking at your daughter, the business owner – well, almost."

At the sound of my voice, his head jerked up. He snatched off one of his gardening gloves. "So you're going ahead with it, then?"

My mouth morphed into a wobbly grin. "Yes."

His mouth curled upwards. "Come here and give your

old man a hug." He bundled me into his arms. "Good luck. I'm very proud of you."

I clung to him. "I haven't done anything yet."

"Oh, but you will."

"I thought you weren't all that keen on the idea this morning."

Dad's brows arched. "I wasn't, but I could see how enthusiastic you were about it. I glimpsed the old Layla, all bubbling over and full of excitement for something. I think that's the first proper smile I've seen from you since Mac died."

He crouched down a little so that his smoky-grey eyes were level with mine. "After you left here this morning, I got to thinking about your plans. I should be delighted that you're as passionate about music as I am."

I smiled. "It's definitely in the genes."

"And you're being so brave about everything," he added. "It's great that you're trying to move on and be positive, after what happened."

My voice cracked. "Thanks, Dad."

"I'll help you in any way I can."

I squeezed him tight, a rush of love invading my chest. "I know you will." I clapped my hands together. "Right then old rocker, put down your gardening gloves. I'm taking you for brunch to celebrate."

Dad flashed me a smile. "Seeing as you're paying, young lady, I'll choose to ignore that use of 'old'."

Chapter Fifteen

The next three weeks vanished in a flurry of paperwork.

I could tell that Norrie, Clem, and many other of the Loch Harris inhabitants thought I'd taken leave of all my senses, but I felt energised and busy. That was what I needed.

I deliberately threw myself deeper into my freelance work, pitching a variety of ideas to my magazine and newspaper contacts, and things were progressing at an impressive rate with the sale of the boathouse, which helped.

As soon as I'd made the decision to accept the money that Mac had bequeathed me, I rang Lois and told her. She was surprised and delighted that I'd changed my mind and was adamant that her big brother would have been enthused about my idea for a music venue.

I wasn't entirely sure about that, seeing as Mac's musical

preferences had always been polar opposite to mine, but I appreciated the sentiment.

"We've been very lucky," Norrie explained one damp late May evening when my dad and I met up with him during a casual sojourn up the lane. "We did think the boathouse might sit there idle for a long while before we got any interest." He nodded at me gruffly. "Oh yes. We're so relieved we got a buyer that quick, especially a sweet girl like Layla." He then dropped his voice and leaned further towards my dad. "Even if she is trying to turn it into some sort of disco."

"A disco?" I snorted to Dad, once Norrie had disappeared back over the brow of the hill. "Where on earth did he get that idea from?"

"Goodness knows. Norrie's a great guy, but he's never been up with the times. He still thinks thrash metal is an element on the periodic table."

I laughed and plunged my hands into the pockets of my rain coat. Then my thoughts strayed to my spiralling to-do list. My smile evaporated.

Dad's voice interrupted my mental running though of all the things I wanted to get on top of. "You don't mind me being honest with you, lovey?"

I turned my attention back to Dad. "No, of course not."

"You don't think this music venture has been a knee-jerk reaction to Mac's death?"

I considered the question. "I was so hurt and angry

about what he did – not telling me about his heart condition and then finding out about him and Hannah."

Another thought suddenly nipped at the edges of my mind. "What if I've taken his money just to spite him? Maybe this is my way of putting two fingers up at my cheating dead fiancé?"

"Listen to me," warned Dad, stopping suddenly. "I know you've got your faults like everyone else, but being spiteful isn't one of them."

I flicked him a look.

"You could have been mercenary," he carried on. "You could have jumped at that money straight away, played the 'we were almost married' card and tried to squeeze even more out of his estate – but you didn't."

I offered my dad a small, grateful smile.

"He left you that money for a reason – OK, maybe it was partly guilt, but now you've decided to do something positive and constructive with it."

I breathed in the damp scent of wet grass. "I'm hoping it will help this place and get Loch Harris back on its feet."

"Precisely. Now stop psychoanalysing everything and enjoy the journey!"

I smiled. "Thanks Dad. You do know I love you, don't you?"

"Let's face it, how could you not?"

I laughed and we linked arms, trudging back towards his cottage on the damp slick of tarmac. "Faith is coming over tonight and we're going to brainstorm what needs doing."

"Well, if anyone can help you get organised, it's her.

And remember what I said, OK? I'll pull in a few favours and speak to my old rocker pals. You'll have class acts performing there in no time."

I gave him a cheeky wink. "Maybe Battalion could make the odd appearance?"

Dad's smile slid off his face and he gently unhooked his arm from mine. "I don't think so, sweetheart."

I stopped for a moment. "What is it? I think it would be a great reunion, Dad. All the guys together—"

"I said no!"

I blinked at him, stung.

"Sorry. Sorry. I just don't think that would be a great idea." He softened his craggy features. "Sometimes, it's best to leave things as they are."

I watched him entwine his arm again with mine.

Chapter Sixteen

"I'm so glad you changed your mind about accepting Mac's money." Faith sighed, all sprawled legs on the sofa. She had come over to help go over the endless list of things I wanted to do, book, check up on, query and research.

"So, you think I'm doing the right thing then?"

Faith stared back at me from under her spiky lashes. "I'm delighted you're staying."

"That isn't what I asked."

She let out a raspy laugh. "OK. So, when you first told me that you were serious about buying Norrie's business, I'll admit I was a bit shocked."

"You weren't the only one. And now?"

Faith delved into the carrier bag she had brought with her and presented me with a box of my favourite white chocolate and macadamia cookies. "Now I just think you're mad."

"Thanks!"

"I'm only teasing."

I padded into the kitchen and fetched two wine glasses from the cupboard. Faith followed, looking like a sleepy Breton catalogue model. "It is going to be a lot of hard work, but if anyone can do it, you can."

She trailed her French manicure across my black and stone kitchen worktop. "Loch Harris could be doing with a bit of a kick up the arse, let's be honest."

Faith watched me glug some white wine into each glass and accepted hers. "I know that a lot of the visitors here often head into town for entertainment."

A naughty grin spread across her pink lips. "I can't say I blame them. Somehow, I don't think Big Bob's repertoire is cutting it."

I leaned against the kitchen worktop, idly crossing and uncrossing my feet.

"I was all set to go," I said, after taking a mouthful of the crisp wine. "I just wanted to get rid of this place."

"And now you've decided to stay."

"I don't think it's so much that I wanted to stay," I admitted after a pause. "It's far more a case that I can't go. Not when I have the chance to take on something so challenging and hopefully help the area. I won't have time to dwell on things."

I raised my glass of sparkly wine to my lips again.

Faith tilted her head, her concerned, pale eyes almost as soft as the oyster silk of her blouse. She'd come over straight from work, and her dark, slim-fitting work trousers rustled slightly as she moved.

I looked at her across the rim of my wine glass. "I went to visit him the other week. Mac."

Faith placed her wine down beside her on the breakfast bar. "You never mentioned that."

I shrugged. "I know this must sound awful, but I never really intended to go back after the funeral. It just kind of happened."

The early evening sky was weaving twists of cloud outside my kitchen window and the hillside was melting into smudges of amber and peach.

I took another big gulp of wine. "I felt let down," I confided. "Standing there, over his grave. I felt betrayed and hurt."

"That's understandable. Anyone would."

"But am I as big a fraud as he was, Faith?"

My best friend's well-plucked eyebrows knitted together. "What do you mean by that?"

I sloshed the wine around in my glass as I spoke. "By accepting that money he left me. I said I wouldn't take it and then I did."

Faith moved closer to me, her expression brimming with reassurance. "You listen to me. What Mac did was dreadful. You were engaged and you thought you had a future together here."

She removed the wine glass from my hand and set it back down on the kitchen top with a decisive clink.

"Maybe it is guilt money, but so sodding what!" She cupped my hands in hers. "A lot of people would have run away from here and gone to lick their wounds and wallow in self-pity."

Faith squeezed my fingers encouragingly. "But you didn't do that. You've decided not only to stay, but to do something that's right out of your comfort zone."

I tipped my head to one side. "I thought this was supposed to be a pep talk."

"It is. I'm just getting started."

"Oh. OK."

Faith rolled her eyes skywards. "You're not splashing all that money on yourself. You're doing something with it to help others."

"Well, that's the plan," I added ruefully. Time would tell if I could achieve it.

Faith looked reminiscent. "I'll never forget how you rushed to my aid when I was the new girl in the class and you rescued my pink fluffy pencil case from Rachel Howson and Cara Wallace."

"Oh, I had to help the incomer, didn't I? You couldn't help it, being a townie."

It was ironic that Faith's family had moved to Loch Harris from the west coast when she was eleven and she had ended up working for our tourist information office.

Faith's long-time fascination with the area meant that her local knowledge was impressive.

Her grin was emphatic. "You'll make a success of this, I know you will. I take it all the paperwork and financial stuff for buying the boathouse is going OK?"

"David Murray is a star," I sighed at her. "He's charging me so-called mate's rates because of Mac and it has taken so much of the pressure off."

"There you are then," said Faith, flashing her bright smile. "Things are going well for you – and about time!"

"I'm a bit concerned about my dad, though."

I indicated for us to flop together on the sofa. Once we'd arranged ourselves with the cushions and topped up our wine, I told Faith about my dad's snappy reaction to my suggestion that his old band have a reunion.

Faith flapped a hand. "Oh, it's probably nothing."

"But you know my dad. He's so laid back about life, he's almost horizontal." I narrowed my eyes. "He bit my head off. It really wasn't like him at all."

Faith swung her wine glass in mid-air. "Harry will have been overtired. Or maybe Tina was on his case about something."

The mention of my mother's name made my back stiffen. "If she had been, he would have said."

"I think you're attaching too much importance to it."

I watched Faith savour another mouthful of white wine.

I wasn't so sure.

"So, what's happening with you and Greg? How did it go when you phoned him?"

Faith blanched. She averted her eyes.

"Oh, for pity's sake! You didn't ring him, did you?"

"I did ring him," she insisted, colouring up.

"Then why do I have a sense of foreboding?"

Faith chewed her lip. "I promise you, I did call him last week, but the conversation didn't go very well."

And I can guess whose fault that was, I thought to myself.

After I sat there for a few moments in silence, arms folded and my eyebrows quizzically arranged, she relented.

"OK, OK. Stop looking at me like I'm a Bond villain!"

I made a series of tutting noises when Faith admitted she had told Greg she wasn't really "in the right place at the moment" to date again.

"How did he take that?"

Faith cringed. "Not very well. He said I was just making excuses because he's a single dad."

I rubbed my forehead. "Well, I don't mean to be rude, but you can see why he would think that."

Faith shook her messy curls violently. "But that's not true. I may be many things, but I'm not shallow." She sighed. "You know what I'm like. I mean, I really do like Greg – a lot."

"Then what is the problem?" I pushed. "Go for it. Stop overthinking things. Forget he's a dad for now and—"

"But that's the point. I can't. Greg and Sam are a unit."

"So you get two handsome men for the price of one."

I hoped for at least a shadow of a smile, but Faith was too distracted. She was closing down again. "I can't take the risk. What if we get too involved and then it all goes tits up? That little boy would be hurt too."

My exasperation was growing. "But that's like saying what if I cross the road and get hit by a number 82 bus?"

Faith flapped her hands. "No," she ground out. "It's best not to go there in the first place."

I flinched at the sadness washing across her face. *Bloody hell. Faith really did like this guy.*

"But look at it from Greg's perspective," I argued. "He's

willing to take a chance on getting to know you better and he's the one with the child, not you."

Faith looked lost. She plastered on a smile. "Let's not talk about this anymore." She forced a jovial tone. "Right, young lady, we've got a music venue to sort out. Chop, chop!"

I opened my mouth to say something else but she held one hand up.

"Come on then," she cajoled. "Where is this to-do list of yours? We've got work to do."

Chapter Seventeen

"**B**loody midges!" grumbled Dad, swatting at a couple of persistent ones fluttering by his head. "When you have this place up and running, Layla, you should supply insect repellent in the summer months."

I gestured to the loch and its gentle, rhythmical sloshing. "I thought that being near water, we might get off lightly."

I turned back to the Sold sign plastered across the front door of the boathouse. An excited ball of tension rolled around my stomach.

It was three days since Dad had barked at me about my Battalion reunion suggestion. I still suspected there was something he wasn't telling me, but decided to choose my moment to broach the subject again. Waiting for a carpenter who was already fifteen minutes late on a cloudy Thursday evening at the start of June wasn't the right time.

As if he had detected my irritation, Alec Carruthers, one of Dad's old school friends, came barrelling up the road in his mud-splattered, bottle-green Land Rover. "Nice night for it," he beamed, getting out of the car and striding towards us.

Alec hoisted his grey beanie further back on his head and surveyed the boathouse. "So it's true then? Layla Devlin is the new owner of this?" As if to emphasise the point, he raised a finger and jabbed it.

"Guilty as charged."

Dad directed a cocked eyebrow at Alec. "Are you ready to go in there?"

Alec performed a jokey bow. "Ladies first."

Rolling his eyes good naturedly, Dad ushered me up the porch steps. I eased the key into the door and opened it. A musty draught coiled outward.

While Alec prowled up and down the empty boathouse, his timber boots thudding on the wooden floor, Dad offered me an encouraging smile. "Don't you worry. Alec is the best. I know he looks like he couldn't find his way to the end of the road, but he's a bloody good chippie."

I supressed any lingering doubts and talked Alec through the shelving we wanted behind the bar, and the broken wooden floorboards needing repair. As we meandered around, gilded rays of light fed in through the windows and pooled at our feet. All I could hear was the sensuous whispers from the Loch water.

Soon, there would be live music, fairy lights strung from the porch and looped all the way along the jetty, and intimate tables and chairs set outside, overlooking the rambling forests.

There would be small frosted bowls with candles on each table inside and out, quilted seats, thick checked curtains to give the interior a homely feel, a fireplace housing crackling logs, a small stage not far away from the bar – for the performers to feel close to the audience – an array of tangy local spirits that hit the back of your throat and melted the chill, a selection of snacks, and native produce of the area. But ultimately, it would be all about the atmosphere – a haven for music lovers, where bands and singers could feel appreciated.

"Oi! Layla!"

I jerked my head round, sending half my hair into my eyes. "Oh! Sorry Alec."

He and Dad swapped grins. "Day dreaming about your little empire?"

Two pops of colour appeared on my cheeks. "Just … making plans."

They nodded their understanding.

"Well, me and the boys will get cracking at 8.30 a.m. sharp tomorrow morning and, with a fair wind, we should be able to hand over to the painter and decorator chappies by the middle of next week."

I clapped my hands together excitedly. "Oh, if you could, that would be wonderful."

"We'll do our best for you."

The three of us began shuffling towards the door.

"Got any ideas for who you're going to feature here then?" asked Alec, balancing his pencil back behind his ear.

"Well, it would be good to have an eclectic mix of artists – folk, rock, grunge…"

"It would be a real coup for you if you could get this Mask fella that's rumoured to have moved here."

"Who?" I asked, puzzled. "I've never heard of him."

Alec puffed out his chest with self-importance. "Oh, my daughter, Heather, has been going on about him. He's some new anonymous singer/songwriter."

"Anonymous?" asked Dad. "How does that work?"

Alec hitched his hooded eyes upwards. "According to the fountain of all knowledge that is my sixteen-year-old, he won't allow himself to be identified. The guy wears some massive hoodie and a black masquerade mask, hence the name." Alec shook his head in mock exasperation. "I wish she'd show as much enthusiasm for her blasted studies as she does for this Mask character. She can recite his ruddy lyrics backwards, but ask her about Robert the Bruce and she's lost."

My curiosity rose. A musician like him would be a marketing dream. "Sorry to interrupt Alec," I said. "I'm sensing a possible PR opportunity. How much do you know about this Mask?"

"Well, Heather has been playing his stuff on repeat for the last week. She said he started off uploading his music online and it's really beginning to catch on. He's got a great voice, mind you."

Alec stepped outside, the setting sun casting a halo effect around his rotund frame. "Rumours are that he's Australian. She keeps on about what amazing eyes he has. Teenage daughters, eh?"

As he climbed into the driving seat, he swung round to look back at me over his shoulder. "According to local gossip, he's bought old Tavish McArthur's place."

Dad's jaw dropped. "Not that dilapidated cottage up by Galen Waterfall?"

"The very one."

Dad's eyebrows arched. "Bloody hell! No disrespect to old Tavish, God rest his soul, but that back garden of his was like something out of a Hammer Horror movie. I offered the stubborn old bugger a hand to get it into some sort of order on more than one occasion, but he wasn't having any of it."

"Well, from what I've heard, it could give Glasgow Botanic Gardens a run for its money now."

Dad laughed. "You are joking."

Alec was earnest. "I'm serious, mate. One of my contacts in the plumbing trade was passing by Coorie Cottage the other night. He said the garden was all brightly coloured flowers and swaying trees. Like an art gallery painting, was his actual words."

He lifted one hand. "Cheerio now!"

A kernel of an idea was tugging at me as we watched him leave.

As soon as Alec had melted into the distance, I spoke to Dad, my enthusiasm firing on all cylinders. "I've got to speak to Heather about this musician. If we could get someone edgy like him on opening night..."

Dad looked pessimistic. "Darling, didn't you hear what Alec just said? The guy wears a mask! He obviously doesn't want to be identified, so I don't think the idea of appearing in front of an audience is going to go down well."

I listened as Dad spoke again. "And if the rumours are true and he has bought the old McArthur place, that's about as secluded as you can get. Maybe that's why he's moved here, to get a bit of peace."

I frowned, keen to remain optimistic. "But he might consider it, because it's a small, new venue close to where he owns a house. It would be a chance to get to know the local community..." A slow grin spread across my face. "I've got to at least try."

Images of blazing publicity articles and news stories flashed in front of me. "I'll do some research about this guy on my own and then see if Heather wants to help me."

A frisson of excitement bolted up my back. I was used to interviewing and dealing with awkward characters. How hard could it be?

Chapter Eighteen

I laced my fingers together behind my head and slumped back against the sofa in frustration.

Good grief! This Mask character was every bit as elusive as the abominable snowman.

I tapped at my laptop keyboard and scrolled down again, but the screen only delivered the same limited information about him; that he'd risen from obscurity to become this emerging singer/songwriter sensation but nobody knew anything about him or his true identity, other than the fact that he was Australian.

There wasn't even a proper photograph of him anywhere on social media. The same images kept reappearing of a tall figure with his features disguised by a baggy, dark hood and a black masquerade mask.

I picked up my mug of tea and took a gulp. He really was to be congratulated. In this day and age, goodness knows how he was managing to stay so elusive. He must have one hell of a PR and management team.

I trawled through several fan discussion boards about him, which ranged from speculation that he was the son of some earl and desperately trying to revolt against his aristocratic family, to the theory that he wasn't just one person but a band of disaffected musicians who were seeking revenge on the record industry that had rejected them.

Recalling what Alec had said about him earlier in the day, I went onto YouTube and entered "Mask Music" in the search field.

A string of still pictures of only his eyes, staring fixedly out from behind his mask, popped up. They were a deep, dark brown.

I tapped on one of his songs called 'Deliverance'. All at once, my cottage was filled with the sound of a soulful electric guitar. It was slow at first, before suddenly launching into a faster tempo.

Then his deep, smoky voice layered over the top of it.

I sank back, drinking in the painful inflections in his vocals. Alec was right. He was a wonderful singer.

When the song slid to an end, I jumped forwards, eager to listen to another one.

I clicked on another of his tracks at random, called 'All Shadows' and was treated to a softer melody this time, all about dreams.

There was no denying this Mask was a very talented and unique musician.

With the Thursday summer evening sky rapidly giving way to charcoal patches of cloud outside the sitting room window, I resumed searching in vain for any other background information about him.

What was it Alec had said about rumours flying that he had bought that secluded old cottage up by Galen Waterfall?

My thoughts travelled to our often harsh winters, when snow and ice clung determinedly to everything and made a lot of the winding verges and roads in the Loch Harris area impassable. If what Alec said was true and Mask had moved in up there, he obviously didn't care too much about being stranded if the weather turned nasty.

I turned back to my search. There were a few similar articles about his songs starting to make an impact on the charts and other excited reports about the amount of hits his music was receiving on social media.

Oh. Hang on!

My fingers paused over one brief article in an indie music magazine. It said:

Reports are very sketchy and we have no way of confirming this story, but elusive singer/songwriter Mask is rumoured to be scouting for homes in the Strathlevin/Loch Harris area of Scotland…

My eyes widened. So it could well be true then?
I eagerly read on.

As is the case with this mysterious performer, we have been unable to either confirm or deny this rumour with his management, Buccaneer, who, yet again, we have been unable to contact.

I picked up my mug of tea from the table and tapped my nails against it. It wouldn't do any harm to look into approaching this Mask about a possible appearance at my new music venue. OK, so it might be a complete waste of my time, but what did I have to lose?

I stared back at the laptop screen. An image of Mask's challenging, dark eyes glowered back at me.

What a coup that would be for me, and for Loch Harris, if we could book someone like him to appear. I fought the nagging doubt that getting a publicity-shy musician to literally show his face was going to be almost impossible.

It was worth a try.

Alec and the boys were starting work on their carpentry at the boathouse first thing in the morning. If I could recruit his daughter, Heather, to help me locate Mask, I'd probably stand a better chance.

After all, it sounded like she was his number one fan.

Then my thoughts travelled to Faith again. Surely there must be something I could do to let her see how obstinate and silly she was being about Greg?

My fingertips tingled as I turned my attention back to my laptop and searched for the Loch Harris Forestry Commission website.

It appeared, all moss greens, sage, and emerald, with pictures of the many tree-lined walkways and wooded paths morphing in and out of one another in the background.

I located the Who We Are section and typed in 'Greg McBride'.

Almost immediately, Greg's attractive grinning face appeared on screen.

I leaned forward and read that Greg and two of his colleagues were based at the log cabin offices on the outskirts of Loch Harris, while the other members of the team were scattered between Finton and North Spey, another slightly larger town a few miles out from us.

I snatched up a yellow Post-it pad beside my laptop and jotted down the address of the log cabin, deciding that I would head straight there tomorrow, once I had dropped by the boathouse.

The next morning delivered a hotchpotch of enthusiastic, early summer bursts of lemon sunshine.

After a shower and a hasty bowl of cereal for breakfast, I got ready to head out. I wanted to try and catch Alec early, before he started to get tired and a bit grumpy. Then I would head off to pay Greg McBride a visit. If he wasn't on a shift, I would leave him a message and hope he would contact me.

Just because my relationship had ended like a Greek tragedy, it didn't mean Faith's had to. I couldn't allow Faith to give up on the possibility of something good without even giving it a bloody try first.

Conflicted ideas jostled inside my head. I mean, perhaps

I could just give things a little nudge in the right direction between her and Greg?

That wasn't interfering, I assured myself. That was simply … interfering.

Oh hell.

You would have thought that after my heart-shattering experience with Mac, I would have had enough of affairs of the heart. But seeing my best friend so down and sounding so flat propelled me into action.

Perhaps I was interfering, but it was either that or do nothing and watch her being miserable. I knew that wasn't an option.

I streaked down the country lane in my car, past Dad's house, with enthusiasm ringing in my ears. I switched on the radio to try and distract myself. This was the most energised I had felt in a long time. Losing Mac in the way that I had had been like having a mortar bomb lobbed into my world.

I tried to clear my mind as I negotiated the twists and bumps that snaked up and around the woodland and swooping hillsides.

Loch Harris was spread out like a dazzling mirror as I swept right and up towards the boathouse.

I parked in the tourist picnic area and cut across the grass. Daisies popped around my feet like mini rays of sunshine and the trees shimmered with the remnants of rain.

I breathed in, savouring the zingy scent of the damp undergrowth. I could hear faint voices travelling from the boathouse and, as I emerged from the trees, the thumping and banging of hammers became louder.

Alec's transit van bearing the name of his business, Tip Top Carpentry, was parked to the left of the boathouse with its rear doors gaping open. The sound of a crackling radio emerged from somewhere inside.

I dashed up the porch steps, stopping for a moment to marvel at the view. I knew I would never grow tired of it.

"Hi Alec," I yelled, sticking my head round the door. I had to raise my voice over the sound of thumping and the disco beat thudding from their radio. "You've hit the ground running then?"

Alec rose up from where he was crouching down by one of the skirting boards. "Morning, Layla. Bloody hell, you're up and about early."

I smiled over at two of his employees, young lads in combats, who were rummaging around in a huge iron toolbox. "The same can be said for you." I took a step forwards. "I don't suppose you could give me Heather's mobile number please?"

Alec gave a nod of his shiny, balding head. "Course I can."

I hesitated for a moment, before deciding that I had to tell him why. "It's just I need to pick Heather's brains about that musician – the guy who calls himself Mask."

Alec was halfway to tugging his mobile out of his dungarees. He gave me a little frown. "Oh?"

"I'm going to write an article about him for a music mag and as she seems to be so enthusiastic about him…"

I tried to conceal the guilty flush in my cheeks. I couldn't tell Alec the real reason why. If I revealed that I was hoping to persuade this musician to appear here when we opened, it would be spread around Loch Harris faster than a bout of seasonal flu.

Alec eyed me for a moment. "It's only she's nuts over this guy as it is, and I don't mean to sound like a Victorian dad, but if she applied half as much energy to her studies right now as she does mooning over this bloke's music…"

I raised one hand. "I won't distract her for too long. I promise." I gave a shrug. "I could even have a little chat with her, if you like. About her studies."

Alec smiled and nodded. He reeled off Heather's mobile number. "That would be great, Layla. She'll no doubt take more notice of you than her old fart of a father."

I laughed and jabbed Heather's number into my phone. "Thanks. And you're not an old fart."

Alec didn't appear convinced. "Since Pam and I split up, it's been a case of good cop, bad cop, and I think you can guess which I am."

He returned to work and I hovered for a few moments longer, watching the three men angling planks of bleached wood. The rich scent of chippings was hazy and homely.

Then the enormity of what I was undertaking decided to punch me in the ribs. I stared around at the empty space, with its floorboards, Formica counter, and shards of Loch Harris peeping in through the windows. I headed out, back down the boathouse steps, taking a moment to compose myself. *Of course, I could do this. This was just a wobble.*

I drew in a big breath of air and attempted to distract

myself by finding a spot with a good enough mobile signal to ring Heather.

Her light, interested voice drifted into my ear and, after we had exchanged a few pleasantries, I explained why I was calling, while Loch Harris murmured nearby.

I knew it would take a couple of days for my right ear to recover from her thrilled shriek.

———————————

I left behind the intermittent banging, thumping, and hammering over the crackle of the portable radio and headed away from the boathouse, towards the Loch Harris Forestry Commission cabin on the other side of the water.

I wasn't sure what I would say to him – assuming he was even working that morning. I'd already decided that if it turned out I'd wasted a trip and he had the day off, I'd simply leave a short note for him with one of his work mates, explaining who I was and asking him to ring me.

I scrambled around in my head as I drove there, attempting to piece together something coherent but persuasive that I could say to him about Faith.

I had to get across that she did really like him but she was used to being in control of situations and, off the record, she was resisting getting involved with him because she had found herself attracted to him so quickly.

Yes. That sounded all right and was a pretty accurate summary of the situation.

The scenery flashed past my window as I made my way under the slivers of sunshine towards the cabin office. Up ahead on the twisting ribbon of road sat a wooden sign with green lettering proclaiming "Loch Harris Forestry Commission" on the left-hand side.

I flicked up the indicator, allowing a tractor to trundle past me, before I swung along a darkened, gravelled route. The trees were clustered together like gossiping heads, bowed in conversation.

The gravel gave way, opening out into a generous parking area that was cushioned with bark.

I parked beside four other vehicles and collected my bag from the passenger seat. The air was stirring with the sound of the rustling undergrowth.

The log-cabin-cum-office was a stout, dark affair. It reminded me a little of the cottage in *Hansel and Gretel*, minus the candy cane door and marzipan roof.

Inside the entrance, I could see a corkboard pinned with various notices about landscape planning, tree surveys, and a timetable of park ranger woodland walks. There was also a bristly brown doormat and a silver stand that housed spare umbrellas.

I stepped inside to be greeted by an interior glass-panelled door.

When I went through that, I was met by a big, smiley, older man in a leather waistcoat. He had been sitting behind a desk covered in paperwork.

The whole interior possessed a cosy lodge feel, with black and white landscape prints dotted on the walls and a dark wooden floor that was decorated with a couple of brightly coloured hessian rugs. There were two other desks, both unoccupied.

"Hi there. Can I help you?"

I asked if Greg McBride was working today and to my relief, I was told he was. "He's just popped out to speak to our red deer ranger. He should only be a few minutes."

I explained who I was and said I'd be grateful if I could have a quick word with him.

The burly man nodded. "Give me a second and I'll radio to let him know you're here."

I watched as he picked up a large walkie-talkie contraption from his desk and spoke into it. There was a series of sizzling crackles before I heard Greg's hesitant reply. "I'm on my way back now anyway."

"I won't keep him long," I insisted, keen to ensure I didn't get Greg into trouble at work.

The man, whose staff badge on his waistcoat announced him as Colin Agnew, gave me a breezy smile. "Oh, don't worry about that, lass. The big chief won't be in till lunchtime today."

He indicated across the office floor to the largest oak desk in the corner. "That's his kingdom over there."

I laughed, while still composing what I was going to say to Greg when I saw him.

No doubt he would think I was an interfering busybody, but the worst thing surely, would be to *not* to try and help Faith and him sort things out.

I knew that, if the roles were reversed, Faith would be the first to get involved – whether I wanted her to or not.

I swallowed as the interior glass door squealed open and Greg appeared.

He studied me for a second, recognition sparking in his hazel eyes. "Hi there."

Colin snatched up a cup of stewed coffee from the top of a pile of papers balanced on his desk. "I'll leave you guys to it for a bit." He dropped his balding head and sauntered out, closing the door behind him.

Greg spoke straight away. "If this is about Faith, you're wasting your time."

I hooked my bag tighter over my shoulder. "What makes you say that?"

"She did, in no uncertain terms."

I tried to smile. "Whatever she said to you, she didn't mean it. She really likes you."

Greg rolled his warm eyes up to the timbered ceiling. "Well, she has a very strange way of showing it."

I watched him stride over to the other smaller vacant desk. There was a photograph of him and Sam in a solid silver frame.

Greg jerked his head towards the picture. "Faith doesn't want to get involved with a single parent." He sank dejectedly into his black swivel chair.

"No, that isn't it at all. Up until now, Faith has had some serious commitment issues."

Greg looked thoughtful. He gestured for me to sit down in the chair opposite.

I hoped I was expressing myself clearly enough. "That's why she's acting a bit weird about all this," I went on. "It's because she really likes you. She's worried in case things go wrong between you and Sam gets hurt too."

Greg rubbed at his clean-shaven chin. "It just seems to me like a whole raft of excuses."

"It isn't," I insisted. "Since she stopped seeing you, Faith hasn't been herself at all."

My fingers reached for my bangle while I carried on talking. "She's been so much more subdued and unhappy since you guys called it a day."

Greg eyed me across the desk. "I didn't call anything off, Layla. It was all her." He shook his blond head, making his quiff tremble. "I think things are best left as they are."

"Even though you really like her too?"

His jaw set. "Sam and I are a team."

"And Faith knows that," I stressed. I got to my feet, feeling dejected.

Was it worth one more shot?

I moved towards the office door, the wooden floor creaking underneath my trainers. "Maybe you should have stressed to Faith that it's not only you who is prepared to take a chance on her?"

Greg frowned across at me. "What do you mean?"

I nodded over at the sunny smiling photograph of Greg and Sam. "You're a team, remember?"

I pulled open the door and hesitated for a moment in the doorway. "Thanks for seeing me."

Chapter Nineteen

Heather bounded out of her house and towards my car the next morning, like a gorgeous teenage puppy on steroids.

She was wearing her pale blonde hair in a French plait and was sporting diamante-studded cropped jeans, but it was the white, V-necked T-shirt, emblazoned with the word 'Mask' and a pair of eyes underneath, that made me smile.

Heather yanked open the passenger door. "Do you like it?" she gushed, pointing one pink nail at her T-shirt. "I had it printed up in Glasgow."

I watched her eagerly settle herself.

"I hope you aren't going to be disappointed," I cautioned her. "These might just be all rumours about him living in old Tavish's cottage." I twisted round in the driver's seat and smiled kindly.

Heather shook her head so ferociously, I thought she would give herself a migraine. I watched her fasten her seat belt. "Amy in my English class, well, her dad is an estate agent with that posh firm in town. He couldn't tell her for definite – something to do with confidentiality – but he wouldn't deny it either."

She flapped her hands. "Amy only told me and we've tried to keep it quiet, otherwise Loch Harris will be overrun with his fans."

I swung the car away from the string of cottages.

"I am SO excited," she bubbled. "What a way to spend Saturday morning! Does my hair look OK? Do you think we'll get to speak to him? I wasn't sure about these trainers..."

She waggled her feet.

Recollections of my heart-wrenching crush on Johnny Depp at her tender age came flooding back. The teenage angst and the fluctuating emotions of despair one minute at the realisation of never meeting him, followed by soaring admiration the next.

"You look lovely," I assured her. "But I don't have to tell you that if the stories are anything to go by, Mask won't be inviting us in for a cuppa and a slice of cake."

Heather looked crestfallen. "No. I suppose you're right."

I indicated left and took us past Loch Harris and out around the winding road that led up to Galen Waterfall.

The Saturday morning sky was now a duck-egg blue, making promises of a warmer and sunlit day to come.

Heather could barely contain herself. "What are we going to say to him, Layla? About your music venue I mean?"

I glanced in the rear-view mirror. "That's assuming he's at home, although I don't think he could really wander around Mrs Fraser's corner shop in a hoodie and masquerade mask, enquiring about the price of tea bags."

Heather grinned at the image.

"I think I'm just going to try and point out to him the mutual benefits of him appearing. It would not only endear him to the community, but it would really benefit the area."

"Have you chosen a name for the club yet?"

"No, but I'm working on it."

Heather's wide blue eyes took in the farmland, spread out like an olive and jade quilted duvet. Then her mouth turned down. "He's not going to agree to appear, is he?"

I let out a sigh that verged on the pessimistic. "Probably not, if what I've read online is true." We pulled up at a set of traffic lights. "But I think we should at least try."

Heather was momentarily cheered again.

Galen Waterfall was spooling down the hillside as we eased around the bend. It reminded me of a shimmering silver dress, sliding its way down the slick rocks.

Heather and I exchanged charged glances as Tavish's Victorian cottage appeared.

"Here goes nothing," I breathed.

Chapter Twenty

The name that Tavish had given the cottage was barely visible beneath a tangle of ivy. On a faded white plaque, the word 'Coorie' was painted across it in black paint.

"Coorie," repeated Heather, frowning.

"It means to cuddle or snuggle in old Scots," I explained. "Don't you youngsters know anything about your Scottish heritage?"

Heather grinned back. "Listen to you. Anyone would think you were ancient. You're not that old, Layla."

"Why, that's very kind of you."

The cottage was a concoction of grey and vanilla stone with angled white-framed windows and a sloping, ghost-grey slate roof. Three narrow steps led up to the matching, solid white door. Its panel of glass was frosted, rendering it impossible to see in. It looked as though it had recently undergone a makeover, with fresh paint.

Heather was fidgeting beside me. She was jumping from

foot to foot so much, I wondered if she needed an urgent visit to the bathroom. "I'm so excited," she squealed. "Do you think he's in?"

I turned my attention to the sash windows, but it was impossible to tell if anyone was at home. The white Venetian blinds were pulled too far down to make out any moving shapes inside.

Heather moved to the side of the house and jabbed a frantic finger. "There's a truck parked down there by the fence."

I walked over and followed her flushed gaze. Sure enough, an inconspicuous black pick-up truck was sitting there, its bodywork gleaming and then fading again under the hide and seek rays of the sun.

"Mask must be in," insisted Heather.

"Well, there's only one way to find out."

We returned to the front of the cottage and made our way up the steps to the front door. I raised an apprehensive hand and rattled the brass letter box. There was silence.

"He's not in, is he?" she sulked after a few moments of us hovering there.

I took a few steps backwards and took in the gleaming coats of snow-white paint on the door and window sills. "It doesn't look like it, although if he's as reclusive as people are saying he is…"

I gave the letterbox a second louder rattle.

Still, the cottage was shrouded in silence, and the only noise we could hear was the odd car trundling behind us on the road and the insistent splash of Galen Waterfall.

I shrugged my shoulders. "Well, I guess that's it then."

Heather groaned and indicated her T-shirt. "This was a right waste of bloody time. I could've spent that money on a new pair of trainers for what I paid for this."

Trying to cast off my disappointment (although to be honest, I wasn't rightly sure what I had expected) I started back towards my car, with Heather trudging behind me.

"Oh my God! Layla, come and see this!"

I twisted round to see Heather pointing to the back of the cottage. "Dad's friend was right about the garden. It's gorgeous!"

Pushing my car keys into my back pocket, I followed her. "Look, maybe we should leave. If he's in, it's not going to look too good if he sees two strangers prowling around..." I drew up behind Heather, my mouth slipping open. "Wow."

It was difficult to know where to look first. Spread out like a palette of bright paint were peony flowers in baby pink and a magnolia, boasting rich butterscotch petals.

Beside those, meconopsis blooms in the prettiest shade of powder blue stretched outwards from the manicured beds. They were like electric poppies, with large saucer-shape petals.

To the right of a clump of sorbet-yellow daffodils was a section of bog myrtle which, when crushed up, delivers a delicious citrusy scent.

My overwhelmed eyes were drawn to the flower bed opposite, where a cluster of black and white dwarf cornel fluttered their veined leaves. They were accompanied by a cushion of pale lilac moss campion that reminded me of butterflies.

Two trees stood further down the freshly cut lime-green lawn. "That's a sessile oak, like the Birnam Oak," I explained to Heather, indicating its long tentacle branches spreading outwards, "and the one opposite it is a sycamore."

I twisted round. "Until Great Birnam Wood to high Dunsinane hill shall—"

Heather frowned. "What?"

"It's a quote from *Macbeth*. You know, William Shakespeare."

"Oh yeah. Right."

I inwardly rolled my eyes.

Behind the two trees sat an herbaceous border groaning with blood-red hollyhocks and white foxgloves. They were surrounded by a sea of gold and tangerine heleniums with velvety petals which were reminiscent of daisies.

It was a masterclass of juxtaposed shapes, colours, and textures, all reaching a climax along a short grey stone path. It was as if a child had gathered all the shades of the rainbow and thrown them haphazardly together.

"It's like something out of a painting," breathed Heather in admiration.

I could smell the spicy, sweet aroma of oregano and the bitter liquorice of fennel, mingling with the buttery perfume of the blooms. "It's beautiful," I agreed. "All of it."

I turned to Heather and jerked my head. "Look, I could stay here all day as well, but I really don't think that's a good idea. How about we come back another day? Hopefully, there will be someone at home."

Heather's blonde plait jerked with frustration. Her mouth turned down at the corners. "OK. Let's go."

We got back to my car and I was just unlocking the door when a deep voice stopped us, booming through the front door. "Who the hell are you? And why were you prowling around my garden?"

Heather and I froze for a moment, thrown by the realisation that there was somebody at home after all. We spun around at the same time.

A tall silhouette was just visible through the pane of frosted glass.

I straightened my back and pinned on a rictus smile. I felt like a child who had been caught with her hand in a jar of Jelly Babies. "I'm sorry to bother you, but we were looking for…" My words were interrupted by the thrilled bubble of Heather, who gushed, "We're looking for the musician Mask."

She bounded towards the shadowy, dark figure behind the door. "Is that you?"

There was a pause that seemed to last for an eternity. "Yes. But what do you want?" he growled in an Australian accent.

Heather let out the biggest scream and grabbed onto my arm. She proceeded to bounce up and down, as if she was on a pogo stick. "Shhh!" I whispered. "Try and calm down a bit until we've spoken properly to him."

I cleared my throat. "I'm opening a live music venue in Loch Harris and I was wondering if you would be agreeable to making a personal appearance…"

I squinted through the glass panes of the door. Realising

I was doing my utmost to get a clearer look at him, he thrust his arm up and hitched a hood down over his features. Now it was impossible to make him out at all.

Bugger!

"I don't do public appearances," he answered shortly from the other side of the door. "I thought that was common knowledge. And you still haven't told me why you were wandering around my garden."

But Heather was too overcome to pick up on Mask's irritation. "Your music is just so wonderful, Mask," sighed Heather, slapping one hand against her heart. "I love the lyrics to 'Refuse Me Nothing'. That's my favourite."

There was a momentary softening to his tone. "Er ... thank you."

"Heather. My name's Heather."

"Thank you, Heather. That's very kind of you."

I pulled at her bare arm as she jumped on the spot. "Oh my God! He just said my name! Did you hear Mask say my name, Layla?"

"Yes, I did," I hissed out of the corner of my mouth. "But I need to speak to him..."

"I can hear every word you say," he barked, his demeanour behind the door like a winter chill. "I'm sorry but the answer is still no. I let my music speak for me and I don't need to prance around on a stage to do that."

My brain scrambled around for something persuasive to say. I couldn't give up yet. "I appreciate what you're saying, but this would be in support of a fledgling music venue... I could install a screen so you couldn't be seen."

The hooded figure leaned in a little closer to the glass.

Heather and I exchanged charged glances and I found myself taking a step backwards.

"What's your name?" he asked.

"Layla Devlin."

"Well, Ms Devlin, I'm not a Punch and Judy puppet that bobs up every now and then."

My optimism was plummeting to the floor. This was not going at all well. "Look, I'm very sorry we were in your garden uninvited, but it's breathtaking and we couldn't resist taking a closer look."

"Thank you." His voice was dripping with sarcasm. "I'm honoured you approve of my horticultural abilities but the answer remains no. I will not appear live at your venue. Now, if you'll excuse me."

I watched his silhouette evaporate.

Heather let out a frustrated groan. "Oh, that's just great. What now?"

"I don't know that we can do anything else," I admitted. "You heard what he said." I jerked my head towards the front door of the cottage again. "It's a pity. I listened to some of his songs the other night and they are beautiful."

Heather sighed into the air. "He's a true artist."

I glanced over at the gushing ribbon of waterfall across the road and then up at the bank of clouds looming. "His music would have been the perfect fit for what I want – something a bit different, but with lots of heart."

I raised my hands helplessly, allowing them to fall back down by my sides. "He might change his mind, but I very much doubt it. I think seeing us in his garden didn't help."

Heather folded her arms, making her series of bracelets jangle. "It's such a shame." We meandered back to my car.

"Yes," I conceded, unlocking the car door. "I don't think he realises how talented he is."

I was too busy negotiating my car away from Coorie Cottage to realise that Mask had remained standing just a little further down his hallway – and had heard every word of our conversation.

———————

There was a deflated mood in the car as I drove Heather back home.

"Well, at least we tried," I said, clicking on the car radio.

Heather glowered out of the passenger-side window. "It would have been so amazing. I just don't understand why he was so against it." She frowned over at me. "Do you think Mask might change his mind?"

"I don't think so. The way he was talking, he'd rather pull out one of his own teeth."

Remembering what Alec had said about Heather's enthusiasm for Mask, rather than her studies, I cleared my throat. I'd promised him I would mention it.

Heather watched me through china-blue eyes as I spoke of her dad's concern about her schoolwork. "I'm not going to tell you what to do with your life, but believe me, Heather, you won't stay sixteen for very long."

I could see her wrinkle up her button nose. "I wouldn't mind working in the music industry. Maybe in public relations."

"Good for you."

I glanced in my rear-view mirror. "I'm sure you'd be great at that, but it's like a lot of careers in entertainment. It's very competitive."

Heather opened her mouth to speak but then clamped it shut.

"I'm not trying to deter you. All I'm saying is, if you do your best and stick at school, you'll stand a far better chance of getting your foot in the door, OK?" I offered her what I hoped was an encouraging smile. "Nobody can ask any more of you than that."

I clicked on the right indicator, the hillsides dashing past the car windows. "Lecture over, OK?"

"OK," she agreed. "I get it."

We drew up outside Heather's grey stone cottage, with its red painted fence and hanging baskets brimming with indigo and lemon pansies.

She clambered out and then bobbed her blonde head back in. "If you do decide to speak to Mask again, can I please come with you?"

"Sure. I don't think I will ask him again, but you can come along and be verbally abused with me if I do take leave of my senses and change my mind." I pinned her to the pavement with a meaningful look. "But that would only be on one condition."

"What?"

"That you promise to try at school." I laughed at her reluctantly accepting look. "See you later."

I drove back to my dad's with ideas for bands and artists I could approach spinning through my mind. It would be a nice touch if Dad were to agree to Battalion reforming, even if it was just for my opening night.

Thinking about my dad, a shadow of a name for my music venue flitted around at the edges of my mind.

When I was much younger, Dad and I had loved to take off to the coast. We would wander along the vanilla beach, peppered with rocks and studded with a swathe of pastel shells that reminded me of colours of ice cream: snowy white, buttercup, faintest peach.

Dad would hold my hand and I'd crouch down, digging them out of the damp sand with my determined little fingers. The conch shells were always my favourite. It was their twisting shape that I loved. I could imagine using it as a musical instrument to call mermaids to the shore.

The conch variety was also so ornate and colourful, like a multi-layered truffle.

The horse conch shell was still the one I liked the best. Its ripples and soft shades were so pretty, like the petticoats of a sumptuous gown.

"The Conch Club," I said out loud. The sound of my own voice, alone in the car, startled me for a moment. I took an excited breath and repeated it.

I drew up outside Dad's house and the car engine slowly died.

I would speak to him about Battalion, tell him about the Mask situation (even if it didn't look like he would appear), and offer to take him for a celebratory drink, now that I had decided on a name for the business.

I locked the car and bounded up the path excitedly.

There was a stillness as I entered the cottage that made me pull up.

My dad was incapable of not having music churning through the house. It would either be him playing an impromptu session on his drum kit or songs sizzling from his radio. At other times, he would be sat like Buddha in the centre of his sitting room, marvelling yet again at his extensive record collection.

But today, there was an unsettling quiet.

A kernel of concern started to grow. "Dad. Dad? Are you there?"

I heaved an inward sigh of relief when I saw Dad in his Harley Davidson T-shirt, sitting in his armchair.

"You OK? Oh, I've got lots to tell you. How about we go out for some lunch?"

My eyes narrowed at Dad's stiff expression. "Dad? What is it?"

He jerked his head sideways.

From out of the connecting kitchen came a figure wreathed in a dark fringed shawl and black trouser suit.

She reminded me of a vampire.

My mother delivered one of her unreadable smiles. "Hello, Layla."

Chapter Twenty-One

I could feel my features hardening.

"What the hell is she doing here?"

Dad jumped up and out of his chair. "She said she needs to speak to you."

"Can you stop talking about me as though I'm not here?" she trilled in her fake London accent.

I folded my arms protectively across my chest. "It's habit. You have been AWOL for the past twenty odd years, Tina." I emphasised her name with as much disdain as I could manage.

Tina flicked her hair back over her shoulders. "I didn't come here to argue."

"Well, that will be a first," growled Dad.

Tina flashed him a disapproving stare. "Aren't I allowed to come and visit my own daughter?"

"Oh, not all this again. I haven't been your daughter since the day you walked out, remember?"

Tina's razor-sharp cheeks flinched under her foundation.

"Let's not go over all that again."

Dad and I swapped knowing looks.

Without being invited, she seated herself on Dad's beige sofa. Her heavily lashed blue eyes swivelled around the sitting room, with its woodchip magnolia walls and black and white prints of Dad as a young drummer.

"That was taken before you got your claws into him," I blurted, moving to stand beside Dad's armchair.

Tina pursed her ruby-slicked lips. "We were happy, weren't we, Harry?"

Dad blinked. "Were we? When was that then, Tina? 2.15 p.m. one Thursday afternoon?"

I snorted into my shoulder, which made Tina scowl through her fringe.

"What do you want, Tina?" asked Dad with an air of weariness. "You said you needed to speak to Layla, and here she is."

My mother shuffled forward on the sofa and laced her fingers together on top of her tasselled effort of a handbag. "A little bird tells me you're going to be a businesswoman."

I thumped my trainer on Dad's russet carpet. "And there we have it. The reason she's dashed up here." I took a couple of steps towards her and she bristled. "What is it, Tina? Ramon getting fed up of writing you blank cheques?"

My mother's fingers picked at the beige tassels dripping from her bag. "Not at all. I simply thought you might benefit from some help."

Dad shook his head in wonder. "What Layla would have benefited from was having her mother around."

A couple of resentful, hot tears glistened behind my

eyes, but I bit them back. There was no way I was going to allow her to see me cry.

"You know how complicated things were," insisted Tina, squirming. "Anyway, I'm not here to drag over the past. I want to help Layla."

Was she serious? How deluded was she? I glowered down at her, trying to contain my temper. "Who told you I was setting up my own business?"

She simpered, which just infuriated me more. "I bet it was that old gossip Susan Mayhew. Am I right?"

"She just thought I should know."

Dad rolled his grey eyes. "And I take it you're staying at Susan's whilst you're up here?"

My mother looked appalled. "Good God, no! I've got a suite at that dinky little hotel in the next town. The one with the drawbridge. Had a wonderful sleep there last night."

I blanched. "You're staying at The Linear? But that's extortionate."

Tina dismissed my statement with a flap of her hand. "Look, investing in your concert hall thingy…"

"It's not a concert hall. It's an intimate music venue."

My mother pinned an indulgent smile on her lips. "Well, whatever it is, I'd like to help you financially. I can afford it."

"You mean, Ramon can," muttered Dad.

I shot her a chilling stare. "I don't need help. Mac left me money in his will."

Tina's beige-smeared eyes widened in her pointed face. "So it's true then?"

Dad and I didn't reply.

"It was good of you to come to Mac's funeral," I ground out after an awkward pause.

Tina's chest heaved. "I would have come, but Ramon and I were so busy with his new restaurant in Covent Garden."

"Well, either way, it's all over with," answered Dad.

Tina rose up onto her spiky black heels. "So that's it? I'm dismissed."

I moved to Dad's sitting room door and yanked it wide open. "I'll call you a taxi."

My mother eyed us both. "It doesn't matter what I do now, does it?"

I hitched my eyebrows up towards my hairline and watched her thrust her handbag under her right arm. "Quite the cosy little unit, you two."

Dad joined me at the door and placed a protective hand on my shoulder. "We had to be."

A flash of something reared up in Tina's eyes.

She started down Dad's hallway, an unfamiliar figure striding past Dad's tumble of walking boots, waterproofs, and assorted photos of us together. She wobbled to a stop in front of one picture of the two of us, ruddy-faced and laughing on one of the Loch Harris hillsides.

She flicked an unfathomable look at my dad but her words were for me. "You and your father should have a talk."

Dad went ashen. He took a lunging step. "Be quiet, Tina."

I swivelled my head between my fractured parents. "What's going on? What's she talking about?"

Tina tugged open Dad's front door. She glanced at me from over her shoulder. "You need to speak to your … dad."

The sharp inflection as she spat out the word 'dad', triggered an odd chill in my stomach.

"I'll call my own taxi," she called out from further down the path.

I slammed the front door closed on her plucked eyebrows, hitched up my mouth, and swung round to look at my dad. "Sounds like we need to have a chat."

My father glowered at his closed front door. "It can wait."

I felt suddenly uneasy. "No, something tells me it can't."

He looked weary all at once. There were smudges of tiredness under his eyes.

"Dad, whatever venomous poison Tina has been spitting this time, I want to know."

He made a puffing noise and rubbed at his face. "Come on. Let's go and sit down."

I sank onto his sofa, pushing one of his striped cushions out of the way, and Dad lowered himself down beside me. I studied his hand as he placed it gently on mine, the contrast of his gnarled drummer and gardener fingers popping against my pale ones.

"I don't want to believe what your mother has just told me."

I observed his usually open smiling face tense up. "Dad, you're worrying me. What is it? What has she been saying now?"

I had grown accustomed to my mother lobbing the odd

emotional bomb at Dad and me – I was certain it was fuelled by jealousy – but it transpired that on this occasion, she had really outdone herself.

Dad let out a bark of dry laughter, as though trying to reassure himself. His eyes searched mine. He took so long to speak, it was as if his words were crawling through treacle. "Your mother has just told me I might not be your biological father."

I curled up my lip. "She said what?" I couldn't comprehend how she could be so wicked. "She really is something else," I spat. "I always suspected Tina was eaten up with jealousy at how close we are but that's despicable, even for her."

My voice died in my throat as I looked at Dad beside me. An odd, tortured expression had taken over his face. I had never seen him look like that before.

Fear and fury felt like they were about to suffocate me. I squeezed his hand, shocked tears springing into the corners of my eyes. They were battling to force themselves down my cheeks, but I bit my lip.

"Don't tell me you believe her? Dad?"

He opened his mouth and closed it again.

No. No. I didn't believe it. Not one word. She was lying.

All I had to do was stare back at my father's features to see mine. We shared the same shade of conker-brown hair, the same quirky cut to our mouths.

I propelled myself up off the sofa and down Dad's hallway towards the front door.

"Layla! Layla! Where are you going?"

I pulled at the front door handle and it opened with a ferocious jerk.

My mother, such as she was, was now just a flash of patent heel as she deposited herself into a waiting taxi.

I wanted to grab hold of her. I wanted to shake the truth out of her bony frame. I imagined sinking my fingers into her designer sleeves and demanding to know why she was such a spiteful cow.

I raced down Dad's path, my sparkly trainers flashing as they slapped over the paved stones. "What is wrong with you?" I screamed at her as she streaked off. "Why would you lie?"

She angled her coiffed head round and out of the taxi window.

"He is my father," I yelled, carrying burning air in my lungs. "Harry is my dad and you're an evil bitch for saying otherwise!"

Chapter Twenty-Two

F rom somewhere behind me, I heard Dad yelling from
the doorway. "Layla. Layla!"

I stood there, hunched over and confused.

All around me, blackbirds were fizzing like fine
champagne and there was the warm scent of honeysuckle.

Everything was as it should be and yet my mother had
just made everything I thought was true implode.

No. She's a liar. A compulsive, spiteful liar.

I whirled round to face Dad.

He looked confused. I shuffled back up the path and
into his arms, and he held me close. I never wanted to
let go.

"I don't believe her," I rattled. "Not a word."

I waited for Dad to tell me he agreed with me, but he
didn't. He hugged me tighter.

I jerked backwards, freeing myself from his arms. "You
think she's telling the truth, don't you?"

He filled the open doorway and dragged a hand

through his hair. "No." It was as if Mum had planted this seed inside my dad's mind and he was battling to uproot it.

I felt as though I'd been punched in the chest. "Oh shit. You do. You suspect she might be telling the truth."

Clarity forced itself to the forefront of my mind. I remembered Dad's reaction when I suggested his band reform and appear at my club. My stomach fell. "Is that why you didn't want to reunite with Battalion?" I began to move the pieces of the puzzle around. "What aren't you telling me?" Another thought struck. I was desperate for the truth. It seemed to be sadly lacking in my life recently. "Dad?"

After an icy pause, I listened to my father admit that he had always harboured suspicions about Mum and Ed, one of the other members of Battalion.

"So, are you trying to tell me Mum and Ed had an affair?"

Dad blinked several times. He didn't want to revisit those memories. "Yes." Frustration shone out of him.

All the doubts and the questions and the assumptions felt as if they were eating me from the inside out.

I choked back fury as the dappled sun cascaded across the planes of his face. I thought I knew the answer to my next question, but I had the burning compunction to ask it anyway.

"Was it Ed she hinted could be my biological father?"

Dad's agony was evident. "Layla…"

I shook my head. Why couldn't the people I loved be straight with me? Mac, my mother, and now my own father.

"Yes," he replied after an agonising pause. "She hinted it could also be him."

My jaw grew slack at the thought of Ed Stockton, the band's surly bass player.

I blinked, struggling to take in the scents and sounds of the Scottish countryside playing out around me in Dad's garden. "And you believe her?"

Dad chewed the inside of his mouth as he considered my question. "This fling they had happened not long after your mother and I got married. I suspected there might have been something between her and Ed at the time, but I didn't want to accept it."

"Why did you never tackle Mum and Ed about it?"

He gave a resigned shrug. "What can I say? I didn't want to face up to the possibility it was true. I loved her."

He reached out his big, capable hands and beckoned me to him before he began to explain that that was why he was reluctant to see Battalion get back together. "I don't have to tell you what band line-ups can be like. Talk about revolving doors."

I nodded my head.

"Me and the boys have had our fallings-out over the years, like most groups, but when Ed threw a real paddy over his song lyrics being called below par and left the band all those years ago, I was relieved."

Dad gave a sad smile that tore at my insides. It seemed so incongruous, standing out here, with the birds lazily flapping through the tree tops. "I thought – I hoped – I had seen the back of him, especially when we recruited a new bass player."

My fuddled brain came up with an image of Ed's replacement. "Gary?"

"That's right," said Dad. "Gary McDermott. He was a lovely guy and much more accommodating than Ed. Unfortunately, he just wasn't in the same league on the bass guitar as Ed."

"And that was why Ed returned to the Battalion line-up?"

Dad's mouth flatlined. "Yep. I could understand it from a music point of view, but personally ... well ... I struggled with the decision."

I thought of the rest of Dad's band members. A dark thought hit me. "Did any of the other guys in the band know about Mum and Ed?"

Dad was emphatic as he stared across at me, a sudden breeze lifting the layers of his hair. "No. I never told them about my suspicions. It really would have all kicked off then." He almost smiled at the memory. "We were a volatile bunch as it was; no need to throw that into the mix."

The fragmented picture in my head was almost complete now. No wonder my dad was so resistant to the band performing for me. He didn't want to see Ed Stockton.

I twisted my amber and jade ring around and around my finger.

"But even if it is true what your mother said – that I might not be your biological father – you are my daughter Layla, and you always will be."

A chill ran through me. I couldn't even begin to process that idea. This wasn't good enough for me. "Ring her," I ordered. "I want you to ring Tina. I need to speak to her."

"Layla..." Dad stopped when he saw my hard expression. "OK."

I followed him back inside the house and I watched him pull up my mother's number on his mobile. I could make out the faint ring from the other end. It seemed to go on for an eternity. "She's not answering."

"Well, try The Linear then."

I fetched my phone out of my back pocket and pulled up the hotel's details on social media.

My chest heaved when the receptionist informed me that my mother had checked out and left about ten minutes previously.

I slammed my phone down on Dad's mahogany hall table. "She's gone."

Then I picked it back up and stuffed it in my pocket. I needed to get away. My head was swimming against a tide that felt like it was pulling me under.

"Layla, what are you doing? Where are you going?"

He started down the steps after me towards my car. "You are in no fit state to drive."

"I need to think, Dad."

The word tasted differently in my mouth as I said it to him – and I hated my mother for that. I dashed a hand down my face. "I'll give you a call later."

I swung my car automatically down the sunlit lane. My insides were like an out-of-control washing machine. I felt as though I didn't recognise myself. The eyes staring back at me from the rear-view mirror were panicked.

I pulled into the parking lot by the boathouse and jerked up my handbrake far harder than I meant to.

After resting my forehead on the steering wheel for a

few moments, I summoned up enough energy to get out of my car and trample up to the boathouse.

The Conch Club.

Its new name circled around my mind, along with Tina's poisonous revelation that my father might not be Harry, but the band's bloody bass player!

I forced one foot in front of the other until I was at the woodchip-strewn porch.

Alec and his colleagues had left for the day and The Conch Club let out an intermittent series of creaks.

I ambled down the jetty and sank onto the end of it. The Loch Harris waters billowed down below, chilly and navy blue, despite it being June.

And it was then that I allowed the fear and pain out. A frustrated sob crawled out of the base of my throat. Was this going to be another lie I hadn't known about, but that I was going to have to deal with?

She's lying, hissed an insistent voice. *She always does.*

But what if she didn't really know who my real father was between Harry and Ed? What if Harry wasn't my dad after all?

I dropped my head and caught a wavering glimpse of my pale face reflecting back up at me in the swirls of the loch.

A tear glided down my cheek as I sat there, my trainers dangling over the water – unaware I was being watched by a man in a black hoodie, who was feeling every bit as conflicted and confused about his life as I was about mine.

Chapter Twenty-Three

I don't know how long I sat there, watching the summer sky melt into a kaleidoscope of baby pink and tangerine.

The hills of Loch Harris were morphing into the promise of an inky silhouette.

Dad had tried to ring me dozens of times, but I'd switched off my mobile. All I wanted was to be alone with my feet dangling from the end of the jetty.

Harry is my father. He is, I assured myself. Tina was just playing her usual, spiteful mind games.

A breeze was picking up across the loch now, making the formerly calm surface stir itself up into small whipped peaks.

I scrambled to my feet and wrapped my arms tighter around myself, wishing I had brought a jacket. Admittedly, that had been the last of my thoughts when I'd bolted away from my dad's place.

I felt drained and insignificant as I made my way past

The Conch Club, as I thought of it now. I said its name over and over again, trying to distract myself from the impending dark.

I had been so excited about the direction my life was finally taking.

Thoughts of Mac and his deceit still burned, but there had been at least a glimmer of a fresh start.

Now this.

I conjured up an image of Ed Stockton. He didn't have my dad's easy charm or confident swagger.

From what I could remember from when I was younger, he had sported the same big rocker hair but there had always been something hesitant about his demeanour.

Was my mother now telling us that she had been sleeping with both of them at the time I was conceived and therefore wasn't sure which one of them was my real father? It would seem so.

I paused in front of The Conch Club, sitting there all dark and closed off, and stuffed my hands into the pockets of my jeans.

The fear of not being my real father must have burned away at the back of Harry's mind for years.

I'd always thought it was simply about the difficult logistics of being a single parent and a musician on the road that had made Battalion take a back seat in his life.

But now it turned out that that wasn't the reason at all. The real reason was that he feared his suspicions all those years ago might have been true.

Why couldn't Tina have just left the past where it was? Why couldn't she have just let Dad and me carry on with our lives as normal? I surmised that when she had seen for herself that neither of us needed her or wanted her, she had decided to unleash her poison again.

Life had always been about Dad and me. We were a team and nothing could ever destroy that.

I reached my car, climbed in, and sat for a moment, trying to fight the gathering lump in my throat. I couldn't let Tina destroy everything. Maybe she was telling the truth and maybe she wasn't, but I wasn't going to allow her to take control of Dad's life or mine as some sort of payback for us getting on just fine without her.

I dashed away a tear with the back of my hand and fired up the engine.

I swung back into Dad's drive and watched as my headlights slid across Dad's windows. I spotted his silhouette dart up from his chair in the sitting room.

"Where the hell have you been?" he shouted, striding towards the passenger side of my car.

I clambered out, shamefaced. "Sorry, Dad, but I needed to get away for a bit."

He cupped my face in his weathered hands. Anger and relief were lighting up his eyes. "I've been ringing you." He took a step backwards and appraised me. "You look cold. Cold and knackered. Come on, I'll make us a cuppa."

He strode back towards the cottage, the open door allowing a flood of orange lamp light to lap down his front steps.

I felt my chest rise and fall and I began to follow him. The odd star looked like shards of glass, emerging now out of the blueberry-coloured sky.

I leaned against Dad's kitchen top as he busied himself with fetching two mugs from the cupboard.

He had his broad back to me. "We need to have a DNA test." He swung round. "I've been thinking about it all while you've been out, and I don't know about you, but I don't want this cloud following us around."

Hearing Dad say it confirmed what I had been thinking too, as I had stared into the sashaying waves of the loch. I couldn't carry on as normal until this was resolved. It would be some unspoken immovable force between us. It would taint everything, even if we pretended that we could ignore it. "But what if it isn't the result we hope it is?"

Dad set down the mugs and pulled me into a hug. "Whatever the result, you are my daughter. End of. But I can't live with this question mark. Can you?"

I pulled back and shook my head. "The thought of finding out ... well ... you know..."

"I know."

I straightened my back. "We'll do the DNA test. You're right. There's no other way."

I watched Dad fill the kettle with a gush of silvery water from the kitchen tap. "I went up to the loch and just sat there. It was so peaceful." I prepared myself for his reaction. "I did a lot of thinking too, Dad, while I was up there." My voice sounded disembodied, as though it didn't belong to me. "And I wondered if you could do me a favour please."

"Of course. What is it?"

I pressed my lips together and gathered myself. I knew what I was about to say would not be well received. I stole a breath. "I'd like you to suggest a reunion with Battalion, and for you to play on the opening night of The Conch Club."

Dad's thick brows dipped. He stood motionless. "Are you joking?"

I think he could tell by my solemn expression that I wasn't.

"But why, love?"

"A variety of reasons. For us, for answers, to throw a sodding great curve ball at Tina, because Battalion was a great band."

My dad looked even more like a big, broad bear in the settling dark. He switched on one of the kitchen under-cabinet lights "But sweetheart, what if it doesn't achieve any of those things? Have you been listening to anything I've told you? What if Ed really is your father?"

I tilted my chin upwards and fought to keep my voice steady. "Maybe he is my biological father, but you will always be my dad."

His quirky mouth sagged at the corners and it made my stomach sink to the floor. "Dad," I repeated. "Dad, please do this for me. For us." My eyes pleaded with his. "We can't leave things like this. You said so yourself. That's what Tina wants. She wants chaos. She wants us in the middle of another drama."

Dad rubbed his chin. "I called her townhouse in London and their housekeeper said she arrived back an hour ago and then she and Ramon buggered off to Gatwick for some last-minute getaway to Italy."

"See what I mean?" I said, following Dad into the cosy glow of his sitting room as he clutched our mugs of tea.

"This is her all over. You might be prepared to let her get the upper hand, but I'm not."

Dad stared back. "You mean we call her bluff?"

"Exactly. We do things our way, not hers. We do a DNA test and Battalion plays at The Conch Club on my opening night."

My father rocked his head back and seemed to search his sitting room ceiling for inspiration. "So, this is your plan, is it? To reunite a group of quarrelling old rockers?"

"It's a chance for us to move on, Dad," I implored. I thought of my mother and my stomach clenched. "This will let Tina see that it doesn't matter what she throws at us, we can deal with it." One of Dad's eyebrows shot up and I could see from the softening in his eyes that he was beginning to agree with me. "And that's the name you've chosen for the boathouse, is it? The Conch Club?"

"Yep. Our shell-collecting sessions gave me the idea."

Dad afforded me a small smile. "I like it. I like it a lot." He sighed. "OK. You win. I'll contact the guys first thing tomorrow. I can't promise anything but..."

"That's fine, Dad. Thank you. And I'll order us a DNA kit."

As I sat opposite him and took a pull of my tea, I was glad we were taking charge of the whole messy situation rather than allowing Tina to dictate the rules.

Dad cradled his mug in his hands. "So does this mean you've given up on trying to secure this Mask guy then?"

I nodded, thinking about the singer's blank refusal to even consider my invitation. "I can safely say that's a non-starter."

Chapter Twenty-Four

I awoke the next morning with a wave of emotions swishing about inside me.

When I had been with Mac, we would spend Sunday mornings sprawled in bed, nursing endless cups of coffee and in a tangle of warm limbs.

I tried not to stare over at the vacant soft pillow beside me. Then my mother's revelation about Dad and Ed reared up again.

Part of me had clung to the hope that I had imagined it all or that it had been some lucid nightmare.

Memories of last night, including the worry and pain in Dad's eyes, told me otherwise.

I huddled further into the bedcovers. I mean, I didn't look anything like Ed Stockton. He had a pointed, confrontational edge to his features, whereas when I looked like my dad; we shared so many similarities, especially the same bemused-looking mouth.

Or maybe that was what I was choosing to see.

I bunched my knees together under the pink and white covers and indulged in another few moments of self-pity, before switching on my phone and scrolling through the dizzying array of DNA kits for sale.

There was one that was a bit more expensive than the others, but boasted excellent reviews. My fingers hovered over the 'Buy Now' key. Refusing to waste any more time, I jabbed in my credit card details and was informed it would arrive within a few days.

Then I tossed my phone back onto the top of my bed and headed for the shower.

The month of June was shooting past in a frenzy of carpentry and assorted phone calls to paint and furniture suppliers.

Alec and his team had repaired the cracks and scuffs in the boathouse skirting boards, installed some new shelving, and replaced Norrie's old shop counter with one made from the most gorgeous, pale blond wood.

They also replaced some of the tired golden hardwood flooring and matched it up with the existing oak.

Once all that was complete, they set to work on making a semi-circular stage out of the same golden oak as the floors.

The stage would protrude out of the right-hand side wall and provide an intimate experience for the audience – at least, that was what I was hoping for.

Alec had also recommended a heating engineer friend of

his, who got to work installing the gorgeous gothic-style limestone fireplace I'd managed to locate for a good price online.

While they had been putting the finishing touches to all that, I had been knee-deep in assorted colour charts.

I wanted The Conch Club to be cosy, but also to reflect its spectacular woodland surroundings.

In the end, I decided to go down the 'inspired by nature route' and opted for a palette of colours in sea-salt pale grey, a subtle mint green, and a peacock blue. I hoped these shades, complete with dashes of navy-blue furnishings, would honour the glassy beauty of Loch Harris and the rambling forests all around us.

I also decided to go for short, Highland-check charcoal lined curtains in a brushed-wool effect for all six windows.

In keeping with the atmosphere I wanted to create, I chose rustic solid oak, high-backed chairs and circular tables to cluster over the floor and around the stage.

For the expanse of jetty at the back, which stretched out towards the loch like a giant wooden smile, Alec advised me to go for furniture made out of slow-growing redwood, protected by an oil-based preservative. "That repels water and protects it," he informed me. "That means you will be OK leaving it sitting outside."

He also suggested that in order to keep the outside furniture in peak condition, it was best to add a further coat of the preservative every twelve months to keep it looking fresh. "I'll recommend one or two of the really good brands for you."

Following Alec's suggestion, I ordered six sets of six-seater tables, complete with two chairs, two-seater benches and rectangular tables, which had a built-in hole to place a parasol.

Dad had grinned at me when I'd pointed this out. "A hole for a parasol? Are you forgetting we live in Scotland?"

I'd also been putting the word out to my music contacts at various newspapers and magazines for bands and artists who might be interested in appearing at The Conch Club in future.

Faith's experience in dealing with advertising and marketing at the tourist office had been invaluable, and she deployed all her skills and contacts so that we were able to plan a publicity drive and persuade local businesses to hand out the fliers we were in the process of designing. Word of mouth would play such a huge part too in the club's success.

The way things were going, I envisaged our opening night to be middle to late August.

I'd pushed any more thoughts about Mask to the back of my mind after I'd approached him about appearing and he'd knocked me back.

It wasn't any of my business if he wanted to rattle around Coorie Cottage all on his own, with just the waterfall for company. Still, it was a pity. He had such a haunting voice and his lyrics were mesmerising.

———————————

The Scottish weather delivered frequent pattering rain, followed by shards of buttery sunshine.

A modest coach party arrived at Loch Harris, well prepared for the unpredictable climate. They were all decked out in light waterproofs and sturdy walking boots.

I had been standing out on the front steps of the boathouse, huddled in my hooded jacket and chatting to Rory, my painter and decorator, when the lone, metallic coach creaked into the picnic area and disgorged its passengers.

I recognised Stuart, the coach driver, as one of Dad's old school friends.

He ambled over, hitching the hood up on his ski jacket. "It had to be bloody pissing down, today of all days."

I indicated the tourists, who were clutching their cameras and pointing at the loch and the spiky scenery that cradled it. "Looks like you'll be kept busy today."

Stuart pulled a face. "It makes a change. Things have been very quiet." Then he smiled at the boathouse, with its door ajar and the glow of pale light emanating out. "Let's hope your new venture brings the punters back to Loch Harris in their droves."

One of Rory's dark brows shot up. "No pressure then, eh, Layla?"

I opened my mouth to reply but my attention was drawn to the sight of my dad striding along the shale path. He offered Rory and Stuart a distracted greeting. "Could I have a quick word please, Layla?"

I excused myself to Rory who darted back inside the boathouse with the colour chart I'd marked up for him, and Stuart marched off to herd his tourists together.

I examined my dad's pensive expression and my

stomach lurched. "What is it? Oh God, what's Tina done now?"

Dad shook his head. "It's nothing to do with your mother this time. Well, in a way, that isn't exactly true."

I steered Dad past the picnic area where the tired grey assortment of benches and tables were stained with the latest falls of rain.

"Dad?"

"I did what you wanted," he offered after a pause. "I managed to get hold of the four other guys in Battalion."

My heart stuttered in my chest. This was what I wanted my dad to do. I'd pleaded with him. I had assured him that we needed to know and that the best thing to do would be to call Tina's bluff.

And yet now…

I buried an apprehensive swallow. "All of them? Even Ed?"

Dad nodded, an odd expression in his eyes.

"What now?"

"I explained about The Conch Club and that you were keen for Battalion to play on opening night."

I tapered my hands up and down the sleeves of my jacket. "I take it you didn't say anything to Ed Stockton about me?"

Dad's frown gave me the answer. "Of course not, Layla. Ed has never mentioned anything in the years I've known him and he certainly didn't say anything when I spoke to him yesterday."

He lowered his voice. "The guy obviously doesn't have a clue about what Tina has been saying."

I glanced up at the steely sky, smudged with the branches of trees. "So what was the outcome?"

Dad pushed his hands into the pockets of his olive-green combats. "All four of them agreed to play with me at your opening night."

Frissons of anticipation and trepidation rocketed through me. "And?" I pushed.

"They're all arriving this Friday in Loch Harris for the weekend. Mikey suggested we turn it into some sort of band reunion."

I fell silent, as if suddenly remembering what was sitting in my jacket pocket. I blinked up at Dad before reaching in and tugging out the blue and white package. "It arrived this morning."

He flicked a concerned expression at the DNA kit and then at me. "It's all happening, isn't it?"

Chapter Twenty-Five

I tried to ignore the rustling of waterproof jackets as the tourists crunched their way back along the path towards their coach.

There was the final rattling and snapping of buttons on cameras and mobile phones.

"They're all definitely coming?" I asked again, shoving the DNA kit back into my pocket and trying to steady the hesitant tone in my voice.

"Yep. All four."

"Where are they all going to stay?"

Dad pushed his hands deeper into the pockets of his combats. "Jack, Mikey, and Stan have just texted me to say they've managed to book into Mrs Clover's B&B."

"And Ed?"

Dad pressed his lips together. "I insisted he stay over at my place."

I stared at my father as another smattering of rain hung suspended from the trees like Christmas decorations. "Do you think that's a good idea, Dad? I mean…"

This was all moving so fast. I wanted to find out for sure who my biological father was, but now that it looked like I would have to address the situation so quickly, the prospect made my stomach twist over.

Dad shrugged his shoulders. "It will give me a chance to talk to him without the other guys around, to finally find out after all these years whether there was something going on between him and your mother."

He read my face. "I thought you wanted closure on this too, sweetheart."

"I do. Really. It's just … now it looks like it could happen, I'm not so sure." I could detect fearful tears behind my eyes. Dad gave me a fierce hug. I bit my lip.

"We need to know. There's no point putting it off. We need to do that DNA test."

He was right. I knew he was.

"Oh, I meant to say to you. Is Faith OK?"

"Why do you ask?"

"I'm not sure. The couple of times I've chatted to her up here, she hasn't seemed her usual chatty self."

I let out a sigh.

Dad frowned. "You've got that look, Layla."

"Which look?"

"The one that says you're plotting and planning something which could have dire consequences for the person or persons involved."

"Why, thanks for your belief in me, Dad."

"Ah! So, I'm right then."

My father knew me better than I knew myself at times.

I stuffed my hands into my jeans pockets and revealed all about Faith really liking single dad Greg, but letting her infamous commitment issues get in the way of her happiness.

"She's making a big mistake, Dad. I think she's trying to conjure up excuses not to get involved, even though she admits she really likes him."

"And she's using the little boy as an excuse too?"

"I think so but she won't admit it, of course. She doesn't want the guilt of disappointing or confusing Sam if things did go wrong. I wasn't going to do anything," I protested, "but even you've noticed how low she is too. I couldn't leave things."

Dad cocked one brown brow at me. "You've already interfered, haven't you?"

"She really does like him and he really likes her. It's obvious."

Dad gave his head a resigned shake. "What's obvious is my daughter trying to interfere. Why didn't you come and speak to your wise old bugger of a father first?"

I crinkled up my freckly nose. "Probably because I knew you would tell me not to. But just because I'm crap at relationships, doesn't mean I should sit back and allow Faith to make a hash of her love life."

Dad disagreed. "Layla, you are not crap at relationships. You're just a bad picker – like me."

"Same thing," I mumbled.

Dad made a puffing noise. "Take my advice, lovey. Don't meddle. Best leave things be."

"But she's my best friend and I've never seen her like this before. Usually she's so laid back and in control of all of this kind of thing, but this is different."

"Even more reason not to get involved," warned Dad. "Now, how about once we're finished here, you rustle me up one of your hot chocolate specials. And don't hold back on the marshmallows."

I agreed.

Dad noticed my hand sliding towards the DNA test secreted in my pocket.

"Come back to mine," I managed. "The sooner we do this test, the better it will be for both of us."

I jerked my head at the sound of Rory calling me into the boathouse to ask me something about a preference for matt or gloss.

"Sure thing," answered Dad. "No point in putting it off."

The hot chocolate tasted just like it usually did – reminiscent of cosy winter nights – but neither Dad nor I were able to enjoy it. The presence of the DNA kit sitting out on my hall table was all-consuming.

Finally, we could put it off no longer,

Dad disappeared into the bathroom with his kit and I gripped my swab in my hand. Lifting it, I swept the inside of my right cheek for several seconds.

Done.

I slid it into the container and picked up the test kit

packaging, its dark blue and white box making my heart thud faster. It looked so innocuous.

Dad returned and, dismissing any more deliberation on what we were doing and the possible outcome, I bundled the two tubes into the padded envelope, together with our signatures of consent.

We had completed our part of the process. Now, I just wanted that envelope and its contents to evaporate.

I reached for my hooded jacket hanging on a hook in the hall. I knew the second postal collection of the day was at 4 p.m. It was now just after 2.30 p.m. so we would easily catch it.

I shrugged on my jacket and collected my phone from the sitting room table. I stuffed it into my pocket and hurried towards the door.

"Just popping down to the post box," I yelled to Dad, waggling the envelope in my hand.

Dad nodded but said nothing.

The post box was located at the bottom of the lane, right before you reached the main square that spread out like a pop-up book.

I walked briskly along the damp grass verge. There had been a heavy shower and puddles glinted up at me from the road.

I huddled a little deeper into my jacket, relieved as the sight of the bright red post box materialised.

When I reached it, I lifted the padded A5-sized envelope. My hand hovered for a moment as I held it up to the gaping black mouth of the post box. I let my fingers go and it slid in, making a satisfying thudding noise as it landed amongst the other items of mail.

I thrust my now empty hands into my jacket pockets. It was like experiencing a release of something – albeit temporary. The next challenge would be when the results were delivered back in a few weeks' time. But I decided not to dwell on that for now.

I couldn't.

I picked up my pace to return to Dad.

I wasn't looking forward to seeing Ed Stockton, for obvious reasons, but Dad insisted I meet up with him and the rest of the Battalion guys on Friday evening for a bite to eat in the other of the two pubs in Loch Harris, The Merry Maid.

Rory had completed his decorating in the boathouse and it was now a sea of peacock-blue and mint-green walls, with panels of salt grey behind the counter.

I loved it.

I locked up and clambered wearily into my car to head back to the cottage to snatch a quick shower and change.

My heart stuttered in my chest at the thought of seeing Ed. I hadn't laid eyes on the man since my twenty-first birthday bash, down by the loch side. It had been a summer's night affair, with a barbeque, flickering tealights, and a ceilidh band.

Oh, this was ridiculous! I was making far too many assumptions. The whole thing could be one giant fabricated lie by my attention-seeking mother.

I pictured Ed at the party eight years ago, smiling at something my father had said as he clutched a glistening bottle of beer. He seemed a decent enough man, but he wasn't the charismatic scene-stealer my dad was.

Looking at the situation from Ed's point of view, it was going to be one a hell of a shock for him to find out that he possibly had a twenty-nine-year-old daughter. The word "possibly" drifted around my head. I clung onto that hope.

As I patted on some eyeshadow, I took a series of deep breaths. I didn't really know Ed. He had never been as open and gregarious as the other guys. But thinking of him in Dad's photos from all those years ago, when Battalion was playing lots of gigs, I pictured his tight curls and denim waistcoats; it made him morph into someone else. This man, whether I liked it or not, might have a more major role in my life.

That was, if he really was my biological father. Even if he was, maybe he wouldn't be interested in having a grown-up daughter.

I frowned at my reflection in the bathroom mirror. Ed and his wife Karen had a couple of grown-up sons. If this was true and Ed was my real dad, what would they think of it all?

I dabbed on some of my favourite lipstick and my shoulders dropped. I had to try and clear my head a bit.

I was just pulling some tendrils around my face when I thought I could hear the faint thrum of a car engine from somewhere outside.

I snatched up my jacket and straw bag from the top of

my bed and went down the hall to fetch my leather ankle boots.

I noticed a package was lodged halfway through my letter box.

It was a small padded brown envelope.

I darted to the right and into my spare room. I peered out of the window, but there was no sign of anyone there. Whoever it was appeared to have already gone.

I moved to the front door and eased the envelope carefully out of the letter box. There was nothing written on it. I gave the envelope a curious squeeze. It felt bulky and angular.

I eased open the flap of the envelope which had been sealed with brown tape, and slid out the contents.

My eyes widened.

Wow. What had made him do that? I hadn't expected that at all.

Chapter Twenty-Six

I nside the envelope were two CDs in plastic cases.

There were no sleeves; only a Post-it note stuck to the inside of the first, which said:

Exclusive new songs for you to play at The Conch Club.

No appearance but hope this is at least a compromise.

Good luck with it all.

M.

I re-read the note twice more before yanking open my front door. I knew Mask wouldn't still be there. It had sounded as though his truck had shot out of the drive and back up the lane, and yet I still hovered for a few moments in the doorway.

I clutched the CDs and glanced about before staring

down at my watch. If I set off to Coorie Cottage now, I could still be back at The Merry Maid for 6.30 p.m. to meet Dad and the rest of the band.

I jumped into my car and set off, pausing at the end of my short drive to slide in the first CD that Mask had sent me.

Why did I feel compelled to go to his house? I looked down at the other CD lying on the passenger seat, sparkling silver.

I was surprised – shocked, but delighted.

OK, so he had made it clear that he wouldn't take to the stage (which hadn't come as any shock, if I was being honest), but the fact that he'd given me a whole raft of his exclusive new material was a real public relations coup for The Conch Club and I was determined to capitalise on it.

I fired the car into second gear as my CD player sprang to life.

While I drove past Loch Harris, which was like a glimmering glass table top, the haunting voice of Mask filled my car.

The timbre in his tone was smoky, as he sang about struggling to put the past behind him. Accompanying his vocals were a couple of guitars that seemed to be crying in unity.

His lyrics bled into my mind and sat there, making me wonder about Mask's life and whether these words were autobiographical.

I wound my way past thrusting hedgerows and moss-peppered walls until Galen Waterfall gushed into view from the left-hand curve of the road.

Why I felt I had to come up to see Mask, I didn't rightly understand.

The second track had drifted into the third, this one titled 'Finding It'. Mask's voice began softly at first, before it launched into a cacophony of drums and guitars. It was amazing.

I took my time parking the car just by the side of Coorie Cottage so I could listen to the song in its entirety. I admired his riot of garden as I let the engine fall silent and the track fizzled to an end.

I set my shoulders back and went up to the front door, knowing that a warm and appreciative thank you note on pretty stationery would have sufficed.

Yet, here I was.

I knocked several times but there was no answer. He wasn't there, or he was pretending he wasn't. Perhaps I could write him that thank you note after all and just post it?

I had only just eased the car door back open, when there was the sound of a spade striking something from further around the corner of the cottage.

I shut the car door again and paused. "Hello?"

Pushing my car keys into the back pocket of my jeans, I walked down past the side of the house.

Mask's truck was stationed on the gravel, its black metallic paintwork glinting.

The sound of a ringing spade seemed to be coming from further up the paved path, past the herbaceous border.

"Hello?"

I steeled myself and tip-tapped along the stones in my boots.

Just ahead of me was a tall figure, shovelling mounds of dirt. Down by his feet was an assortment of new shrubs waiting to be planted.

He was dressed in a loose navy cotton shirt and dark combats.

I couldn't make out his features from where I was, but his thick, collar-length dark hair furled upwards. He was focused on what he was doing and the spade glittered and flashed as he scooped out more earth and bent to pick up a fat, florally shrub.

I watched him snatch up a bottle of water from beside him and take a grateful gulp.

I waited until he had dumped the bottle back down beside his Timberland boots. "Mask? Sorry to disturb you, but I wondered—"

The figure swung round, alarm etched on his features. He had a strong jaw and deep, dark eyes that were framed with arched, black brows. He also possessed a vivid red scar that ran like a deep river down the right-hand side of his face.

I froze with embarrassment as he thrust one arm over his features in an attempt to conceal himself. His spade clanged down onto the path as he roared, "What the hell do you think you're doing?"

Chapter Twenty-Seven

My cheeks lit up.

"Oh. Er ... I'm so sorry."

He kept his right arm positioned over the right-hand side of his face. "Do you always creep up on people like this?"

"I wasn't creeping," I mumbled, trying not to stare. "I tried the front door but there was no answer."

His spade glinted down by his feet. "What do you want, Ms Devlin?"

Oh. The formality was back. He was annoyed.

I took a few tentative steps forwards, which made Mask do the exact opposite. He eyed me with suspicion.

I stopped and clasped and unclasped my fingers. "I just wanted to say thank you for the CDs. That was very unexpected, but very kind of you."

Mask twisted his face away from me. He paused. "Excuse me for one minute."

He strode away from me, vanishing into Coorie Cottage

and emerging moments later in his black mask and hoodie.

Mask appraised me. "And you came up all this way just to say thank you in person?"

I gave an unsettled shrug. "It isn't that far. It only took me fifteen minutes as there isn't much traffic at this time of the evening..." I could hear myself rattling on and fell silent. There was a trickle of blood weaving down from a cut on his wrist.

"You're bleeding."

Mask followed my eyes. "It's nothing," he brushed off. "I must have caught my skin on that holly bush when you crept up on me."

Crept up?

My expression tightened. "I didn't creep up on you."

He muttered something incomprehensible.

"Have you got a plaster handy? You really should put something on that cut."

Now it was Mask's turn for his mouth to contort. "I don't require open-heart surgery. It's fine."

I watched another drizzle of blood travel down his wrist and moved back towards my car. I rummaged in the glove compartment, finding my tube of antiseptic cream and a couple of plasters.

Aware of Mask watching, I tore off one of the plasters and moved towards him.

"What are you doing?"

I gestured to his wrist. "Here. Put some of this on it and then the plaster."

Mask's dark eyes bored into mine. "Not only a businesswoman, but a qualified general practitioner?"

I pulled my lips in at his sarcasm and thrust the plaster and tube of antiseptic cream at him. "I haven't got anything for rudeness unfortunately, but this should help that cut."

Mask blinked at me before making an irritated sighing noise and struggling to tug off his other gardening glove.

"Let me help."

His Australian growl was terse. "I can manage."

With the rich perfume of Mask's garden coiling around me, I rolled my eyes and took his wrist. "Yes, I can see that. Here."

He eyed me curiously while I smeared some antiseptic on the cut. "Don't worry, my hands are clean. I've just come out of the shower."

Heat travelled up my neck when I realised what I'd just said. I was certain I saw the faintest flicker of amusement cross his mouth. I trained my eyes on Mask's wrist, asking him to keep still while I peeled off the plaster and placed it over the cut.

"It didn't require attention," he protested again, "but thank you."

I struggled to look at him, still feeling somewhat self-conscious after my throwaway 'shower' remark. "No problem."

He jerked his dark head at my outfit. "Going out?"

I glanced down at my sparkly jeans and pink shirt and nodded.

There was a lock of crisp black hair that had escaped from under his hood and which was now flopping forwards onto his forehead.

He moved closer to me. It was just enough to make me

shrivel a little under his fixed gaze.

"So, as I was saying, I just dropped by to say thank you for your CDs. That was very thoughtful of you."

He shrugged. "You're welcome."

I fiddled with my watch strap as the sun above our heads dipped behind the tangle of trees. "I listened to a couple of tracks on my way here. Your lyrics are wonderful."

His clenched jaw softened a margin. "Thank you." His accent was melodic.

"I'm impressed you found my address."

Mask folded his arms. "I have my ways."

The silence was palpable. "Right," I exclaimed, clapping my hands together, "I'd better be off."

For some inexplicable reason, I started to walk backwards towards my car. "Thank you again for the CDs. They are definitely on the playlist for opening night."

I realised I must have looked like I had some sort of medical condition and drew up. "You're more than welcome to come along. Barring any major mishaps, it looks like opening night is going to be Saturday 29th August."

Mask flicked me a look. "I don't think so, but thank you very much anyway for the invitation." Then he nodded at my outfit. "Pink to make the boys wink."

It took me a few moments to register. "Oh yes. I'm just meeting up with my dad and the rest of his band mates for something to eat. It's a reunion kind of thing."

He pushed his hands into the pockets of his combats. "Your dad's a musician?"

"He was. He played the drums in a fairly successful

Seventies' rock band, called Battalion."

Mask inclined his head. "Didn't they have a couple of top twenty hits back in the day?"

"That's right. They did pretty well for a while and then kids and wives came along and things took a bit of a dive for them."

"A reunion, eh? Should be fun."

Not when I've got to confront the chance that my father may not be my father, but the band's bass guitarist instead.

I plastered on a strained smile. "That's one word for it."

His eyes narrowed behind his black mask.

"Anyway, I had better be off. Bye then, and thanks again."

I walked quickly towards the car, recalling the red lightning flash down the side of Mask's right cheek that I had accidentally seen when I arrived.

I wonder how he got that? Well, however it had got there, he obviously didn't want anyone seeing it. As far as I was concerned, it wasn't all that bad, although that was easy for me to say. I wasn't the one staring at it each day in the mirror.

I fastened my seat belt, aware that Mask had left his garden path and was strolling back up the lawn. His hood was lifting ever so gently in the evening breeze.

He continued to stand there as I reversed out of Coorie Cottage to head back to Loch Harris.

I switched on my CD player and his rich, rumbly voice came through the speakers again.

As I drove past the spiky mountainsides, I tried not to dwell on the DNA test result and the arrival of Ed Stockton.

Chapter Twenty-Eight

All the way back to The Merry Maid, I kept visualising Mask and his facial scar.

I pulled into the car park at the pub and leaned my arms on top of the steering wheel for a few moments.

My cheeks grew hot at the memory of Mask's fury at me catching a glimpse of his face and then my embarrassing remark about just getting out of the shower.

Maybe I shouldn't have gone up to Coorie Cottage after all, but I really did appreciate him giving me those CDs.

My mind swished back to how he had looked at me when I had first arrived and seen him in the garden. It was the way he'd thrown his arm across his scar and the flash of temper and fear in his eyes.

I stared out my car window at The Merry Maid. Cosy lights popped inside and there was the thrum of music and conversation seeping out of the partially open glass doors.

I hitched my bag up from the passenger side and slung it over my shoulder, before locking the car door.

The Merry Maid was all white pebble dash and thatched roof and I could see silhouettes flitting around inside.

Burying a ball of apprehension, I walked in, scanning the sea of heads for my dad. A strange, distant feeling washed over me. I remembered all the times I'd seen Dad with the guys in the past, chatting and swapping sentimental stories, cackling with laughter about misdemeanours they had got up to in their younger days, belting out the lyrics of their favourite songs.

Now I'd be viewing Ed from a totally different perspective.

The interior of The Merry Maid consisted of Tudor-inspired black beams and solid white pillars that acted as partitions for several booths in maroon leather, with polished mahogany tables and bench seating. An old jukebox was pumping out Seventies classic rock in the far corner (I could guess who had selected it).

The pub clientele were predominantly stalwarts of the Loch Harris community, who would cluster around the tables to exchange tales of their youth, complain about hikers parking in front of their driveways or challenge each other to protracted games of chess.

The Merry Maid was a moment captured in time, but the bar food was tasty and generous.

The sight of Dad made me stiffen. He was laughing over in the corner at something someone had said and his eyes flicked upwards when he spotted me. He stood and gestured me over.

I arranged my tense expression into a smile and moved

across the pub floor to where he and the rest of the members of Battalion were sitting.

Dad hovered, a proud smile enveloping his face. "There's my girl."

Our eyes exchanged a knowing look.

Mikey, Stan, and Jack jumped to their feet, exclaiming about how well I looked, before offering their condolences about Mac. They were all clad in faded rock T-shirts and denim. Stan continued to sport his trademark grey baker-boy cap atop his balding head.

After delivering hugs and pecks on the cheek to the three of them, Ed squeezed out from the end of the bench. I noticed that the table was already littered with several half-empty beer glasses.

I found myself staring, examining every crevice of Ed Stockton's face, from the sharpness of his chin to the slight bump across the top of his nose. He still possessed his riot of brown curls, but there were shots of silver in there now too.

I looked nothing like him. Nothing at all. Or maybe I did and I just didn't want to acknowledge it.

A knot started to tangle itself in my stomach.

I stiffened as Ed gave me a brief hug. "How's things?" I faltered, trying to act normally.

"Good, Layla, thanks. Sorry about Mac. Karen sends her best."

Pictures of his unassuming wife reared up in front of me. If what my mother was saying was the truth, there were going to be innocent people caught up in all this crossfire.

I aimed a look over at Dad, who was observing me

and Ed.

As we all resumed seats and the rest of the guys bunched up to allow me to sit down, I wondered whether trawling over the past was such a good idea after all. I had had twenty-nine years of ignorant bliss. Harry had raised me, ferried me to my dance classes when I was all sugar-pink tutus and my ballet bag was bigger than I was, helped me through meltdowns for my exams, comforted me when I was a seething mess of teenage hormones. He had cried and grinned all the way through my graduation ceremony and taught me to drive in his old Chevrolet pick-up truck.

I smiled fleetingly at the memory of him as we bounced over the old fields at the back of Grandma and Grandpa's cottage, me crunching the gears and Dad rolling his eyes heavenwards and hissing, "For pity's sake, Layla, please be careful with her!"

Nothing could steal that from me.

I dragged my eyes away from the laminated pub menus Jack had plucked from the end of the table and pushed across to each of us.

Dad was laughing at something Stan was saying as he sat beside him. He had his head tipped back and his grey eyes were crinkling at the corners.

Then I snatched a glance along my side of the table to where Mikey was telling Ed a story about the time he'd found a Battalion fan trying to scale the first floor of the B&B they had been staying at in Aberdeen. "She'd really had a few," he lamented, "so I gave the poor girl a black coffee and then she started telling me about this guy at work who she was mad on."

Ed's mouth twitched with mild amusement.

"So what's everybody having?" I asked, my attention switching back to the menu.

Mikey watched me prepare to write down the food order. "This is just like old times. It's great!"

Jack peered down the table and folded his arms. "I thought you said you never wanted to be in a band again." Jack pointed a finger at Mikey. "Do you know, Layla, five minutes before you arrived, this one was saying that he wants Battalion to be a regular thing again?"

I smiled and caught Dad's eye.

"I've got two ex-wives to support," argued Mikey.

"Well that's not our fault, is it?" piped up Stan. "If you'd think with your brain rather than another part of your anatomy, you wouldn't have to graft all hours in that music shop of yours."

Mikey flicked up one brow. "It's not my fault I'm irresistible to women."

"And in which parallel universe is this?" asked Jack, rolling his eyes.

I couldn't help but laugh at the witty banter bouncing backwards and forwards like a tennis ball at a Wimbledon final. It was helping to distract me a little from the paternal issue I was facing.

I glanced down the table to Ed who was sitting there gawping at his phone and not participating much in the conversation.

"Not joining in then, Edward?" asked Mikey, noticing his silence.

"I'm just texting Karen," he confessed, brandishing his mobile as proof.

Mike pulled a comedic face. "You've been let off the leash for a couple of days, man. Make the most of it."

Ed snapped his head up from his screen. "We're not all like you, Mikey."

What a hypocrite!

Mikey picked up his pint glass and grinned over the top of it. "You can say that again."

I fired a meaningful look over at Dad and went to open my mouth, but Dad frowned at me and made a brief "Shhh" motion with his mouth.

While the rest of the guys discussed what beer they would have with their meal, Dad leaned across to me. "Don't worry," he hissed. "I'll handle it."

My lips ground together. "Did you hear that comment from Ed? That's rich coming from him. He's got the cheek to have a go at Mikey when he had a fling with Mum."

Dad put one finger to his mouth. "We'll sort this. I promise."

Finally, I nodded.

Dad sank back against the bench, plastering a smile on as Mikey began telling him about a session musician they knew from years back who had treated himself to a flashy brand-new Mazda and a hair transplant.

I eased my way out from behind the table and negotiated my way to the bar with our scribbled food order.

I was finishing chatting to the friendly student behind the bar when Dad materialised at my shoulder.

"You OK?" he whispered.

"Yes, I guess so. It's all so weird, though."

Over the buzz of the jukebox, which saw a song from The Beatles fizzle to an end and another from The Rolling Stones take over, Dad threw a look over his shoulder at his cluster of bandmates.

Mikey was explaining something about his vocal range while Jack was pointing over at him and gleefully pointing out his greying haze of stubble.

"I don't know what I'm going to say to Ed about all this," admitted Dad after a lengthy pause. "But I know we can't leave things as they are."

I gave a resigned nod. "I know you're right. And anyway, that would be far too risky a strategy with Cruella lurking around."

"That's your own mother you're talking about."

"Yes. And?"

Dad smiled briefly and then frowned. "I was kind of hoping she and Ramon would stay in Italy for a bit longer to give us a bit of breathing space."

I thanked the bubbly girl behind the bar as she placed our drinks on a tray. "Yes, why is there never a volcanic eruption when you want one?"

Once the drinks had been received with a chorus of hearty noises and the piping hot array of soups and cod and fries were delivered to our table, we tucked in with gusto.

Well, the rest of them did.

Dad and I found ourselves jabbing our forks at our slices of breaded fish and chunky golden fries in nervous anticipation.

We had no idea how Ed would react to the news that I

might be his daughter. Maybe he would simply attempt to laugh it off and deny ever having had a fling with my mother at all?

I managed to stomach a few more mouthfuls of food and then pushed my plate across the table. The other guys had already demolished their meals and were slumped back in their seats, patting their bellies and proclaiming that in their younger days they could eat a smorgasbord of calorie-laden delights and not put on an ounce.

"It was all that prancing about on stage we did," mused Mikey with longing. "We would just sweat it off."

"Prancing about?" echoed Stan. "Speak for yourself, mate. You lead singers might prance, but us rhythm guitarists don't."

There was a series of guffaws and protests from Mikey, but my attention was drawn to Norrie and Clem who were clattering in through the pub door. "It's all happening round here tonight," exclaimed Norrie, surveying the crowded pub and shuffling through the throng towards us.

"Aye, it's a busy Friday night," agreed Dad, taking a gulp from his pint glass.

"Oh, I'm not talking about in here," said Norrie with importance. "I'm talking about all that carry-on up at old Tavish's place, Coorie Cottage."

My head snapped round. "What do you mean?"

Norrie smoothed his wisps of grey hair over his crown. "I was only talking to young Tom and that police sidekick of his in the car park a few minutes ago. Apparently, there's some sort of commotion and they've been summoned up there now."

Chapter Twenty-Nine

I swung round in my seat and the conversation at our table lulled. "The police have gone up to Coorie Cottage?"

Dad frowned as he took a considered gulp of his beer. "A break-in?"

Clem, who was standing beside Norrie, slid out of her aubergine cardigan and draped it over one arm. "All Tom would say was that it sounded like some sort of disturbance."

At this point, my imagination decided to go full throttle. Images of Mask struck over the head by some opportunist thief flooded screaming into my head.

From a table close by, two local farmers were gossiping. "I heard that some reclusive weirdo is living up there now."

"Aye," agreed Norrie. "I heard that too. Supposed to be some musician or other that's holed himself up there." He performed a disinterested shrug. "It's probably a few of the local teenagers having a laugh, that's all."

My back went rigid and my community spirit kicked in. "What, so it's OK for a group of local idiots to intimidate a newcomer, Norrie? And someone is labelled a weirdo simply because they don't want to associate with the likes of you, Ewan Tate?"

Ewan smirked over at his ruddy-faced companion. Norrie's eyes widened at my remark.

"Layla," warned Dad across the top of the empty beer glasses. But I didn't reply. Instead, I offered my apologies to Jack and Stan as I jumped to my feet and squeezed past their denim-clad legs.

Dad stared up at me. "Where are you going?"

I fixed him with a determined look. "Up to Coorie Cottage."

Dad opened his mouth to say something, but I was already waggling my half-empty glass of orange juice. "I haven't had any alcohol as I brought my car."

I could feel the Battalion guys gawping up at me while I stood there, still prickling at Ewan Tate's ignorant remark and Norrie's bluff comment.

"I am sorry," I smiled apologetically at the guys. I fumbled around in my shoulder bag for my car keys. "I'll be back as soon as I can."

Dad was concerned. "It's getting dark, love."

"I'll be fine, Dad. I know these roads well. I had a good teacher, remember?"

Mikey leaned in close to Dad's shoulder and hissed theatrically, "Can't think where she gets her stubborn streak from, Harry."

I felt my attention wander from my dad to Ed, who was

sitting in the corner. His fingers were tapering up and down his half-finished beer glass.

I snapped my gaze back to my father.

"And what are you intending to do when you get there?" argued Dad.

I let my hands rise and fall. "I'm not sure. I just ... Look, I'll see you all in a bit."

I was clattering out of the double doors, leaving behind the chink of glasses and the strains of a Queen song, when there was a commotion behind me. "Hang on, Layla," grumbled Dad, downing the dregs of amber liquid swilling about in his pint. "I'm coming with you."

He gave Ed, Mikey, Jack, and Stan an apologetic grimace. "Keep the jukebox warm, lads. We won't be long."

Dad laughed off the jokes about him being a lightweight and followed me out of the cosy glow of the pub.

"You didn't have to come, Dad."

He shrugged on his leather jacket. "I know I didn't have to. To be honest, I'm struggling to keep up with Mikey and Stan. They're like bloody fish."

I broke into a smile. "Well, you weren't doing a bad impression of it from where I was sitting."

I slid into the driver's side and waited for Dad to secure his seat belt.

"Right. Come on then," he urged. "Let's go and see what's happening with this musician friend of yours."

I flicked my indicator right. Describing Mask as a friend was a bit of a stretch, but I didn't bother to correct him.

Chapter Thirty

My car headlights picked out the silhouettes of the hedgerows and plumes of trees as we made our way to Coorie Cottage.

Dad shot me a curious glance from the passenger seat. "And why exactly are you dashing up here on your white charger, Layla?"

I blinked. "I don't know what you mean."

Dad rested one arm along the window. "You hardly know this Mask guy. You don't even know what this disturbance is and yet you're rushing up to his house."

I indicated right, taking the open road past the dark shimmer of Loch Harris. "I'm just being neighbourly."

"And?"

Galen Waterfall slid into view down the rock face, through the black night.

A police car was stationed in front of the cottage and Tom and a female colleague were clambering out.

Dad was still studying me, waiting for a response.

"Mask gave me two CDs of his exclusive new songs to play at the launch night of The Conch Club." Dad's brows rose with surprise. "I guess I also feel a bit sorry for him, living up here alone."

"Maybe it's his choice."

Something niggled at me. A voice inside my head wasn't convinced about that.

As the ignition wound to a halt, Dad smiled over. "You were always a soft-hearted soul, even as a kid. You definitely didn't inherit that from your mother."

We jumped out, slamming the car doors. Tom and his blonde police companion were peering at us as we approached. "Hi Layla," puzzled Tom. "What are you doing up here?"

"I was kind of wondering the same thing," mumbled Dad, shaking hands with Tom and the female officer.

I hooked my thumbs into the pockets of my glittery jeans. "Is everything OK? It's just I sort of know the person who's living here now."

"You didn't answer my question," twinkled Tom. "And it's not like you just live around the corner."

"Well, I suppose nobody does," I pointed out. "At least not in this area. The guy who lives here is on his own; I thought I should make sure he was OK."

The policewoman shone a torch down past the cottage to the garden. It illuminated the waggling branches of flowers and leaves in various silhouettes of shape and height. "Looks like someone has green fingers," she remarked, scanning the darkened garden.

"You should see it in the daytime," I replied. "It's stunning."

The female police officer clicked off her torch. "One of our colleagues at the station received a call from a passing motorist to say that there seemed to be some sort of commotion taking place outside the cottage."

"Well officers, I'm afraid you've had a wasted journey."

We snapped our heads round to look at Mask, who was partially concealed by his open front door.

The four of us shuffled closer, making him retreat further back behind the door. A shadow fell across his masked face and thick shock of dark hair. He wasn't wearing a hooded top this time.

Mask's chocolate brown eyes fell on me. "Ms Devlin?" He angled his head to one side, his voice taut. "This is becoming a bit of a habit."

Two stripes of heat rose in my cheeks. "I was in the local pub with my dad and heard there had been some sort of incident up here, so I thought…"

Mask's mouth flatlined. "Thought what? That you'd break the monotony of a thrilling night in the local hostelry to have another nosey about?"

Embarrassment flared in my chest. *Sarcastic sod.*

Tom flashed me a look of sympathy. "There's no need to be rude, sir. Ms Devlin was just being neighbourly, that's all. Now, we had a report—"

"I just told you, officer. Everything is fine. Whoever reported an incident must have thought they saw something when they clearly didn't."

The blonde police officer didn't appear convinced and

answered Mask's insistence with a cynical hitch of an eyebrow.

Neither was I.

"Well, if you'll excuse me," added Mask tightly. "Have a good evening and again, I apologise for your time having been wasted."

Dad loitered at my shoulder. "Come on, sweetheart. False alarm." Then he threw a glare at Mask and called back to him. "And may I suggest, sir, that you show more gratitude in future, especially when someone is concerned for your welfare?"

I dropped my gaze. "Don't, Dad. Please leave it."

Mask's eyes burned into me, before he banged his front door closed.

I watched the police car depart first in a blur of lime-green and white.

Dad eyed me across the roof of my car. "You OK, lovey?"

I settled myself and waited until he had shut his door. "Yes, Dad. I'm OK."

He pulled a face. "If that's the sort of thanks you get from that man for showing concern, I wouldn't bother in future."

I looked back at Coorie Cottage. "Maybe you're right."

From out of the corner of my eye, I could see Mask's tall silhouette hovering behind his front door. "I still think he was lying."

I turned left, the spools of Galen Waterfall disappearing behind us. "I think he did have some sort of disagreement or altercation with someone and he's trying to cover it up."

Dad stretched his legs. "All I know is that he shouldn't have been so bloody rude to my daughter."

I smiled for an instant.

"Now don't give it any more thought," instructed Dad, staring out of the window at the black silhouetted countryside. "You concentrate on The Conch Club."

He glanced across at me from the passenger seat. "He's given you those songs, so you use them for opening night. But I wouldn't have anything more to do with him, if you can help it."

One minute Mask was giving me those beautiful songs he'd written, the next he was snarling at me. My face flushed hot again at the memory.

Maybe Dad was right and I should just leave him to fester up in Coorie Cottage, with only the squirrels for company.

I felt sorry for the squirrels.

Chapter Thirty-One

I pulled up outside The Merry Maid again.

A couple tumbled out of the door in a clumsy embrace and shared a conspiratorial giggle.

Dad examined me. "Aren't you coming back in?"

"No, I'd really rather just call it a night, if you don't mind."

"You aren't dwelling on that rude sod's comments just now, are you? Emerging singer or not, he had no right talking to you like that, especially when you were just being kind."

The truth was, as we'd approached the pub again, I had been hit with images of Ed Stockton. "I'm not in the mood to see Ed again this evening," I admitted. "Don't get me wrong, part of me does want to know the truth…"

"But part of you would rather remain in ignorant bliss," nodded Dad's shadowy profile beside me. "Oh, I get that, believe me. I feel the same way."

He reached his hand over and gave my fingers a

squeeze. "But we both know deep down that that until this is settled, we'll always be wondering."

I kept staring out of the windscreen at the pub car park, with its hanging baskets suspended from a couple of lampposts. "You're right. I know you are."

Then I turned to him. "It might sound a bit stupid, but part of me was almost grateful to Mask tonight. At least that … thing – whatever it was – up at Coorie Cottage provided a temporary distraction."

Dad's light-grey eyes softened in the dark as I leaned across and gave him an awkward hug. "Love you, Dad." Then I blinked back a tear. "Right. Go on. Get back to your gang of fellow reprobates."

Dad grinned. "I see you've got the measure of us."

I smiled after him as he stalked back towards the pub entrance. I wound down my car window. "Give me a ring later if you want a lift home."

Dad flapped my offer away. As he opened the door, a burst of raucous laughter shot out. "We'll get a taxi."

My stomach delivered a forward roll. "When will you talk to Ed?"

"Tomorrow."

"I want to be there, if that's OK."

He considered for a moment. "Of course you do. I'll get you to come round before we speak to him."

And then, with a small wave, he disappeared back inside.

I'd only just wrapped myself up in my towelling dressing gown and pyjamas and put the kettle on to make an indulgent hot chocolate, when my eyes were drawn to my calendar hanging on the opposite kitchen wall.

Below June's picture of a sun-drenched antique bookshop in Edinburgh, was a small, heart-shaped motif beside the 29th.

A sinking sensation overcame me. The anniversary of when Mac and I had first met.

I had been so preoccupied with The Conch Club and brooding about Ed that the date had been stealthily creeping up on me and I'd failed to notice it until now.

I fought to ignore memories of Mac and me flirting in the restaurant as I tried to interview him. I recalled my attempts to ask him questions about his novels being met with persistent demands for my phone number and that lopsided grin of his.

I sloshed hot water from the kettle into my mug and stirred it hard. Then I shuffled into the sitting room.

Snatching up my mobile from my coffee table, I pulled up Faith's number. I knew I should have confided in my best friend much sooner about Ed Stockton, but I had been struggling to get my head around it myself.

I was desperate to unload my worries. Faith answered and had barely uttered a word before I launched into my story about Mum's revelation.

"Why the hell didn't you tell me about all this before?" gasped Faith into my ear, once I'd poured my heart out to her. "Layla, best friends tell each other everything – or at least I thought they did."

"They do," I insisted. "I always have done, but this came out of nowhere."

I played with the belt of my dressing gown. "This will sound stupid, but I thought that if I didn't speak about it, then it might not really happen."

Faith was her usual pragmatic character. "I mean, you haven't had the DNA test results yet, so I wouldn't go jumping to conclusions. And even if it does turn out that Ed is your biological father, Harry will always be your dad. When are you due to receive the test results?"

"A few weeks, so not long in the scheme of things, although it feels like forever at the moment." I waggled my toes in their grey and white fluffy socks. "For a brief moment, there was a part of me that didn't want to know, but looking back on it now, I don't think Dad and I had much choice. It would have been hanging around us both and tainting everything."

"And Ed," she ventured. "Does he know that there's a chance you might be his daughter?"

"Apparently not. He's staying with Dad till Sunday, so Dad said he's going to discuss it with him tomorrow and I've said I want to be there."

There were more supportive murmurings from Faith, and then I told her about Mask.

"So all those rumours swirling around here are true then?" she breathed. "Wow."

"Yes, but even though he was bloody rude to me tonight, please don't spread it around that he's moved here, otherwise we'll be overrun with hormonal teenage girls." I smiled down the phone at Faith. "Can you imagine the likes of Norrie and Clem if Loch Harris had groupies to contend with, as well as city types rambling everywhere?"

Faith laughed and promised me she wouldn't say anything. "This Mask sounds a right complex character, though. One minute he's giving you exclusive songs for your music venue and the next he's telling you to bugger off." She made a grunting noise. "Typical bloody artist. Moody and unpredictable."

"He was probably annoyed that I saw him ... without his mask."

She dropped her voice, even though we were both alone in our respective houses. "What does he look like?"

"He has a scar on his cheek and it's clear he was horrified when he realised I'd happened to see it."

"Well, I wouldn't give him a second thought," she sniffed. "Disturbance or no disturbance, he shouldn't have spoken to you like that. If he wants to go all Phantom of the Opera up there, let him get on with it."

Despite myself, I let out a short laugh. Then my eyes fell on the calendar again. "And what with the twenty-ninth of this month being three years since Mac and I first met..." I let my words tail off.

"Would you like me to come over and stay the night? It'll take me two minutes to throw a few bits in my bag."

"No, it's fine," I assured her. "Thanks for the offer but I'm going to head off to bed in a minute with the latest Sophie Kinsella." I paused before I spoke again. "And how are you?"

Now it was her turn to take a breath. "I'm OK."

"Just OK?"

"Look, if this is your way of trying to speak to me again about Greg, please don't. That's all in the past and I made up my mind about all that a while back."

Faith didn't sound at all convinced. She swiftly changed the subject. "Promise me you will ring me tomorrow once you and Harry have spoken to Ed."

I assured her I would call her and then we wished each other a good night.

Chapter Thirty-Two

I slept fitfully.

First I was convinced that Harry was still my biological dad, and then his craggy, open face would morph into Ed's.

I decided it didn't bloody well matter because Harry would always be my dad, regardless of the outcome of the DNA test. He had been there when it counted. We were a team.

After showering and trying to calm my jittery stomach by nibbling on some buttered toast, I tried my best to focus on my to-do list.

Progress on The Conch Club had slid recently, due to all the commotion and fallout from Tina's story, so I set to work again. First, I rang the furniture suppliers and confirmed delivery of the two squashy sea-green leather sofas I had ordered.

Then I dropped reminder emails to some of my music contacts that I had made at a few of the industry magazines, asking for recommendations of any more bands or artists who would be willing to play live. I already had half a dozen groups who had contacted me after my posts on social media, and who were already allocated performance slots, and two solo singers were asking if they could give me a ring.

Faith had also been her usual, reliable self and was liaising with food and drink suppliers on my behalf.

My thoughts moved from my new business and strayed to Mask. The petulant side of me wanted to tell him exactly where he could stick his exclusive tracks, but I knew I would have to play his songs on opening night now. The word was getting around and there was a real buzz.

As for Battalion, they would appear first.

I swallowed my apprehension. *Oh God*. That was providing my dad's band didn't implode before then. Finding out he could be my dad might send Ed running in the opposite direction.

Oh well. I had plenty of time to mope over that.

For now, I had to get some work done before Dad rang to get me round to the cottage so we could both speak to Ed.

Things were gradually slotting together, at least from the practical side.

The Conch Club was freshly decorated and the sound system had been installed by one of Dad's studio recording pals from Glasgow. Now it was a case of filling out all the Health and Safety forms, liaising with Environmental Health, and ensuring our Licence to sell alcohol was approved too.

I'd drafted out interview questions for possible bar staff and there were eight people with catering experience who had applied for the two positions I had advertised. I'd explained that The Conch Club would be primarily about the music and the atmosphere, but that I wanted to offer tasty, Scottish-inspired finger foods and snacks, not main meals.

With any luck, my launch date of Saturday, the 29th of August, would still be achievable.

As well as letting arrangements for The Conch Club slide a tad, I'd also been a little less productive with my freelance writing, something I intended to remedy.

I was in the process of finishing a freelance commission I'd secured about the challenges of home working compared to an office-based job when my mobile rang.

Dad's grinning image popped up on my screen.

My stomach lurched.

We exchanged pointless chit-chat and then Dad invited me to come over. "I think we should talk to him sooner rather than later, don't you, Layla?"

"Where is he now?"

"Just having a shower. We're all a bit delicate this morning."

"And the rest of the guys?"

"Probably still slumped in their B&B. You'd think at our age we would learn," groaned Dad. "Orange juice from now on."

I asked Dad to give me twenty minutes to finish off my article. Once I'd rung off, my eyes blurred at my scribbled notes. Thank goodness I'd got it almost completed.

Once I'd finished checking it for spelling mistakes, I rattled off a brief email to the Features Editor, attached the document, and pressed 'Send'.

Saturday morning sunshine trickled through the glass of my front door while I pulled on my leather jacket, hooked my straw bag over my shoulder, and shoved in my mobile.

I would walk the short distance down the lane to Dad's and clear my head. I adjusted the collar of my shirt in the hall mirror, trying not to dwell on the concerned edge in my eyes.

Then, forcing a brittle smile at my reflection, I set off.

"What are you saying?"

Ed's bewildered expression swung from Dad to me and back again. "Are you telling me I could be her father?"

Dad leaned forward in his chair, his fingers knotting themselves together. "Yes, we're trying to say you could be Layla's biological father."

"Or at least, that's what my mum is saying," I added, irritated that despite me sitting opposite him, he'd referred to me as 'her'.

Ed slumped back in Dad's dark brown armchair. I could see the colour slipping from his face. "But ... but Tina's never mentioned anything before..."

Dad and I swapped charged glances.

"It's true then," said Dad after a considered pause. "You did have an affair with her."

Ed's right hand reached up and started tugging at his

ball of faded brown curls. "Yes ... no ... I mean ... oh shit!"
He let out an agonised breath so deep I thought he was
experiencing an asthma attack. "I'm so sorry, Harry. You
were a mate. You still are, but you know what a good-
looking woman Tina was. Still is. I suppose I was
flattered..."

"Was it a one-night stand?" I croaked, trying to assemble
the pieces of the story in my mind.

Ed looked over at me as though he had forgotten I was
still there. He hunched over and examined my features, like
I was an unusual museum artefact. "No," he answered.
"But our fling didn't last long. Maybe a few weeks."

His honesty, though appreciated, stabbed me in the
stomach. "So not exactly Romeo and Juliet then?"

Dad frowned over at me. "Layla."

"How can you be so sodding calm about all this, Dad?" I
erupted, jumping to my feet. "One of your band mates was
shagging your wife."

Ed dropped his hooded, pale blue eyes to the carpet.

Dad's cool gaze regarded Ed and asked him when it
happened.

"Do we really have to do all this now?" Ed whined.
"What is it going to achieve?"

I glowered down at him from where I stood. "Well, if I
am your biological daughter, I think we've got the right to
know."

Ed drank in my facial features. I could feel my mouth
hardening.

He swallowed before he spoke again to my dad. "You
and Tina had been married about two years by then."

I gave my head a shake, but said nothing.

Dad snorted with derision. "Nothing that woman has done, or does, surprises me anymore."

Ed was staring off into the middle distance, his attention focused on Dad's sitting room wall. "Karen and the boys..."

"Is that all you can say?" barked Dad, the pain swimming in his stare. "Layla is the one you should be thinking about right now."

I stared down at my dad.

"And you betrayed me too, Ed," he managed. "You betrayed a friend."

We both blinked as Ed jumped up from his chair, panic about the situation he could be facing catching up with him. "Look, I'm not denying we had a bit of a thing, but there's no way I could be your dad."

He darted into the hallway where his battered sports bag was sitting. "I'm sorry, mate. I really am. And Layla..."

His raspy voice tailed off as he slung his holdall over his right shoulder.

"Where the hell are you going, Ed?" asked Dad. "You can't just up and walk off, not after all this."

Ed marched off down Dad's hallway and yanked open the front door. "I don't need to know anything. It happened thirty years ago."

"But you can't just walk off like this," repeated Dad, running out of the door and positioning himself in front of Ed, barring his way. He gestured over to me. "I promised Layla that Battalion would play at the opening night of The Conch Club next month."

Ed frowned. "What's done is done."

Panic and anger swelled within me as I watched Ed's gangly figure head out of Dad's gate and begin the short walk down the country lane to the village. "That's right, Ed," I called, trying to stem the hurt in my voice. "Just go and leave Harry to pick up the pieces. You let him down once and you're doing it again."

Dad shot out his hand and gave my arm a squeeze. "Let him go, love."

Surprise overtook me as Ed stopped on the other side of the sunlit hedge.

"Can't you at least be professional about the band?"

Ed remained standing in the lane, self-conscious and awkward.

Dad lifted his hands and let them fall back down by his sides. "I agree. If the DNA test declares you as Layla's biological father, then what you do about that is up to you. Just don't let her down by dropping out of Battalion before her opening night."

Dad's voice took on a sharper edge as it travelled across his garden. "It's the least you can do for her."

Ed's shoulders slumped.

"I can't. I'm sorry."

We watched him stride off down the lane.

Chapter Thirty-Three

Lunch was a sombre affair for Dad and me.

I heated up a goat's cheese and tomato quiche he had stashed in his freezer, while Dad prepared some salad. We made a gallant effort to eat it, but after the dramatic events that had taken place with Ed earlier that morning, we realised we weren't hungry.

"I can't believe you're being so reasonable about all this, Dad."

He lowered his fork and surveyed me from across the kitchen table. "What can I do, love? Shout at him? Give Ed a broken nose? It happened thirty years ago. What would that achieve now?"

He sat back for a moment. "Don't get me wrong. When your mother told me that you might not be mine, I felt like wringing both their necks."

Dad speared some lettuce.

"Tina always managed to cover her lies well." Dad gave

a brief, wry smile. "Your mother also had a very low boredom threshold."

"I had noticed."

I watched my father pick up his fork and take a pensive mouthful of quiche. "I loved her," he said simply.

A crushing, empathic pain erupted in my chest. "She didn't deserve you."

"Not that you're biased or anything."

I took a sip of my iced water. "I can't believe he's refused to play with you guys again."

Dad shook his head. "I think It's guilt. It's a struggle for him to face me, let alone the other guys when they find out."

This was not going to be an easy situation, but Dad had always told me that Battalion had experienced loads of 'creative differences' and internal squabbles over the years; I viewed this situation between him and Ed as just another hurdle to get over.

I lowered my glass back onto its hessian coaster. "He owes you, Dad." I set my shoulders. "I will persuade Ed to be part of Battalion again, even if it's just for those couple of hours on opening night."

Dad let out a dry laugh. "You definitely get that determined streak from your mum."

Once I'd helped Dad clear up after lunch, I ambled back up the lane towards my house.

Dad was about to ring Stan, Jack, and Mikey and invite them to come over to his place for a jam session and to discuss what tracks they wanted to play on my launch night. He said he also wanted to explain the situation with Ed, who had dropped Dad a brief text about an hour after he'd left to say he had managed to get a room at The Merry Maid.

To be honest, he could have said he was camping out by the shores of Loch Harris in a bin liner and I wouldn't have cared.

I offered to hang on until all the guys arrived, but Dad insisted I go.

I was grateful in many ways. I had an uneasy feeling that there was going to be testosterone-filled arguing for a while.

I just hoped Dad and the other guys would be able to remain professional, not stand by and watch Battalion implode. That wasn't the solution, especially as The Conch Club was due to open in a few weeks and there was a growing buzz in the area about 'the original line-up of the local old rockers' getting back together.

The early afternoon sky carried the promise of sunshine after a burst of brief showers.

I breathed in the heady scent of damp grass and tried to assemble my thoughts into some sort of coherent order.

It seemed so long ago now since I'd lost Mac, in some ways. Although, if I was being honest with myself, I'd lost him to Hannah well before he'd had his fatal heart attack.

Now I felt as though I were losing my identity too.

I rounded the corner where the hedges that framed the lane frothed into a deep curve.

A shiny black pick-up truck was parked on the edge of the pavement outside my cottage.

My eyes widened with surprise as I spotted a tall figure, clad in a navy-blue hoodie and light-coloured jeans, posting something through my letter box.

He must have heard my trainers scuffing along the chipped stones, because he swung round.

It was Mask.

Chapter Thirty-Four

There was a charged silence, broken only by the rattle of my letter box as whatever Mask had delivered skittered onto the mat.

His hood was down, exposing a few seconds' glimpse of his thick, dark hair and heavily lashed, deep-brown eyes.

He wasn't wearing his mask either, so I was able to snatch a fleeting glimpse of his stubbled chin and the angry red scar that crackled down from his arched right brow to near his mouth.

He jerked his hood up and over his features to conceal himself. "You seem to make a habit of creeping up on people, Ms Devlin."

I blinked at him. "I'm sorry." Then I realised the situation. "Hang on. Why am I apologising? You're the one lurking about at my front door."

I strode up towards my cottage, fishing about in my bag for the front door key.

"I'm not lurking," he replied in his indignant Australian

twang. He was standing to my right, but took a couple of steps backwards.

I opened my front door to see a white envelope lying face down on my mat.

Mask gestured to the envelope. "I dropped by to deliver that."

"What is it?"

"Well, unless you possess X-ray vision, you won't know until you open it."

I threw him a dark look and bent down to pick it up. I turned the envelope over in my hands. 'Layla' was written on it, in bold, dark pen.

I started to tear it open, when Mask made my heart jump into my throat. "What are you doing?" he snapped.

I glowered over at him. "I'm opening it. I thought that was what you were supposed to do with a sealed envelope."

A grunt emerged from under his hood. "Very droll, Ms Devlin, but I'd rather you read it after I've gone."

This was ridiculous!

First he gives me a verbal tongue lashing the other night for simply being neighbourly, and then he writes me some sort of note, delivers it personally – and then asks me not to open it while in his presence?

I lowered the envelope to my side. "Can I ask why you'd prefer me not to open it in front of you?"

There was a brief flash of hot brown eyes. "It refers to my behaviour the other evening."

I watched as the emerging sun sidled out from behind the trees across the lane. "Is this a letter of apology?"

"I wouldn't go that far."

"Then what is it?"

Mask thrust his hands into the pockets of his hoodie. "It's a note."

"Yes. I had gathered that much. About what?"

"Oh, for pity's sake," he growled. "All right. It's to say sorry for my behaviour."

He jutted out his chin a little, but the rest of his face was concealed by shadow. "I shouldn't have spoken to you in the way that I did. I know you were only concerned for my welfare."

"Thank you," I faltered. "I appreciate that."

I raised the envelope again.

"I would still rather you open my note after I've left," he insisted.

I nodded. "OK. So … would you like to come in for a coffee, now that you're here?"

Mask remained to my right, his feet firmly planted on the gravel. I could see him weighing up his options. "All right. Thank you," he muttered, after a pause.

I started down the hall and propped his note against a ceramic vase which Faith had bought me as a housewarming gift.

As I pottered about in the kitchen, spooning coffee into two mugs, Mask loitered in my sitting room. His hood remained stubbornly up, concealing his face.

I set the mugs of steaming hot coffee on the table between us and watched him sink into my armchair opposite.

I so wanted him to remove his hood and wondered

whether I should suggest it, when his long fingers tapered around his mug and he took a grateful sip. "Good coffee," he rumbled.

I sat back against my cushions on the sofa, trying not to give the impression that I was imagining him outside the confines of his hoodie.

"Pretty house," he said over the rim of his mug.

I cleared my throat, wondering what Heather would make of the sight of her musical hero drinking coffee in my sitting room. No doubt she would spontaneously combust.

"How is your wrist now?"

I caught a flicker of Mask's spidery lashes as he glanced down at where he had cut himself. The plaster was gone and the skin was healing nicely.

"I don't think I'll lose the use of my arm, if that's what you mean."

I sighed in frustration. "Do you always have to be so grouchy?"

"And do you always have to be so neighbourly?"

I was sure I caught a glimmer of a smile teasing his lips.

I took a sip of my coffee, enjoying the rich taste. "So has everything been OK since the other night?"

Mask's mug screeched to a halt halfway to his lips. "Is this your way of trying to find out what happened that evening?"

"I'm sorry?"

Mask clattered his mug down on my glass-topped coffee table. The banter between us had vanished. "Is this what the coffee and cosy chat is all about? Inviting me in for an interrogation?"

My lips parted in shock. "No, of course not! I was only making conversation."

"Next you'll be asking me about my scar and why I wear these things." He tugged at his hoodie for effect. "I don't do touchy-feely," he ground out. "Only music helps me cope with my guilt and even then—"

His shoulders stiffened as he realised what he had said.

Mask snatched his mug back up and took a final large gulp. "Thank you for the coffee, Ms Devlin. I really should be going."

I sat there, stunned, as he stormed out of my house.

Chapter Thirty-Five

I hurried to my front door and jerked it open.

Mask's truck was already indicating right out of my drive and then set off down the lane in a streak of black gloss.

What was he hiding? What guilt?

I closed my eyes for a moment in frustration. *Shit.* I hadn't meant to touch on something sensitive.

Feeling annoyed with myself, I noticed Mask's note propped up against the vase on my hall table.

I picked up the white envelope and eased it open. It contained one sheet of expensive-looking writing paper. It made a brief whisper as I unfolded it and began to read:

Layla,

Please accept my apologies for my attitude the other evening.

I realise that you were only showing concern and I should have shown my gratitude.

As you might have guessed, I don't find it easy to express my emotions – that's where my music comes in.

Hope you are continuing to enjoy the exclusive CDs I gave you and that they are warmly received on the opening night of The Conch Club.

Wishing you every success,

Mask

My eyes scanned his writing again, picking up on the sincere brevity of his words.

I refolded the paper and slid it back into its envelope. Then I leaned it back against my vase.

I still suspected something had taken place up at Coorie Cottage the other night. It must have. Why was he so defensive about it if it had been an innocent misunderstanding?

And what was that strange guilt comment he had made just now, before he realised what he was saying and closed himself off again?

My imagination was halted by the melodic trill of my mobile. Faith's warm grin appeared on my screen. "So how did it go with Harry and Ed?"

"Horribly. He clammed up, quit the band, and stormed off."

Faith was every bit as sympathetic as I expected. "He might change his mind – Ed, I mean. It's bound to have come as a shock for him too, finding out you might be his daughter."

I set my mouth into a firm line. "Well, Faith, I'm determined to change his mind for him. I know I can't force him back with the band, but I'm not intending to give up yet."

"I also had a visit from Mask. He was here when I arrived home, leaving me a note. I invited him in but it all went badly."

Faith listened as I shared the details, interjecting with her usual murmurs and noises of understanding.

"Maybe I offended him," I suggested, biting my lip. "When he got up all of a sudden and shot off, I felt so embarrassed."

"Sounds like he was the embarrassed one," Faith pointed out. "He was obviously hoping you wouldn't be there." She paused. "I don't know anything about him," ventured Faith, "but it sounds to me as though he might be trying to deal with one or two issues, especially when you consider that he hides himself away up by Galen Waterfall all the time. I don't mean to sound harsh, lovely, but what with Mac's death, The Conch Club, and now the Harry and Ed situation, you really have more than enough to deal with right now."

She dropped her voice a little lower, allowing me to detect the faint sound of a Spanish gentleman enquiring about hiking maps of the area and a chirping telephone in the tourist office background. "Whatever is going on up at Coorie Cottage isn't your responsibility, Layla."

I opened my mouth to speak again, but a third voice interrupted down the line and addressed Faith in almost apologetic tones.

"I should let you go," I said. "I don't want you getting into trouble at work because of me."

There was a stony silence, followed by Faith muttering to the disembodied, female voice. Then she turned her attention back to me, apologetic. "Sorry about that. You forget I'm the office manager, so I can't reprimand myself, can I?"

I smiled to myself.

Faith's voice was carrying an element of excitement. "OK, so that was Danielle telling me that an Australian woman came in here first thing this morning, just before I started my shift, asking all sorts of questions about Coorie Cottage and its new occupier."

I sat up a little straighter. "What sort of questions?"

There were a few more murmured exchanges between Faith and Danielle, which I was struggling to make out.

Faith then spoke to me again. "Danielle says she had a pretty aggressive attitude. She wanted to know if Mask was seen a lot in the village and what the locals thought of him, that kind of thing."

A thought struck me. "Do you think she could be a journalist?"

"That's what I wondered too, but Danielle said she was certain she wasn't. She didn't introduce herself as one either, although that might have been deliberate. Oh, I wish

I hadn't told you now," she groaned, trepidation dawning in her husky voice. "I can hear your spidey senses tingling from here."

"Don't worry," I assured her insincerely. "I've got to concentrate on The Conch Club."

Faith made a snorting sound. "Yeah, right. Why don't I believe you? You've always been a terrible actress, Layla Devlin."

Sure enough, for the rest of the day, I couldn't help but wonder about this mysterious Australian woman and what connection she might have to Mask.

Was she the one he had confronted up at Coorie Cottage the other evening?

Chapter Thirty-Six

I was slumped on the sofa nibbling on a bar of dark chocolate but not savouring its bitter, delectable taste like I usually did.

Dad must have spoken to the boys in the band by now about Ed and our situation. Realistically, he had no choice.

Visions of long-haired, shouty, fifty-something men drifted into my imagination and I cringed.

Part of me really didn't want to ring my father. Even mentioning the situation seemed to bring it to life. When I didn't talk about Ed, when I didn't have to think about him, it disappeared into the recesses of my mind for a while.

I was stealing myself to ring Dad when there was a knock on the door.

Dad was hunched on the doorstep, his hands buried in the pockets of his leather jacket. There were tired smudges under his eyes.

I scooped him into a hug and guided him inside, where he sank into one of my armchairs.

"I thought there was going to be a bloodbath," he admitted. "When I told Jack, Stan, and Mikey, they went from shock to infuriation within a matter of seconds."

I curled my feet underneath me, trying to stem the hammering in my chest. "Nothing violent happened, did it?"

"If you don't count Mikey threatening to wrap his microphone around Ed's neck, then no."

"Oh..."

Dad dismissed my concern with a flap of his hand. "Don't worry, love. It was all posturing. I mean, the other lads were being loyal to me and I think things could have turned ugly, but when I reminded them about you and what you've been through with Mac..." Dad's flint grey eyes flashed. "You've had enough people letting you down – your mother, Mac – you don't need any more."

My heart swelled with love and appreciation. "Thanks Dad."

He laced and unlaced his drummer's fingers. "I'm not saying things are going to blow over easily, especially after Mikey spotted Ed in the village this afternoon and accused him of being a sanctimonious shit." Dad tried to smile, but it didn't reach his eyes. "I'm so sorry sweetheart, but I can't see Ed changing his mind about appearing with the rest of us."

Furious tears pricked the corners of my eyes as I surveyed my dad's weary smile. He didn't deserve any of this.

The more I considered the situation, the more I wanted a

definitive answer – even if it turned out not to be the one I wanted.

How long had Ed known my father? Forty years? They had slept on uncomfortable floorboards between gigs. They had played in countless dingy pubs boasting sticky, beer-soaked carpets and jaded audiences.

Dad had done everything he could to make Battalion a successful band, and although the fame they had experienced had been fleeting, the recognition they had received had been largely down to my father.

The least Ed could do was give my dad and the rest of the guys an evening to remember at The Conch Club, whether I really was his daughter or not.

July rolled around in a flurry of lists being ticked off, rewritten, or added to, accompanied by puffs of frustration.

Faith's help continued to be priceless. Whenever the tourist office experienced a lull in visitors, she used the time she had to ring tradespeople on my behalf or confirm delivery dates and times.

I'd managed to whittle down the number of candidates of potential staff to six and after informal interviews, I selected three full-time employees and two part-timers to begin with.

Alec had spoken to one of his friends, an artist by the name of Molly Evers, and she had produced the most gorgeous sign – a scalloped-edged rectangle of pale treated wood with 'The Conch Club' scrawled across the sea-blue banner in sweet vanilla lettering. To the right of the name was a depiction of a pretty ruffled conch shell which Molly had painted in gold and tangerine.

I loved it.

Dad and Alec hovered outside the boathouse, shuffling each end of the sign between them, like a modern-day Laurel & Hardy.

Before Alec had arrived, complete with a fried egg roll that had my tummy groaning with desire, Dad had told me the guys would be returning that weekend for another jam session. "Even though the gig is off, we really enjoyed meeting up like old times and we all agreed we wanted to do it again." Dad had performed a big eye roll. "They've decided to camp this time up in that campsite not far from Galen Waterfall."

"And what about Ed?" I'd asked.

"He's coming as well."

"But he said he wouldn't play with Battalion again."

"Turns out he hasn't told Karen and the boys yet about you, or that he's quit the band," Dad said, his voice layered with meaning. When he saw my expression blossom with hope, he'd added, "Oh, he's still got no intention of playing with us, but you know what a gossip Stan's missus is and she and Karen are best mates."

I'd let out a grunt. "So he's coming along with the lads for the weekend as usual, so Karen doesn't get suspicious."

"It looks that way," Dad had agreed, "but I'm trying not to think about it too much."

Now, I squinted upwards as Dad and Alec raised the sign between them and angled it this way and that.

I knew I was playing a very dangerous game, but despite Dad repeatedly telling me to make it public knowledge that Battalion would not now be appearing on opening night, I'd resisted.

I wasn't about to give up. Not yet. I had unofficially put another rock band from Fife on standby, just in case they were needed, but I refused to think like that for now. I still had a couple of weeks left to try and reason with Ed.

The boathouse was now painted in a glossy butterscotch, with the exception of the new window frames and doorway. I'd opted for an azure blue for these, to create a brightly coloured beach-hut effect, to tie in with the name.

The sparkling new windows reflected the spearing trees and craggy hillsides. The jetty, now slicked in matching paint, stretched out like a wooden carpet to the edge of the loch.

"Maybe just left a little please, Dad," I called up to them. "Alec, would you mind maybe nudging the sign a fraction to the right please?"

I watched, trying to conceal my amusement, while Dad rolled his eyes good naturedly and Alec attempted to conceal his growing frustration.

Alec and Dad heaved sighs of relief when I thrust my thumb up at them. "That's it! That's perfect."

Alec finished securing the banner with several thumps of the hammer protruding out of his back pocket, and then he and Dad clambered down their respective ladders.

Alec dashed his dusty hands down the front of his paint-splattered khaki shorts. "Thanks for having a word with

Heather. She hasn't transformed into a bookworm overnight but she's definitely making more of an effort."

"Not a problem," I smiled. "She's a sweet girl."

Alec plucked his mobile phone out of his other pocket and gave it a couple of idle jabs. "That she is – unless anyone dares to criticise that Mask character."

"Oh, I think parents and teenagers often have disagreements about music."

Alec frowned at his mobile screen and pushed it back into his pocket. "It wasn't me she had a recent slanging match with about him. It was some stranger in the village."

I stared at him, intrigued. "Was it a woman, by any chance?"

Alec nodded. "Yes, it was. According to Norrie and Clem, our Heather gave her a right mouthful, 'cos she dared to say this Mask guy should be driven out of town."

Dad frowned over at me, searching for a reaction.

"Do you know who she was, Alec?" I asked. "This woman, I mean?"

"Lord knows. Heather said she's never seen her before but that she must be a tourist as she had an Australian accent."

It was too much of a coincidence. It must be the same person who had been asking in the tourist office about him.

"What did this woman actually say?" I pushed, my curiosity fired up on all cylinders.

Alec made his way across the grass towards the car park and picnic area, where his transit van was sitting underneath a canopy of trees. "Heather said she asked her what she knew about him moving to Loch Harris. Then she started going on about him being a right nasty piece of work, capable of all sorts."

Dad and I swapped charged glances.

"Did she elaborate?" asked Dad.

Alec raised his bushy eyebrows up to the sky, which was becoming stippled with clouds. "I don't think she got the chance with our Heather."

We waved Alec off with our grateful thanks as his van disappeared. I turned to look at my father.

"You need to concentrate on your new business," he said. "I know that look, Layla."

"What look?"

"That one," he warned. "It's admirable that you care about other people – even when they do behave like insensitive cretins. But did you hear what Alec said? That woman accused this Mask of being dangerous."

"Dad..." I began, preparing to try and reason with him.

He glanced down at his battered old wrist watch. "When did you say your drinks menus were being delivered?"

A thought occurred to me as I appreciated the sign now shining above the new pale wood and glass entrance. I should ask Faith and Danielle to keep a look out for this mysterious Australian woman. They literally were the gatekeepers of Loch Harris in the tourist office. They also knew the owners of all the local B&Bs, hotels and camp sites. If this woman were staying locally (which was very likely, considering we were pretty remote out here), they stood a much better chance of finding out more about her than I did.

I decided to drop Faith a text.

"Layla? Layla!"

I swung round.

One of Dad's eyebrows was hitched up to his hairline. "Where are you?"

I blushed and pinned on a smile. "Sorry. Just daydreaming for a minute."

He frowned from under his floppy fringe, as he stood on the wooden steps leading up to The Conch Club. "I can see that. I was asking you when your drinks menus were being delivered here?"

I checked the time on my watch. It was 10 a.m. now. "In about an hour."

Dad nodded. "OK. So plenty of time for me to pop into the village and grab us two takeaway coffees then."

I hovered by the partially open door and waited until Dad jumped into his silver jeep and streaked off down the road.

Then I sent a text to Faith.

I'd just pressed 'Send' and slung my phone into my back jeans pocket, when I spotted a flash of red jacket and a glimmer of a Royal Mail van out of the corner of my eye. It was Arthur, our local postman.

"You'll be giving Sir Alan Sugar a run for his money, if you carry on like this," he joked, rummaging around in the mail sack suspended from his shoulder.

"I'm running before I can walk, Arthur."

He nodded at The Conch Club. "I was just passing and thought I'd drop by and take a look. It's grand. You can be sure Fiona and I will be some of your first patrons. We're so looking forward to seeing your dad and the lads doing their thing on stage again."

I was struggling to smile.

"Oh, before I go, this came for you. Seeing as I was passing, thought I would drop it in. That's all for today, I'm afraid. Cheerio now."

Arthur bustled back over the grass and towards his van. He had handed me a slim white envelope, which I turned over in my hands, my thoughts still with The Conch Club.

But all thoughts fled when the name of the DNA testing organisation jumped up at me from the top left-hand corner in blocky blue lettering.

Oh no. Oh no. It was the results.

Chapter Thirty-Seven

D ad had only just returned from the village, proudly clutching two lattes and two warm croissants.

"Food for the workers," he beamed, handing me my cardboard cup and croissant, which was nestled in a brown bag. "Well, one of us is working."

My mouth had turned to sandpaper.

Oh God. This was it. I set down the cup of coffee and the croissant on the step beside me. "Arthur just dropped by," I gulped. "He brought this."

I showed Dad the envelope. His shoulders sank. "Is that it?"

I ran my trembling fingers around the four edges of the envelope and did the briefest of nods.

I wanted to know. Dad wanted to know. I supposed Ed did too.

I peered down at the plastic window of the envelope, with my name and address staring back at me.

My stomach lurched and swooped. I could see Dad and

Ed's faces mingling and interchanging in front of me. This involved them every bit as much as it did me.

These past few months – the betrayal by Mac, my mother's revelation – it was all pressing down on me. But then I angled myself round on the wooden step. The Conch Club sat behind me, full of the promise of laughter and music that would echo around the hills and the woods here.

Despite the pain and the deception, I had come so far. I had pushed through and I had achieved something.

"Go on," urged Dad, tense beside me. "Open it." He seized one of my hands in his. "Whatever it says, it will be fine. *We* will be fine, OK?"

My heart was zinging around my chest like an out-of-control pinball machine.

I steeled myself and took one long breath. The scent of the leaves and fresh water was glorious.

Dad fiddled with the collar of his long-sleeved polo shirt beside me. "It's like the Oscars."

I slid open the envelope with one trembly finger. My hand fumbled inside, pulling out the folded letter. It made a crackling sound as I flapped it open.

The air lodged itself in my ribcage, while I impatiently scanned the letter. The beginning of it consisted of references to scientific data. My attention focused on the second paragraph.

Mr Harold George Devlin is not excluded as the biological father of Ms Layla Rosalind Devlin, with a Probable Paternity Ratio of 99.99%."

I buried a gasp and thrust the letter at Dad. I didn't know what to say, so I just gave a nod of my head and a tiny smile. The relief and happiness sweeping through me was overwhelming.

Dad scanned the letter. He didn't say anything for a moment. He just sat there, contemplating its contents, before turning, pulling me to him, and planting a kiss on the top of my head. His voice crackled. "It's all right. Everything's all right."

Dad reached for his mobile. "I had better ring Ed. I promised I would tell him as soon as we knew."

I reached for the coffee beside me and held it, allowing the warm sensation to seep into my fingers.

Ed answered after a few rings and I listened as Dad relayed the DNA results to him. When the call was over, Dad lowered his phone and appraised me. "I think Ed's a bit disappointed about not being your dad after all." Dad stretched out his legs. "He admitted that he wasn't too sure how he was feeling right now." He rubbed his forehead. "I think part of him had started to come around to the idea of having a grown-up daughter."

My eyes widened. "Well, that wasn't the reaction I expected."

Dad agreed with me. "I don't think Ed's reaction was what he expected either."

We sat together for a few more moments in quiet contemplation, with only shafts of papery sunlight slithering through the branches for company.

Eventually, I gave Dad a playful frown and broke off a

bit of my croissant. "It's hungry work, directing the position of signs."

"I bet it is."

I popped another piece into my mouth and slid my eyes down to my mobile, which was sitting beside me. In all the drama of the DNA results arriving, I realised Faith hadn't responded to my text yet. I knew she would though. My best friend was nothing if not reliable.

Sitting here, next to Dad, with the water slapping against the end of the jetty and the faint crackle of tree branches, reminded me of when I was little. I had feared that those memories would be stolen from me. Now I treasured them even more.

I glanced at my watch, determined for our lives to move on and for things to get back to normal. Dad handed me back the letter and I grinned before folding it up and putting it in my back pocket. "Molly should be here soon to deliver the menus," I said to Dad.

My mobile chose that moment to let out an indignant beep, signalling that I had received a text.

I grabbed my phone, thinking it might be Faith, but it was Molly, saying there had been a traffic-light failure on the road from her house in nearby Finton and she apologised, explaining that she would be ten minutes late.

I had never met Molly before, but Alec assured me her artwork was first class. When I took a look at her website, her originality and her passion were evident, and she had shown that in the sign she had produced for me. The woman appeared to be able to turn her hand to almost anything.

Dad and I were chatting about possible solo singers I could scout when a Ford Transit Connect in school bus yellow swung into the tourist parking area opposite and eased into an available space by the picnic tables.

We observed a curvy redhead climb out and move round to the passenger side, from where she fetched a rectangular box.

As she approached, her curls bounced around her shoulders and the ankle-length camel maxi-dress she was wearing fluttered over a pair of jewelled sandals.

She was like something out of a Rubens painting, all creamy skin and voluptuous curves.

Dad made me jump as he sprang to his feet like he'd just received an electrical charge. His eyes were widening so much they were at risk of falling out of his face.

"Layla?" she asked in a dusky voice.

"That's me," I grinned, walking towards her and offering an outstretched hand. "You must be Molly."

"And I'm Harry Devlin, Layla's Dad."

I buried a smile at the sight of my blushing father, eagerly thrusting his hand towards Molly.

She drank in my dad. "Hello Harry. Very nice to meet you." Her hazel eyes crinkled at the corners and as I stood there, observing their exchange of flushed smiles, I estimated her to be in her early to mid-forties.

"So," I exclaimed, clapping my hands together, "I take it the drinks and snacks menus are in that box?"

"They sure are."

Molly flushed with appreciation as I thanked her for the

sign and pointed up at it above the entrance. "I love it. It's perfect."

"It certainly is," insisted Dad, bathing Molly in a million-dollar smile.

Molly's appreciative blush deepened. "Thank you. That's lovely to hear."

She snapped the white cardboard lid from the box and handed it to me. "I produced a total of twenty in all," she explained, "but have only charged you mate's rates for the dozen you ordered originally, because you know Alec."

She shot a glance up at my dad. "I think it's always better to have too many than not enough, especially in somewhere like a bar."

"Oh absolutely," nodded Dad. In fact, he was nodding so much he was in danger of giving himself a crick in the neck.

Molly could have told my father that she was the getaway driver for a criminal mastermind and he would have congratulated her.

I shot Dad a knowing look and pulled the drinks and snacks menus out. "Oh, it's lovely!"

Molly had made it a long, parchment-like affair in soft vanilla, complete with gold lettering.

All our offerings were on there, dancing in front of my eyes in sweeping, looping text – everything from our Irish coffee with a distinct, Scottish whisky twist and roasted coffee from Costa Rica and Guatemala, to loose leaf teas, and rich drams and amber ales that made the tastebuds pop.

Below the beverages section was a choice of Scottish-inspired snacks: Dunsyre blue cheese with oatcakes; Scottish smoked salmon & avocado fromage; shrimp bites with salad, and pear & parmesan honey crostini.

For a sweet tooth, I'd decided to offer pecan or butter shortbread, marmalade cake, and Scottish snowball drop cakes, all of which would be the perfect accompaniment to a cup of strong coffee or a pot of tea.

Molly enthused about the tasty treats. She pointed a finger and said, "It's making me hungry just reading that again."

I frowned down at the list. "I hope I've covered all the bases. I want tourists to get a flavour of Scotland, but I didn't want to go all out on the food front. After all, The Conch Club is supposed to be about the music and the location."

"Don't worry about that," assured Dad, still gazing at Molly's open, pretty features. "You can always tweak the food side of things later if you have to."

"Totally," agreed Molly, her cheeks fizzing at my father's undivided attention.

I marvelled again at the glittery lettering and the impression of a conch shell that Molly had painted in the top right corner. All the colours complimented the palette she had used for the main sign.

"Oh, excuse me," I rushed as my phone rang and Faith's picture flashed up on my screen. "I won't be a minute."

Dad appeared only too delighted to have Molly to himself, so I left them chatting and sidled down the steps to plonk myself on a random rock. "I take it you got my text OK?"

"I did, and I have some news of your mysterious Australian lady."

My heart fluttered. "And I've got some news for you too."

There was then a bit of a commotion erupting down the line as Danielle began pestering Faith about there being too few maps detailing the local woodland walks. "I only put out a new batch the other day," I heard her moan, "and yet there's only two left now and look at the state of them! They're all bloody crumpled!"

I could detect frustration in Faith's disembodied voice. "Sorry about this, Layla." She let out a ragged sigh. "Look, Danielle, we can't electronically tag every single guidebook, map, and leaflet in here..."

"Would it be easier if I popped by?" I suggested, getting to my feet and brushing down my jeans.

"That's probably best."

I dashed past Dad and Molly and snatched up my bag from inside the doorway. I fetched my keys from the inside pocket and jangled them round one finger. I couldn't wait to tell Faith about the DNA results. "I've just got to drop by the tourist office and see Faith for a few moments. I won't be long."

The two of them were oblivious. Molly was laughing at something Dad had said.

"That's fine, darling," said Dad distractedly. "You take your time."

Chapter Thirty-Eight

I parked close to where canvas draped stalls were being set up for the monthly farmers' market and headed across the sunlit square towards the tourist office.

It shone bright white in the July sunshine, its floor-to-ceiling windows displaying token Loch Harris-embossed gifts.

I was about to go in when my phone started ringing in the bottom of my bag. I paused and plucked it out. I didn't recognise the mobile number glowing on the screen.

My jaw dropped when I realised Greg McBride was talking to me.

"I'm sorry to bother you," he apologised, "but I've been thinking so much about what you said to me a few weeks ago, and as for Faith ... well, she's on my mind all the time."

I glanced around and waved at Faith through the tourist office window. "Does this mean what I think it means?"

I could hear Greg gulping. "Yes, it does. I'm going to try and persuade her to give us another go."

My stomach pirouetted in sympathy for him. "So what's the plan?"

"We – as in Sam and I – are going to head down to the tourist office now. No point in delaying. I've farted around for long enough."

"So has she," I answered. "I'm actually just going into the tourist office to see Faith now."

"You're kidding! Right, do you think you could hang on a bit longer then?" asked Greg in a pleading tone. "I might need some back up."

I knew Faith would want to drown me as a witch after all this, but I found myself agreeing. After all, I had been the one to instigate this turn of events. "What made you change your mind, Greg?"

I could almost hear a nervous smile playing on his lips. "You did. I've been mulling over what you said about Faith's fear of commitment and the fact that Sam and I are a team."

He let out a short laugh. "It's up to me and my boy to let her see we're worth taking a chance on."

A lump collected in my throat. "Well, she's a very lucky lady."

Greg ended the call by saying that he and Sam were almost ready and they could be there within twenty minutes.

I set my shoulders and tried not to look guilty as I went in, rattling the little doorbell.

The tourist office was quiet. Faith was standing behind

the counter, fiddling with the collar of her lacy blouse while a Nordic couple shuffled around her carefully organised display.

"Not busy then?" I asked, indicating the stony atmosphere. Only the sound of a lilting fiddle from their concealed speakers broke the peace.

Probably a good thing if Greg was planning on some big gesture.

"I've seen more life at the Women's Institute Christmas party," grunted Faith. "The sooner you get that nightclub of yours up and running the better."

"It's not a nightclub," I sniffed. "It's a music venue."

"Well whatever it is, I'm sure it will help to bring more tourists here. We'll probably be overrun with them."

"Not that you're putting pressure on me or anything."

Faith smiled.

"No Danielle?" I asked, noting her chair was empty.

Faith said goodbye to the backpacking couple who took a campsites leaflet and departed with a cheery wave.

"She's just popped out to get us some more postage stamps."

I lingered by the desk, strumming my fingers on top of it. I was bursting with anticipation on both counts now.

Faith stared at my hand and then at me. "Are you all right?"

I flinched and tried not to look down at my watch for the eighth time in the last five minutes. "Yes, I'm fine."

Inside, my nerves were galloping in sympathy for Greg. What on earth was he planning to do?

Oh shit! What if Faith was still adamant that she and

Greg were a non-starter? This could all end in humiliation and it would be my fault.

Faith narrowed her blue eyes at me. "Are you sure you're OK?"

My lips twisted into a strained smile. "Of course, I am. I just told you I'm all right. Why?"

"You just seem a bit on edge today."

I flapped my right hand, sending my rose-gold bangle sliding up and down my wrist. "No, I'm fine. I think it's all the stuff I've still got to do. It's preying on my mind a bit."

"Oh, don't you worry about any of that. You know you've always got me to call on if there are other things to do."

You won't be offering to help me in a few minutes. You'll be offering to wring my neck.

I knew I had to try and gather myself together. Even Danielle – not the most observant person in the world – would notice my odd behaviour when she got back.

Tell her now about the DNA result, hissed a voice in my head. Then she might only slightly kill you when Greg walks in.

As Danielle still wasn't back from the post office, I snatched the opportunity. "Dad and I just received the DNA results." A wide grin broke out across my face. "They confirmed he *is* my biological father."

Faith's hand flew to her mouth. She shot round from the counter and gathered me into her arms. "I knew it! I just knew it! Bloody hell! Why didn't you tell me as soon as you got through the door? I'm thrilled for you – and for your dad."

She scanned my face. "And Ed? Does he know?"

I answered that yes, he did. "Dad reckoned he was a bit conflicted about the result and that a bit of him had been coming round to the idea of having a daughter."

Faith glowed with happiness for me. "Well, you and Harry make sure you celebrate tonight."

I confirmed that indeed we would. Then I noticed the time on the tourist office clock and glanced towards the door. My nerves for Greg and Sam were beginning to jingle like Christmas bells.

Why the hell hadn't I listened to Dad to begin with? Why had I insisted on getting involved? *Because you are a nosey, interfering cow,* came a warning voice.

I found my attention wandering again. I angled my body away from the desk so that I had a clearer view through the window.

Every time I so much as glimpsed a blond guy, my stomach catapulted into my throat.

I managed a distracted smile at Danielle as she barrelled through the front door with her swathe of postage stamps.

Where was Greg? Had he reflected on it and decided he wasn't prepared to take the risk? I hoped he hadn't. Faith, Greg, and Sam would make such an adorable little family.

Faith's irritated voice made me blink. "Layla, Danielle was just about to tell you what info she has on this Australian woman, but you haven't been listening to a word she just said." Faith's concern was evident. "Something is clearly bothering you. You have told me everything, haven't you?"

She blinked emphatically, aware that Danielle was now present.

"Yes, I've told you everything," I blustered. *Sort of.* Panicked, I pointed at the burnt-orange sofa and chairs in front of the window, where many of the tourists would sit and peruse the collection of leaflets and maps before setting off.

"Is that new?"

"What, the furniture?" interjected a puzzled Danielle. "God, no. We've had that in here for years."

"Oh," I flapped. "It goes to show how observant I am then."

Faith was really studying me now. She shot a troubled look at Danielle, who raised her eyebrows and shrugged.

Mentally willing Greg and Sam to arrive so this nightmare could be over, I began to gush about the boathouse colour scheme, when two blond heads appeared out of the corner of my eye.

Going by Faith's stunned expression, there was no doubt it was Greg and Sam.

I inched around, as though a huge tarantula was crawling up my back.

My apprehension melted at the sight of father and son hovering there. They were both dressed in similar outfits: dark blue jeans, leather jackets, and desert boots.

They were like two handsome bookends and looked adorable. Greg was obviously going for the top end of the irresistibly cute spectrum. As far as I was concerned, he'd achieved that and then some.

Don't look at me, Greg, I mentally whispered to him. *If Faith sees, she'll know straight away.*

Too late.

Greg delivered the swiftest glance over to me, but Faith pounced on it. Her jaw dropped. "You knew about this!" she gasped, her tone accusatory. "That's why you've been so jumpy."

She switched her attention from me to Greg and Sam. "I don't know what Layla has been saying, but—"

"Will you just hear me out please, Faith? All I ask is that you listen to what I have to say."

Faith was scarlet. She swallowed and risked the briefest glance down at Sam, who was gazing up at her out of long-lashed, blue eyes. Then he offered her the widest grin that revealed a dimple in his right cheek, the same as his father.

Faith returned a watery smile. "This is unfair," she managed. "You brought Sam."

"He and I come as a pair," Greg reminded her gently. He squeezed Sam's hand beside him. "And that's the whole point of this, Faith. I know we only went out together a couple of times, but I really like you and I think you feel the same about me."

Danielle's hand fluttered to her throat.

Greg's expression was open and appealing. "I'm prepared to take a chance on us and see how things go. I think you could have real fun with Sam and me."

It was then that I noticed Greg squeeze Sam's hand and the little boy burst out, "Please go out with Daddy again. He has been very sad."

I swallowed a smile and flicked my gaze at Faith for her

reaction. She was biting her lip. "And of course, that was in no way rehearsed."

Greg winked at her. "Of course not."

Faith turned her attention to me. "You knew about all this, didn't you?"

I held my hands up in mock surrender. "I only found out about half an hour ago. I didn't know about the cute routine they had planned. Honest."

Greg jumped to my defence and agreed that I was innocent – well, sort of.

Faith's blue eyes clouded over.

Greg kept staring at her. "Well, what's your answer?"

Danielle afforded my best friend an encouraging nudge. "How can you resist the two of them? Talk about adorable!"

Faith made a noise that was a cross between a giggle and a sob. "I still think you know more about this than you're letting on, Devlin."

I made my eyes huge. "Me?"

She shook her head. "That's the problem. I can't resist, especially not now."

She hurried out from behind the counter and threw her arms around Greg's neck, before they shared a tender kiss, much to Sam's amusement.

Then Faith lowered herself to the four-year-old boy's height. She took his hand and shook it, before giving him a hug.

"Right," said Greg after a few moments, as he scooped up Sam into his muscular arms. "How about you come round to ours tonight and Sam and I will make you dinner?"

Faith's cheeks popped with colour. "I'd like that very much."

Once they'd confirmed the time and left, Faith studied me. "Right now I don't know whether to hug you or bar you from the premises."

I grinned back at her. "You know you want to hug me."

She threw her arms around me and playfully flicked the end of my ponytail. "You really are a pain in the arse at times."

"Thank you."

Then the real reason why I'd dropped by to see Faith came screeching back into my mind. "Now that all the excitement is over, how about this mystery Australian lady?"

Faith looked at Danielle. "Go on then, Poirot. Tell Layla what you told me."

Bursting with anticipation, the younger woman could hardly contain her excitement. "OK, so I was tidying up our window display earlier this morning ... you should have seen it. I mean, you couldn't describe Coleen as an office cleaner..."

Faith's pale blue eyes rolled in her head. "Just get on with it please."

Danielle coloured. She glared at Faith and squared her shoulders. "All right. All right!"

She flapped her hands about, giving a flash of her French manicure. "Do you know Wendy Goodman? She started her own little bed and breakfast here several weeks back?"

I recalled seeing an article about her in the *Loch Harris Informer* last month.

Before I had the opportunity to answer, Danielle's dark eyes shone as she told me Wendy had dropped into the tourist office earlier that morning to pick up a few more leaflets about where to locate the best of the local wildlife.

"I mean," sniggered Danielle, "you can catch plenty of the local wildlife round here on a Friday night, if you know where to look."

I waited until she had recovered from laughing at her own joke. "You were saying?"

She cleared her throat and didn't dare look up at Faith. "Oh yeah. Well, I was having a chat to her about how her B&B was going and she said it was slow, but that she had this new guest staying with her who seemed to be a bit of a strange one."

"In what way?" I asked, intrigued.

Danielle leaned forwards, delivering a waft of strong citrusy perfume. She revealed that Wendy's new guest was an Australian woman who seemed to be very preoccupied with Coorie Cottage and, more importantly, who was living there.

"Wendy assured me she didn't tell her that that reclusive musician guy was living up there," said Danielle.

"And I believe her," added Faith.

"But Wendy said this woman keeps coming and going at funny hours and has been asking round some of the local businesses about him," said Danielle. "Not only that, but she even remarked to my boyfriend's boss over at the garage that this Mask fellow is dangerous and not to be trusted."

I looked from Danielle to Faith. "Dangerous? I don't believe that."

But why would someone go around saying such things?

"Do you think this woman night have been up at Coorie Cottage that time when the police were summoned?" I asked Danielle.

Danielle's eyes grew wide. "I heard about that and I did mention it to Wendy."

"And?"

Danielle flicked a loaded gaze at Faith and me. "Wendy said her new house guest was out till late on that Friday evening and came back looking all harassed. She remembered the date and the time because her brother-in-law rang to tell her that her sister had just given birth."

Danielle beamed through her cinnamon freckles. "Her B&B is in Fallow Lane."

I adjusted the strap of my bag and clanked the wooden counter shut behind me, "Oh, I know the place. Thanks. That's great."

Faith drew her red-slicked lips into a disapproving line.

"Why are you looking at me like that?" I asked.

Faith leaned her arms on the counter and appraised me with a twinkle. "You just can't help yourself, can you?"

Chapter Thirty-Nine

Wendy's bed and breakfast was situated only ten minutes' walk away from the little cluster of shops and down a cobbled close. I left my car and hurried there on foot.

The glossy black front door was unlocked so I let myself in.

I dinged the gold bell on top of the reception desk and picked up on the subtle drone of bagpipes coming from two secreted speakers.

There was a squeak of an opening door from somewhere behind me and a well-groomed blonde lady appeared. "Can I help you?"

As she moved closer, her soft blue eyes narrowed, as if she were struggling to place me from somewhere.

I introduced myself and she confirmed she was Wendy Goodman and shook my hand. "Ah, Harry's girl," she smiled, "and how's your music venue coming along? It's not long till it opens?"

"That's right. Yes, it's been a lot of work, as I'm sure you can appreciate, but everyone has been so helpful. We open at the end of August."

Wendy nodded approvingly. "Only a few weeks then. That's good. Lord knows we need a new injection of something round here."

"Business a bit slow?"

Wendy's lips contorted. "If it gets any slower, it will come to a complete halt."

I adjusted the strap of my fringed bag over my shoulder. "So, not many guests staying with you at the minute?"

"Two," she sighed. "It's hardly worth opening the dining room for breakfast."

She pointed a lacquered nail over to the right, to a room where creamy tablecloths were spread out over several square tables.

"These guests," I ventured, "do you mind me asking if one of them happens to be an Australian woman?"

Wendy blinked at me. "Yes, she is."

I gazed over her shoulder and up the carpeted staircase. "I don't suppose this lady happens to be in her room at the moment?"

Brief disappointment tugged at me when Wendy told me she had gone out straight after breakfast.

"Do you know how long she intends to stay for?"

"She hasn't said, but I get the impression she isn't in any hurry to leave."

Wendy eyed me for a moment. "I'm sure you can appreciate, Layla, that it wouldn't be right for me to give out details of my guests."

"Oh, of course not," I agreed with a fierce nod. "All I wondered was if this lady had been asking you about Coorie Cottage at all ... or about who lives there?"

Wendy debated my question for a few moments, then glanced around before leaning closer. Her voice dropped to a hush. "Yes, she has." Her gold earrings jiggled against the side of her neck. "She seemed really preoccupied with this ... Mask, is it?"

"Did she say why?"

"Not at all. All she said was that he's not the innocent, tortured soul he pretends to be."

My optimism started to flourish. "I know you can't give me her name—"

"I'm sorry, I can't."

"All I'm trying to do is help someone, Wendy. I assure you it's not for anything sinister."

She bit her lip.

"I don't know what's going on or what happened up there on that Friday night, but I've got a feeling your new guest might have some idea."

Sensing that Wendy was weakening, I hit her with the Loch Harris mantra. "After all, what are we always saying we are proud of round here? Our sense of community."

Wendy gave a defeated sigh. "Honestly, young lady, you're just like your dad. You could charm the birds out of the trees."

I grinned. "Is that a yes?"

She didn't answer, but marched over and slid behind the reception desk. She flipped open a leather guest book and flicked over a couple of pages. "My guest book happens to have fallen open and I'm just about to take a brief sojourn in the dining room. I'll give you thirty seconds to look at the name at the bottom of the left-hand page."

I thanked her but she was already disappearing into the dining room, her white leather loafers flashing.

I dived behind the desk and ran one finger down the page to locate the woman's name.

There it was. Beside it, she had scribbled her country of residence. Australia.

I took a Post-it from Wendy's desk and jotted it down. Then I thrust the note into my pocket.

Chapter Forty

M y window wipers dashed the pearls of rain from my car windscreen.

The shower had cleared the summer air and sunlight was sweeping across the landscape, changing the hillsides with a kaleidoscope of colours.

Mask's voice warmed me on the drive to Coorie Cottage, swimming out of the CD player like honey.

I drove past the campsite where the Battalion guys would be staying this coming weekend, past the spiky green woodland and on towards the silvery rush of Galen Waterfall.

As if on cue, Mask finished singing.

I'd texted Dad before I set off, telling him I had to pick up a few bits of shopping and that I would be back shortly.

If I told him I'd ventured up to Coorie Cottage again to see Mask, he would have done his utmost to talk me out of it.

I eased to a halt in front of the cottage and steeled myself.

My fingers reached into my back jeans pocket and brushed the top of the Post-it note. I felt an obligation to tell Mask that someone was going around Loch Harris verbally attacking his character.

No doubt he would accuse me of interfering – all things considered, perhaps I was – but I needed to know why this woman was saying awful things about him.

I reached his front door and knocked twice. My hand hovered as I prepared to knock for a third time; I could hear Mask singing from somewhere close by. His dusky vocals sent a bold shiver down my back.

I was startled by the sudden physical effect he had on me. I took a deep breath.

It sounded as though he was out in the garden again.

This time, the sound of me walking down the side of the house must have travelled, because his singing came to an abrupt halt.

Mask's tall silhouette was standing over a sprouting bush, knotted with bright red berries that reminded me of Christmas baubles. I could make out his hand reaching to pull his hood up.

There was a cold silence. "And to what do I owe the pleasure this time, Ms Devlin?"

His Antipodean drawl was dripping in sarcasm.

I squared my shoulders. "I need to speak to you."

He was gruff. "About what?"

I rolled my eyes. Why did he have to be so mistrusting and confrontational? Then I thought about that vivid red scar running down the right side of his face and concluded that I wouldn't know how I might react to people after suffering a wound like that.

"That's a lovely plant," I observed, pointing at the glistening berries dripping from its branches.

Mask glanced over his shoulder. "It's a viburnum cranberry bush. The songbirds like them." I think he detected my curiosity, because he sighed and continued. "My father was a very keen gardener. I used to spend hours with him in our postage stamp of a garden in Port Macquarie."

When I asked him where that was, he explained it was a laid-back coastal town north of Sydney.

Mask cast his dark gaze downwards for a few moments. He reached down to stroke a desert rose. It was similar to a daffodil, but instead of the lemon sorbet colours, it boasted frilly white petals, edged with faint sugar-pink. "I like to bring a splash of Australia to Scotland." He paused. "When I'm tending to my garden, I feel like I can lose myself and forget things for a little while."

I admired a cluster of flowers, which Mask explained were Australian Swan River daisies. Their delicate mauve, white, and blue flowers softened the edge of the grey paved path.

"They can escape and find their way through walls and crevices almost anywhere."

I gazed up at him. There was something melancholy about the way he said it – perhaps even some envy for what these small but persistent buds could achieve when they set their mind to it.

"After my father died, I looked after the garden. My mother loved it, but didn't have the heart to tend to it."

"But you did."

"It was a struggle," he confessed. "But I promised Dad I would."

"And when did you realise you had inherited his green fingers?"

Mask's mouth softened. "I'm nowhere near as talented a gardener as my father was."

I cast one appreciative hand over the throng of bell-shaped flowers, rosette foliage, and fans of sage-green leaves. "You're kidding, right? This is a haven."

I could have sworn Mask was almost bashful for the briefest moment. "Thank you."

"Is your mum still alive?"

Mask paused. "No, she passed away a year after my dad. I think she gave up after she lost him."

"Oh, I'm so sorry. It must have been true love."

Mask's jaw clenched. "If you say so." He folded his arms. "I don't think you came up here to ask about my gardening expertise though."

What was it about this man? Whenever I thought I was making some progress with him, he would close down. "My father is a landscape gardener," I said, immediately regretting it. He didn't appear that impressed.

I cleared my throat. "I came up to see you about a mysterious Australian woman who's been asking around about you."

His brown eyes narrowed. "What are you talking about?"

"I have a name," I blurted. "I know who she is."

Mask tilted his head to one side as he considered this. "Someone has been asking about me in the village?"

Good grief, he was so frustrating! "All right. If you want to be an awkward sod, that's fine by me." I pulled the Post-it from my back pocket and unfolded it. "OK, so the name I have for this woman is Belle Raven."

"What did you say?" His deep brown eyes smouldered from under the shadows of his hood.

"Belle Raven," I repeated in a much smaller voice.

"Is this some sort of joke?"

I thrust the note towards him but he didn't take it. "That's the name she gave at the B&B she's staying at."

He took two long strides so that he was now looming over me. Confusion and alarm radiated off him. "I think you should leave."

I opened my mouth but he cut me off. "I said I want you to leave. Now!"

"I was just trying to help you. This woman has been saying lots of cruel things. Was she the one who was trying to cause trouble for you the other evening?"

He didn't answer. He just seethed under his hood.

"You might not be familiar with a thing called community spirit but that's what we share around here."

"I think that's a euphemism for being nosey."

I almost laughed at the irony of it. He sounded like Mac, saying that. I challenged his hot, dark gaze. "How to win friends and influence people. You've really got this nailed, haven't you?"

I didn't need him to be grateful, but a shred of civility would be nice.

Mask's square jaw jutted out from under his hood. "I didn't move to the middle of nowhere to have tea parties."

"I gathered that much."

"I want you to leave. Now!"

My face burned.

I screwed up the note in my hand and hurled it at his trainer-clad feet. "Maybe she's right about you."

Mask jerked his hood further down over his features as I slammed my car into reverse and drove away.

What I didn't see was him drop down to snatch up the Post-it note and close his eyes in anger and frustration.

Chapter Forty-One

I stomped over the grass and back up the porch steps to The Conch Club.

Molly had gone but my dad was still wearing a flustered glow. He was checking one of the window locks and spun round to watch me.

I clod-hopped over the wood floor and past the furniture, still swathed in its protective plastic sheeting.

Dad's brows knitted together when I launched into a verbal tirade about Mask and said that I'd decided I wouldn't be featuring his music on opening night.

Dad's mouth twitched. "You can't do that, darling. It looks like you've already lost Battalion and you've already mentioned your exclusive play of his new material in your advertising."

I rubbed my bare arms and made a groaning sound. Dad had a good point. I'd left several voicemail messages for Ed, trying to persuade him to change his mind and re-join the group, even if it was only for one night at The Conch Club. He hadn't called me back.

If I dropped Mask's music now as well, it would do my reputation no good at all.

As if reading my mind, Dad warned me of the consequences. "If you pull him now, punters may think you're untrustworthy. Is that really what you want when you're trying to launch a new business?"

I frowned over at the peacock-blue walls and the semi-circular stage. "No, of course not."

Dad finished adjusting the window lock and shot me a look from over his shoulder. "I take it he's upset you again."

I couldn't tell Dad that I'd ventured up to Coorie Cottage again. He would sport his infamous told-you-so face and that would make me realise even more what an impulsive idiot I was.

"Oh, forget I mentioned anything," I said, flapping my hands about. "So, what happened between you and Molly?"

At the mention of her name, my father's long expression melted into a soppy grin. "We've exchanged phone numbers and I'm taking her out next week."

"Fast work, Dad. Well done."

He went on to explain that she was a widow with no children. "Think I'll take her to that nice new bistro on the road to Finton. Molly said she hasn't been there yet either."

I was very impressed at his assertiveness. "Good for you!"

I followed him out of the boathouse. He jangled the keys

and made sure the door was locked. "The boys have all confirmed they're coming back here on Friday morning to spend the weekend. It was supposed to be another rehearsal." Dad's disappointment was clear. "Mikey suggested we recruit another bass player, but it's too short notice. Ed knows all the songs and he can play those riffs blindfold."

I offered a sympathetic smile. "Ed's still coming too though, I take it?"

Dad gave the tiniest of nods.

"And they're all staying together at that campsite near Galen Waterfall?"

One of Dad's eyebrows hitched itself up. "Yep. Should be cosy."

I chewed the inside of my bottom lip. I had to try and speak to Ed.

Dad was doing all he could to be pragmatic about the band not playing on opening night, but I could see how much it meant to him. If Ed was ignoring my calls, then I would go to the campsite on Friday and speak to him there.

I had to give it one more try.

The next couple of days dissolved in a succession of phone calls to bands confirming details of their future appearances and signing off on contracts for our drinks and snacks suppliers.

I also had a couple of deadlines screaming at me on my to-do list for my freelance writing.

Faith was there, as dependable as ever. She instructed

me to press on with my writing deadlines, while she took charge of invoices from the food suppliers.

I'd only finished heaving a hysterical sigh of relief at what I'd managed to achieve when my mobile pinged on my writing desk.

It was Dad, checking to see if I was OK. He had added at the end of his text that the boys had arrived at the campsite and would meet up at his later, once they had got settled.

I replied to his text with some general chat and ended with a couple of kisses.

Slumping back in my chair, I stared out as the lazy July sky pricked the tops of the trees.

I glanced up at my wooden clock on the wall. It was approaching 11 a.m. I switched off my computer and hooked my bag up and over my arm.

In my oval hall mirror, I noted grey smudges under my eyes. I had been staring at my computer screen for so long I was surprised my head hadn't contorted into a rectangular shape.

I reached into the side pocket of my bag and put on some lipstick and a couple of blobs of rosy blusher. It was like trying to add splashes of colour to a negative photograph.

I reached up to the coat stand and plucked my leather jacket from its hook. As I did so, my attention was drawn to something poking out from under the slats of my shoe rack.

I crouched down and retrieved one of Mac's scarves, which must have fallen there when I was sorting out his things. It was one he would often wear during the fiercer winter weather.

I fingered its woollen texture before holding it up to my nose. It didn't smell of him at all; I could detect none of the heavily scented, musky aftershave he always favoured.

I couldn't contemplate that he had been gone for four months now.

I held it aloft, before folding it up into a neat square and slotting it back under the shoe rack.

Galen Campsite was pricked with several tents, their multi-colours flapping softly in the morning breeze.

I was aware that Coorie Cottage was only a fifteen-minute walk up the road, but I vanquished pictures of Mask from my mind, especially the ones from Wednesday afternoon of him ungrateful and snarling.

I locked the car and left it in the visitor's car park and scanned the blanket of grass.

My attention settled on Mikey and Jack first, who had erected their camouflage-print effort and were relaxing, savouring cups of coffee.

Stan, meanwhile, was shaking out his red sleeping bag and barking something indecipherable over at Ed.

Ed vanished back inside his tent, which was navy blue with one plastic window.

Right. This was my opportunity to try and reason with Ed and let him see why this performance was so important. *Come on. Get on with it!*

Pressing my lips together, I marched up to their semi-circle of camping gear.

"Hello you!" beamed Mikey, planting a coffee-flavoured kiss on my cheek. "I didn't think roughing it was your style."

I returned Jack's affectionate hug. "It's not."

Their eyes followed mine over to Ed's fluttering tent.

"Are you OK?" whispered Stan, wandering over to squeeze my hand. "Your dad told us everything." He was such a caring man. He would need to be, as he was a counsellor in his day job.

I squinted under the persistent rays of sun that were fighting their way through a bank of cloud, and cursed myself for not bringing my sunglasses.

"I know he did. I'm glad. There have been enough secrets."

I studied each of them in turn: Mikey with his craggy charisma, Jack's intent, pale gaze, and Stan in a black Def Leppard T-shirt.

I put on a confident smile. "I've come to try and change Ed's mind about playing in the band on opening night."

Mikey, Jack, and Stan swapped pessimistic looks.

"Good luck with that one," muttered Mikey. "I wouldn't be too optimistic though, if I were you. He's a stubborn bugger."

Jack nodded and started to say something as Ed's curly head poked out of his tent flap. His expression stiffened when he saw me. "Layla."

I planted my feet into the damp grass. "I wondered if we could have a word please."

Reluctantly, Ed emerged. His eye contact with the other

guys was non-existent. "I don't think there's anything else left to say."

My gaze burned steadily into him. "Sorry, but I disagree."

"So do we," piped up Mikey. "You could at least hear the lass out."

Ed's jaw tightened. "Who asked you anyway?"

"Whoa, whoa!" Stan stepped between them, his hands raised in the air in a surrender position. "Come on guys. Cool it." He turned back to me. "Does Harry know you're here, Layla?"

I shook my head. "All I'm asking is for five minutes of your time, Ed."

Apprehension was scrawled all over his features, but under the weight of Jack, Mikey, and Stan's disapproval, Ed finally gave out an irritated grunt. "OK. Give me a second."

He dived back through the flaps of his tent and returned wearing a pair of silver and amber wraparound sunglasses.

The rest of the band observed the pair of us awkwardly walking off, side by side.

Chapter Forty-Two

The woodland closed in as we left behind the stippled tents and odd camper van.

"I know why you want to talk to me," Ed admitted after a long pause, "but the answer is still no."

A bolt of disappointment coursed through me as we trampled over the grass.

I couldn't help myself. "Can't you see how selfish you're being? The rest of the guys have been really looking forward to playing at The Conch Club and it's a big deal for me too." Thoughts of Ed and my mother sneaking around behind Dad's back all those years ago played out in front of me. "Don't you think you owe us that much?"

Ed stopped walking. "Look, Layla, I'm really sorry about what happened. I should never have got involved with your mother. But bloody hell! It was thirty years ago."

He shuffled from foot to foot before moving off again, keeping his eyes concealed behind his sunglasses. I followed up behind him and we moved past an old fence that was thirsty for a coat of fresh paint.

The whole situation was one giant tangle of lies and deception, which was still having repercussions all these years later.

"You know you're not my biological father after all," I reasoned, hoping that this angle might cast some quiet optimism over the proceedings. "But don't you understand how tough this paternity situation has been on Harry and me?"

Ed fanned my frustration by increasing his walking pace. "Can't you just accept all this for what it is and move on? I made a mistake and just want to forget about it."

Was this man for real?

I'd never felt I knew Ed as well as Mikey, Stan, or Jack. The other three were always more gregarious, but Ed managed to give off a detached vibe. He was the pensive, self-conscious one out of them all, but his selfish attitude towards my dad, the other boys in the band, and me right now was stoking my anger.

I glared after him as he stepped over the remnants of an old tree trunk and thrashed through some overhanging branches. "Don't you think you ought to take off those sunglasses?"

It was like trying to have an in-depth conversation with a marathon runner.

"I often get migraines if I experience too much sunlight," he called over his shoulder.

I sighed. *Of course you do.*

"Well, things can't be left like this," I reasoned, struggling to keep an even tone to my voice.

I moved on again, ducking under some low branches and adjusting the strap of my shoulder bag. Ed was a shard of white T-shirt ahead of me now, ducking and dipping between the leaves that stuck out like pointing fingers.

"Please Ed, can't you give it some more thought..."

"Aaaargh! Shit!"

Suddenly, Ed was sprawled on the ground, legs akimbo. He whipped off his sunglasses and threw them to the ground.

"What's wrong?"

"Shit! Shit!"

I hurried over to him and knelt down. "What is it?"

Ed grimaced. "I've twisted my ankle on that sodding tree stump. I didn't see it."

"No wonder. I did tell you to remove your sunglasses."

Ed muttered something and winced.

"Can you put any pressure on it?" I asked, shrugging off my bag. "Here."

After a couple of clumsy attempts, I managed to angle him upright. Ed clung onto me. "I think I've really bruised it." He squeezed his eyes shut. "Bugger! I've left my mobile in the tent."

"I've got mine."

I rummaged in my bag and attempted to retrieve a signal. There wasn't one. So much for ringing one of the guys or Dad and asking for help.

"It's quite a way back to the campsite, but I'll try to help you as much as I can."

Ed let out a long groan. "I can't hobble back to the site in this state. Don't you know anyone that might live round here? I thought you were all about community in this part of the world."

I retrieved his sunglasses from the ground and thrust them towards him while balancing myself so that he could lean against me. "It's a remote area."

I shifted his weight and angled his right arm tighter around my neck. It felt so heavy and uncomfortable but I would have to endure.

Visions of the two of us blundering about all day in the woods made me want to cry out in frustration.

Then a noise startled me. It seemed to be coming from somewhere beyond the crude path we had been negotiating.

I listened carefully, hope blossoming. I realised it was Galen Waterfall, jangling like silver bells. "There is one person I know who stays in a cottage just beyond those trees."

Oh, bloody hell.

The prospect of having to ask Mask for anything again made dread and resentment pool in my stomach. But what was the alternative? Stay here, trapped in this woodland, with a hobbling selfish bass-guitarist throwback from the 1970s?

I took a determined breath. "Come on. We can get help there."

Chapter Forty-Three

Closing my ears to Ed's incessant whimpering wasn't easy, especially as he was leaning against me.

I guided him along, gripping onto the arm he had draped around my shoulders.

Fortunately, the unofficial woodland walk we were on wasn't a steep one.

"Not far now," I cajoled, fantasising about the bottle of still water languishing at the bottom of my bag. I was tempted to stop and give us a both a quick drink, but fought the temptation. Ed and I seemed to have developed a satisfactory if somewhat odd rhythm and were making steady progress that I was loath to interrupt.

At least it wasn't raining. That would have topped events off perfectly.

Ed shuffled his uninjured left foot and I made sure he was supported under his arm. I took a weary breath. "Nearly there."

He aimed a suspicious look at me, but his pale

expression relaxed a little when we emerged, clammy and exhausted, onto the edge of the road.

Behind us, the woods were a sea of green plumed branches.

Galen Waterfall gushed down the rocks and I guided Ed over to the slick, glistening stones to splash our faces.

I cupped my hands and supped the water swilling against my fingers. Ed slumped against the rock face. "Thank you."

I blinked at him.

"I mean, thank you for helping me."

I gave a faint nod. "You're welcome."

I pointed across the quiet road to Coorie Cottage. "We can get help over there."

Ed didn't appear convinced. "Is there anyone home? All the blinds are closed."

"Don't worry about that. They always are."

I dashed my wet hands down the front of my jeans. "Come on."

Ed was dubious. "Do you know the person who lives there?"

"Yes. Well, in a manner of speaking." If anyone thought they knew the real Mask, I would be very keen to meet them.

I gathered what little strength I had left before slipping my bag over my other shoulder and assisting the hobbling Ed across the road. I'd taken a sneaky look at my mobile at the waterfall but there still wasn't any reception.

Going to Coorie Cottage was our only option.

It was a relief when we reached Mask's front door. The windows glinted and the sun sparkled off the red, tiled roof.

Ed leaned against the side fence while I went up the steps to the door. He had to be in, or perhaps tending to his garden. If he wasn't, we would have no alternative but to wait until he returned.

I strained my ears and thought I could hear the whisper of a guitar from somewhere inside. I lifted my hand to knock on the door when Mask's silhouette appeared behind the glass.

Before he could say anything, I gushed with relief, "Mask, it's me. Layla Devlin. I need help. It's an emergency."

His deep Antipodean voice rumbled back through the closed door. "Is this your way of trying to gain entry to my house?"

Indignation shot through me. I narrowed my eyes and glanced over my shoulder at Ed who was slumped against the picket fence. "No, it bloody well isn't! I've got a man here with an injured ankle!"

I expected another caustic retort, but there was silence and then a fumbling sound. Through the front-door glass, I could make out his fingers reaching up to his face and then his hood was pulled upright. He must have been putting his mask back on.

The black door swung open. Mask stood there with his arms folded like a black-clad Ninja warrior.

I dashed back down the steps to assist Ed. He shrank backwards at the sight of Mask glowering down at him from the door.

"Are you sure this isn't the Bates Motel?" he hissed under his breath.

I couldn't help laughing. "Don't worry. He likes to make out he's a tough guy, but he's a pussycat really."

Ed looked doubtful.

"OK," I conceded, "maybe a sabre-toothed tiger."

"Are you two going to come in or are you going to have a tea party out there?" growled Mask. He watched me help Ed adjust his body weight and angle one arm again around my neck. "Oh, for goodness' sake, Ms Devlin. You're going to put your back out. Look. Stop there. Let me help."

My eyes popped with surprise as an irritated Mask strode over and ably assisted Ed up the steps.

I followed up the rear, amused by Ed's slack-jawed expression. Here he was, with a bruised foot or sprained ankle, being helped into a strange house by a man in a black masquerade mask.

Mask vanished inside the cottage with Ed. Moments later, he reappeared. His black hot eyes gazed steadily back at me. "Well, Ms Devlin, are you planning to join us or not?"

Chapter Forty-Four

M ask took Ed into his sitting room, off the hall to the right.

I could see Ed was making every effort not to stare up at his concealed face.

The hallway I was standing in was a plain vanilla affair with a pale wooden floor, while the sitting room was all steel-grey walls and matching carpet, dotted with black furniture.

Ed was now sprawled on Mask's squashy leather sofa, with two silver satin cushions supporting his back.

There was very little light filtering in through the closed venetian blinds, but what there was highlighted a dark Gothic-style fireplace with smouldering logs popping in the grate.

There was one black and white print above it, showing Sydney Harbour Bridge glittering like a strand of tinsel against the night sky. He certainly preferred the minimalist look.

A charcoal shelf ran along the opposite wall, housing a selection of musicians' biographies.

Mask's voice interrupted me as he spoke to Ed. "Here," he said, "put this bag of peas on your foot."

Ed thanked him and placed the frozen item against his sock. He let out a noise that was a combination of satisfied groan and delicate whimper.

Mask studied me. "Where were you trying to get to?"

"We were taking a walk through the campsite woods when I did this," interrupted Ed. "I'm staying with friends there for the weekend."

Describing the rest of the guys in Battalion as friends right now was pushing it, considering the current situation, but I didn't comment.

Mask loomed there, surveying Ed for a few more moments.

"Can I have a word?" he asked me, jerking his hood to indicate that we would be leaving the sitting room.

I followed him into his kitchen, which was located at the end of the hallway. It consisted of a marbled breakfast bar with chrome appliances, cream accents, and off-white cupboards.

Mask pushed the kitchen door closed behind me. "If your boyfriend isn't capable of negotiating a simple forest walk, I'd advise something more sedate next time."

I stared up at him. "Boyfriend?"

Mask's dark eyes washed over my bemused expression. "It's none of my business of course, but when people who are ill-equipped take off on ridiculous jaunts—"

A smile flickered across my lips. "Hang on. You think

I'm going out with Ed?" Mask's jaw tightened as I burst into a weary giggle. "You think we're a couple? I can assure you that we aren't."

Mask snatched two glasses from a cupboard and filled them with water. He thrust one at me and then took the other in to Ed, only to return with it seconds later. "Christopher Columbus is asleep. Stepping over twigs must have taken it out of him."

He glanced over his shoulder, indicating the sitting room as he closed the kitchen door again. "So if he isn't your partner, then who is he?"

I frowned as the puffs of cloud knitted together outside the kitchen window. At least the hessian roller blind in here was drawn up, presumably because the kitchen was located at the rear of the cottage and offered more privacy. "Why are you so interested to know who he is?"

Mask shrugged. "I'm just curious. You come to my door, looking dishevelled, with a strange man draped all over you."

I could feel my resentment bubbling. "For your information – not that it's any of your business – I happen to be dishevelled because I was helping Ed through thick undergrowth."

Mask continued to examine me.

"And he wasn't draped all over me, as you so colourfully put it. I'm not bloody psychic! How was I to know he'd injure his foot?" I snatched up my tumbler of water and took a sip. "If I'd known that, I would have packed my portable crutch."

I could have sworn Mask's mouth twitched for a second.

Annoyance sizzled in my veins. "Why the hell am I explaining myself to you anyway? You aren't exactly an open book."

"I don't follow."

I bit back an ironic snort. "That figures. You hide behind that mask, conceal yourself under that hood…"

Mask's angular jaw throbbed and I noticed the faintest peppering of stubble on his chin. "I don't hide."

"Well, that isn't the impression you're giving out."

I swung round to reach for the kitchen door handle when Mask's hand shot out and touched my bare arm. His fingers teased my skin. The sensation made me gasp out loud. Embarrassed, I turned it into a cough.

Mask gazed down at his fingers and snatched his hand away, as though he had been burnt. "You still haven't told me why you were in the woods with this guy."

I shoved my hands into the back pockets of my jeans. *Why was he so keen to know about Ed?*

I took in the faint, shadowy angles of his features under the hood. "Maybe I will tell you one day, when you decide to confide in me about all this." I lifted a hand and flapped it at his mask. "I tried to help you and all I got in return was my offer thrown back in my face."

I placed my hand on the door handle. "Trust is a two-way thing, you know."

I pulled open the door, catching a flickering movement out of the corner of my eye and the sound of slithering fabric.

"Oh, for pity's sake. You are so frustrating. Layla, turn around. Please."

I stopped, momentary shock springing through me at hearing him call me by my first name.

I turned, my eyes widening.

His hood was down and the black mask was hanging limp in his right hand.

Chapter Forty-Five

I'd caught a glimpse of Mask's face before, but that was from a distance when I'd surprised him in the garden.

Now, he was standing right in front of me, an odd expression pooling in those dark, spiky-lashed eyes. I could see his features clearly.

His black hair was in messy waves, reaching to the nape of his neck, and there was a quizzical slant to his eyebrows. His features carried a determined defiance.

My attention slid to the scar rivering down the right side of his cheek. I recalled from briefly seeing it before that it reached from his brow to the corner of his stern mouth, but close up, it seemed to melt away. It was unable to compete with the rest of his compelling, handsome features.

He ruffled a hand through his hair. "Satisfied?"

I swallowed, fighting to compose myself. "What do you want me to say?"

He shrugged, his shoulders rising and falling under his hooded top.

"How did it happen?"

Mask's face closed with pain. "One step at a time, Layla."

We hovered opposite one another, the meaning of what had just happened travelling backwards and forwards between us. It must have been a major event for him, to reveal his scar like that.

I detected another faint throb in his jaw as he continued to watch me.

I slipped out of the kitchen to check on Ed, who had turned over and was cuddling one of Mask's silk cushions. When I returned to see Mask seconds later, I closed the kitchen door behind me.

I had to tell him about Ed. OK, so he hadn't confided in me yet about how he had come to bear his scar, but the very fact that he had revealed it to me in the first place was undoubtedly a huge step – and he had decided to take it.

I let out a long breath of air as Mask indicated for me to sit opposite him at his breakfast bar and brought over two fresh glasses of water, clanking with ice cubes.

And that was when I unleashed my story in his sun-washed kitchen.

Mask listened. His moody features displayed a range of emotions, his scar only prominent to me when he angled his head in a certain way. "So your mother had an affair with that man currently sleeping on my sofa?"

I toyed with the russet and lime leaf ring on my finger that Dad had given me for my twenty-first. "Yep."

"And you were out strolling with him, taking in the countryside?"

I pulled a face. "I was trying to reason with him. Like I just told you, he's refusing to re-join the band to play on my opening night."

A dull throb decided to lay claim to my left temple at that point. I took a sip of my water, the ice cubes bumping against the front of my teeth. "I thought I'd try and have another word with him about it today when they all came back to Loch Harris for the weekend, which was originally supposed to be for another rehearsal."

"And that's why you were out walking with him?"

I nodded and then wished I hadn't. My head felt heavy.

"That's a bit selfish of him, isn't it?"

I sighed. "I think so, but then maybe I'm the one being selfish."

Mask examined me and blinked his spiky black lashes. "I don't think that's a word that could describe you."

My stomach did a weird squirm as I stared back at his handsome face, with its riverine red scar. "I don't notice it," I blurted. "Your scar, I mean." I wanted him to know that.

Mask dropped his eyes for a few seconds before looking back up at me. "You look a little tired. Why don't you go and take a seat in my spare room for a few minutes?"

"But the guys back at the campsite will be wondering where we are."

Mask rose from his kitchen stool, all long legs and flashing eyes. "I'll drop you both back there once you've recovered a bit."

My fingers reached up to my face. I felt as attractive as a melting waxwork. "I'm sorry we're causing you so much trouble."

Mask flicked me a look I couldn't decipher. "Not at all. I wouldn't have offered otherwise."

"Thank you."

He eased open the kitchen door and we both went along the hall to the sitting room. Ed was still sprawled on Mask's sofa like a puppet on invisible strings.

He let out a snort.

"A vision of loveliness," muttered Mask dryly.

There was a closed door back down the hallway and to the left of the kitchen. I'd spotted it before, assuming it was a cloakroom or cupboard.

Mask popped the gilded handle and guided me into his spare room, which was more like a music studio.

There was a small window at the back wall with the obligatory blind, but it was hitched halfway up. Milky light fed through, striking a piano in the corner, as well as a keyboard and two guitars. A microphone, threaded on a long stand, was seated beside them.

There were notebooks stacked on top of the piano and an old quilted bottle-green armchair in front of it, as well as a traditional piano stool.

Mask angled the chair away from his piano and reached for a blue and green tartan blanket that was draped over the back of it.

He urged me to sit down and I sank into its squishy cosiness.

"Here," he said, giving the blanket a shake and placing it over me. "It can get a little cool in this room."

"I'm twenty-nine, not ninety-nine," I joked.

His quizzical eyebrows shot up. "Just do as you're told for once. An alien concept, I know, but roll with it."

He disappeared out of the open door and returned moments later, clutching a mug of strong tea. "I've pepped it up with a little sugar."

I gratefully accepted it and took a long sip. "Thank you."

Mask nodded. "Finish your tea and then rest for a bit."

I watched him vanish from the doorway and took several more gulps of the hot, sweet tea. It hit the back of my throat, but tasted wonderful.

Stripes of mellow sunlight shimmied by my feet.

I drained the last of the tea and placed the mug on a nearside table, before flopping my head back and shutting my eyes for a moment. Images of Mac, The Conch Club, my dad, and Ed melted together behind my eyelids.

It was only when I heard Mask's voice that my eyes leaped open again and I pushed myself upright in the chair. I must have nodded off.

I blinked several times and pushed away the blanket. It slid off my knees and onto the carpet.

I rose out of the chair and moved towards the partially open music-room door. Ed was speaking now, his voice wafting down the hall to me. It was insistent, but Mask cut across what he was saying. "You need to do this for Layla. For her and her father."

My mouth fell open and I leaned one shoulder against the magnolia wall. Bloody hell! Mask was speaking to Ed, and it sounded like he was trying to persuade him to play on my opening night with the rest of the guys.

I squeezed through the gap of the open door, keen not to make any unnecessary noise.

I tiptoed towards the sitting room, the breath clouding at the base of my throat. Through the narrow crack, I could see Ed sitting on the edge of Mask's sofa with a wary expression.

Ed faltered. "But what I did … I feel so guilty about it all now, having an affair with a mate's wife. Then there was all this with Harry and Layla having to take a DNA test. I can't face it. I thought it might stay in the past – Tina and I, I mean – but what I did … what we did … it's all too much for me to deal with."

From somewhere in the room, Mask gave a frustrated sigh. "There you go again. Thinking only of yourself. What about Harry and Layla? Surely they've been through the ringer more than anyone during all of this?"

My heart clattered against my chest as I leaned back against the wall. What Mask was doing … what he was trying to do to help me…

I chewed my lip and refocused on the conversation taking place just inches away from me.

I angled one eye through the slim gap again and saw Mask move into my line of sight for a few seconds. He was sporting his black velvet mask again and the grey hoodie was up and over his face.

"Some secrets should stay in the past," snarled Ed, a guilty flint in his eyes. "If Tina wasn't such a vindictive cow…" Ed stared up at Mask, suddenly sounding braver than he looked. "And anyway, why are you so interested? It's got nothing to do with you."

Mask leaned forward, his concealed profile edging towards Ed. "I guess you have a point. But I don't like to see good people treated badly."

My stomach lurched as Mask moved in even closer and Ed shrank backwards. "You had a fling with Layla's mother."

Ed's pale blue eyes narrowed in his pinched face. "I'm not proud of what I did."

"Well, now is an opportunity to do something positive to atone for that mistake."

I swallowed a bubble of emotion as Mask spoke again. His Australian accent was laden with determination. "Layla is … Layla is a very special woman. The way I see it, you can at least show Layla and her father that you want to do something for them."

He took a step backwards and I lost sight of him through the sliver of the door.

"Nobody is asking you to re-join the band permanently. This is for one night. Don't you think you owe them at least that much? You would be doing the right thing for both of them."

Mask appeared briefly again through the crack in the door. "Whether you like it or not, you threatened their little family unit and they've had to fight to come back from it."

Ed swallowed and bunched up his fists.

Mask's words echoed around my head and I watched through wide, shocked eyes as he slid into view again. "You've got a chance after almost thirty years to put things right. Or at least, try to make amends." Mask gave the briefest shake of his head. "I wish I had that sort of opportunity."

What did he mean by that?

Ed uncoiled himself from the sofa and stood, his hands pushed into his jeans pockets.

They didn't exchange any more words, but both started towards the sitting room door, Ed limping slightly.

Stifling an emotional lump in my throat, I bolted back down the hall and into the music room before either of them realised I had been standing there.

Chapter Forty-Six

"**B**loody hell! We were about to scramble huskies and a helicopter!" yelled Mikey from across the campsite. "Where have you two been? Up Ben Nevis?"

Stan whipped off his mirrored sunglasses. "Harry has been going out of his mind with worry, Layla. We rang him to see if he knew where you both had got to."

Jack emerged from his tent and squinted past my shoulder. "Christ, Ed. What happened to you?"

A silence descended when they noticed the hooded, masked figure.

"He stumbled over a tree trunk," I explained in a rush, trying to fill the quiet. "He's OK but his foot is a bit bruised. We managed to get help."

The campsite tents flip-flapped as Mask maintained a discreet distance. "I'll be off, Layla." He lifted a hand to the other guys and then began to stride back towards his truck.

"Hang on," I called after him.

Behind us, the guys from the band clustered together in

a semi-circle and did their best impression of trying not to stare over at the imposing, mysterious stranger.

Mask's eyes blazed down at me and I cleared my throat. "I wanted to say thank you for all your help today."

"You're welcome."

I debated inwardly whether to confess that I knew about his valiant attempt to persuade Ed to perform with Battalion for me, before thinking better of it. I didn't want Mask to think of me creeping around his home and spying on him.

We hovered opposite one another, as the sound of a sizzling camp fire travelled up from nearby.

"Mask," I burst out, my fingers tumbling over one another. "What is the relevance of the name Belle Raven?"

Mask let out a dry laugh. "You aren't backward at coming forward, are you?"

A blush swept across my cheeks. "I'm sorry. It's just that you helped Ed and me today, and so I'd like to help you if I can."

Mask's chest heaved under the zip of his dark grey hoodie.

I could visualise his features from earlier, and all its arrogant angles.

"I won't get any peace if I don't tell you," he ground out. "That I know only too well." His mouth flatlined. "OK. You win. *Belle Raven* was the name of my first album."

"So this woman must be some sort of obsessed fan."

Mask let out an exasperated grunt. "That's where I think you could be wrong. That album was never released."

Mask and I moved a little further away, to where there

was a canopy of shimmering trees. "*Belle Raven* was named for my mother, Belle, and a boat my grandfather had owned called *Raven Warrior*. It was a working title for the album."

I frowned.

"Why was the album never released?"

His answer was brusque. "I had my reasons."

"So, not many people would have known about this album then?"

Mask's eyes narrowed. "That's right."

I grasped at the vain hope that he would confide in me again, the way I had with him about Dad and Ed. "So who the hell is this woman who is going by the name of Belle Raven?"

"I wish I knew. Thanks for trying to help."

He turned and strode back to his pick-up truck without another word.

Chapter Forty-Seven

I watched Mask leave and an odd squirming sensation took over my stomach.

There were so many questions demanding answers. How *did* Mask get his scar? Who was this Australian woman in town, and why was she using the name of his unreleased first album? And why had the album never been released in the first place?

"Layla?"

I spun round at the sound of Ed's hesitant voice from across the grass. He was squirming in a vivid green and yellow stripy plastic chair. His bruised foot was raised and propped up on a cooler box that was draped with a blanket. Mikey, Jack, and Stan were lurking close by.

Ed muttered something to them and one by one they vanished back inside their respective tents.

I wandered over. "How's the foot now?"

"I'll live."

I loitered beside him until Mikey emerged out of his tent

with another collapsible chair thrust under one arm. "Here you go, Layla."

He flexed it open, eyed Ed, and then vanished back through the flapping canvas.

I sat next to Ed.

"Thanks again for helping me this morning." He angled his elbows along the arms of his chair. "I wouldn't have blamed you if you had decided to knobble my other foot."

I found myself smiling.

I squinted up at the mid-afternoon sky, which was refusing to promise any more sunshine. It looked like we might have received our quota for the day.

"Yes. Well, I've got my reputation at The Conch Club to think about. I can't have the punters thinking I abandon poor bass guitarists in the wilds of Loch Harris when they're in desperate need of help."

Ed gave a snort. "In my case, I don't think many folks would have blamed you if you did." He dropped his eyes to the knees of his jeans and picked at an imaginary thread. "I feel like such a dick. The boys just explained to me who Mask is." He flopped his head back against the camping chair. "I'd heard of the guy of course, but I was so concerned about myself and my bloody foot..."

"Don't worry," I assured him. "Mask isn't one for idle chat."

I saw Ed's chest heave under the clean red T-shirt he'd changed into. There was a stutter in our conversation.

I dragged a weary hand down my face. "I could be doing with a hot shower. Oh, and I'd better ring Dad myself."

I knew Jack had spoken to him to tell him Ed and I were both OK, but knowing my father like I did, he wouldn't be satisfied until he had interrogated me himself.

Ed adjusted his propped-up leg. "Harry is a wonderful dad."

I eased myself out of my chair and tried to disguise the emotion in my voice. "Yes, he is."

I lifted my hand in an awkward wave. "Look after that foot, Ed."

I stooped over and peeked into each of the three tents, waving at the other guys, and had only made a few feet's progress over the fluttering carpet of grass towards the car park, when Ed's voice called after me. "Layla. Stop."

My shoulder bag clattered against my right side as I spun round.

"At least my foot isn't broken," he faltered, after a pause. He broke into a smile. "I won't have to hobble about on stage on your opening night and can let rip with the rest of them."

Chapter Forty-Eight

"How do I look?" beamed Dad, failing to conceal the flecks of tension in his silvery grey eyes.

He had chosen a pale blue cotton long-sleeved shirt and a pair of smart navy trousers.

I noted he had also followed my advice and had a trim at the local barber's. His hair was still a mix of longer layers in chocolate brown with a sift of grey running through, but it was much tidier.

"You'll sweep Molly off her feet," I grinned. "What time are you picking her up?"

Dad peered down at his watch for the tenth time in the last half an hour. "Seven-thirty. I'll set off in a minute. I don't want to be late."

I pressed my lips together.

Finton, where Molly lived, was fifteen minutes away from Loch Harris. He could have hung on for at least another twenty minutes. Bless him. He was jangling with excitement and nerves.

Dad gazed over my shoulder at my phone. "Crikey, Layla. Are all those emails to do with The Conch Club?"

I shifted round on Dad's sofa. "Apart from these two, trying to sell me Viagra."

He laughed and collected his car keys from the coffee table. "OK, sweetheart. I'm off. Pace yourself, all right?"

I performed a mock salute.

"And please don't forget to lock up on your way out."

He dashed a kiss against my cheek and vanished out the front door in a swirl of dusky aftershave.

I snapped my mobile shut and flicked on Dad's hall lamp for when the dirty stop out eventually made it home.

Autumn was still several weeks away and the trees would soon be shifting and twisting into shades of amber and russet. There would be that familiar, earthy tinge to the air too, which reminded me of pumpkins and fireworks.

My pink and white Converse trainers took me back up the lane.

Dad had been surprised but delighted when I told him of Ed's decision to re-join the band on the big night, and had insisted on putting all of them up at his place when they came for the show. Yes, even Ed.

It would be cramped, it would be beer-fuelled, and testosterone would be raging, but it was agreed by all that it was a good idea.

As I rounded the corner of the lane, the roof of my cottage poked through the tangle of tree tops, but all I could see in my mind was Mask. I fought to ignore the zinging sensation in my stomach. I would get home, rustle myself up a nutmeg-flavoured hot chocolate and work through my emails.

I let myself in and reached for my table lamp in the hall. I kicked off my shoes and watched them skitter across the carpet. Having thrown on my pyjamas and savoured the swirls of cream lacing the top of my mug of hot chocolate, I settled myself down in front of my computer at the rear of my sitting room.

I'd just finished replying to a Glasgow newspaper with background information on the members of Battalion when my phone screen lit up with a mobile number I didn't recognise.

I heaved a frustrated sigh and answered it.

It was Wendy Goodman, owner of the River Lawn Bed & Breakfast. "My Australian guest that you've been concerned about," she babbled in hushed tones. "I think there's something going on with her."

I sat up straighter in my swivel chair. "Wendy? Are you OK? Slow down."

"I overheard her by accident," she gulped, her breathing heavy in my ear. "She was in her room tonight, talking to someone on her phone."

I waited until Wendy was a little more composed. "Was she walking about Mask?"

"Yes. Definitely."

"Could you make out what she was saying?"

Wendy paused before speaking again. "She said she was going to head up to Coorie Cottage tonight to confront him."

I blinked. "Confront Mask? About what?"

"I've no idea."

I jumped out of my chair and began to pace. "Do you know what time she was planning to go up there?"

"She said around eight-thirty. She still has a hire car."

My imagination screeched into overdrive. *Oh hell.* Maybe she was some crazed fan after all, who thought he was ignoring her.

Although Mask had said his first album *Belle Raven* had never been released, if she was an ardent fan of his, she would most likely know that, which might explain why she was going by that particular name.

"I don't have a mobile number for him," I said, beginning to panic. "And even if I did, the phone reception up there is awful." I swung around, my hair flying loose. "Is this woman still in her room?"

"Yes, I made an excuse about having to check she had clean towels."

I whipped my wrist up to check my watch. It was 7.45 p.m. This woman was intending to be at Coorie Cottage in forty-five minutes' time. I knew that if I was quick and threw some clothes on, I could be out the door in five minutes and on the road.

Something told me I had to get there before she did.

Chapter Forty-Nine

As I got ready to head out, Wendy's departing words circled my mind. "Don't you think you ought to notify the police, in case things kick off?"

I suspected Wendy might have been binge-watching too many gritty crime dramas, but I appreciated her concern and knew she was talking sense. Nevertheless, I shuddered at the thought of police cars and sirens wailing into the night and swarming all over Coorie Cottage.

While I pulled my shoes on with one hand, I scrolled through my contacts to locate local policeman Tom Bateman's number with the other.

Tom had been so caring and compassionate when Mac died, and he had been enthusiastic and helpful when I had been commissioned to write a feature about 'A Day in the Life of a Countryside Copper' for a Sunday newspaper supplement.

Considering we'd also been at school together, I felt like

I wasn't being presumptuous … well, hopefully not too much, anyway.

Tom's home phone rang out, but I did manage to reach him on his mobile. "But I've just come off duty," he moaned into my ear, "and I promised Douglas we'd have a quiet night in with a takeaway."

My silence was deafening.

"Oh Layla," he ground out. "You owe me big time for this."

I slid on my denim jacket. "Thank you so much, Tom. A bottle of plonk and a takeaway will be on me. I'm on my way to pick you up now."

I steered my car over to the kerb where Tom was waiting under one of the town square's street lights.

He gave his close-cropped dark head a mild shake as he clambered into the passenger seat. "Let me get this straight. We're heading up to Coorie Cottage again, because of a hunch."

I flicked a look sideways at Tom as I indicated out onto the main road. Roofs pricked the starry sky and silhouettes of moss-dotted brick walls and farmhouses slid past.

He listened while I expanded about Wendy's Australian guest, the album title name this woman was using and my feeling that she had been responsible for the previous disturbance up at Mask's cottage.

Tom considered what I had told him. "A stalker?"

I negotiated the country road, noting how the darkness

made the hills appear like great slumbering giants. "I wondered about the stalker thing too."

"And why are you so bothered, Ms Devlin?"

My attention flitted to my rear-view mirror, even though I knew there was no traffic currently behind me. "What do you mean?"

Tom's full lips twitched. "Even at school you were always the one who would rescue an insect or stand up for the shy kids."

I blushed. "And your point is?"

"I know you're a compassionate soul, but this is different." Tom fired me a look out of the corner of his hazel eyes. "This is the second time you've shot up to Coorie Cottage to help this guy – or at least, the second time I know about."

I wriggled in my seat. "It's called being neighbourly."

Tom's eyebrows twitched. "Is it now?"

I ignored his comment and swung my car around the corner.

There was an orange glow coming from Mask's sitting room window and his pick-up truck was stationed, as usual, down by the left side of the cottage.

Apart from us, there was no other vehicle to be seen.

"This woman has a car," I said, easing to a stop and turning off the ignition. "Wendy said she'd hired one."

We climbed out and I locked my car, the scent of a burnished night mingling with my trepidation. I wasn't sure what I thought I would be able to do, but the compunction to help Mask – to show him that someone cared – was overwhelming.

When I knocked on his front door, a hall light came on and I could see his tall figure wavering through the glass. "It's Layla and I have Tom Bateman, a local police officer, with me."

From what I could make out through the bevelled panes of glass, Mask was pulling on a hoodie that he had retrieved from a hook on his coat rack.

The door eased open and Mask materialised behind it.

Tom was beside me on the step and eyed him with a quizzical stare.

"Is there something wrong?"

I noted he hadn't put on his mask, but the hood he was wearing was tugged forwards as far as it would go, which made it impossible for us to see his features. All that was visible was the very odd flash of his black dark-lashed eyes.

"There could be," I admitted, sharing a glance with Tom.

Tom offered a slight smile. "May we come in, sir?"

Mask's attention travelled between Tom and me for several more seconds before he took a step backwards. "All right. Please go into the sitting room."

Mask was just closing the front door when there was a squealing of tyres from outside and a shrill voice erupted through the darkness.

"Murderer!" someone screamed. "You're nothing but a murderer!"

Chapter Fifty

Mask barrelled out of his door and stopped on the top step.

His shoulders stiffened.

A woman dressed in a blue fleece and beige trousers and walking boots was jumping out of a revving white Ford Ka. She had bobbed red hair and her freckled face was contorted in fury.

Beside her in the passenger seat was another woman. She appeared entranced by the proceedings that were unfolding through the windscreen.

She clambered out. I could see that she was a few years younger than her companion. She was sporting a pink and yellow beret, which rested further back on top of straw-blonde choppy hair, and was dressed like a student in a pair of glossy black Doc Marten boots.

At first I struggled to comprehend the awful things that were being shouted. Then I noticed her delve into the rainbow bag over her shoulder and retrieve a notebook and pen. She must be a journalist.

My attention travelled back to the redhead.

She slammed shut her car door and jabbed an accusing finger at Mask. "That's him! Go on, Shelley. Ask him!"

Shelley, the beret-wearing blonde, approached Mask. "Rafe?" she asked, excitement rising in her voice. "Are you Rafe Buchanan?"

Under the dark sky, Tom and I swivelled on the step to look at Mask but he didn't reply. He just stood there like a mannequin.

The redheaded woman bared her teeth at him. "Of course it's him! I told you it was. He's nothing but a murderer!"

There was that word again. I flinched, trying to pretend I hadn't heard it.

Tom marched down the granite steps towards her. "Excuse me, but you can't go throwing accusations like that around."

"Accusations? That's a laugh. He's guilty." Her hard, ghostly eyes slid over Tom. "And who the hell are you anyway?"

"Police Constable Tom Bateman."

Her white chin jutted forward. She glowered up at me. "And who is she?"

For a moment, I couldn't articulate anything. My mind felt as though it were battling through a thick fog. Why was she saying these terrible things? And why was Mask not protesting? Why wasn't he yelling at her to stop?

I willed Mask to look at me, to reassure me. But he

didn't. His hood remained pulled over his features. There was an air of defeat around him.

"I'm Layla Devlin," I replied, gathering myself together. "And I take it you're…" I paused for effect. "Belle Raven?"

She appeared thrown that I knew. She dashed a lock of hair out of her eyes. "The most important thing is that he knows who I am, don't you, Rafe?"

Mask's body language was stiff and he struggled to speak. "I want you to leave. Now."

"I bet you do," she scoffed. "Not nice when your past comes back to haunt you, is it?"

What past? What was she talking about?

Beside her, Shelley was scribbling something in her notebook. She fixed Rafe with a faux-conciliatory gaze. "I'm Shelley Fraser. Look, Mr Buchanan, why don't you just agree to speak to me? It will be easier for everyone that way."

The redhead indicated to Shelley and said, as though we hadn't already guessed, "She's a journalist."

I eyed the girl. "Who with?"

"What?"

"What paper are you with?"

The blonde girl blanched. "Er … *The Loch Harris Tribune.*"

I frowned over at her. I was on friendly terms with the staff there but I didn't recognise her. Maybe she was a new recruit.

I turned back to Mask and inwardly pleaded with him to tell me what was going on. *Rafe Buchanan? Was that his real name?*

But he refused to even look at me. Instead, he retreated back into his doorway. Then he turned his annoyance on me. "Is this why you two came up here this evening? You knew that she would be coming?"

I rubbed my brow, frustration and fear gnawing at me. "I wanted to help you. I found out this Belle Raven character was intending to come up here and—"

Mask's dark eyes glittered in the shadows. "I want you all to leave. Right now."

My mouth popped open. "But can't you tell me what's going on? Maybe I can help."

I shrank backwards at his snarling tone. "I'm not a sodding charity case, Layla! What? Does it make you feel better about yourself to help the local weirdo?"

I swallowed hard. "I've never thought of you that way. I never would."

Tom placed a hand on my shoulder. "Come on. Let's go."

I hesitated, my stomach rolling.

"And as for you two," barked Tom to the two women through the dark, "I suggest you leave right away, unless you fancy a night in the cells."

The Australian woman snatched open her door. "You haven't heard the last of this, Rafe. Even though you've run away to Scotland, you can't escape what you did."

Mask watched the reporter dart back inside the car. I could see his chest rising and falling under his hooded top. "It wasn't my fault," he erupted, baring a flash of white even teeth. His breathing was ragged. "I did what I could!"

I made a move towards him, but his cold stare dared me to go any further.

"Layla," said Tom, an edge to his mild Scottish burr. "Let's go."

Mask fired me the briefest look as he retreated back into the cottage, and as he banged the door, the optimistic feeling that I was finally getting to know him trickled away, leaving only a painful thud in my chest.

It turned out I didn't know him at all.

Chapter Fifty-One

I dropped Tom outside his flat on the outskirts of the town square.

As I drove away, his warning rang in my ears. "Don't get involved, Layla. If there has been any criminality, it's up to the law to address it."

I had opened my mouth to argue, but Tom stuck his head through the open window.

"Sometimes people don't want to be helped. Or at least, they want to try and deal with things on their own first."

I had nodded, but still wasn't convinced.

My bruised feelings crowded in on me as I pulled up outside my cottage and killed the engine.

I sat for a moment in the car with the dark pressing in on all sides. Why was I so affected by tonight's events? Why did I feel so deflated? It couldn't be true, could it? Mask couldn't have actually murdered someone?

I let myself inside and clicked on the hall lamp, sinking down onto the carpet and yanking off my shoes. I had buggered things up spectacularly, charging up to Coorie Cottage with Tom like we were Batman and Robin.

What had I expected to achieve? Make a citizen's arrest of that woman? Save the day? Have Mask sweep me into his arms?

Whoa.

I rocked back on the hall floor, staring at my boots lying in a tangled heap in front of me. *Where the hell did that come from?*

I was tired. I was emotional. I was bursting with apprehension over the opening of The Conch Club.

I balled my fists and rubbed at my eyes for a few seconds, only to flinch when my mobile chirruped in my bag. It was Dad.

"How did your date with Molly go?" I asked, pushing my voice into what I hoped was a normal range.

"Oh Layla." I could hear him smiling into my ear. "She's an amazing woman – gorgeous, funny, talented…"

I imagined his tanned face flushed with excitement and those pale grey eyes of his twinkling. "You're on for a second date then?"

"You betcha," enthused Dad. "I explained to her that the guys are coming back tomorrow for the weekend for another band rehearsal, but I'm taking her out on Monday night."

He fell silent for a moment. "Are you OK, love?"

I sat up straighter in the hall. "Of course I am." Crikey, he was good. I was certain I had drawn on all my best acting skills and yet Dad still sensed a certain reticence in my tone. Must be a superpower you are awarded when you become a parent.

"Well, as long as you're sure," said Dad, not sounding reassured. "You get to bed. I'm worried you're taking on too much."

"Isn't it supposed to be me who says that to you?"

I couldn't burden him with my woes. It wasn't fair, especially as he was so happy. Dad hadn't had a date for eons and I knew I would feel awful if I took the gloss off his wonderful evening with Molly.

I listened to him chuckle into my ear. "I think you might be onto something there."

I wished him a good night and rang off. I paused for a few moments, gazing down at the blank black screen of my phone. Then I plopped it back into my bag.

Once I'd wriggled out of my top and trousers and tossed them into my wicker laundry basket, I threw on an old T-shirt and tracksuit bottoms.

I clattered about in my kitchen, the noise of the brewing kettle oddly comforting while I tried not to replay tonight's events in my head. All I could see was the haunted edge in Mask's eyes when he saw that mysterious woman.

Or was it horror that some previous crime from his past was finally catching up with him?

No. Surely not.

It couldn't be true about Mask. I just wouldn't accept it. She must have made some sort of serious mistake.

I swirled my camomile tea bag round and round in the mug, lost in a cobweb of thoughts and assumptions. But if she hadn't been certain of what she was saying, why take a local reporter along with her?

I considered Shelley again. I had never heard of her at the local paper, nor seen a byline of hers in it.

I dumped the used tea bag in the bin before taking the mug into the sitting room. What the hell should I do? I wanted to know about Mask, didn't I?

I just wish he'd felt he could have told me himself.

I fired up my computer, my fingers hovering over the black keyboard before I sat back for a moment in my swivel chair and stared at the screen.

Did I really want to do this?

I lowered my hands to touch the keys. How could I not do it? I had to see if I could find out anything about Mask's past.

I steeled myself and tapped the name 'Rafe Buchanan' into the search engine.

Chapter Fifty-Two

My eyes were met at first by a distinguished-looking elderly gent who had won some prestigious gardening competition in Canada, and another Rafe Buchanan who had lived in Ireland 200 years ago.

I tapped my mouse and scrolled down the page a little further.

An image made me shoot forward in my chair.

What was that?

It was a photograph of a handsome, dark-haired man holding a Rio Natural acoustic guitar. There was no scar running down the right side of his face.

I enlarged the photograph and leaned in closer to the screen. Oh, bloody hell! It was him! It was Mask.

I scanned the caption of the photograph.

Up and coming singer/songwriter Rafe Buchanan (34) pictured at his gig in The Roundhouse, Sydney on Saturday night.

The picture had appeared in *The Sydney Enquirer* newspaper on Monday 19 December 2016.

I was so preoccupied with the easy charm he was exuding, exacerbated by his white loose cotton shirt, tweed waistcoat, and faded jeans, I almost didn't notice two women's faces in the crowd behind him.

Then one sprang out at me.

I reached for my mug of tea and squinted at the picture again. There was something familiar about the pointed angle to her chin...

"Shit. It's her!" I said aloud. "It's the Australian woman from tonight."

Her red hair was longer in the photo and not styled in the severe bob she favoured now, but it was definitely her.

As I examined the picture again, I could make out the recognisable, abrupt tilt to her nose. My attention swivelled from where she was positioned behind Rafe to another woman hovering in the crowd beside her. She was pretty, with an open expression and long, swishy brunette hair. She was gazing at Rafe with what could only be described as adoration.

I clicked away from the photograph and searched further down the page for more references to Rafe Buchanan.

My eyes were beginning to feel gritty and threatening to surrender to sleep, but I pushed on.

Next to appear was a review of his never released debut album *Belle Raven*, in a Melbourne-based independent music magazine called *Making Waves*.

The critic had described his music as "haunting, with

lyrics that speak to the soul. A paradise for the senses". He had gone on to award it a glowing five stars out of five. So why hadn't it been released?

I frowned and moved the cursor further down the screen. There were more references to this eagerly anticipated album by the music press, as well as mentions of successful gigs in Australia and New Zealand.

There were also reports about how Rafe's music videos were finding an audience on social media and the fact that this talented musician, who had played the grottiest pubs and busked on street corners, was finally on the threshold of something big.

And then nothing.

My eyebrows rocketed in disbelief at my computer screen. All the hype, all the acclaim, all the promise of a huge music career had vanished.

At one time lauded as the next Ed Sheeran, he'd simply disappeared. It was as though Rafe Buchanan had evaporated.

Frustrated, I clicked my mouse and slid through another series of pages. But there was nothing further, and definitely nothing pertaining to any crimes either.

There were no reports of his arrest. There were no fevered articles about court cases or tawdry accusations.

A kernel of worry insisted on pushing its way up. What if he had done something awful, but escaped from Australia to Scotland? I acknowledged it was possible, but refused to give it credence.

Perhaps Rafe had experienced some sort of mental breakdown and had chosen to avoid the limelight?

Or maybe this Belle Raven woman was a spurned lover after all, trying to get revenge on him by ruining his career?

But that still didn't answer the question of how he'd got his scar.

My mind was reeling with all sorts of questions and possibilities.

I flopped back in my chair and ran a hand down my face.

It was too late to call Wendy at her bed and breakfast now. But first thing tomorrow morning I would ring her. I had to speak to her again about that guest.

Chapter Fifty-Three

Afrer finishing some business for The Conch Club opening, I rang Wendy.

Before I could give her a potted explanation of last night's events, she burst my bubble of growing optimism. "She's gone."

"What?"

"Belle Raven – or whatever her real name is. She's left. Checked out."

I shoved my half-eaten bowl of cereal across the kitchen table. "You have got to be joking. When was this?"

"First thing this morning. She must have sneaked out while I was preparing breakfast."

Wendy went on to explain that the woman had paid for her stay in full, in cash, and deposited her payment and her room key in an envelope behind the reception desk.

"Oh shit! Now what do I do?"

My mind fluttered back to last night and the so-called

female reporter who had accompanied her. "You don't know where she might have gone?"

"Nope, sorry. But I could ask around some of the other bed and breakfast owners in the area?"

"Thanks Wendy. That would be great."

I hung up and began rifling through the contacts on my phone, searching for the telephone number of the local newspaper, only to be told when I rang that Shelley Fraser was not employed as a reporter there.

According to the paper's editor, she kept pestering them for a job as a journalist and promising them exclusive scoops, which never materialised or had any substance.

I crossed my fingers that there was nothing in Mask's history that would be of benefit to her.

I took a mouthful of soggy cereal and grimaced.

The remainder of Thursday saw me making a series of calls to suppliers, confirming the delivery of LED candles and jars for each table in The Conch Club, as well as alcohol, soft drinks, and snacks.

Faith took on the job of ensuring the local advertising was all in place and that fellow Loch Harris businesses were displaying the posters and handing out the fliers she had designed.

I also pitched a few freelance article ideas to some magazine editors I knew.

Who knows, I thought to myself, *The Conch Club might become so successful, that I won't have to continue with my freelance journalism*. But when I considered this further, I knew that was impossible. I enjoyed writing far too much to abandon it.

Friday swung around, bringing with it frequent showers and damp leaves.

The late July rain hung like pearls suspended from the trees and knotted branches. The air was brisk, laced with the zinging scent of wet grass.

I bet the Battalion guys will be relieved they aren't camping up by Galen Waterfall in this, I thought to myself with a brief smile.

My thoughts then zipped to Rafe – it was strange, referring to him like that…

Was it worth giving the local car hire company a ring, to see if they had any details about this Belle Raven woman?

Even though I felt guilty for abandoning a half-written email to a folk singer in Dundee who was enquiring about a future spot at the club, I looked up the number for the Loch Harris car rental company, Wheelie Good.

I suspected it was company policy not to divulge personal information about their customers, but I decided that as I was fumbling around for any leads, it wouldn't hurt to ask anyway.

I rolled my eyes at my flickering computer screen as the woman I spoke to delivered her well-rehearsed diatribe about client confidentiality and refused to tell me anything.

The air in my chest deflated like a balloon. I decided to

try a different tack. "You're telling me that nobody by the name of Belle Raven has hired a car from your recently?"

"As I told you, madam," sighed the bored voice, "I'm not permitted to say."

"Right," I replied after a moment. "I thought as much. Sorry to trouble you." I was about to hang up when I decided to try again, more urgently this time. "Look, I'm not exaggerating when I say that this woman is … well, I think she could be a threat to someone's safety."

There was a sigh into my ear from the other end of the line. "You did say the name she was going under was Belle Raven?"

I held my mobile a little tighter to my right ear. "That's correct. As you might have guessed, that isn't her real name."

She let out a low breath and I could hear her tapping at her computer keyboard. "Well, what I can tell you is that I've been tasked with electronically filing hires for the last three weeks – oh, joy – and that name hasn't appeared."

So she must have used her real name to hire a car or she had used another car hire firm.

The receptionist sounded sympathetic. "Sorry."

I put down my phone and pulled a frustrated face. If she was so intent on causing Rafe grief, surely she wouldn't just up and leave Loch Harris like that? Perhaps that was just what she wanted people to think.

Wendy had promised to ask around the local hotels and bed and breakfast places to see if she had booked into one of them. I would just have to be patient and wait to hear back from her.

In the meantime, I'd offered to rustle up some sandwiches and filled rolls to take round to Dad's for us all to have for lunch.

I fetched the seeded brown bread I'd bought, together with a bag of floury baps, and raided my fridge for tomatoes, cucumber, salmon, tuna, and a tub of egg and cress.

While I swept a knife across the top of the glowing yellow butter, I struggled not to dwell on a dark-eyed musician. It wasn't easy.

There were barks of laughter, intermittent twangs of guitar strings, and thrashes of drums emerging from Dad's garage by the side of his cottage when I arrived.

The garage door was flung open and inside there were cables slithering around the concrete floor.

Dad was stationed behind his glittery drum kit, spinning the sticks idly between his fingers. Mikey was adjusting his microphone stand and, positioned either side of him, were Ed and Stan on bass and rhythm guitars respectively. To the left of Ed was Jack on keyboards.

I took a couple of steps backwards so they wouldn't see me and hovered by the side of the garage. I could feel the vibrations from their stirring guitars reverberating through me while I leaned there against the wall.

"OK guys," said Mikey. "Let's go again after three."

I heard him mutter and then Dad's drum solo cranked

up in volume before Mikey's raspy, rocker voice began singing and Ed and Stan's guitars broke in over the top.

Mikey's vocals continued to rise and fall until Jack performed a frenzied chorus on his keyboard. It reminded me of rainwater striking my cottage roof.

"Guys. Guys!" shouted Dad all at once over the music. "Stop a sec."

The song screeched to a halt. "Come on," urged Dad. "We can do better than this for my girl, can't we?"

A whoosh of emotion and grateful pride shot through me like a whirling hurricane.

I hitched the strap of my bag higher onto my shoulder and prepared to appear from around the corner of the garage.

Ed's next words made me stop in my tracks. "Layla is a credit to you, Harry. She's a wonderful young woman."

There were murmurs of agreement from the others, which made my throat constrict even more.

I composed myself and then barrelled round to greet them as though I had just arrived. "Hi guys," I beamed, sniffing back a stray tear that was desperate to escape down my cheek. "Sounding great."

Mikey performed a mock bow. "You're too kind."

Dad eased himself out from behind his drum kit. "I think we're getting there."

"Yeah," muttered Jack, idly plonking at his keyboard. "A certain someone has exacting standards."

The other band members all turned to look at my dad and I laughed at his surprised expression. "Power going to his head, then?"

"Just a bit," smiled Ed.

I surveyed them all and clapped my hands. "Right. I hope you're all hungry, as I've made enough sandwiches and filled rolls to feed the Loch Harris pipe band."

As I watched Dad and the rest of the guys stride out of the garage towards the cottage, all denim and faded T-shirts, I knew that on opening night they would do not only me but also The Conch Club proud.

Chapter Fifty-Four

After lunch, the air was still carrying the promise of more showers and the burgeoning steel sky was testament to that, but from inside the garage came snorts of laughter and then Battalion cranked up their guitar playing. There was a series of sharp drum thrashes and then Mikey's gravelly voice erupted, singing lyrics about love at first sight.

It was obvious they were like a bunch of kids enjoying themselves.

I shouted out from Dad's cottage doorway that coffee and tea would be on the way soon and my message was greeted with enthusiastic shouts and thumbs up.

In the meantime, I took the opportunity to check out my emails on my phone. I found myself distracted by Faith's update on ticket sales for opening night (thank goodness I'd hired that huge marquee for the inevitable overspill.) There was also a positive response from a magazine features editor about my suggestion to cover the story of the former soldier who rescued abandoned dogs from war-torn countries.

Then I scrolled down further to deal with a reply from the lighting hire arm of the marquee company, asking me to confirm what style of lights I would prefer.

I sank back on Dad's sofa and tapped through their online catalogue until I located my preferences of the silver star-shaped lights for the boathouse itself and the heavier white carriage lights to decorate the jetty.

I had only just dashed off an email to the dog rescuer, requesting to interview him, when my mobile rang.

I didn't recognise the number.

My body hardened when I realised it was Shelley Fraser

"How did you get this number?" I prickled, pushing myself upright on Dad's couch.

Her tone was light. "I dropped by your cottage just the other day but you weren't at home. Then I tried your nearest neighbours. They were very helpful."

Clem and Norrie.

"I think they assumed I wanted to speak to you about publicity for your new business."

Yes, and I bet you failed to put them right on that score, I concluded darkly. I set my shoulders. "I rang the local paper. Apparently you aren't employed by them."

There was a pregnant pause down the line. "Well, not yet," she blustered. "But I'm sure I will be if I can successfully follow up on the juicy stuff."

I bet she would too.

My voice was dismissive. "Look, I really don't know why you're contacting me."

I could hear her smug smile. "Well, you seemed rather chummy with Mr Buchanan."

Chummy?

I took a thoughtful breath. I had to keep my emotions in check when dealing with her. "We're acquaintances, that's all."

"Right, and you are aware that Angela Burrows is making extremely serious claims about Mr Buchanan?"

My brow furrowed. "I was there, remember? I did hear what she said." It took a moment for my brain to catch up. My optimism grew. "Hang on. Angela Burrows? Is that the name of the woman you were with?"

Shelley Fraser sounded flustered and annoyed at herself for revealing more of her story than she had intended to. Her tone was dismissive as she tried to recover herself and focus on me. "What do you know about Rafe Buchanan's background?"

"You tell me," I parried back. "You're the aspiring reporter with all the answers."

"Ms Burrows claims Mr Buchanan murdered someone close to her."

From outside, the throbbing sound of music from Dad's garage made me start. It seemed to emphasise her words.

I faltered, trying to conceal the returning trepidation from the other night. Someone close to her? "Why aren't you speaking to Angela Burrows?"

Shelley's voice became defensive. "I can't locate her. She's gone off grid."

Off grid? What was she? An MI5 spook?

"Don't you think that's rather suspicious?" I pushed, detecting a frisson of hesitancy. "Surely if there was a real story there, this woman would have kept in touch with you?"

Shelley fell quiet.

"Well, doesn't that tell you something?"

Shelly started to talk again but I interrupted. "I think this Angela Burrows has got a hidden agenda of some kind and she was trying to use you to get at Rafe Buchanan."

Sensing I was starting to throw her off-balance, I carried on. "It's obvious, isn't it? As soon as you asked her for proof of what she was saying, she got nervous and disappeared."

I jumped up, my insides whirring around. "Sorry, Ms Fraser, but I can't help you. Oh, and here's some advice. Next time you try to follow up a story, I suggest you check out the validity of your sources first."

She started to say something else but I terminated the call.

Shelley Fraser was blundering about in the dark. She was only armed with the briefest of information – no facts – and now that this Angela Burrows had done a disappearing act on her, presumably to deal with things on her own terms, Shelley was trying to claw a story out of the ashes.

But it still begged one question. Why was this woman so desperate to sully Rafe's name?

If Rafe was guilty of something awful, why hadn't this Angela called him out on it, instead of going to a second-rate freelance reporter and then doing a disappearing act?

Dark thoughts gnawed at the edges of my mind.

Perhaps it was because she was seeking out some sort of retribution of her own.

I gathered up my bag. I was going to look into this Angela Burrows myself.

Chapter Fifty-Five

As I strode past the garage, the guys were taking a break and discussing the state of the music charts.

Dad spotted me. "Where are you off to?"

"Just got a couple of things to chat over with Faith. I won't be long."

Mikey did a cheeky wink. "Hope you're back in time to make us that brew you promised."

I pointed my hand towards Dad's cottage. "You know where the kettle is."

Their laughter and teasing noises grew quieter as I headed back down the lane to retrieve my car. There had been another light shower and everything from the trees to the hedges looked like they had been polished to a high finish.

I had got as far as Norrie and Clem's front garden hedge when Norrie bobbed up from the front lawn. "All going well with your disco, lass?"

I tried not to laugh, but couldn't be bothered to explain. "Yes, it's all on track, thanks Norrie. You and Clem OK?"

"We're hanging together."

I started to move off, but Norrie wouldn't be deterred. "Have you heard the latest rumours about that Mask character? Terrible business."

I paused and swung round. I thought I could guess what they might be, but still asked the question anyway. "What rumours?"

Norrie beckoned me closer to his hedge. It was spotted with the remnants of shiny raindrops. "Rumours are rife that he murdered someone."

My mouth flatlined. This Angela Burrows/Belle Raven character was certainly doing all she could to make sure Mask was the talk of Loch Harris. I greeted his comment with what I hoped was an authentic-sounding, dry laugh. "Who's been saying that?"

He dropped his voice to an audible whisper, even though the only company we had was the surrounding trees and grass verges. "Some woman who's staying at a friend of our Sophie's."

I shot forward, almost sending myself toppling into Norrie's manicured hedge. "Sophie?"

Norrie studied me as though I were trying to communicate with him in Mandarin. "Sophie. Our daughter-in-law. Married to our Ross?"

The optimism in my voice was fighting to escape. "Oh. Of course. Right. And does Sophie's friend own a hotel or...?"

"A new wee bed and breakfast place near Finton,"

clarified Norrie. "Sophie said it's a sweet wee place, all hanging baskets and floral curtains."

Was it her? I tried to sound calm. "You don't happen to know what this woman looks like or remember her name? The guest, I mean?"

"What woman? For God's sake man, the poor lass is getting soaked!" Clem asked, bustling up behind Norrie.

I glanced up at the sky, only just realising that another shower was beginning to splat onto the lane and me. I couldn't let it deter me.

"Clem, you don't happen to know who this woman is who's staying with Sophie's friend at her B&B?"

Clem hit Norrie with one of her disapproving glares. "I can see someone has been gossiping again. Honestly man, you can't hold your own water!"

"I'm not gossiping, woman. I'm merely making polite conversation."

"Aye, sure you are," said Clem, pinching her mouth.

I hopped from foot to foot in agitation, unphased by the summer rain. "This woman," I began as patiently as I could muster. "The one who Sophie was talking about. Do you know who she is?"

Clem's ample bosom strained under the confines of her buttoned coat. "I don't, but I can ring our Sophie and ask her."

I thanked her and she delivered a wry smile. "I take it from the eager look on your face that you'd like me to ring her now?"

I placed my hands together in a praying motion. "I'd be really grateful."

Clem pulled her silver mobile out of her coat pocket and tapped a couple of buttons.

Fortunately, the rain was dissipating now and an almost marmalade hue was sliding across the sky.

Clem chatted to her daughter-in-law for a few moments about the weather and whether her car had passed its MOT. Then she got around to asking her about her friend's B&B and the Australian guest.

"Yes," said Clem into her mobile. "That's right. The woman you were talking about."

Clem made a few murmurs under my watchful gaze. "Yes, love. The one with the Australian accent. What does she look like?"

Clem shot me a few sideways glances while focussing on what Sophie was telling her. "OK love. Thank you. See you soon."

Her greying hair bobbed up and down as she terminated the call with a "Oh and give our love to Ross."

She thrust her phone back into her coat pocket, her powdery, round face bursting with importance.

"Well, get on with it, woman," moaned Norrie. "The lass has no time for your theatricals."

Clem ignored her husband. "The woman's name is Meredith Stone."

I blinked several times at her. "Not Angela Burrows?"

Clem shook her head. "Sophie was round visiting Nicola at the B&B this morning. She said that was definitely the name she gave."

Either this was a different woman or she had assumed

another false name. "And she was definitely interested in Mask?"

Clem sniffed. "Sophie said she was making snide comments about him and asking lots of questions."

My growing pessimism faded. It must be her. This must be another pseudonym she was using. "Like what, Clem? What did she want to know?"

Clem elaborated that this Meredith Stone was keen to know if Mask had bought Coorie Cottage or whether he was renting it, if any locals knew his music management team, and even whether he had a girlfriend.

"She's obsessed with him," I muttered to myself.

I refocused on Clem. "Did Sophie describe what this Meredith Stone looks like?"

"She said she's a short, stout redhead. Hair in a wavy bob, I think ... Layla, where are you going?"

But I was already bolting back up the soggy lane towards Dad's cottage. I would tell him and the guys I was going to have to go out for a bit longer than I thought. "Thanks ever so much," I called, running backwards to give them a wave. "You've both been very helpful."

Chapter Fifty-Six

I marched back down the lane after saying goodbye to the guys and promising to try and return to Dad's later that evening to join them all for a Friday night takeaway.

Inwardly, I had decided that it would depend on what I could uncover about this Meredith Stone/Angela Burrows person.

I dumped my bag in my hallway and then moved through to my bedroom and bombed around, throwing off my damp socks and jeans.

Once I'd eased into a T-shirt and shorts, I sat at my desk in my sitting room.

How many aliases was this woman using? And why? What was so important to her that she was going to so much trouble to conceal her identity?

The dappled late afternoon sun wriggled its way through the clouds and into the sitting room as I entered in the name 'Angela Burrows' into the search engine.

My breathing lurched in my chest.

Images of many different Angela Burrows appeared, but, unsurprisingly, none of them was an Australian redhead. Furthermore, any that were listed were either elderly or deceased.

I frowned at the screen and typed in her latest moniker, Meredith Stone. That wasn't her either. The name did, however, bring up a glossy picture of an older, glamorous woman. She was all carefully coiffed dark hair and adorned in eye-catching silver jewels.

I was preparing to move away from the photograph, which was taken from a Sunday newspaper gossip column, when I spotted a link to an article accompanying the picture.

I clicked on it and that led me to a piece written in April 2009:

Celebrated philanthropist Meredith Stone is pictured at her 60th birthday party at her luxury home on the Gold Coast, looking as immaculate as ever.

When asked about her stunning necklace and earrings she had chosen to wear for the evening, Meredith informed me that they were the work of a young Australian designer, Hazel Jennings...

I admired the glittering strand of snowflake-like jewels pressing against her neck and a pair of matching, angular earrings peeking out from behind her lion's mane of black hair.

I was about to move the cursor away from the article

when my attention zoomed in on a picture close to the reporter's byline.

It was a small head and shoulders shot of a beaming, pale-skinned young woman with folds of red waves down to her shoulders.

Underneath the picture, it said:

Jewellery designer Hazel Jennings (23)

My fingers froze above my keyboard. It was her. There was no doubt.

With my heart hammering, I sat back in my swivel chair and studied her youthful exuberance as it shone out at me from the screen. It was a complete contrast to the snarling, accusatory version I'd witnessed up at Coorie Cottage.

I leaned forward again, fired up to see what else I could locate about her, but the information was sparse, with the rest of the article only mentioning that she was born in Melbourne, had a sister called Emily (a dancer), and that she had gained a scholarship to a prestigious fashion college based in Sydney.

I printed off a copy of the whole article and returned to my screen saver, which was an image of a snow-drizzled Loch Harris. Then I scooped up my mobile from the top of my desk.

Hazel Jennings deserved a visit.

Chapter Fifty-Seven

I looked up the location of the bed and breakfast place online. It was called The Beech Tree and was situated just off the main street in Finton, overlooking farmland.

Finton was an even smaller town than Loch Harris, so I knew I shouldn't have too much difficulty in finding it.

I drove away from my cottage, piecing together what I was planning to say to Hazel Jennings. I mean, realistically, what could I say? I had no idea why she seemed so intent on persecuting Rafe, but hoped I would be able to prize it out of her.

A picture of her face contorting as she screamed "Murderer!" at Rafe shimmered into my head and I tried to blink it away.

I clicked on my radio, forgetting that I had left one of Rafe's CDs in there.

I stared at my apprehensive reflection in the rear-view mirror as his dusky, melodic voice filled the inside of my car.

What on earth was I doing? I had my business just about to open shortly and yet here I was, charging about the area like Miss Marple. Thank goodness I had most things for The Conch Club in hand now and Faith watching my back so efficiently.

Dad and Faith would often tease me about being a manic list-maker, but if I didn't do it, goodness knows what a pickle I would be in, especially with all this DNA test worry that had taken place, and now the Rafe debacle.

A carved wooden sign proclaiming 'Welcome to Finton' appeared on the grass verge, taking me past three old stone crofts and through the main street that consisted of a bevelled-windowed post office and several shops huddled together.

I drove on until I reached the end of the row of glinting shop windows and ended up looking out over a patchwork blanket of bottle-green and sage-coloured fields. Sheep wandered and jostled each other like blobs of noisy cotton wool.

I looked to my left. There it was. The Beech Tree Bed & Breakfast.

I slowed down, taking in the chintz curtains at the sash windows and two hanging baskets of lavender heather swinging either side of the porched entrance. A green picket fence ran around the front, framing a modest patch of grass and a bird table. The whole effect reminded me of a doll's house.

Parking at the rear of the place, I pulled my denim jacket tighter around me.

I squared my shoulders and walked around to the

entrance, still inwardly deliberating about what I was going to say.

The door was unlocked and a bright table lamp threw out a welcoming hue.

What if this Hazel Jennings isn't in? murmured a doubting voice in my ear. Maybe she's moved on again?

I plastered on a smile as an attractive, curvy brunette strolled towards me in a navy V-neck sweater and silver knotted scarf. This must be Nicola, Sophie's friend. "Can I help you?"

"I hope so. I'm looking for a lady who I understand might be a guest of yours – Meredith Stone?"

She appraised me out of wary, dark eyes. "Can I ask what it's in connection with?"

Bingo! So, she was a guest here.

A combination of realisation and trepidation tripped through my chest. I couldn't blow this. Not now.

I flapped my hand in the air as if to stress it was a matter of minor importance. "Oh, she was sitting near me in a café in Loch Harris this afternoon and left her sunglasses on the table."

I delivered what I intended was a friendly smile. "By the time I realised, she had already gone but she'd stitched her name into her sunglasses case…"

My eyes alighted on a sprinkling of Beech Tree business cards on top of the hall table by the lamp. "And I found one of your business cards on the floor beneath her table. It must have fallen out of her bag when she got up to leave."

The woman returned my smile and shot out her hand.

"Well that's very kind of you. If you give me her sunglasses, I'll pass them on to her."

Oh bugger.

I could feel my mouth twitching. "That's sweet of you, but we had a chat and I wouldn't mind asking her for her contact details back in Australia. It would be nice to keep in touch."

The brunette stood her ground in the middle of her blue and green tartan carpet. "I'm sorry but, as I'm sure you will appreciate, we can't allow people to simply wander in here and try to gain access to our guests and their rooms."

I pushed my hands deeper into my trouser pockets. This woman had missed her calling. She would make a wonderful bodyguard. "Look, Miss..."

"Crawford. Nicola Crawford."

"Nicola," I began again, in my best persuasive voice. "I do appreciate that you have to be cautious, but all I'm asking is that I'm allowed to return Ms Stone's sunglasses in person."

Nicola's attention swung away from me to look upwards, to where there was a short staircase. A door had just banged shut and there was the sound of feet padding down towards us. "Ah, Miss Stone," she smiled, indicating her head towards me. "Perfect timing! There's someone here to see you. She has your sunglasses that you mislaid today."

I fought to keep calm as Hazel Jennings's puzzled voice wafted over in my direction. "I haven't lost any sunglasses..." Her pale, freckled complexion lost more colour when she recognised me.

I pinned her to the spot with a calculating smile. "Hello Ms Stone. How are you?"

She blinked at me out of alarmed blue eyes. "Er ... hello."

I tilted my chin. "I was just explaining to Nicola here that I was hoping to catch up with you again. For a little chat."

I sounded, at least to my own ears, like a convincing and confident woman. Inside was a different story. My heart was zinging around my chest like an out-of-control pinball.

"Oh, would you mind coming back another time?" she blustered, leaning one hand on the carved staircase. "I've done a lot of walking today and I'm wiped out."

There was a charged silence as Nicola surveyed our verbal exchanges with an element of suspicion.

"That is a pity," I pushed, playing with the strap of my shoulder bag. "I wanted to tell you that Hazel Jennings sends her regards."

I watched as Hazel's eyes grew large. She gripped the staircase tighter and inhaled. "Really? Oh, well, that's wonderful."

I cocked one eyebrow at her.

She slid a frightened look at Nicola and then back to me. "Why don't you pop up to my room for a quick coffee then?"

"Thank you. That would be lovely," I replied through a forced grin. "I'm sure there will be lots for us to talk about."

Chapter Fifty-Eight

I followed Hazel up the short flight of stairs to where there was a small corridor of guest rooms.

My imagination started to ramp up visions of her knocking me down the stairs or clubbing me over the head with a candle stick holder as soon as we entered her room.

I mentally rolled my eyes up to the cornice ceiling. This isn't an episode of *Murder, She Wrote*.

Despite this, I ensured I didn't turn my back on her and stood a discreet distance away as she produced her room key from her skirt pocket.

Her room was much like the rest of the place. A set of lemon flower-sprigged curtains framed the window that overlooked the quilted landscape of fields and to the right of that was a small en suite bathroom.

I positioned myself in the centre of the room.

She closed the door with a click. "I don't know what you're doing here." She folded her freckled arms. "If you need to speak to anyone, it's that weirdo musician."

I shook my head. "He isn't a weirdo." A burning defence mechanism kicked in, a surging conviction to defend Rafe.

Hazel smirked. "Oh, and you know so much about him, I suppose."

"I know enough." I tilted my head to one side. "He isn't the one going around Loch Harris using about a dozen different aliases."

She delivered an indifferent shrug. "I had no option but to keep changing my name. I have to achieve what I set out to do."

I frowned over at her. "And what have you set out to do?"

I thrust one hand into my shoulder bag and produced the copy of the Meredith Stone magazine article.

Hazel's eyes darted from me to the paper in my hand and back again. I offered it to her and she hesitated before snatching it from my grasp.

She scanned the article, the previous arrogant edge to her features melting away. "So what?"

"This proves you're using someone else's name. You're really Hazel Jennings, jewellery designer."

Without seeking her permission, I sank down into a nearby armchair. "What did you mean that night when you accused Rafe of being a murderer?"

Her lips, slicked with a frosted-pink lipstick, ground together. "What do you think I meant? I would have thought that was obvious."

"I don't believe it."

She moved to the other side of the bed and sat. "So Rafe

Buchanan has got you fooled too. He always had a real way with the ladies."

"He hasn't got me fooled at all," I snapped, my frustration and worry growing. "I like to think I'm a good judge of character…"

Mac chose, at the moment, to appear in my mind and my voice tailed off.

I swallowed and locked eyes with her.

A triumphant glint hovered there. "Having doubts already?"

I shrugged off my shoulder bag and dumped it down beside my feet. "How do I know you're not making all of this up? You could be a spurned fan of his or some sort of stalker."

Her smirk faded. "I'm not making anything up. I have proof."

She turned and bent down to a small bedside cupboard. Pulling open the polished wooden door, she took out a section of newspaper.

"I suggest you read this." She shoved it towards me.

Now it was my turn to look from her to the newspaper cutting she was gripping in her hand.

I took it from her. There were various articles on the page taken from *The Sydney Enquirer*, dated 22 May 2016, one of which had been circled in black pen.

I lowered my gaze and began to read.

FATAL COLLISION KILLS DANCER

A talented dancer from Melbourne was killed last night in a car accident, after having just departed from her engagement party at The Hyde Park Hotel in Sydney.

Emily Jennings and her fiancé, Rafe Buchanan, were travelling on the Pacific Highway to their home in Terrigal, when their silver Toyota Corolla was struck by a delivery truck.

Mr Buchanan managed to escape from the vehicle, but Ms Jennings sustained serious injuries and died at the scene...

I blinked as the text loomed up at me. *Oh God.* So Rafe had been engaged to Hazel's sister and she had been killed in this awful accident.

"So there's your answer," Hazel said, examining my shocked expression. "Well, part of it."

I slowly lowered the article. "What are you talking about?"

Hazel raised her chin. "He left my sister to die."

"What?"

She regarded me steadily with her glassy, marble-like gaze. "That article doesn't tell the whole story."

Her voice wavered. "Rafe Buchanan saved himself and left Emily. Now, he's going to pay for what he did."

Chapter Fifty-Nine

C onfusion and fear pressed down on my shoulders. "It doesn't say that here. It doesn't say anything like that at all."

Hazel sank down on the edge of the bed and laced her fingers together in her lap. "Well, it wouldn't, would it? Not all the facts were known then."

I realised I had let the newspaper cutting slip out of my hand and it had fluttered down to land on the paisley carpet.

I was struggling. "What facts?"

She made a frustrated sighing noise. "He made it out of that accident alive and without a scratch."

I shook my head so fiercely that my plait jumped against my back. "That's not true. Rafe has a vivid red scar down the right side of his face. He must have sustained that during the crash."

Hazel narrowed her cold eyes. "You're lying."

"I'm not," I insisted. "I've seen it myself." I tried to

appeal to her common sense as I slotted pieces of the story together in my own head.

"That must be why Rafe became a recluse, why he didn't release his debut album, why he disappeared from the music scene for a long time, and why he wears that mask – why he hides from the world behind it."

Hazel got up and paced backwards and forwards in front of me. "I don't believe you," she announced, chewing her bottom lip. "After the crash, we never saw Rafe again. He didn't even have the balls to come to Emily's funeral." The fury in her words echoed around the room. "If that isn't guilt, I don't know what is."

I opened my mouth to speak, but Hazel challenged me with an icy stare. "My sister died and he walked away." She angled her head towards the window. "Now he's living as this Mask character. He's got women like you swooning all over him—"

"I'm not swooning," I bit back, but Hazel ignored me, tangled up in her own web of grief and anger.

Her gaze hardened as she stared ahead at the sweeping countryside and she spun round to face me. "Well, if he thinks he can just live his life and forget all about what he did to Emily and to our family, he's sadly mistaken." Her voice was resentful.

She returned her attention to the middle distance, captivated for a moment by the squares of rich fields laid out through the window. "I'm going to tell everyone what than man is capable of. Let's see how well his flourishing music career does then."

Chapter Sixty

My skin prickled at the sight of this woman's grief and resentment gnawing away at her from the inside out.

I knew I had to speak to Rafe. I had to hear the story from him.

Whether he would be prepared to discuss it with me was anyone's guess, but I had to try. He had made the decision to reveal his scar to me. That must mean we had an element of trust between us. It had meant so much.

I rose slowly from the chair and slung my bag back over my shoulder. I was struggling to digest it all.

Hazel appraised me. "Where are you going?"

I maintained as much of a steady voice as I could manage. "I'm going to head home," I lied. "And I'm so very sorry about your sister."

Hazel's plucked brows dipped. "You must think I'm stupid. You're going to see him, aren't you?"

I moved towards the closed door and closed my fingers around the cool handle. I was determined to sound calm. "No. I told you, I'm going to go home. You've given me a lot to think about."

I hoped my words were said with enough conviction to placate her.

I maintained eye contact and, after a lengthy pause, she gave the lightest of nods. "I'm sorry, but you needed to know the truth about him." Then she broke into a smile, which wrong-footed me. "I know he's very handsome and charming, but don't feel bad. He manages to fool everyone. He even fooled me once…"

What did that mean? A sudden, slow-burning realisation took hold and wouldn't let go. Was that Hazel's way of saying she had been in love with Rafe? Did she still love him?

I popped open the door.

She straightened her shoulders. "Drive home safely."

I was relieved to escape the confines of Hazel's guest room, to dart back down the stairs and out into the descending Friday night darkness.

I leaned against my car and gulped in several breaths of the cool air. My brain felt scrambled.

It was awful what had happened to Emily, and I could understand why Hazel was so consumed by grief over the death of her sister. But what she was accusing Rafe of…

I caught sight of myself in my car window. What if what Hazel said was true? What if Rafe had left that poor girl to perish in the car?

But then I thought back to Hazel's irrational behaviour and her refusal to consider Rafe as a victim too. She hadn't seen his face.

Everything was jockeying in my head for prime position.

I climbed into my car and switched on the headlights. They dazzled like giant eyes, illuminating the dry-stone wall in front of me.

I clutched at the steering wheel. Why was I so keen to speak to Rafe about all this, anyway? Why was it so important for me to believe the best of him?

I fired up the car engine and took off back towards Loch Harris, before taking the diversion towards Galen Waterfall.

I knew what I wanted to think – my heart was screaming at me – yet, beneath this, there was now an incessant murmuring, a droning voice that wouldn't leave me alone.

You don't know what really happened. You can't know.

I swiped one frustrated hand across my forehead and concentrated as much as I could on the road snaking ahead of me.

My headlights picked out the waterfall as it gushed down the rockface in the dark, with Coorie Cottage's lights seeping through the cracks in Rafe's blinds on the opposite side of the road.

I parked, listened to the car engine fade, and snatched

my bag from the passenger seat. My eyes slid up to my rear-view mirror. I had chewed most of my lipstick off.

With my stomach turning itself over, I stalked towards Rafe's front door to talk to him about Emily. More importantly, to talk about him.

Chapter Sixty-One

R afe's voice almost blended in with the sound of Galen Waterfall. Judging from the direction the music was coming from, it seemed he was in the garden, strumming his acoustic guitar.

"Rafe? Rafe, it's me. Layla."

His tall shape emerged from near the herbaceous border, pushing back his hood and smoothing his hair.

It was a simple action. One of trust. It made my heart clench.

But did I trust him, still?

Of course I did, I concluded sharply.

My head buzzed as he pinned me to the spot with his black eyes. "Is everything all right?"

"Yes. No. I'm not sure." I felt a sudden chill and wrapped my arms around myself. "I need to talk to you. About Emily."

His handsome face closed down. My attention strayed to his scar.

"I take it you've been talking to Hazel Jennings."

I blinked up at him. "There was someone here that first time, wasn't there, when Tom and I turned up? It was her."

He held my gaze but said nothing for a few moments.

Rafe's beloved garden, with its heavenly scents, shades, and shapes, swayed behind him.

"Yes, I thought there was someone hanging around outside. I thought I heard Hazel trying to talk to me through the front door." He whipped a frustrated hand through his hair. "I thought I was going crazy." He sighed and carried on. "So I went out to check, but I couldn't see anyone and just assumed it was my imagination playing tricks on me."

Rafe rubbed at his chin. "Then when you and your police officer friends arrived here, saying that a passing motorist had seen someone prowling around, I didn't know what to think."

My eyes moved across his handsome, pensive face.

Rafe stared listlessly over my shoulder and out into the descending night.

I gestured to his scar. "You showed me that," I faltered. "I told you about my dad and Ed. Why won't you confide in me again?"

Rafe's jaw throbbed. It was bearing the faintest dash of stubble. A whoosh of relief entered my chest as he indicated for me to follow him into the cottage, which was warmly drenched in swathes of lamplight.

I sank down onto his two-seater sofa in the sitting room and Rafe took up the chair opposite. "You look cold."

"I'm fine," I lied, eager to hear him talk. "So ... Emily..."

Rafe delivered a defeated nod, before shrugging off his navy hoodie. He looked as though he was struggling to make sense himself of what he was about to tell me.

"It was the twenty-first of May, four years ago. Emily and I were in the car on the way home from our engagement party. We were laughing and brimming with optimism for the future. Our engagement party had been a sea of glowing, celebratory faces of family and friends. Now we were returning home, with a carload of presents decked out in silver bows and shiny wrapping.

"Emily stared across from the passenger seat at me with one of her looks that always made me smile. 'When are you going to write a song about me?' she asked. I grinned at her. 'What a damned cheek! Every song I write is about you,' I said. Emily laughed. 'Yeah, right. You're so full of bullshit, Buchanan,' she said. She always called me that. I winked at her. 'Why, thank you.' I narrowed my eyes as I continued to stare into my rear-view mirror. The guy behind was getting a bit close and Emily swivelled, peering over her shoulder at the looming lorry.

"I hit the brake to make him ease off but he didn't. I dipped down a little in the driver's seat to get a different angle in the rear-view mirror, but the articulated lorry's cab and the interruption of lights along the freeway wasn't making it at all easy for me to make out the driver, and an uneasy sensation settled in my stomach. I could tell Emily was scared, so I rearranged my concerned expression into one that I hoped was supreme confidence and told her it was nothing to worry about. He was just driving like a bit of a dick.

"Changing my mind about the slowing down theory, I decided to adopt a more dramatic approach. With the lane of the freeway ahead of us clear of traffic, I subtly pressed down on the accelerator and Emily's hands clawed at either side of her seat. I shot out my hand and squeezed hers, telling her everything was going to be fine…"

It felt like my own breath was choking me. I sank back against Rafe's sofa.

"And then what happened?"

His voice was brimming with pain. "I should have done more, Layla. I felt as if I were watching events unfold through a sea of treacle. The driver of the lorry, unbeknownst to us at the time, had taken too many sleeping tablets after a slew of restless nights on the road. His foot slammed down on the accelerator and by the time the freeway lights shone behind his flickering eyelids, the chrome beast he was fighting to control was already ploughing into our car."

Rafe's unwavering gaze reflected the burnished flames of his log fire.

"There was the worst sound ever – like a thudding and bouncing that shook our insides. Our car rolled over a couple of times like a dice. I thought Emily would scream, cry for me to help her, reach out to me … I begged for her to yell, to call my name, to reach out for me, but she didn't.

"I threw out both my arms, trying to find her. She was just beside me, after all. But my hands just grabbed air."

Rafe rubbed his hands on his knees as he sat there, hunched over.

"We eventually landed upside down on the other side of

the freeway. The air in the car was suddenly so still and quiet. There was the odd creak and splintering sound, but nothing else. I tried to move but there was this pain shooting through my body and then an excruciating sensation on the right side of my face."

He lifted one finger and traced it down his scar, as if to illustrate the point.

"I managed to wriggle out of my seat belt. All I could think of was Emily."

My voice was a whisper. "But she was gone?"

Rafe's eyelids fluttered closed for a moment. "Not at that point. I started to scream at her. I shook her. I begged her to look at me. I managed to free her from her seat belt and reached to feel her pulse. She was slumped forwards like a ragdoll. Her pulse was very faint, but there was one. I felt it. I began to try and move her, but then a pair of hands grabbed me from behind and pulled me out. I screamed at them, begged them to take their hands off me. I told them she was still alive, barely, but still breathing. But they wouldn't let me go back in to help her."

He thumped his fists down. "I begged them to let me return to her, but they held me back. Do you realise how that felt? I could have saved her, Layla."

Rafe's eyes bore angrily into the flames of his log fire. "She died moments later."

He thrust his finger towards his scar. "See this thing on my face? It's nothing. It's nothing compared to the guilt I carry around with me over what happened to Emily."

I wanted to embrace him as he sat there, rigid with pain, I wanted to tell him that none of what had happened to

Emily was his fault.

My heart ached for him. This weight he was carrying around with him must be unbearable.

"Rafe, you mustn't feel guilty…"

"I walked away with this," he ground out. "Emily lost her life."

"But you also walked away full of all this remorse. And you shouldn't have."

Rafe gave his head a shake. "Don't you see? I promised Emily I would always keep her safe, but I didn't."

Without thinking, I propelled myself up from the sofa and walked over to him. I knelt down in front of his long legs. "You weren't to know what was going to happen. You weren't responsible for that driver taking too many sleeping pills."

He looked at me but said nothing.

"What happened to him? The lorry driver, I mean?"

"Died of his injuries two days later." He raised his chin and stared down at me, his mouth a flat line. His dark brows thundered above his eyes.

"Is that why you didn't end up releasing your first album and why you live like you do? Because of the accident?"

Rafe didn't deny it.

"I want to help you," I choked. "No one should be made to feel like this, least of all you."

I slowly stood, watching as Rafe did the same. I could feel my breath catching in the base of my throat as his hot gaze swept me from head to toe.

"Thank you, Layla, but I think it's best that you leave."

My brows furrowed at him. "Why? What is it?"

He stalked out of his sitting room and down the flickering hallway to the front door. He tugged it open and walked back towards the garden as I followed. Pausing, Rafe pushed his hands into his trouser pockets and gave a slight shiver. "I'm not good to be around."

"Who told you that?"

"No one."

"Then why say it?"

His brown eyes grew hard. "Because it's true! I lost Emily and I'm not prepared to lose you—" He drew himself up.

"What?" I asked in a whisper. "Rafe, please talk to me. You won't lose me."

"How can you possibly know that?"

My chest rose and fell under my denim jacket. "I just do."

His attention followed my hand as I raised it to his cheek. I sensed him flinch at first. Then his body relaxed as my fingers slowly traced over his ragged wound from the tip of his brow right down to the edge of his lips.

"Rafe," I breathed into the night air, aware of the silhouetted trees and trembling plants surrounding us. There was the dusky, heady scent of heather.

I gazed up at him, spellbound by the depth of his eyes.

He angled his head so that his scarred cheek was resting against the palm of my hand. "I warned you, Layla," he growled. "I'm not good to be around."

His eyelids fluttered closed for a moment. His long, sooty lashes rested on his cheekbones. Then his lips grazed my wrist and I let out a gasp, before managing to say, "Maybe you should let other people be the judge of that."

I allowed my fingers to stroke a stray hair that was furling over his ear. "What happened to Emily was tragic, but it wasn't your fault."

Now it was Rafe's turn to touch my face. He did it as though he were frightened at first – slowly and deliberately. He traced one finger down my cheek until it stopped beside my lips. His eyes locked on my mouth and I struggled to breathe.

The silence was broken by Rafe suddenly murmuring, "Oh Layla," before claiming my lips with his.

I pushed myself against him and tasted the heat of his mouth. His hands kneaded and pressed against my back and I reciprocated by sliding my fingers underneath his top, caressing him and investigating the curves and planes of his body.

His muscles slid under his warm skin and I moaned, causing Rafe to draw me even tighter to him.

I wanted to make all his pain and torment go away. No one deserved to feel so twisted with guilt and remorse, especially someone like him.

Our pace became more frantic, our breathing urgent as we greedily kissed over and over.

It was only when a ragged squeal of tyres broke the silence of the night that we sprang apart. Yellow headlights dazzled out of the dark, like two angry eyes.

My heart stilled as Hazel came stumbling out of her car. Her features were pale and contorted. "I knew it!" she screamed at our startled expressions. "I just knew it!"

Chapter Sixty-Two

"**K**new what?" challenged Rafe. "What are you talking about?"

Hazel jabbed an accusing finger at me. "Snow White over there. She's another poor, deluded bitch who has fallen for the Rafe Buchanan charisma."

I tried to placate her. "Look, Hazel, it's terrible what happened to your sister…"

"And it was his fault," she barked, eyeing Rafe. "Like a coward, he left her to die in that car!"

"Hazel, I didn't want to leave Emily. I tried to get back into the car to pull her out, but rescuers held me back."

She took a few deliberate steps closer, her light eyes wide and unwavering. "Oh, don't give me that! She died in that accident and you walked away."

"Oh, for pity's sake," I ground out. "I didn't lie to you about Rafe."

I turned my head around to look at him, but he was already thundering towards her.

Hazel shrank back at the sight of Rafe's clenched jaw.

He loomed over her and whipped his handsome face to the left. The night breeze rippled through his black hair.

Hazel's eyebrows rose towards her hairline when she saw Rafe's vivid wound. "I sustained this during the accident. I don't want pity. I just want you to know that I didn't walk away unscathed."

Hazel's jaw grew slack while Rafe went on to explain that he had also attended Emily's funeral. "You just didn't see me," he confessed. "None of you did. But I can assure you I was there."

Hazel struggled to focus as she digested what Rafe had just told her. She took a breath before unpredictable anger and disbelief reared up in her again. "But where did you go? After the accident, I mean. You just vanished."

Rafe glanced over at me. "I felt guilty about it all, as though I didn't deserve to be happy. Emily was gone and I couldn't save her. Why should things just go on as normal for me?"

A slow realisation began to tease me as I watched Hazel take a step towards Rafe. Her expression seemed to be melting in front of my eyes, like raindrops on a sunny day.

She continued to study him. "I had no idea," she murmured, drinking in his face. Then she reached out a hand and began stroking his arm.

Rafe, surprised by her sudden tenderness, sprang away.

"You know," she carried on, oblivious to my dawning expression only feet away, "we're two lost souls, aren't we, Rafe? We have so much in common, you and I." She dropped her gaze to the ground, before raising her eyes back to him. "We both lost Emily."

Hazel played with a few strands of red hair that had escaped from her up-do. "You must have realised how I always felt about you. I knew I shouldn't have, what with you being with my sister, but…" She allowed the rest of her words to vanish into the dark air. "I always hoped you would notice me."

My thoughts returned to that photo I'd found.

All the pieces of this tragic jigsaw were moving into position.

Hazel was in love with Rafe. She always had been.

Chapter Sixty-Three

R afe looked utterly confused. "Sorry?"

Hazel remained rooted to the spot in front of a horrified Rafe. The enraged, spiteful glint in her eyes had gone and she was gazing up at him in adoration.

"It was the only way I could accept that you didn't want me, Rafe. By convincing myself that you caused Emily's death."

A hopeful smile broke out on her face, as the evening breeze fluttered the hem of her skirt. "But now I've seen how much you've been suffering and what Emily's death did to you, I know there's hope for us. We need to be together."

All the odd comments Hazel had been making, the hidden inferences, and the desire to punish Rafe. That's why Hazel had been so intent on pursuing him, why she had wanted him to suffer. She had been harbouring jealousy for years over Emily being in a relationship with him.

Rafe's dark eyes widened as he began to come to the same conclusion. He took a few steps away from her.

Hazel's smile contorted into despair. "You have to understand Rafe, I only contacted that pathetic journalist because I didn't know the truth. I was desperate." She stretched out both her hands towards Rafe in a pleading motion. "I'm so sorry."

He rubbed his forehead. "I told you all the truth from the beginning, but you chose to believe the worst of me. And now you think I could..." Rafe's disgust was evident. "Do you know how much it has taken for me to try to resurrect my love of music, Hazel? I've had to adopt this Mask persona, just to try and cope with each and every day."

"I'm sorry," she gulped and threw her arms out to him. "I would never have wanted you to punish yourself this way, had I known the truth. But I really do love you, you know. I always have."

I tried to understand Hazel's logic.

"We could make each other happy," she insisted. "I know we could. We would be a comfort to one another."

"Please leave, Hazel. Now."

She swiped at her tearful cheeks with one hand. "You want me to go?"

Rafe clenched his jaw. "I think that's best."

"You don't mean that. You're just confused." Her fingers tumbled over each other.

She snapped her head over to where I was. "She won't make you happy, Rafe. Not like I would."

Rafe's jaw was like concrete. "I won't tell you again, Hazel. Just go."

She hovered for another moment, a lost look drifting through her eyes, before reluctantly moving back towards her hire car. "I'll email that local reporter," she muttered. "I'll tell her there's no story here."

"Thank you," said Rafe, in a barely audible whisper.

Hazel awarded me an indecipherable sidelong glance before clambering back into her car, switching on her headlights, and leaving.

Rafe shot me a relieved look, before striding back over to me and reaching out one hand to clasp in mine.

I furled my fingers around his. "Thank goodness that's over. You can try to move on properly now."

Rafe shook his head in disbelief. "I can't believe that just happened. Emily would be horrified if she knew Hazel was trying to accuse me of causing her death."

We stood there admiring Coorie Cottage, its cosy lights welcoming in the darkness. "Maybe now after talking to you, Hazel will realise what real harm she could have caused." I gazed up at him, admiring his handsome profile. "I know you think I'm just saying this," I began, "but I don't notice your scar. Especially not now."

As I drank Rafe in, with his shaggy, dark head and generous mouth, the pain of losing Mac – and his deception – evaporated.

Rafe pulled me back towards the garden with him, just as the furious roar of a car engine erupted behind us.

Hazel had swung the car around, switched off its headlights and stopped there, facing us, with the engine still running. Her freckled face was oddly composed and her glassy eyes shone like those of a lifeless doll.

I could make out both of her hands clamped to the top of the steering wheel as the car engine revved and Hazel pushed the vehicle into gear, slamming her foot down on the accelerator.

She fired the headlights back on, suddenly dazzling us. We raised our hands to our eyes and stumbled backwards. There was a squeal of tyres while she bore down on us.

"Layla!"

Chapter Sixty-Four

Rafe threw himself at me, encircling my waist with his arms and propelling me to the ground.

Tufts of grass and dirt rose up from the driveway as Hazel's car shot past in a shiny streak and slammed to a halt.

We raised our heads, preparing to scramble to our feet, when Hazel's face, twisted with rage appeared out of the open car window. She ground her jaw at the sight of Rafe and me lying in a tangle of limbs.

We scrambled backwards, reaching out for one another, in fear that she intended to screech towards us again.

"Hazel! For Christ's sake, stop!"

Rafe's yell made her gasp. She clutched at the steering wheel, her knuckles turning white. Then she gave a horrified, wounded cry which seemed to reverberate around the surrounding hillside.

"I'm sorry. I'm so sorry," she gasped. The car remained still for a moment, before Hazel switched off the engine.

Rafe and I rose to our feet, refusing to take our eyes away from the car or its sobbing occupant.

Rafe dusted down his jeans. "Shit! Are you all right, Layla?"

"Yes," I managed. "Thanks to you. Are you?"

He didn't reply. He just blinked down at me, an odd, trance-like edge taking over his features.

Hazel had her head thrown back in the seat, her chest rising and falling. She was gasping for air between racked sobs.

I took a few tentative steps towards the car door. The interior of the car was dark, except for the odd glowing light on the dashboard. Rafe's concern for me crackled in the night air. "Layla! What are you doing?"

I lifted one finger and put it to my mouth.

Hazel sensed me there and turned her head slowly, as if it was physically painful to do so.

"Let me help you."

I eased open the door and took a step back. I didn't want to alarm her.

Hazel's teary eyes travelled the length of me. Finally, she placed one sandal-clad foot out, followed by the other.

"There you go. Take it steady."

She blinked at me, her summer outfit crumpled.

Rafe watched as I took her by one arm and steered her gently towards Coorie Cottage.

"I'm going to make you a cup of tea, OK?"

She clung to my arm, taking ginger steps in the dark, and allowed me to manoeuvre her into Rafe's sitting room and onto his couch. Hazel lost herself as Rafe helped me make her a cup of tea.

She accepted it from me with whispered thanks and cradled it between her trembling fingers. Rafe sank down opposite her and I took up a place beside her on the sofa.

Hazel moved the mug to her lips as if to take a sip. "I don't know who I am anymore."

I shot a concerned glance over at Rafe.

"I don't recognise who I've become."

My voice was low. "Hazel, you lost your sister. You're struggling with your grief."

She shook her head, her up-do threatening to fall down at any moment. "I needed someone to blame, someone to hold responsible."

Her pale eyes flitted across to Rafe. "I was jealous that Emily had you, and when she died I just felt so guilty that I had been harbouring all these feelings for my sister's fiancé."

Rafe dropped his gaze for a moment.

"I don't know how I got there, through all that grief. It all seems an insane blur now."

I watched her put the mug of tea to her lips and take a nervous sip. "Emily wouldn't want to see you like this. I'm sure it would break her heart."

She turned to me, her face crumpling. I quickly removed the tea from her hand and set it down on the table. Hazel folded into my shoulder, letting out agonising tears against my T-shirt.

Once her breathing had steadied, I dropped my face to

her level. She swiped across her eyes with her hand. "I'm sorry. I'm so sorry." She held my eyes with hers, desperate to be believed. "I'm going to take control of my life. For Emily."

She flicked an embarrassed look at Rafe from under her lashes. "I'm going to return to Australia as soon as I can. Get some counselling and talk to my parents."

I squeezed her arm. "Emily would be very, very proud of you."

Once we were certain Hazel was composed enough, I offered to drive her back to her B&B and Rafe called the care hire company and arranged for Hazel's vehicle to be collected the next morning.

I settled Hazel into the passenger seat of my car and she offered me a grateful but watery smile.

I returned to Coorie Cottage and found Rafe.

I crouched down to stroke his cheek but he sprang backwards in his chair and averted his gaze.

"Rafe?"

"I'm tired," he confessed, not bringing himself to look at me. "You should go. Drive home safely, and thank you for what you did this evening."

"Get this down you."

I eyed the tumbler of whisky Faith was handing me.

"Go on. You've almost been run over. It'll be good for

the shock."

I propped myself up against my pillows. "Since when did you become a doctor?"

"Just drink the bloody thing!"

I gulped the rich golden alcohol down in one gulp and started as the bitter liquid struck the back of my throat. I let out a couple of raspy coughs. "Where did you find this?"

Faith shuffled her bottom as she sat beside me on the bed. "It must have been part of Mac's secret stash. It was lurking at the back of one of your kitchen cupboards, alongside two bottles of vodka." Faith narrowed her eyes at me. "Don't you think you should see a doctor?"

"What, for a bruised arse?"

She shook her strawberry-blonde head in exasperation. "For the shock. You've really been through the wringer tonight. It's not every day someone tries to run you over. And you should have rung me," she stated, her gold bangles sliding up and down her arm. "You shouldn't have driven home from there on your own after that."

I picked at the seam of my coffee-coloured duvet cover. "I wasn't on my own. For some of the time Hazel was next to me."

Faith looked annoyed. "A lot of people wouldn't have done what you did. Still, as long as you and Rafe are OK..."

The taste of his mouth still lingered on mine as Faith said his name.

"Oh shit," I wailed, as a single tear slid down my face and plopped onto my covers.

Faith seized both of my hands in hers. "I know you've

had a terrible shock, but there's something else you're not telling me, isn't there?"

My shoulders sagged under my purple pyjama top. "Rafe and I kissed."

Faith's eyebrows arched. "OK."

I tipped my head back against my brass headboard. "It was wonderful. I've never been kissed like that before. Not even by Mac."

Faith appeared suitably impressed. "Wow. OK. So, what's the problem?"

My chest heaved under the covers. "I think he regretted it, once we'd done it. The way he looked at me when I was leaving with Hazel ... he was so distant and detached."

Faith dismissed my doubts and insisted I was reading too much into it. "He almost saw you run down by someone who nearly became his sister-in-law. If that didn't have an effect on him, I'd be very surprised."

Yet I could clearly recall the change in him and his standoffishness when I moved to stroke his face as I was leaving. He could barely bring himself to look at me.

My heart sank with embarrassment at the recollection of it.

"Are you sure you don't want me to ring Harry?"

"No, definitely not. I'm fine. I think my pride is bruised more than anything."

Faith moved to speak, but I silenced her with a forced smile. "I'll tell him once the guys from the band have gone home on Sunday. I know he'll be furious with me for not telling him straight away, but he'll get over it."

Faith leaned over to my bedside table and picked up the

glass of white wine she had deposited there for herself. "You should have called the police, you know. That woman could have killed you both."

She took a gulp of the crisp golden wine and savoured it.

"Hazel needs professional help and she has realised that. I don't think getting arrested would have been the answer."

I cursed myself for allowing Rafe to send me into a tailspin in the first place. It was true what I had said to Faith. I had never been kissed like that before. The intensity and fire of it had been overwhelming.

I closed my eyes for a few moments in an attempt to dislodge the memory of it and how Rafe made me feel. It wasn't working.

I propped one of my pillows higher. "And you're sure Hazel has left the area?"

Faith curled up her mouth at the mention of the woman's name. "Totally. I made up some cock and bull story about Hazel Jennings leaving an expensive engraved pen in the tourist office. Norrie fell for it and got Sophie to check with The Beech Tree."

She took another satisfied gulp of her wine. "The woman who owns the place – Nicola – said Hazel packed all her things and checked out this evening."

Faith waggled her wine glass in the air. "She got Nicola to organise a taxi for her to the airport."

She examined me out of her concerned light-blue eyes. "From what you've said, this Jennings woman was obsessed with Rafe."

"Oh, no doubt about that. I think what with the death of

her sister and her conflicting feelings for Rafe, everything simply just got too much for her."

Hopefully getting help would show Hazel the way forward.

Faith eyed my empty whisky tumbler under the glow of my bedside lamp. "Fancy another?"

"No thanks. I don't want to be pissed and bruised."

I watched Faith head towards my bedroom door, and called her name. She turned around.

"Thank you for everything you've done."

She blushed prettily. "No worries."

I stretched my legs under the covers. "I don't want you going home late on your own. You should head off soon."

Faith planted her hands on her hips in defiant mode. "I've been necking white wine, remember? I'll stay the night, if that's OK with you. I'm not due in at the tourist office till lunchtime tomorrow anyway."

"Of course it's OK. The spare room bed is all made up."

Faith started out of the bedroom door again, before pulling up. "But I draw the line at smearing arnica cream on your arse. There have to be some limits."

I let out a snort of laughter at that graphic image, only to wince as my bruised buttocks let out a bark of indignation. "Ouch! So, how are things going with the lovely lumberjack?"

Faith tilted her head to one side. "I take it you mean Greg? We had a lovely dinner, and Sam was charming too. He wanted us to have fish fingers and spaghetti hoops, but Greg managed to persuade him that a roast chicken might be better."

"And?"

"And we're taking things nice and steady. Greg's mum has offered to babysit Sam one night next week, so the two of us thought we'd try that Italian place in North Spey."

She blushed at my smug grin and meandered off into the kitchen.

Faith had left my mobile on the bedside table and as I lay there, my head replaying tonight's events, my phone lit up with an incoming call.

Rafe's name appeared on the glowing screen. My stomach made a swooping sensation. I remembered how Rafe had insisted on jabbing his mobile number into my contacts when I'd insisted on returning Hazel to her B&B.

I hesitated, debating whether to answer it or not. Eventually I surrendered and took the call. His voice made me shift uncomfortably in bed. "I wanted to check you were OK."

I gathered myself together and stared into the middle distance. "I'm fine, thank you. My best friend, Faith, is staying over tonight to keep an eye on me."

There was a long pause at the end of the line.

"I'm just a bit bruised," I added, in an attempt to fill the quiet. "No doubt a good night's sleep and a hot bath in the morning will do the trick."

I could hear Faith moving around in the kitchen. "How are you?" I asked him.

"A bit sore, like you, but otherwise I'm all right."

I willed him to mention our moment. Would he say something about that kiss?

But instead he cleared his throat and declared in his

deep Australian accent, "I'm going to contact Hazel's parents. I'll leave it up to Hazel as to how she wants to approach things, but I think I should alert them to the fact that she's in a delicate state of mind at the moment and needs their support."

"That sounds like a good idea."

"So anyway, I'd better go and let you get some rest. Take care Layla and have a good night."

I felt overcome by waves of disappointment. So that was it. As far as he was concerned, our kiss was banished to the past and didn't warrant another mention. "Thanks Rafe," I managed. "You have a good night too."

I ended the call and bit back a tear, before thumping my mobile down on the bedcovers in frustration.

Chapter Sixty-Five

"So, all the tickets have gone for opening night," grinned Faith, "but I've kept a reserve list like you asked me to, in case there are any last-minute dropouts."

She turned to the scribbled notes she'd made on a lined pad by her computer. "And all the invitations we sent out have now received positive RSVPs..." Her enthusiasm dribbled to a halt. "Are you all right? Layla?"

I pulled my attention away from the tourist office door. "Do you think I'm doing the right thing?"

"Aren't you leaving it a bit late to be having regrets now?"

Faith was right. This was all about looking forward and not back. I flapped one hand and smiled. "Ignore me. It's just a touch of nerves, that's all."

"And there isn't anything or anyone else lurking in your mind?"

I straightened my spine. "Like who?"

Faith smiled. "Oh, come on."

"If you mean Rafe, then no."

That wasn't entirely true. If I were being honest with myself, I felt like a right idiot. Since his phone call on Friday night, I'd received a couple of brief texts over the weekend from him, asking how I was, but that was all.

Our kiss had been a heat-of-the-moment thing. That must have been all it was. A combination of charged emotions.

It hadn't meant anything. Well, at least for Rafe it hadn't.

I decorated my face with an indifferent smile, or at least what I hoped was a convincing impression of one. "I've put all that behind me."

Faith's lips curled up at one side. "Uh-huh."

I pushed one of the pens lying on her desk around for something to do. A large part of me secretly wished I wasn't having to play Rafe's music on opening night. As I said it to myself, I cringed. It sounded so childish, but having to sit there and listen to him singing his beautiful lyrics wasn't going to be easy.

I would keep myself busy, I decided. There would be a lot to keep on top of and Dad's band were playing their set first.

"Dad's got another date with Molly tonight," I said, changing the direction of our conversation. "He's like a jittery seventeen-year-old, bless him."

"You like her?"

"She's lovely. Molly is exactly what Dad needs, after being married to the Loch Harris equivalent of the Wicked Witch."

Danielle changed the music in the tourist office from a

soothing Celtic panpipes number to a rigorous Virginian reel.

I buried a smile as Faith rolled her eyes up to the spotlights dotted around the ceiling. "Is your mum coming to the opening?"

I widened my grey eyes in horror. "I bloody well hope not. You didn't send her an invite, did you?"

Faith pulled a condescending look. "As if. I know what a prolonged and painful death you would inflict on me if I had."

She beamed as she added, "Greg said he would bring Sam along for a little while to the opening, until his boredom threshold kicks in. Then his grandparents said they would take him."

The bell of the tourist office door tinkled and an elderly couple wandered in.

"I think Tina will invite herself anyway," I said. "You can bet that local fiend of hers has been keeping her informed of developments."

"You said fiend. Did you mean friend?"

"No, I didn't. I knew exactly what I meant."

Faith laughed. "Maybe it would be a good thing if Tina does show up." She wriggled her eyebrows. "She'll not only see what you've achieved with The Conch Club, but also that she wasn't able to destroy your relationship with Harry. Or Ed, for that matter."

Maybe Faith had a point. I hadn't thought of it like that.

Our heads swung round in unison as the door swung open again, bringing with it this time a murmuring cluster of student types. They were decked out in crackly waterproofs.

"We're definitely busier than we were," Faith said with satisfaction. She pointed one finger at me. "And that's down to you."

I blushed and began to protest, but Faith was having none of it. "Ever since we started promoting The Conch Club, Loch Harris has begun to show signs of life again."

I planted a kiss on her cheek, waved goodbye to Danielle and headed for the door.

"Don't underestimate what you've achieved, OK?" Faith called with affection at my retreating back.

I turned and mouthed "Thanks," before heading off across the town square. Sure enough, there did appear to be more people mingling around as of late.

Tourists were exclaiming at the shop windows that boasted everything from Harris tartan to decorated cupcakes and hiking equipment.

Trainers, boat shoes, and walking boots were slapping over the cobbles and snaking their way down the network of lanes, past the assorted tourist accommodation, bevelled windows, and hanging baskets that were clotted with heather. It was a gratifying sight.

I set off away from the main street, towards the country lane that took me home. I was glad now that I hadn't brought my car. The walk back would clear my mind and allow me to run through my checklist.

I reminded myself to give the coffee-machine hire company a ring to confirm details of the lease I had arranged with them. I also wanted to check that the coasters

I'd ordered from an Edinburgh artist would arrive on Thursday as agreed. I'd opted for a white and gold conch design, with a sturdy cork reverse. I thought they would look so pretty on each table.

As I walked along, I realised my bruising was getting better. There was only an odd, dull ache in my bottom now when I moved. Dad had been livid when I'd told him on Saturday morning about my near miss at Coorie Cottage, but I'd managed to distract him with talk of Molly and he grudgingly agreed to forgive me.

I had got as far as the carved wooden sign and illustrated map that welcomed visitors to Loch Harris and boasted of our network of mysterious caves, population of red deer and oak woodland, when I stopped to let a truck slide past me with a pyramid of logs piled up in its rear trailer.

It was as I was standing on the grass verge, appreciating the beauty of the place, that I realised that even if I had physically moved away from Loch Harris, my heart never would have left.

Chapter Sixty-Six

I stretched out my shoulders and smiled down the phone. "So, all set for your hot date tonight with the luscious Molly?"

"You bet I am. She wants to go and see this new Ryan Reynolds romantic comedy at the cinema."

I laughed. "I didn't think romcoms were your thing."

"They're not," confessed Dad darkly, "but I've made her promise that she'll come with me to see the next *Star Trek*." He paused. "And talking of matters of the heart, how are you?"

My hand hovered over my mouse. I knew Dad was alluding to Rafe. "I'm doing OK. Why do you ask?"

Dad's hesitancy made me turn away from the flickering screen of my computer.

"You're not too upset then? I thought you might be when you heard."

I swivelled my chair to glance out of my sitting room window. "Upset about what, Dad?"

It sounded like Dad swore under his breath. "Oh. You haven't heard then? I mean, it might not be true."

I moved a little further away from my desk. "Dad, what is it? You're talking in riddles."

"It might just be idle gossip," he assured me. "You know what the folks round here can be like."

My curiosity was piqued and my frustration was growing. I was about to push him when he blurted, "Victor Prentice the estate agent, was in the newspaper shop at the same time as me this afternoon."

"Yes. And?"

Dad's words came out in a sympathetic rush. "He said Rafe Buchanan is considering selling up."

A stab of shock hit me in the chest. "Sorry?"

Dad repeated what he said and I sat still for a moment. A whirlwind of emotions caught me off guard. "Oh. OK. Right."

My initial surprise gave way to pain and hurt. So Rafe was thinking about selling Coorie Cottage and moving away from Loch Harris.

Then I had been right. That kiss we had shared – that intimate moment, the fact that he showed his scar to me – it all meant nothing to him. I had honestly thought there was something growing between us.

"Layla. Layla? Are you still there?"

My dad's concerned voice made me start. "Yes. Sorry, Dad. I'm here."

There was a weighted silence from his end. "Are you all right? I thought you might have heard already." I heard him mutter "Shit!" to himself.

I blinked back tears and raised my chin in a defiant gesture. Pity I didn't actually feel it. "Don't worry about it, Dad. Honestly."

I reached for my water and watched the cube of ice nudging against the side of the glass. But was it such a shock? Was it really so unexpected? He was the next big thing in the music world. His alter ego, Mask, was slaying social media and creeping up the charts.

Rafe wanted to leave Loch Harris behind. After the Hazel Jennings incident, he had probably decided that this rural living wasn't for him after all. Maybe he had come to the conclusion and finally realised the truth; that he wasn't responsible for what had happened to Emily and wished to move on somewhere else, with someone else.

That someone else obviously isn't you, hissed a voice in my head.

I took a gulp of water and put it back down on the coaster on my desk.

"Layla, talk to me," said Dad into my ear. "I know how much you liked him."

I forced out a laugh. "Oh, it wasn't like that. We were friends, that's all."

Dad fell silent, before managing a simple, "Right."

I didn't want to prolong this conversation. It was making me conjure up images of Rafe greedily kissing me and his breathing growing ragged as I cupped my hand against his scarred cheek.

I had been so bloody stupid, reading into the situation and seeing things that simply weren't there. I was inconsequential to Rafe. What I had thought we had didn't exist. It didn't matter. I didn't matter.

I pressed my eyelids closed. I had to keep busy and put all that in the past. I was going to tear myself up inside if I didn't. I had to take on board the advice I'd given Hazel. I arranged a tight smile on my face, even though Dad couldn't see me. "Anyway, I'd better go. I've got more emails to check."

"Sure. I know you're up against it before the big opening."

There was an uneasy silence between us again.

"Enjoy your romcom," I said with fake joviality. "Please say hi to Molly for me and don't eat all the popcorn."

"Oh, I won't. I'll be on my best behaviour."

Dad started to ask me again if I was all right, but I couldn't answer.

I sat still for a few moments after having ended the call, blinking back the hurt in my eyes and willing images of Rafe to go away.

The wounded part of me didn't want to play those sodding songs of his on the opening Saturday night, but I knew I was being childish. I had a new business I wanted to make a success of. I had to deliver on my promises, no matter what.

Chapter Sixty-Seven

The remainder of August was a blur of repeated visits to the boathouse to check on the arrival of stock and have informal meetings with my new members of staff, not to mention confirming arrangements for opening night, such as the delivery of lights, catering, and the arrival of the marquee.

I was also very enthusiastic about seeing the team modelling the new Conch Club outfits I'd ordered for them.

Danielle had tipped me off about one of her friends, Rachel, who was a fashion student in Glasgow. She was keen to earn some extra cash, and I was keen to secure a smart and easily washable work outfit for my staff at a competitive rate.

I wanted a simple, classy design for the team to wear that didn't look like a uniform. So Rachel came up with a black, long-sleeved shirt for the guys, shot with discreet silver stripes and slim-fitting dress trousers.

For the girls, strappy black tops overlaid with a little bolero and teamed with a knee-length pencil skirt bearing the same silver pattern as their male colleagues' shirts.

There was unanimous agreement that, as they would be constantly on their feet, black loafers would be the most sensible option.

When they emerged from the boathouse toilets, strutting and putting on exaggerated pouts (and that was just the guys) I beamed with satisfaction. They all looked dapper and professional, but still approachable.

Faith was a godsend, dealing with any last-minute emails that she could on my behalf, while she kept the tourist office ticking over.

Even Danielle, known for her somewhat scatty approach to work, was a great help too, stepping in and handling the tourist office so that Faith could help me.

I hadn't received any more text messages from Rafe since our kiss, and that suited me fine. Or at least, that's what I kept trying to convince myself.

My heart tempted me to contact him, even if it was simply to establish why he was thinking of moving away. But as soon as I eyed my phone, my pride would kick in and my head would scream, *Don't you dare! He didn't even have the decency to tell you himself that he was considering moving.*

Dad had an eventful date with Molly, even if he did fall asleep for the last ten minutes of the movie and missed Ryan Reynolds sweeping his love interest away in a speedboat.

My father had been horrified, but Molly had dismissed his snores with a wide grin and they'd been out together a dozen more times since then.

"I hope Molly's coming along on the big night," I told him.

He assured me that she was. "I'm intending to impress her with my rock star moves."

"Well, just make sure you don't take forty winks in the middle of your set."

On the Thursday evening, two nights before the grand opening, I was nursing a glass of ruby-red wine and dashing off the last few paragraphs of my phone interview with a local breeder of prize-winning birds to submit to a commissioning features editor.

I looked up when I heard a knock on the front door.

It was Jack.

I indicated my checked pyjamas and my hair tied on top of my head in a messy pineapple.

"Don't worry," he smiled. "You still look better than your dad."

I laughed. "I won't tell him you said that. Come on in."

Jack ambled into my sitting room. "Rehearsals are going well but your dad has made one huge mistake that we, as his fellow band members, feel we can't ignore."

My stomach plummeted to the floor. Oh no. What had happened now? These creative types were so unpredictable!

Jack kept his face straight. "He's run out of milk for the tea."

I hit his arm playfully. "Don't ever do that again. I think I've just aged ten years."

Jack grinned as I headed over to the fridge and plucked out a spare pint of milk. "Here you go."

He thanked me and cradled the milk against his grey and white sweatshirt. "I'd better get back to your dad's. Goodness knows what they'll be sounding like down there without their wizard on keyboards." I walked Jack to the front door. "And how are things going with you and that musician everyone is talking about?' he asked. "I heard his latest single has gone straight into the top ten."

I huddled deeper into my fluffy dressing gown. "Oh, that was nothing."

Jack blinked at me. "Really?"

I struggled to contort my expression into one of indifference. "We had a moment about a month ago," I confessed. "Or at least I thought we did. I must have read more into it than there was because, according to the rumours, he's moving away from the area."

Jack processed that, the lamp light casting shadows against the angles of his face.

"And you haven't tried to speak to … Mask, is it?"

"Rafe," I said after a pause, his name hurting my lips. "His real name is Rafe."

I shook my head, almost dislodging my topknot. "I opened myself up to him after what happened with Mac. I wanted to take a chance on him. I honestly thought he felt the same way, but I haven't seen him since. How wrong can you be?"

I embraced Jack and pecked him on the cheek. "Give my love to Dad, Mikey, Ed, and Stan. No doubt I'll see you tomorrow."

Jack appraised me from my door step. "Well, if you ask me, the guy is an idiot."

I know who the idiot is, I thought, affording Jack a small wave and closing my door against the stars prickling in the sky.

———————————

Saturday was proving to be frantic.

As soon as I'd woken up, realisation kicked in with full force.

Oh hell. Today was the day.

I lay in bed, frozen with nerves.

Since Mac's death and the truth about his deception with Hannah, the last few months had seen me making a series of decisions that had led to tonight.

Visions of the old boathouse, transformed from a tired, ramshackle tackle shop into a music venue decorated in a palette of blues and strung with fairy lights, flashed in front of me.

There was little time for reminiscing, however, as I had to double-check stock, ensure the lights all worked, watch the erection of the marquee – likely with a combination of fear and excitement – and mull over Rafe's songs, which would be played after Battalion had appeared.

A couple of times over the past twenty-four hours I had caught myself idly checking my phone for texts. Rafe knew The Conch Club was opening this evening and yet he hadn't even sent me a good luck text.

A stab of disappointment pricked me in the chest but I refused to engage with it. He was probably too busy having Coorie Cottage valued, or packing up his worldly goods, to grant me a second thought.

After a quick shower, hair wash and nibbling some cereal, I dressed in my old denims and drove to the boathouse. There had been a couple of heavy showers overnight, so the woodland was laced with damp, but the forecast for the rest of the day was settled. As long as there weren't any further downpours, that was fine with me.

As I eased my car to a stop in front of the picnic tables outside the club, there came the sound of laughter and shouting.

I gathered my bag from the passenger seat and clambered out. My Converse trainers squeaked over the damp grass.

What greeted me, as I stepped out of the bank of trees and towards The Conch Club, was the sight of a billowing, white marquee being erected by a cluster of student types.

Adam and Richie had said they would be able to recruit a few of their friends to help out, and I had enthusiastically agreed with the promise to pay them a competitive rate each for their trouble.

Faith was already there, emerging from the boathouse as she chatted to Molly. "The electrician is stringing all the fairy lights up now," she grinned. "Oh Layla, you should see them. They're gorgeous."

She steered me by the elbow through The Conch Club, which was a sea of squashy new furniture and decorated in the most beautiful shades of blue, reflected out of the rear patio doors that I had asked to be fitted.

The water was calmer today, like a lapping lake of silver, and the jetty looked amazing, with the tables and chairs now in situ.

"You wait till tonight," Faith bubbled beside me. "If it looks this fantastic during the day, it's going to look even more incredible this evening."

We headed back into the boathouse. Marie and Lewis were unpacking glasses from brown cardboard boxes, while Connor was stocking the mirrored shelves behind the bar with bottles of wine.

The air was filled with clinking and rattling.

I saw Faith blossom into a wide smile as Greg appeared, carrying another box of glasses towards the bar. "I hope you don't mind, but Greg offered to help out and I thought we could be doing with some extra hands."

I waved at him. We actually had tons of extra help, but the sight of her so happy and brimming with contentment was worth it.

Faith pointed to another box sitting on the floor in front of the curved bar. "The table tealights are in there."

I ripped apart the brown tape. Nestled inside were dozens of tiny circular white candles, encased in glass, but on the front of each glass vessel was a small impression of a conch shell. They were gorgeous.

I beamed to myself and started placing one on each of the inside tables first, before venturing out onto the jetty to decorate the tables there.

"It's all coming together," grinned Dad, materialising at my shoulder.

We stood back to admire the interior of glossy, circular tables, quilted seats and swathes of tartan curtains. "It seems to be. You guys all set for tonight then?"

Dad moved to say something but we were interrupted by heavy feet negotiating the wooden floor. It was Jack. "Well, we would be, but we seem to have temporarily lost our bass player."

Dad frowned. "What do you mean?"

"There's no sign of Ed." Jack offered me an awkward smile and then turned back to my dad. "Stan just noticed his car has vanished from the picnic area."

A random thought entered my head. No. Surely not. "You don't think he's had second thoughts about performing this evening?"

Jack pulled a face. "I wouldn't have thought so. He's been fine about it all since then."

Dad's mouth tightened with annoyance. "Well, whatever it is, it would have been nice of him to say when he would be back." He glowered down at his watch. "This place opens in six hours and I'm not happy with the ending of 'You're Trouble'. I'm sure we could sharpen that up."

Jack offered Dad a matey pat on the back. "Don't worry, Harry. Everything will be fine."

Dad's mood visibly darkened. "It'd bloody better be."

Faith, busy placing the drinks and snacks menu on each

table, wandered over and watched Dad march back outside. "Harry's normally so laid back about everything."

Jack nodded. "I know, but it's not every day your daughter launches her own business." He smiled at me. "I think your dad's in more of a state than you are."

"Don't bet on it," I grimaced.

Jack moved off. "I'll catch up with Stan and Mikey, to see if The Invisible Man has reappeared yet."

When he had gone, I let out a ragged gasp to Faith. "This is all we need. One of our performers going missing hours before their band is due on stage. Ed assured me he was fine about it all now."

Faith squeezed my hand. "Try not to sweat it. I bet there's some innocent explanation."

"You think?"

"It's more than likely he's got some errand he had to go on."

"An errand?" I repeated, my anxiety growing.

Faith stifled a laugh. "You know what I mean. It'll be something and nothing. You wait. Give it half an hour and he'll show up again."

I reached up to my shoulder and picked at the band securing the end of my plait. I wasn't so sure. Why not say something to Jack, Stan, Mikey, or Dad then, instead of vanishing in the middle of the Loch Harris countryside?

I knew Battalion hadn't played live for years and the guys had admitted that they were all a bit rusty, but surely he wouldn't let me down now?

Faith read my panicking thoughts. "Come on, you," she urged. "Let's try out the new coffee machine."

I nodded and followed Faith over to the bar where the new chrome coffee contraption was all plugged in and ready for action.

I would have preferred it to have been a curly-haired, pointy-chinned bass player.

Chapter Sixty-Eight

"Where the hell have you been?" snapped Dad, two hours later. "We were about to call out sodding Loch Harris Mountain Rescue!"

Ed locked the door of his car and hovered beside it, looking uncomfortable. "Sorry lads. Sorry Layla. There was something I had to do."

Dad eyed him with that angular brow of his, but Ed wasn't forthcoming about where he'd been or what he'd been doing.

"Right," exclaimed Mikey, with a fierce clap of his hands to rally the troops. "Now that Christopher Columbus here has returned, maybe we can get some last-minute rehearsal time in?"

There was a distinct air of tension as the reunited members of Battalion stalked away from the picnic area and back into The Conch Club.

I eyed the flapping marquee under the pearly sky.

Hopefully, there would be no more cause for panic. It was already 3 p.m. and the plan was to make sure everything was in place, with one final check before we all took off to get ready.

"Layla," came the hesitant voice of Richie from the boathouse steps. I turned my attention away from the marquee. "We don't seem to have any liquid soap for the toilets."

By the time I'd jumped in the car and dashed around to the local corner shop to buy an armful of hand soap, I had just enough time to return and witness the testing of the jetty fairy lights by one of Dad's drinking buddies, who was an electrician.

It was time to go and get ready, but before I did I snatched a final glance at the zingy, new interior of the boathouse.

From the semi-circular, blond-wood stage, to the rich checked curtains in Harris tartan and the walls in peacock-blue ... I had actually managed to do it – with the help of Mac.

For the first time in a long time, I found myself managing to contain my emotions when I thought of him. The twisting, burning feelings of deception and hurt were almost non-existent now. Perhaps that was because of Rafe.

I set my shoulders and began locking up the glass-panelled door to The Conch Club. There would be time enough to think about Rafe when his exclusive new tracks were being played here tonight.

Trying not to dwell on how I would react to that or what I would feel, I shifted the strap of my denim shoulder bag and relegated Rafe to the recesses of my mind.

It was time to go and get my glad rags on.

Chapter Sixty-Nine

After taking a prolonged shower and washing my hair, I rifled through my wardrobe, colours and materials clashing and rubbing against one another on the hangers, until I located what I was looking for.

I'd treated myself to an expensive dress months ago, which I had intended to wear to Mac's birthday party next year. When he died, I had relegated it to the back of my wardrobe.

My hands reached tentatively into the darker recesses of my wardrobe, until my fingers connected with a sliver of beige and gold. I pulled at the hanger, bringing with it the long-sleeved sequinned belted dress. It had a V-neckline and shimmered down to my knees.

I held it up against my dressing gown and twisted it this way and that.

I had also bought a pair of strappy gold shoes and a matching quilted clutch bag to go with it.

I rough dried my hair, then scrunched it until it was all

tousled and wavy, before pinning it up either side for a dressier look.

Once I'd finished my make-up, I reached for the dress, which slithered over my head and down my body. I tied the belt and stepped back to admire the way it glinted when I moved.

I switched on my bedside lamp for when I returned home later and did the same in the hallway. The early evening sky was still carrying a lavender hue.

The plan was to light up the jetty and the boathouse around 7 p.m. so that by the time the darkness had completely descended around 8 p.m., The Conch Club and surrounding area would already be fully bathed in a wash of silver.

I opened my front door and gave a tiny shiver. There was a hint of an autumnal chill in the air, so I darted back to the bedroom to locate my cream shawl. At least that should stave off the breeze which would travel in across Loch Harris later. With its lace embroidery running along the fringes, it looked rather dressy.

I peered down at my feet. I'd painted my toes in a flash of burgundy polish, but knew I would be struggling by the end of the night if I insisted on keeping on these killer heels.

Congratulating myself on being sensible, I grabbed a carrier bag from the kitchen and made my way back up the hallway towards my shoe rack.

My trusty pair of lace-up long brown boots were sitting beside my trainers. They weren't as glamorous as what I was wearing, but at least they wouldn't clash with my dress once the heels became unbearable.

I hitched my clutch bag back under my arm and paused.

The culmination of all the decisions I'd made over the past few months was reaching a peak now. It was strange, but as I opened the door, I could almost imagine Mac standing there, wishing me good luck in that gruff burr of his.

———————————

The sky above Loch Harris was taking on a sleepy, pearly sheen as I parked my car by the picnic tables and took a moment to myself.

The Conch Club was glowing. The carriage lights threw out amber rays onto the grass and the huge white marquee bursting through the trees.

From inside the boathouse, I could make out Battalion having a final run through of their set and the odd shadowy figure flitting backwards and forwards behind the windows.

I examined my face in the rear-view mirror. Oh God. I looked like a terrified rabbit caught in headlights.

I wiped a smudge of black mascara away from under my right eye and secured my kirby grips again.

My stomach was rolling from left to right, as though I were trying to steady an out-of-control ship.

Well, here goes.

I gathered up my clutch bag and shawl from the passenger seat and reached down for the carrier bag containing my boots from the footwell.

As I locked the car, I spied Adam, Lewis, and Connor

flitting in and out of the marquee flap, carrying trays of glasses. I also recognised the odd Loch Harris resident beginning to arrive and mill around, clutching glasses of sparkling, pale-gold champagne and exclaiming their relief about the weather being kind.

"Layla!"

Faith skipped down the steps of the boathouse, resplendent in a red and white striped shift dress and ruby-coloured Mary Jane shoes.

"Wow! I grinned at her. "You look terrific!"

She didn't appear convinced. Faith reached up and pulled at her hair, which she'd teased into a strawberry-blonde ponytail. "Are you sure? I think I look like a tube of toothpaste."

"Don't be daft. You look wonderful."

She nodded at me and planted her hands on her hips. "Talk about being the belle of the ball. You look gorgeous!"

Then she made a beckoning motion. "Come in and take a look. Your dad and the guys are rehearsing and the caterers have set up the buffet in the marquee."

With excitement pumping through me, I stepped through the buzzing entrance. Up on the stage, Dad and the rest of Battalion were gathered in a semi-circle, discussing how they could make one of their song intros more upbeat.

My heart charged across my chest with pride. The five of them were all dressed in smart shirts and trousers.

Jack must have sensed Faith and me observing them, because he turned and said something to the rest of the guys. They all switched their attention towards us and delivered enthusiastic compliments about both our outfits.

"You lot have scrubbed up nicely," I teased. "I almost didn't recognise any of you."

"Thanks very much," joked Mikey. "The same could be said for you, young lady."

My staff were flitting about, just blurs of smart black in their outfits, as they made sure the tables and chairs were lit with the tealights and that each table was adorned with a drinks and snacks menu.

Through the patio doors at the rear of the boathouse, the flicker of lights on the external tables was like a line of dancing fairies.

Faith and I made our way back outside and began heading for the marquee. But she drew up suddenly, her creamy skin blossoming into a fetching shade of baby pink.

I didn't have to turn around; I knew who was making her blush.

When I did turn, I grinned. Greg was walking up the shale path, all suited and booted in steel grey, with Sam galloping ahead of him in a smart little waistcoat, matching trousers, and a sky-blue shirt.

"Doesn't he look adorable?" cooed Faith to me out of the corner of her mouth.

"Which one?"

"Both of them."

I pecked Greg on the cheek and thanked him for his help earlier. Then I ruffled Sam's crown of golden hair and left them to it.

The sky was crisp and welcoming – a stunning evening in Scotland, when the hills appeared to be shapeshifting under the lilac light.

I entered the marquee, to be greeted by trestle tables adorned with platters of Scottish salmon and cream cheese mini-bagels, crusty-bread sandwiches oozing with seafood, and an array of oatcakes topped with everything from plum tomatoes to mozzarella.

Beside that was another table, but this one was decorated with an array of mini-desserts, including raspberry cranachan and shortbread cookies, Scottish oaty walnut & raisin flapjacks and Scottish macaroon snowballs.

When Faith appeared with Greg and Sam, she did her best to encourage me to eat something by thrusting a plate and napkin under my nose, but I struggled.

I glanced down at my watch. It was almost 6 p.m. and time for the official opening of The Conch Club.

Faith followed me out of the marquee, and I recognised so many of the expectant faces gathering together outside the entrance. There was: Heather and her mum and dad, Alec and Pam; Molly, dressed in a full-length orange dress and colouring up every time she and Dad exchanged glances; Danielle from the tourist office with her boyfriend Josh; my dad's assorted drinking buddies from the local watering holes; most of the local business people from Loch Harris; and of course, Jack, Stan, Mikey, and Ed.

Norrie and Clem were swigging their champagne amongst the throng too, and behind them I noticed Mac's sister, Lois, who blew me a kiss and waved.

I made a gesture to indicate I'd speak to her in a few minutes.

Even David Murray, Mac's solicitor, had accepted my invitation. He hovered close to Lois, making conversation with her and glancing approvingly around himself every so often.

I approached the steps of the boathouse and climbed up them carefully in my gold heels.

When I reached the top, I realised I was scanning the upturned smiling faces. *Who are you looking for?* whispered a mischievous voice inside my head. *Rafe, perhaps?*

I arranged my mouth into a smile.

Dad appeared behind me and gave me an encouraging pat on the shoulder.

I opened my mouth, ready to welcome everyone on this Saturday evening in August with the scent of pine needles lacing the air, when I found myself muttering, "Oh shit. She's here."

Dad took a step closer. "Who?"

"Madame Guillotine. Mum."

"Where?"

"Surprised you can't see her," I ground out of the corner of my mouth. "She's over there to the right of the crowd. I think some of the neighbouring trees have just withered and died."

Dad tried not to laugh and followed my gaze.

Tina was lurking like a black-clad praying mantis with her partner in crime, Alison, hanging by her side.

"Just ignore her," hissed Dad. "Go on, lass. Everyone's waiting for you to speak."

I gazed at all the happy, relaxed expressions eyeing me and cleared my throat. Then I tightened the shawl draped around my shoulders. "I won't go on for long," I assured the gathering. "I'm sure you'll be relieved to hear that."

"You don't take after your father then," piped up Mikey a few feet away from me. Ed, standing beside him in a lemon shirt, smiled and dropped his eyes to the grass. There was a chorus of cheers and laughter.

"Anyway," I started again, giving Mikey a playful scowl, "I really wanted to say thank you to all of you for coming along tonight and showing your support. As many of you will know, the last few months haven't been easy, but we got there."

I clapped my hands together and then Faith handed me a champagne flute. The gold liquid popped against the glass as I held it aloft. "Here's to The Conch Club, and to Loch Harris and its wonderful community."

There was a loud cheer and the air filled with the vibrant clinking of glasses.

"Right," I began, pointing to the cosy interior behind me, "first up tonight is Battalion. Please grab a seat and give them a huge round of applause."

The guys and Dad darted past me and inside so they could take up their positions on stage. The tealights waved and danced on the tables, while chairs were scraped back and guests took their seats.

I stood at the back of the room beside Faith.

Outside, Loch Harris swayed in the evening breeze and all around me, the carriage lights glowed like miniature jewels. Another hour and then we could have the grand switch on of the fairy lights adorning the entrance and jetty.

"Layla, you've done *so* well."

I could feel my body stiffen as my mother emerged into my line of sight, all glossy red highlights and spray tan.

"No thanks to you," I replied, eyeing her sequinned jacket and black split skirt. She reminded me of some second-rate cruise ship entertainer.

She made a move to speak again, but I thrust my face closer to hers. She was wreathed in a musky perfume. "Sorry to disappoint you, but you didn't manage to drive a wedge between Dad and me."

Faith and I swapped satisfied smiles.

"You see, Dad and I decided to take a DNA test and it turns out that Harry *is* my biological father."

She tried to conceal her surprise but failed, her thin brows darting upwards, as though trying to escape from her face. She gathered herself together. "It must have been such an awful time for you all."

"Yes, you would have liked that," I rallied, "but we dealt with it."

I could see her mind whirring. "Things must be rather awkward now with Ed."

I let out a short laugh. "Oh, you would have loved that, wouldn't you?" I leaned in a little closer to her. "As a matter of fact, your tawdry little revelation seems to have cleared the air. Dad and Ed will never be best friends, but they've moved on."

I raised my chin and stared past her glittery shoulder to watch Dad and the band prepare to play their first song. "Now, if you'll excuse me, I've got a business to launch."

Faith gave Mum a frosty grimace.

Setting her shoulders, Tina glowered. "Your father has filled your head with poison about me."

"Not at all," I answered simply. "I was able to deduce

from an early age what a self-centred, vacuous individual you are. I didn't need anyone else to tell me."

My mother swallowed and turned on her patent heel. She muttered something unintelligible, before barging her way through the crowd and out the door. Her lapdog Alison scurried at her heels.

"Right guys," boomed Mikey. "Let's go!"

There was a riot of whoops and loud applause.

I was overcome with emotion as I watched my dad thrash the drums before Mikey launched into their first track.

Jack played the keyboard with his usual pizazz, Stan carried an air of solid, quiet confidence, and Mikey flirted unashamedly with the female members of the audience. But it was Ed's odd behaviour that caught my eye.

His attention kept flicking towards the door.

"Does Ed seem all right to you?" I whispered in Faith's ear.

She tilted her ponytail to one side. "I thought he seemed a bit distracted earlier."

I turned to look at her. "His wife is here. I spotted her earlier in the marquee." I peered across the silhouetted heads of the crowd in front of us and shrugged. "Oh, it's probably nothing. More likely a bit of nerves."

Battalion continued to wow the crowd with a selection of their best songs, delivering the vibrant rock tunes for which they were best known.

When they finished their second encore and soaked up the adulation, a dull sensation took over. This was what I had been dreading. It would soon be time to play Rafe's exclusive material.

I delved into my clutch bag which I'd secreted behind the bar and checked my texts. There was nothing from Rafe, not even a polite 'Hope all goes well tonight'.

That told me all I needed to know.

It was almost seven o'clock and all the fairy lights outside the entrance would flicker into life shortly.

Trying not to register my hurt over Rafe, I made my way onto the stage and suggested to the audience that they might like to step outside for a few moments to see the grand switch on.

The assembled crowd reached for their mobile phones from bags and jackets and held them aloft in anticipation. There were appreciative gasps and words of delight as the silver fairy lights, like snowflakes, flickered to life in a burst of light.

They framed the doorway and beamed entrance of The Conch Club, lacing and looping their way along and down the side of the old boathouse, before stretching along the jetty and out towards the loch.

I addressed the buzzing crowd. "Ladies and gentleman, please join us back inside for an exclusive play of new material by the musician Mask."

"Whoo-hoo!" whooped Heather, her blonde plaits flying about her shoulders.

I walked back into the boathouse and nodded at Adam, who was manning the bar. He switched on the CD player and the sound of Rafe's velvety voice drifted through the room.

His lyrics were gorgeous, suiting the lilting guitar before the rhythm picked up and drums and a bass guitar joined in.

As quiet conversation rumbled and the crowd drank in the music, Faith and Greg leaned on the bar beside me. Greg's mum had arrived and whisked a rather indignant Sam away, so Faith and Greg could enjoy the rest of the evening together.

Faith gave my shoulder a playful nudge. "It's all going great."

"Everybody seems to be enjoying themselves," I conceded.

She offered me a considered look. "Are you?"

"Am I what?"

"Enjoying yourself?"

"Of course I am," I insisted through an overly bright smile. I fell silent as Rafe's first song drifted to an end and then the second track, a particular favourite of mine, sprang into life.

I shut my eyes for a moment. This was ridiculous. What was the point in wasting my time thinking about someone who clearly didn't care about me?

I swung round and snatched up my shawl, which I'd thrown over the back of an empty chair beside me. "I'm going to get some air," I announced, arranging it around my shoulders. "I'll be back in ten minutes."

Faith didn't reply.

"Is that OK?" I asked, expecting her to answer me. "If you could keep an eye on things in here..."

I looked up from smoothing my shawl but neither she

nor Greg were paying any attention to me. They were too preoccupied studying something over my shoulder.

"Faith?"

I narrowed my eyes at their odd expressions and turned around, picking up on a growing commotion taking place only feet away by the boathouse door.

My heart stilled.

Chapter Seventy

A tall, shadowy figure in an upturned hood was standing beside Ed.

They were surrounded by staring members of the audience and audible muttering.

"Layla's over there," said Ed, an apprehensive smile tugging at the corners of his wide mouth.

I watched, trying to process what was taking place right in front of me under the glowing lights and the hush of clinking glasses.

The figure moved. I caught a glimpse of a dark mask.

"Oh my God!" shrieked Heather over everyone's head. "It's him! It's Mask. Can I get a selfie?"

Rafe turned towards her and smiled nervously. "Sure."

Heather let out a prolonged squeal and I blinked over at her and then at him.

Rafe was pinning me to the spot with his gaze. He hovered a few feet away from me, before raising one hand and slowly tugging down his hood.

Oblivious to the dozens of wide eyes that had settled on him, he shrugged off his grey hoodie and draped it over the back of a vacant chair. There was a moment's hesitation before his fingers reached up and pulled at his mask. It fell away from his face and into his right hand.

He dumped that on the chair too. Excited chatter swirled up into the air.

Rafe stood in front of me now, in a beige waistcoat and dark trousers. His white shirt sleeves were rolled to his elbows.

My heart twisted in on itself.

"Layla," he faltered, "do you think I could have a word with you in private please?"

My eyes swept him from head to toe, struggling to process what he was doing here and why.

"Go outside," advised Faith. She indicated the jetty. "It's quiet out there at the moment."

I snatched up my shawl and led the way, with Rafe following close behind. The crowd parted for us.

I hugged myself in my cream shawl and clattered over the wooden jetty towards the loch. I hadn't expected to see Rafe again. I didn't know what to think.

I drew up close to the jetty edge, where the waves of silver water danced with each other in the shadowy darkness. There was the promise of autumn now in the air.

Over my shoulder, I could sense intrigued faces at the closed patio doors, pretending they weren't watching us.

Rafe studied the tealights on each deserted wooden table. "You've done a terrific job. The place looks great. Magical, even."

"Thank you."

I tried not to stare as he appeared beside me. His scar melted away while I looked at him. For me, it didn't exist.

He shot me a sideways glance and then trained his attention across the water. "I've behaved like a prize twat."

I didn't disagree with him.

"This is where you're supposed to assure me that no, I haven't."

I bit my lip and continued to stare ahead.

"Layla," he started, turning to face me. "You look beautiful."

I swallowed and raised my chin.

"And you saved me. You and that garden."

My brows dipped. "Sorry?"

Rafe fidgeted on the spot. "I came here to Loch Harris to escape. After what happened with Emily, I blamed myself and thought I didn't deserve…"

"To be happy?"

"Yes."

Rafe rifled a hand through his hair, sending it into irresistible, black plumes. "When Ed came to see me earlier today—"

I whirled round, almost slapping him with my shawl. "Ed? What was Ed doing going to see you?"

"He told me about the results of the DNA test," admitted Rafe. "He seemed a bit disappointed, if I'm being honest. He told me that he'd lost out on having a wonderful, beautiful girl like you as his daughter."

Rafe pushed both his hands into the front pockets of his trousers. "When Hazel almost ran you over up at the cottage, all I could think of was losing you like I had Emily."

I felt like I couldn't breathe properly. My chest heaved under my sparkly dress. "Go on."

"If anything had happened to you, I knew it would be my fault and I just couldn't risk going through pain like that again."

My eyes smarted. I was desperate to touch the scar on his handsome face and assure him that he was worth taking a risk on.

"When Ed came to talk to me today, he told me how you helped him that day in the woods."

Rafe's eyes lingered longer than necessary on my lips. "He also reminded me what I'd said to him about playing with the band tonight, instead of cutting and running." A smile flickered at the corners of his mouth. "He said, as it turned out, he wouldn't be able to play a part in your life, but that I could, and that I was a dick if I threw that chance away."

His gaze burned. "You saved me, Layla, but I was too much of a coward to admit it to myself."

I played with the fringing of my shawl. "So, is it true?" I managed. "That you're planning on moving away from Loch Harris?"

Rafe cast his gaze downwards for a moment. "Well, that kind of depends on you." He traced a finger against my cheek and I shivered. He tilted my chin upwards so I couldn't escape the intensity of his black lash-fringed eyes. "I want you, Layla. I want to give this – us – a go. I can't leave Loch Harris. I can't leave you. Not now."

Then a mischievous grin overtook his features. It lit up his whole face and made my stomach leap. "And I really want to put a gazebo up in the garden, anyway."

My lips smiled against his, before his mouth claimed mine over and over and I clung to him, kissing him back and revelling in the taste of him.

The pain and despondency of Mac's betrayal, the desire to escape the memories of him and what I'd thought we had in Loch Harris, the stress of launching The Conch Club and the endless business decisions, the fear over Harry not being my real father … they all melted away into the night.

It was all about new beginnings for Rafe and me.

But first, I had Ed to thank.

Epilogue

Two Years later, Terrigal, Australia

I padded out towards the panoramic window of our two-storey holiday home on Ocean View Drive.

It was all timber and glass, with a sun deck and generous garden for Rafe to indulge his green fingers. Outside, the waves charged onto the honey sand and a gull weaved its way through the azure sky.

"Huh! It's OK for some," teased Rafe. "I wish I had time to stand and daydream, Mrs Buchanan."

He came and stood beside me. "I need to finish off the lyrics to that song so I can add it to my new album, and I have a radio interview scheduled for this afternoon."

I grinned at him. "Well, that's what happens when you achieve three top five singles."

Rafe gave me a wink. He looked wonderful, with his caramel suntan and the sexy beard he had grown, yet I was pleased the top part of his scar was still visible.

It made him who he was.

"Love you," he grinned, vanishing out into the hall.

My mobile let out a shrill ring from our bedroom dressing table, interrupting the tranquillity.

I darted in to answer it.

My heart leaped when I saw it was Faith calling. "We're coming Down Under for a visit!" she squealed. "Greg has been accruing some leave, so we thought we could bring Sam over when he begins his school holidays in June." She paused. "That's if you want to see us?"

I let out a gasp of excitement. "Are you kidding me? That's wonderful! Let me know what flights and dates you're looking at so we can get the vacation plans underway. I hope Mikey is still looking after The Conch Club?"

Faith let out a throaty laugh. "She's in very safe hands. It's all going great, although he keeps insisting on performing for the Friday night crowd." She let out a playful moan. "It's all right for some people, splitting their time between Australia and Scotland."

"When do you expect the honeymooners to arrive?"

I watched as a cyclist glided along past the beach, the sunlight sparking against their silver spokes. "Dad texted me well over an hour ago to say he and Molly had picked up their hire car at the airport and are on their way here."

I could almost hear Faith smiling down the line. "And how is the writing going?"

"Good," I replied. "I've been commissioned to write a monthly column for a women's magazine. It's all about what it's like being a Scottish woman living in Australia. They've called it 'Great Scot'!"

Faith made a noise that was between a laugh and a groan.

"And I've secured more freelance work with a couple of local newspapers."

"That's amazing! I had better get to bed now though. Greg has an early start tomorrow. Can't wait to see you both. Good morning and good night!"

When I turned, Rafe was looking at me expectantly from the doorway. "Anything exciting?"

I grinned at him. "That was Faith. She was asking if she, Greg, and Sam could come and visit once the school summer holidays start."

Rafe strode over and delivered a lingering kiss. "That's great. We'll have to take Sam whale watching."

He glanced down at his watch. "I don't think it will be too much longer before Harry and Molly arrive." He smiled. "I can't believe your dad played with Battalion at his own wedding reception. You would think he would have been happy just getting married."

"You can't keep an old rocker down."

Rafe was disappearing into his recording studio down the hallway when there was the sound of a car engine growling outside.

I dashed to the front of the house and peered over the balcony, grinning and waving at Dad and Molly.

"They're here!" called Rafe, bounding down the spiral staircase.

I waited until he had opened the front door and was

heading out to greet them, before I slipped back into the bedroom and tugged open the drawer of my bedside table.

My stomach turned over with excitement. The positive pregnancy test, with its bold blue line, grinned up at me.

Rafe Buchanan and Harry Devlin.

Boy, do I have some exciting news for both of you.

Acknowledgments

Huge thanks as always to my wonderful agent Selwa Anthony and to Linda Anthony. You are two phenomenal ladies.

I cannot put into words how honoured and delighted I am that the amazing Charlotte Ledger at HarperCollins and her fab team saw something promising in this book and sprinkled it with their magic. I will be forever grateful.

Thank you also to Jo, Amanda and Geraldine for being such supportive and special friends.

And to my boys: Lawrence, Daniel, Ethan and Cooper – love you so much.

YOUR NUMBER ONE STOP

ONE MORE CHAPTER

FOR PAGETURNING BOOKS

One More Chapter is an
award-winning global
division of HarperCollins.

Sign up to our newsletter to get our
latest eBook deals and stay up to date
with our weekly Book Club!
<u>Subscribe here.</u>

Meet the team at
<u>www.onemorechapter.com</u>

Follow us!
 @OneMoreChapter_
 @OneMoreChapter
 @onemorechapterhc

Do you write unputdownable fiction?
We love to hear from new voices.
Find out how to submit your novel at
<u>www.onemorechapter.com/submissions</u>